I0730983

# Strands

# Strands

ELENA GRAF

**PURPLE HAND PRESS**

Purple Hand Press
www.purplehandpress.com
© 2022 by Elena Graf



This is a work of fiction. Names, characters, places and incidents are the product of the author's imagination or used fictitiously, and any resemblance to actual persons, living or dead, businesses, institutions, companies, events, or locales is entirely coincidental.

Trade Paperback Edition
ISBN 978-1-953195-12-8
Kindle Edition
ISBN 978-1-953195-13-5
ePub Edition
ISBN 978-1-953195-14-2

Cover photo: belchonock © 123RF.com
Editor: Elaine Mattern

06.27.2023

*To the healthcare workers who heroically
fight the good fight*

# 1

"Liz!" The stunningly clear voice carried over the water beating against the tiles. Liz shut off the faucet and squeezed most of the water out of her hair before turning around. Through the steam, she could make out a dark figure standing at the end of the enormous shower. The vapor swirled and began to clear, revealing a small, red-haired woman with her hands on her hips.

"Yes, Lucy?" Liz asked in her most patient voice.

Lucy smiled as if that would make everything better. Usually, it did, but a steaming hot shower was one of Liz's guilty pleasures. Interrupting it was unforgivable. "I'm sorry to bother you. Are you almost done?"

"I am now, it seems." Liz dried her face and wrapped the towel around her waist. She gingerly stepped across the wet tiles. "Are you leaving now?"

"Not yet. I need to talk to you first."

Liz came out of the shower and stood on the bath mat. "What's so important that it can't wait?"

"I called to schedule a physical and found out that you're no longer my doctor!"

With the edge of her hand, Liz cut away a drop of water running down her cheek. "Lucy, I kept trying to tell you..."

"I know. I know. I didn't want to believe it. Can we talk?"

"Now?"

Lucy's green eyes pleaded. "I promised Ginny I'd get right back to her." The efficient woman who ran Liz's practice hated to leave open appointments. Keeping her waiting was never a good idea.

"Let me put on some clothes."

Lucy gave Liz's naked breasts an admiring look. "I don't know. I think I like you this way."

"You're not serious. You're all dressed. You even have your collar on." Liz nudged Lucy aside, so she could pass.

"I have that funeral this morning. There have been so many of them lately, not only postponements from the lockdown, but new ones every week. The old are deprived of their families and friends and just give up." Lucy shook her head sadly. "There's so much pain out there."

"Obviously, you can't be late for a funeral." Liz stood on the fuzzy rug in front of the sink to dry herself more thoroughly. Despite the shower, she wasn't completely awake. "Maybe this conversation should wait until later."

She wondered why Lucy, who was usually the first to object when an ethical line was crossed, couldn't accept the change. But where other people only saw black and white, Lucy saw myriad shades of gray. Her impulse was always to offer compassion, no matter what the rules said. When Liz had lost her mother and couldn't process her grief, Lucy had agreed to talk to her—as a friend, she'd emphasized, not as a psychotherapist. They both knew they were walking a fine line but decided it was acceptable. In a small town like Hobbs, people's lives eventually become intertwined like the strands of a rope.

Lucy was watching her. Somehow, she always knew when Liz had disappeared into her thoughts. "Liz?" she asked gently to bring her back.

"Give me a few minutes to throw on some clothes. If you make me a cup of coffee, I'll love you forever."

"You'd better love me forever. You asked me to marry you."

"Lucy, you've got that backwards. *You* asked *me* to marry you."

"I did, didn't I? Best thing I ever did," said Lucy, then looked thoughtful. "No, becoming a priest was the best thing I ever did."

"I'll remind you of that after a rough vestry meeting."

"We're meeting today."

"Thanks for the warning."

After Lucy left, Liz toweled her hair. Since the pandemic had begun, the white hairs had been encroaching on the iron grays. When Liz had complained, her stylist had said, "You don't know how lucky you are. People pay me to get that color!" Yanking a comb through the tangled waves, Liz wondered if she should ask the woman to cut her hair even shorter. Her friend Sam had shaved hers on one side. Liz was tempted to do the same, but she doubted Lucy would approve.

While she dressed, Liz tried to compose a concise explanation of why she could no longer be Lucy's doctor. In her capacity as chief of surgery, Liz had often lectured the junior staff about the pitfalls of treating close friends and relatives. Emotional involvement could compromise objectivity, especially when a doctor was under pressure to make a quick medical decision. Training doctors to think under any conditions was supposedly the purpose of all those brutal, long shifts, but they were a thing of the past. Now, residency programs limited the number of hours a physician could be on duty, supposedly for patient safety. Liz didn't completely approve, but since she was no longer responsible for training young doctors, it didn't matter.

She put on a T-shirt and shorts although the September morning was cool. Summer in Maine was too brief, and wearing summer clothes allowed at least the pretense of holding back the season. She shrugged on a hoodie for additional warmth.

When she came into the kitchen, the single-serve coffee maker was dribbling dark liquid into her favorite cup. "I waited until I heard your feet on the stairs," Lucy said, bringing the cup to the table. "I didn't want your coffee to get cold." Liz bent to thank Lucy with a kiss and decided to nibble her ear too. "Stop," said Lucy, raising her shoulder in defense. "Don't think you can seduce your way out of this conversation."

"Lucy, we've talked about this," said Liz, sitting down at the table. "Obviously, you weren't paying attention."

"I guess not," Lucy said, looking reflective. "I heard what you said, but I didn't want to believe it. You're the best doctor I ever had. I don't want to lose you. I trust you, Liz. You even kept my secret when I was dating your best friend."

"Your medical history is no one's business. You thought the adoption was sealed, so why would you expect your daughter to show up?"

"I should have told Erika about Emily. She was hurt when she found out."

"But she got over it quickly. She was always so reasonable."

"Unlike you. You're so darn stubborn. Liz, please. Can't you make an exception for me?" Lucy's lower lip protruded slightly. At such moments, the confident pastor and insightful therapist vanished, and Liz could see a much younger Lucy.

"No, Lucy, and you know why. You don't always like my medical advice. Why is this such a big deal?"

"It makes me feel safe to have you as my doctor. Maggie always said she felt protected from the cancer because you were there."

"I'm a doctor, not a guardian angel," said Liz, scowling as she stirred cream into her coffee. "I hope she remembers to get her screenings without me nagging her." When she looked up, she saw Lucy looking at her with concern. "I know, I have to forgive her, and I'm working on it. Having an affair with a man was the one thing I couldn't forgive."

"She was only trying to get your attention."

"No, she wasn't. She was trying to get back at me for kissing you."

"People's motives for having an affair are complicated. Maybe she did want to punish you. More likely she felt unappreciated or worried that her looks were fading. Maybe she needed the attention of a younger person as an ego-boost. That's not uncommon at our age. Maybe she just needed sex."

"I doubt that. The tamoxifen suppresses her hormones. And if it was sex she wanted, I was more than willing to provide it."

"Whatever her reasons, sleeping with that man was a bad choice. She knew she was using him and hurting you, which was why she asked me for absolution. She probably hoped it would make the guilt go away, but it doesn't work like that."

"But that's what they taught us. The priest says the magic words, and your sins are forgiven…just like that." Liz snapped her fingers for emphasis. "White hair or no, Maggie is still the good Catholic girl I knew in college."

"We're all stuck with baggage from our childhood. We might spend a lifetime processing it."

"Processing it," Liz repeated with disgust, "sounds like meat." Liz got up and took two hard-boiled eggs out of the refrigerator. "Want one?"

Lucy shook her head. "I don't have a lot of time this morning, and I have to call Ginny back. Who should I ask to do my physical?"

"Cathy said she'd take you as a patient. You like Cathy. You've seen her when I wasn't available." Lucy pouted. "Oh, please, Lucy. This is the way it is. Stop giving me a hard time!"

Lucy composed her face and looked perfectly adult again. "All right, you're no longer an option, but Ginny asked if I wanted to wait until the new doctor comes. What new doctor?"

"I've been interviewing candidates to join the practice. I've pretty much narrowed it down to one person. She's a New Yorker too. Probably why we clicked."

Lucy put down her coffee cup and stared. "You're hiring a new doctor? Are you thinking of retiring?"

"No, not yet." Liz cracked a hard-boiled egg on the tabletop and carefully peeled it into a napkin. "You think I'd do something that big and not talk to you about it?"

"You're not the world's best communicator. I don't expect you to tell me everything, but yes, I would expect you to tell me something that important."

"When I'm ready to retire, you'll be the first to know. We need more help. Cathy is cutting back on her hours. She's overwhelmed with two teenagers, each involved in different activities. With all the new construction in Hobbs, we have an influx of new people. I thought of hiring another PA, but eventually, I will retire, so hiring another physician makes more sense." Liz paused, realizing she was explaining her reasoning to herself as much as to Lucy, who was listening with her usual deep attention. "She's an internist with impressive credentials, but her group practice was absorbed into a big health network. She says she's done with the bureaucracy and wants to leave New York."

"Sounds like you," Lucy observed.

"Yes, except I was older when I decided to leave the rat race. She's only fifty, which makes her young enough to replace me when I finally do retire."

"And when will that be?"

Liz shrugged. "Maybe when you retire."

"I don't have to retire until I'm seventy. I'm only fifty-seven."

"Uh huh." Liz cracked open the other egg and peeled it. "Would you be willing to come to dinner with Dr. Hsu…to give me your opinion as a shrink?"

Lucy gave her a sharp look. "Liz, I asked you to stop using that word. It's disrespectful. Just because I agreed to marry you doesn't mean you can backslide. I don't intend to spend my time with you doing behavior modification."

"Sorry," said Liz and bit into the egg.

"When is this dinner?"

"Next Tuesday. We're eating at Nathan's. I know you like that place. I thought I told you."

"No, you didn't, but I wish you would tell me what's going on, so I don't always find out at the last minute. You need to open your mouth and talk." Lucy tapped her fingers to her thumb to imitate lips moving.

"I know, but I'm used to keeping my mouth shut for professional reasons."

"So am I, but there are some things you need to discuss with your partner. Sex isn't the only way to express love." Liz imagined Lucy giving the same practical advice to couples during marital counseling. "What time is this dinner date?"

"Seven. Afterwards, you can come back with me and stay the night."

"Liz, I appreciate your hospitality, but I need to be at home sometimes. I do have a home, remember?"

"After we get married, we'll live here, of course."

"Of course!" Lucy repeated with faux shock. "When did we decide that?"

"*We* didn't, but we need to talk about where we're going to live. Don't we?"

"Yes, we do. And then, *we* will decide together."

Liz got up to get another cup of coffee. "I see you're wearing your engagement ring today. Is this funeral a dress-up occasion?"

"No more than usual. I put on your grandmother's ring because I have that vestry meeting today." Lucy extended her fingers to admire the huge, showy diamond. "I'm hoping the glitter attracts enough attention to prompt some questions. Then, I'll casually explain that we're engaged."

"You're staging an engagement announcement? Isn't that rather devious?"

Lucy shrugged. "I don't want to make a big thing of it."

"Afraid of their judgment?"

"Maybe a little. People were fond of Erika. They're fond of you too, but some people might think it's too soon. I want to ease them into the idea." Lucy looked at her phone. "Liz, I need to go. Come to my house tonight." Liz deadpanned while Lucy studied her face. "Yes, I know. You hate sleeping in the queen-sized bed," said Lucy, "but Liz, you built that bed, and it's very comfortable. I can find you in it, not like that king-sized monstrosity you have upstairs. Come over when you finish your office hours. Okay?"

Liz knew that this small compromise would earn her a few points. "Okay."

She was rewarded with an extended kiss. When their lips parted, Lucy added a quick peck. "See you later, sexy thing. Be good. Or at least, try."

❋❋❋

Melissa Morgenstern watched the priest head to her SUV. Lucy wore her collar under her cardigan. Off to work, Melissa assumed. Lucy had been spending most nights with the doctor, probably because the location was more private than her own house on the beach. Set far back from the road, Liz's place was hidden from their few neighbors by dense trees. Most of the time, Melissa treasured the quiet and solitude of the pine forest, but she often missed the expansive view of the salt marsh from her mother's house in town.

After watching Lucy's car head down the driveway, Melissa reluctantly returned her eyes to her laptop. What the ladies did next door was none of her business, but Melissa often envied their neighbors because they seemed to know exactly what they wanted. Clearly, it was each other, which was confirmed by Liz's adoring look whenever Lucy came into the room.

Melissa wished Courtney would look at her that way. Occasionally she did when they made love, but otherwise, she carefully controlled where her eyes fell and their expression, especially when her daughter was nearby. Ironically, Kaylee seemed more relaxed about her mother's relationship with a woman than she was. Young people had grown up seeing gays and lesbians on TV, in the news, everywhere. No wonder they didn't consider it strange.

Of course, Melissa knew the position of assistant principal of a small-town elementary school was a sensitive one, but in public, Courtney acted like she hardly knew her. Courtney was her first closeted girlfriend. Not that Melissa put a sign on her office door declaring her sexual preference, but everyone at her law firm knew. Before the virus had ended socializing, Melissa had always invited her girlfriends to the holiday office party. When her clients brought their spouses to a dinner meeting, Melissa always brought her partner too…if she had one. Even the clients from conservative states, who made no secret of their politics, seemed fine with sharing a meal with a lesbian couple. It probably helped that Melissa and her girlfriends were indistinguishable from other professional women and didn't look especially gay.

There were some places where Courtney felt at ease. Her landlord occasionally invited them over for a couples' night. Liz's culinary repertoire was considerably more sophisticated than Courtney's. Melissa's palate had been spoiled by client dinners at Boston's top-drawer restaurants. Courtney's meals were prepared with love, and the cuisine in the local restaurants was honest and tasty, but it was fun to get dressed up and enjoy a fancy dinner. Occasionally, Melissa cooked a gourmet recipe she found online, but Courtney did most of the cooking. She said she didn't mind because it had become a habit when she was married.

Melissa felt a hand over hers. "Mind if I sit with you while Kaylee showers?" Courtney's brown eyes smiled warmly. Her blond hair was still a little damp from the shower. "I hope I'm not interrupting anything important."

"No, I was just looking over my schedule for today."

"I'm so glad they're letting you work from home again. Now that you don't have to get up before sunrise to catch the train, I can sleep longer too."

"It's not generosity on their part. The spike in infections forced them. Mike wasn't happy about letting me work remotely, but the train is crowded, and people don't always wear a mask. He finally admitted that working from home makes no difference in the business I bring into the firm."

"Well, if he ever asks me, I'll tell him I've never seen anyone work so hard." Melissa basked in Courtney's generous loyalty—one of her most endearing traits. "I only wish we had more space for you to work."

"I could move back to my mother's. She gave me a room to use as an office."

Courtney squeezed her hand. "No, I like having you here, especially because you're home when Kaylee gets off the bus. She's a teenager now. I trust her, but you know how it works at that age." She studied Melissa's face. "You miss all the space you used to have in your mother's house, don't you?"

Melissa shrugged. "Funny. I was just thinking about the view of the salt marsh." She saw a flicker of anxiety in Courtney's eyes. "Don't worry. I'm not moving back in with Mom. With Jack there, I'd feel like an intruder in their love nest."

"Doug is finally paying child support again. Maybe we should start looking for a bigger place."

The idea of more room was appealing, but Melissa finally had her finances under control, now that she didn't have to commute every day. She patted Courtney's hand. "Let's wait until the summer people are gone and the rents come down. You seem much calmer about money since you moved in here."

"I am. I've even caught up on my student loan and saved a few dollars. Liz won't take money for rent. We're not going to get a better deal than this."

"So, let's sit tight and see what happens. Right now, everything is in flux." Melissa sat back and sighed, realizing how uncomfortable uncertainty made her. She was a planner and liked to know what exactly was coming next. "Lucy is always telling me to relax and go with the flow. I'd love to, except I can't even see which way the flow is going."

"I know what you mean. Since I left my marriage, everything has been chaotic. For years, I packed lunch for Doug and me, and we headed to school together. On the way, we'd drop Kaylee off, first at daycare, then at school. The routine was boring at times, but I knew one day would be pretty much like the last." Courtney's blond brows dipped to the base of her nose. "Isn't it strange how things go along smoothly for years, and then everything gets shaken up?"

"I'm not a big fan of change, but sometimes, it's a good thing."

A quick smile came to Courtney's face. "Really? Name one good thing about it."

Melissa knew exactly what she was angling to hear. "We got together."

"I was hoping you'd say that. Sometimes, I think you're not sure."

"For a while there, I wasn't. Everything seemed to be against us. Mike wanted me back in the office. You needed a place to live. Mom wouldn't let us move in with her. Then Doug showed up."

Courtney had been studying her face while she spoke. "You're still worried about the bi thing, aren't you?"

Melissa squirmed a little. She didn't want to lie to Courtney's face. "I'm getting there."

"Just because I've been attracted to men in the past doesn't mean I want to be with one now. I'm with you, only you." Courtney frowned. "I'm sorry I ever told you."

"After Doug showed up, it was kind of obvious."

"Melissa, I hate labels. We label kids in school to make sure they get the right services, but then it sticks for the rest of their lives."

"If you hate labels, why do you insist on calling yourself bi? Why not just say you're gay?"

"Because it's not my truth!" Courtney protested. She pulled back the hand that had been gently stroking Melissa's.

The door to the sleeping nook slid open, "Mom, when are we going to leave?" Kaylee was all dressed for school and looked impatient.

Courtney spun around to look in Kaylee's direction. Melissa hoped the girl hadn't heard them talking. Living in such a tight space made private conversations difficult. "We should talk about this when we're alone," whispered Melissa.

"I think that would be a good idea. I have to go," said Courtney, still sounding annoyed.

When she got up, Melissa reached out to grab her wrist before she could get away. "Courtney, don't be angry."

"I have to go," Courtney repeated, pulling away, but she came back to land a cold kiss on Melissa's cheek. "See you later."

Melissa listened to their feet on the stairs into the garage. She felt bad sending Courtney off to school after an argument. What a shitty way to start the day. Melissa wondered why she had mentioned Doug. Courtney's ex could be annoying at times, especially when he was reminiscing about their marriage, but otherwise, the guy couldn't be nicer. He always spoke to Melissa respectfully. He seemed to genuinely care about his daughter. Now that he lived nearby, he often took Kaylee for weekends, providing his ex-wife and her new lover with some much-needed privacy. So, why did Courtney get prickly whenever he came up in conversation? She didn't seem to have feelings for him except wishing he would go away.

Melissa wondered why Courtney couldn't just say she loved women now. Melissa had to concede it was a selfish wish, which had more to do with her own insecurity than anything Courtney was doing. She hadn't shown the least interest in Doug or any other man. Arguing about a label was stupid. It changed nothing and only put Courtney on edge.

She hated to add to Courtney's stress, especially when things at school were already so crazy. People had been demonstrating against the mask mandate even before the new term had opened. In another state, a protestor had threatened the school board members with a gun. When the report was broadcast on the evening news, Courtney was white with terror. She tried to hide her worry, but it was obviously taking a toll. Now, Melissa had added to her burden with a stupid argument about being bi. Courtney would be busy when she got to school, but Melissa texted her a red heart, hoping she would see it on her break.

Before digging into the morning's tasks, Melissa poured herself another cup of coffee. Harriet Keene had finally sent over the paperwork for Hobbs Family Practice. Drafting the agreement shouldn't have taken so long, but a corporate agreement with so many contingencies was out of Harriet's wheelhouse. She mostly handled business permits and real estate transactions; sometimes, simple wills and divorces. There was time pressure on finalizing the contracts now that Liz was ready to hire a new doctor. Melissa reviewed the places where she'd stuck sticky notes, finding she still had questions for Liz. She glanced out the window. The big Ford pickup still sat in the driveway, which meant Liz hadn't left for the office yet, so Melissa called her.

"Hey, Liz. I'm reviewing the contracts for the practice. Do you have a few minutes to answer some questions?"

There was a slight hesitation. "Sure, but I don't have a lot of time. I'll open the door through the garage for you."

Liz appeared at the door wearing khakis, a perfectly ironed button-down shirt, and a blazer, but her feet were bare. "Come in," she said, opening the door wider. Liz was the consummate hostess. The fact that she didn't offer Melissa a cup of coffee meant that she really was pressed for time.

"The orange tags are my questions for you," explained Melissa handing her the documents.

"Come into my office." While Liz flipped through the pages, Melissa studied the photographs and awards on the walls. She knew that her neighbor hadn't always been the senior doctor at Hobbs Family Practice. In a former life, she'd been a famous surgeon and well-known author. "Yes, I want the real property to become part of the assets of the corporation when I leave the practice." Liz flipped to the next tag. "Yes, I want the corporation to be bound by the succession plan." She looked up. "Is that it?"

"The blue tags are for Harriet."

Liz slid the papers across her desk. "Tell her I'll set something up for later in the week."

"Okay. Can you give me a clue what it's about, so I don't look stupid when she asks me?"

"She knows. But I'll tell you. You know all my other business." Liz looked at her through her brows. "You know that Lucy and I are engaged."

"Yes, but I've kept it to myself, like you asked."

"That's good because I haven't even told my friends. I only told Harriet because she's my lawyer. She keeps pushing me to draw up a prenup like the one I had with my first wife. Admittedly, it made the divorce go smoothly, but I don't feel I need one with Lucy."

In her work as a trust attorney, Melissa was known for her expertise in financial planning, but because of the age difference and Liz's professional success, Melissa looked up to her. She was flattered to be asked for her advice. "Does Lucy have significant assets?" Melissa asked.

"She does. After she recovered the earnings her agent embezzled, she found a legitimate financial advisor, who really grew her investments. Her wife left her well off, and the beach house is worth quite a bit, as you might expect. Erika had an insurance policy to pay off the mortgage, so Lucy owns it free and clear. Yes, I would call her assets significant."

"She has a daughter, and I assume you have heirs. Prenups are a good idea for people with wealth. Better to sort things out when there is good will between the parties."

"I know all the reasonable arguments, and I was willing to listen to Harriet when I married my first wife because I wasn't really sure. I have absolutely no doubts about marrying Lucy."

"That's how you feel now," Melissa cautioned. "As you know, situations can change. Feelings can change."

"I want to enter this relationship in good faith, and I think Lucy feels the same."

Melissa found herself crossing her arms on her chest, mirroring Liz's posture. "If you're both so certain, why not do a prenup?"

"I want Lucy to know I trust her…and she can trust me, no ifs, ands, or buts."

Melissa studied Liz's resolute face. "I could make lots of arguments that might change your mind, but it sounds like you've already decided."

"Yes, I guess I have," she said, nodding. "Thanks, Melissa. You've been very helpful."

"But I didn't do anything."

"Yes, you did. You let me think out loud, but you need to leave now, because I have to go," said Liz briskly.

By now, Melissa knew Liz well enough not to be offended by the abrupt dismissal. Besides, it was probably time for Melissa to be at her makeshift desk in the garage apartment. When she checked her phone to see if there were any messages, she saw one from Courtney—a string of red hearts.

❋❋❋

Brenda Harrison could feel her wife's eyes on her while she buttoned her shirt. She flipped up the collar and looped the regulation navy tie around her neck. "I guess seeing me in my uniform doesn't bother you anymore."

"No, I've accepted it. It's part of you…like having blond hair and blue eyes…and being white."

"I can change being a cop, but I can't change being white."

"White is how God made you, and I wouldn't ask you to give up your job because you love being a cop. That's why I tried to talk you out of re-signing. And aren't you glad Olivia wouldn't go along with it, especially now that your heart is almost back to normal?"

"I would have lost all that pension money. I owe Olivia for refusing my resignation."

"Sometimes, she can be decent," Cherie said, idly smoothing the bedsheet with her hands. Brenda admired her wife's attempt at kindness toward the town manager, especially knowing how much she disliked her.

"Olivia is not my favorite person," said Brenda, engaging Cherie's gaze in the mirror, "but she has her moments, like all of us."

"I still don't trust her." Cherie wasn't alone in her skepticism. As the former CEO of the big hedge fund she'd founded, Olivia Enright was used to getting her way. Pushy, overbearing behavior never went over well with Mainers, who were mostly 'live-and-let-live' people. Most of the residents of Hobbs were "from away" but tried to learn the local customs. Not Olivia. She thought she was superior and made sure everyone knew it.

"She saved my job," said Brenda, thinking back to when her COVID-related heart problems first surfaced. At first, she wouldn't listen to Liz, who was hopeful that she would recover. Everyone tried to talk her out of quitting her job, but only Olivia had the power to prevent her resignation. No matter how much Olivia annoyed her, Brenda would always be grateful. "And I'm one of the lucky ones. Many COVID long haulers are still out of commission. Liz says they may never get better. Scary."

"We're just beginning to see how big a problem that will be. We've been so busy handling the outbreaks, we haven't had time to think about the long-term effects. I don't know how we'll deal with all those chronic cases." Cherie got out of bed and put a robe over her nightgown. She mocked a shiver. "It's right chilly this morning. Why did I ever think it was a good idea to move to Maine?"

"Because your father was a Mainer, and he wanted to die at home."

"Yes, exactly. Daddy was so homesick for this place, but he's gone now, so why did I stay?"

"Because Liz gave you a good job."

Cherie's full lips curved into a sly smile. "You know that's not the reason."

"You stayed because you love me."

"Damn right, I do," said Cherie, standing on her toes to give Brenda a kiss. "Come downstairs, Chief Harrison, and your wife will make you a nice big breakfast with all the fixings."

"You don't need to do that. It's your day off. You could have slept in today."

"I know, but I don't want my Brenda heading off to work without a good breakfast in her belly." She gave Brenda's midriff a gentle poke. "Which is getting more impressive by the day. I see you've moved your belt a notch. Come down, and I'll fry you up a couple of eggs. And how about that nice ham I made the other night? Mmm. I think I'll make some for myself too. Maybe a nice ham-and-cheese omelet. What do you say?"

Brenda smiled, watching Cherie's face as she concocted the breakfast menu. Her wife was the most natural cook she'd ever met. All she had to do was taste a dish, and she knew exactly how to make it.

After Cherie left, Brenda carefully adjusted her tie and inserted the Hobbs Police tie pin. She snapped on her epaulets and threaded through the cross belt. Finally, she put on her collar insignia and stood back to inspect her image in the mirror. She always tried to look sharp to set an example for her officers.

This uniform wasn't NYPD blue like Brenda and generations of Harrisons before her had worn, but Hobbs PD gray made her equally proud, especially the collar stars and sleeve chevrons designating her rank as chief of police. She'd had to work her way up from patrol officer, even though she'd made lieutenant before she took retirement and left New York. She hadn't minded because she'd been looking for a lower-stress job, and that's how they did things in Hobbs.

Brenda thought of how close she'd come to giving up the uniform and even her life. She had never felt so sick in her life. For a while, she'd needed an oxygen tank to breathe. Fortunately, Liz and Cherie took good care of her. Cherie still felt guilty because she'd been an asymptomatic carrier, who'd infected Brenda and her father before she knew. Emphysema had left Jean-Paul Bois vulnerable, so the disease took him fast. Cherie would probably never forgive herself for her part in his death or giving Brenda the virus.

"Brenda! Are you coming down soon?" shouted Cherie up the stairs. The tantalizing smell of coffee wafting up from the kitchen made Brenda crave a cup. She grabbed her service shoes from the closet and hurried downstairs.

Cherie was pouring her a cup of coffee when she came into the kitchen. "Two eggs or three?"

"Two's plenty. How come everyone's worried about cholesterol except you?"

"You don't get much cholesterol from food. Eggs are okay."

Brenda sat back in her chair. "I like eggs, so that makes me happy. It's nice to have a doctor in the house."

"I'm not a doctor, just a physician's assistant," Cherie gently corrected. "I don't know half of what Liz carries around in that brain of hers." Cherie gave Brenda a kiss on the top of the head. "Honey, you need a dye job. Your dark roots looked cool, but now, they're coming in gray."

"I'll do it this weekend. It grows so fast in the summer."

"I just want my hero to look her best. Don't you have those departmental awards coming up? Your photo will be in the paper. Olivia worries about how her people look to the public."

"I'm not one of her 'people,'" muttered Brenda.

"She's the town manager and you report to her, so yes you are."

Cherie didn't need any encouragement in her dislike of Olivia, so Brenda changed the subject.

"When is Liz hiring that new doctor?"

"Sounds like soon. One of the candidates is doing per diem work this week."

"You really don't mind having two doctors to support?"

Cherie shrugged. "I'll have more patients, but that's good. It means the practice is growing and my job is more secure. For a while there, when we had to close the office during the lockdown, I was worried I might be let go."

"But Liz kept paying everyone. She's a real mensch."

"A what?"

Brenda was surprised. She thought everyone knew that word. "It's Yiddish for a decent person who does the right thing."

"That's Liz all right." Cherie looked up from beating the bowl of eggs. "Mensch. Huh? I'm picking up a lot of those New York words from you."

"Maybe I'll learn to speak New Orleans."

"That's good. When we start our family, I want it to represent both of us."

"Cherie…" Brenda tried to think of a gentle way to say that starting a family in their fifties wasn't a good idea.

"Yes, I know. You think I'm too old to carry a baby, but I'm healthy and still fertile. Cathy says if that's what we want to do, we should get going."

This topic was even more volatile than Olivia's high-and-mighty attitude. Brenda decided to let it go.

Cherie sang softly as she watched the omelet cook. She always had a tune in her head. Just hearing her voice in her house could bring a smile to Brenda's face. After Marcia died and during all those years alone, Brenda never thought she'd meet anyone special again. And then, there was gorgeous, sexy, smart Cherie to love her. Brenda wasn't an especially religious person, but she murmured a little prayer of gratitude.

***

Sam McKinnon combed back her chestnut hair with her fingers. Feeling daring, she'd let it grow long on one side and shaved the other. While her hair remained the original color, and she was young enough to carry it off, she figured she might as well experiment. It might be her last chance before she looked ridiculous. At sixty, she knew she was already pushing it.

"How long will you be working on the renovation of Liz's office?" Olivia asked, pouring Sam a cup of coffee.

"I have no idea."

"That's an informative answer," Oliva said, topping off her own coffee. "Surely, you know, and you're not telling me for some reason I can't even guess."

"There is a reason, which is, I don't know myself. Building materials are in short supply. Many of the things we need are on backorder. No one can give me any information." Sam hated defending herself to Olivia, whose penetrating blue eyes sometimes made her feel like she was back in grade school.

"Does Liz know there will be a big delay?"

"Yes, I told her. I didn't even want to break ground until I knew I could get what we need, but you know how Liz is. She wants everything ready for that new doctor she's hiring."

"It's part of her succession planning," said Olivia. "Melissa Morgenstern suggested it. She's helping get the practice set up so that it won't be swallowed up by the Southern Med network."

"I keep hearing about this, but I don't understand. When our architectural firm was bought out by a bigger one, it turned out to be a good thing. We could hire more architects and take on more clients with less overhead."

"That's a benefit of mergers, but it doesn't always work that way. Liz bought Hobbs Family Practice because she likes the idea of being an old-fashioned, independent doctor. It's a romantic idea, but I don't know how practical it is in today's world."

"If you'd heard her complaints when she was chief of surgery at Yale, you'd understand. She said there was too much policy and PR, and patient care was shoved into the background."

"Well, she would know," said Olivia, mixing blueberries into her yogurt. "Will I see you tonight?"

"I have to mow my lawn. It's supposed to rain tomorrow."

Olivia's expression softened. "Maybe you could come over afterwards."

"Thanks, but if I have time after I finish the lawn, I'd like to get in some fishing."

"Please, Samantha. You're so busy I hardly ever see you."

Sam's patience, calmly maintained for months, shattered. "Olivia, why are so fucking demanding! Don't you understand that I have other things to do? Give me some space!" She threw her napkin on the table and got up.

"Wait! I'll make you some breakfast," said Olivia, following her through the living room.

"I'll pick something up," Sam called over her shoulder. She forced herself to close the front door normally, but she hurried to her truck before Olivia got the idea to come out of the house. Sam didn't want to be roped into extending the conversation.

The morning air was chilly. Sam wished she'd remembered to bring her jacket, but she didn't want to face Olivia again. The sweatshirt in the truck was dusty from tiling work, but it was better than nothing, so she pulled it over her head. As she climbed into the cab, her phone vibrated in her pocket. She was tempted to ignore it, thinking it must be Olivia, but the caller ID showed it was from the SIPs company. Hopefully, it didn't mean yet another delay. She didn't want to leave the foundation open all winter.

"Samantha McKinnon?"

"That's me."

"I wanted to give you a heads up that we're loading your panels on the trucks today for delivery tomorrow."

"Nice of you to give me so much advance warning."

"Sorry, but we never know ourselves."

"I'll see if I can get my crew in place. Everybody's busy. They're building like crazy here."

"They're building like crazy everywhere," the man said. "I've got the crane for tomorrow, so I put you in right away. Should I send my crew if you can't round up yours?"

"Let me see what I can do. I'll call you back in an hour."

Sam gazed out the window while she considered who to call first. The phone rang again. This time, it was Olivia. Sam thought about letting it go into voice mail, then decided to answer it. "Not now, Olivia. My SIPs are coming tomorrow, and I need to find my crew. Most of them took other work while I've been waiting for the panels."

"All right, I'll let you go. Work comes first."

"The panels are for Liz's project, and they're loading them on the trucks as we speak. Look. I'm sorry I was short with you, but, dammit, give me some breathing room! I'll talk to you later." She tapped off the call before Olivia could respond.

While Sam drove to Liz's office, she mentally planned how to finish the prep work. Fortunately, with structural insulated panels, it was minimal. She liked to work with them for light construction because they cut down on labor costs and ensured uniformity. She'd also used them for the original structure she'd designed when Liz had first bought the practice. The new wing would have more offices, exam rooms, and a staff locker room and bathroom. Sam had wanted to build this section right from the beginning, but Liz was worried about the risk of buying a practice in a small town and put Sam on a tight budget. Afterward, she complained that the uncomfortable bargain furniture made her patients squirm. Somehow, Sam had resisted saying, "I told you so."

When she arrived at Hobbs Family Practice, she was glad to see the big, gray truck in the parking lot. Placing the panels would be noisy, and she needed to warn Liz, who hated surprises.

Ginny, the practice manager, smiled behind the plexiglass. Sam had originally designed the business office to be open. Because of the pandemic, the staff was now walled off from the patients, which made the check-in area look cold and unwelcoming.

"Hi, Sam. I bet you're looking for Liz. Unfortunately, she's busy right now."

"Oh, Ginny, please. I really need to talk to her…just for a minute."

Ginny frowned in disapproval, but she picked up the office phone. "She's with the new doctor. She won't be happy about being interrupted."

"I'm sorry, but I just heard that the panels are coming tomorrow, which means this place will be really noisy."

Ginny's expression suddenly changed, which meant her boss had picked up on the other end. "Hi, Liz. I'm sorry to bother you, but Sam McKinnon is here. She needs to see you about the building project. Yes, she said it's important." Ginny rolled her eyes as she listened. "Okay. I'll send her right down." She hung up the phone. "She growled, but she'll see you."

"She always growls. Thanks, Ginny." Sam patted the counter before she headed down the hall.

The door opened before she could knock. "Make it fast, Sam. I'm really busy here."

Sam glanced into the office where an attractive Asian woman sat. Sam's first lover had been Japanese, and ever since, she'd had a weakness for Asian women. She felt herself blushing while the intelligent, dark eyes gave her a careful once over. She wished she were wearing something better than a dusty sweatshirt and paint-splashed jeans.

"Amy, this is Samantha McKinnon. She's the architect on the renovation project." Liz turned to Sam. "Dr. Hsu is thinking about joining our practice."

Dr. Hsu smiled coyly. "Liz, I hope we're past the 'thinking about it' phase."

Liz folded her arms on her chest. "Well, Sam? What's so important that it can't wait?"

"Your panels are coming tomorrow. I didn't expect them for weeks because of the shortages, but this morning I got a call that they're loading them on the truck. Nice of them to give me advance notice," Sam said sarcastically. Liz pointed to the open visitor's chair. "No, I can't stay. I have to find my crew. They signed on to other jobs while I was waiting for the SIPs to be fabricated. I only came to warn you because installing the panels could be disruptive."

"Will we need to close the office?" asked Liz, frowning. Sam could guess why she looked worried. Things had finally gotten back to normal at Hobbs Family Practice. Shutting the office during the lockdown had nearly bankrupted Liz. Even now, some patients were afraid to come into the office, fearing infection from the virus.

"It will be noisy," Sam explained, "but it shouldn't affect the inside of the building much. You might feel the vibration when the panels land. The crane could block the parking lot. I'll do my best to manage the traffic."

"I'm sure you'll handle it, Sam," said Liz, still standing with her arms folded, clearly impatient to get back to her meeting.

"That's all I wanted to say. If you have any questions, call me. But now, I need to find my men and see if they're available." Sam smiled at the new doctor. "Nice to meet you, Dr. Hsu."

"Please call me Amy. Nice to meet you too, Samantha."

"It's Sam to my friends. Will you be around tomorrow?" Sam asked hopefully.

"I will. I'm working per diem all this week." The woman's smile was beguiling, and Sam couldn't help but return it. After she shut the door, she was still grinning. She managed to remember to thank Ginny on her way out.

*****

Lucy secretly enjoyed watching the vestry members do a double take. Their eyes were transfixed by the enormous diamond that had once belonged to Liz's grandmother. Erika had used the antique ring in her very public proposal at the Webhanet Playhouse cast party, but Lucy had rarely worn it. Liz had donated the family heirloom because Erika had accidently dropped her mother's engagement ring into the garbage disposal. Liz had expertly opened the plumbing and recovered the sapphire, but the ring was mangled. Erika eventually had the stone mounted in a new setting, and Lucy wore it next to her wedding ring over the course of their brief marriage. The diamond ring had remained in Lucy's jewelry box because Erika didn't want to offend her friend by attempting to return it. When Liz asked for it back, Lucy could easily guess why, but she didn't want to spoil the surprise by saying it aloud.

"Can we come to order?" Abbie, the senior warden said, rapping her knuckles on the mahogany table. "Ladies and gentlemen, order, please!" The murmuring and pointing stopped. Abbie turned in Lucy's direction. "Mother Lucy, will you please start us off with a prayer?"

Every head bowed reverently. This vestry was a pious bunch. The buzzing over the ring resumed as soon as the prayer ended. Lucy had to use her theater-sized voice to get their attention. "Hello, everyone. Glad you all could make it this afternoon."

"Lucy, it looks like you have an announcement." Abbie's eyes focused on the big diamond. "Who's the lucky person, or should we guess?"

"I'm sure no one needs to guess that Dr. Stolz and I have agreed to marry. We haven't set a date yet, but when we do, you will be among the first to know."

There was instant applause and a chorus of congratulations. The verger blew Lucy a kiss from the other end of the table. The people sitting beside Lucy patted her shoulders.

But not everyone seemed happy about the news. Olivia Enright frowned slightly. Tom Simmons was deadpanning. Lucy had expected some pushback from the group, but she'd been counting on Olivia and Tom to support her. Tom was the associate rector. His friendship with Liz and Erika went back decades. Olivia was one of Lucy's staunchest allies. Thanks to her, St. Margaret's, with its too-large, historical church, now had a healthy endowment.

The knowledge that the finances were on firm footing allowed Lucy's mind to wander during the treasurer's report. She had to pay attention while the vestry discussed when wine might be included in communion again. Everyone agreed it was still too dangerous to bring back the common cup. The return of masks was similarly unpopular but deemed necessary. Lucy half-listened to the reports of the altar guild and the harvest fair committee, but Olivia's disapproving frown kept distracting her.

Finally, Tom said the closing prayer. Without a goodbye, Olivia headed straight to the door. Tom hung back, obviously waiting for Lucy, while people offered her congratulations and hugs. After everyone else had left, he remained, standing by the door.

"Tom, I can see you have something on your mind," Lucy said, gathering her papers.

Tom smiled as he approached. "I do, Lucy, but first, let me offer my congratulations on your engagement." He bent to kiss her cheek.

"Thank you, Tom. It actually happened a few weeks ago, when Liz and I were in New York."

"I'm surprised that you could keep it a secret for so long. Not you, Lucy. I know you're discreet, but Liz? Of course, as a doctor, she needs to keep secrets too. I admit that I'm a little disappointed she didn't confide in me."

"Don't be. I asked her to keep it to herself."

"Really?" Tom looked at Lucy with surprise. "If it's a good thing, why not share the news?"

"I wanted to share it, especially with my friends, but I waited to see what Liz would do."

"What do you mean?"

"I wanted to give her time to get used to the idea."

Tom looked around to make sure no one was nearby. "Let's go to your office to talk about it."

"Smart idea."

Lucy headed out, and Tom fell into step beside her. Once inside Lucy's office, he closed the door. "You don't really think Liz would change her mind, do you?"

"No, but just in case, I wanted to give her an out. Liz doesn't like to be backed into a corner, even when she does it herself. I don't think she would have proposed to Maggie Fitzgerald if the cancer hadn't forced her hand." Lucy put her bags down in her desk chair and took one of the visitors' chairs.

"Like Erika, Liz was raised to have a strong sense of duty. She has old-fashioned ideas about morality."

"One of the things I like most about her."

"Me too." Tom took a seat beside Lucy. "You do think Liz is serious about this marriage?"

Lucy thought for a moment before answering. "I do, but I had to propose to her. The words just wouldn't come out of her mouth." Lucy smiled at the memory of Liz, tongue-tied while they sat at dinner in an elegant Manhattan restaurant. "She's serious enough to have her grand-mother's ring resized for me." Lucy extended her fingers so Tom could admire the ring.

"Altering a family heirloom that obviously means a great deal to her is a big step," Tom said, releasing Lucy's hand. "But are you sure, Lucy? Loneliness and grief can drive a person into a connection that may not be right for the long term."

"Tom, you're one of the few who know I've loved Liz for a long time. Being intimate with her has revealed parts of her personality that I never knew existed, but it's about much more than sex." Lucy glanced at Tom, whose face was suddenly stony. "I'm sorry, Tom. Too much information?"

"Lucy, you know you can always talk to me about anything. Maybe it's presumptuous, but when I heard the news, I'd hoped you would ask me to officiate at your wedding. We'll talk about your intimate life in your pre-nuptial counseling. Besides, I've been in this business a long time. Nothing anyone could say would shock me."

Lucy searched his kind face. The white beard made it harder to read his facial expressions, but she could see that his lips were compressed. "You have other concerns."

"Oh, Lucy, I know I'm crossing the line, and I don't want to offend you." He offered a weak smile. "You are my boss, after all."

"That doesn't matter. This is between friends."

Tom idly stroked his knees as he thought. "I don't want you to feel pressured to marry because of your role as a priest. I think that's why you pushed Erika into marriage. Happily, that turned out well."

"I have no regrets about the marriage…except that it was too short."

"And that brings me to my next concern. Isn't it too soon?"

Lucy had expected this objection, but she thought carefully before she responded because she respected Tom. He deserved more than a rehearsed answer. "I'm sure many people will think so, which is another reason I hesitated to make an announcement. I never want anyone to think I'm disrespecting Erika's memory or didn't love her. I miss her so much!" Tears formed in Lucy's eyes.

Respectfully, Tom gave her a moment to deal with the strong emotions and compose herself. "Lucy, people will judge you no matter what you do. As the rector of St. Margaret's, you're held to a higher standard. But you're well established now, so I wouldn't worry too much about what people think."

"But you're still frowning."

Tom sighed. "Liz still seems so angry. Maggie's betrayal really touched a nerve. That hurt goes back to their college days, so it's deeply entrenched. I pray that she learns to forgive her…for her own sake, if nothing else."

"I pray too. Forgiveness is essential for them both to go forward, but, honestly, Maggie doesn't help herself. She's isolated herself from her friends in Hobbs, including me. She used to call me her best friend. I never understood why she didn't try to meet Liz halfway. I find fishing messy and smelly, but I know how much Liz loves it, so I go out with her. It's a small price to pay for the pleasure of her company."

"Maggie gets seasick, so I can understand her reluctance."

"But there were other things they could have done together. She even complains about camping…in a cabin that's as comfortable as a hotel!"

"Lucy, we're talking about your marriage. A postmortem on theirs isn't going to help."

"Yes, it will, because I can see the pitfalls ahead. Maggie let Liz get away with a lot in that relationship. I've made it clear that I won't tolerate that kind of behavior."

Tom laughed and offered a fist bump. "You go, girl! Set boundaries right from the start."

"Mostly, I haven't had to. Despite what you've said, Liz isn't 'immune to reform.' I've seen changes in her."

"Liz is an intelligent woman. If it suits her purposes, she'll modify her behavior. Being with you is a strong incentive, but be careful, Lucy, don't make her into a project. You're her partner, not her therapist."

"I'm not intentionally modifying her behavior, but you know how it is, Tom. We all bring our roles into our relationships. Liz would prefer I'd check my priesthood at the bedroom door. She offers medical advice during sex."

Tom roared with laughter. "Somehow that doesn't surprise me, nor the fact that she is quickly adapting to your cues. It's never too late to grow, and Liz is quite a remarkable woman, so different from the hard-driving, ambitious woman I met forty years ago. You will be a good influence on her, Lucy, especially because she admires and respects you. You can do so much good in her life if she allows it. I hope she will do the same for you."

"She already has. I don't know if I could have finished my book without her help…and yours."

"When it's published, you will have a big impact beyond our little Maine parish."

"Tom, I know you don't want to hurt my feelings, but are your concerns important enough to prevent you from marrying us?"

Tom smiled broadly. "Not at all, and I didn't mean to suggest they were. But does Liz know the marriage will come under greater scrutiny because she's divorced? That you'll have to wait a year after the divorce papers were filed?"

"We haven't set a date. I doubt Liz will be in any rush. Besides, waiting would be more respectful to Erika's memory."

"I agree. It sounds like you've thought of everything." Tom leaned on his knees as he rose to leave. "Thank you for listening, Lucy. I only wanted to clear the air and keep the lines of communication open. Our friendship means a great deal to me."

"Thank you for the gift of your honesty, Tom."

He gave her shoulder an affectionate squeeze. "I'll let you go home. It's been a busy day."

Lucy watched him go. She hoped the conversation had reassured him. She valued Tom's steady support in his role as associate rector, but she treasured his advice as a friend.

When Lucy got home, she savored the simple pleasure of being in her own space. The modest house seemed too big now that Emily had gone off to Yale, but Lucy loved it because Erika had remodeled it specifically for them. Lately, Liz had been encouraging Lucy to sell the house to capitalize on the rising home prices, but Lucy wasn't ready to let go of the place where she still strongly felt Erika's presence.

Lucy found Liz in the kitchen, preparing a salad for dinner. The other dinner ingredients and utensils were carefully staged on the countertop.

The pots and pans Liz needed were set out on the stove. She approached cooking a meal like surgery.

"Did the vestry ooh and aah over the big rock on your hand?" asked Liz, bending to kiss Lucy. She wasn't satisfied with one kiss and came back for another.

"It certainly got their attention…as planned."

"Any pushback?"

"Only from Olivia, who frowned and bolted from the meeting. And Tom, but he was kind."

"Oh? What's Tom's problem?" asked Liz, lowering the flame before tossing sliced zucchini into the frying pan.

"He's worried that you're still angry with Maggie."

"Well, I am."

"I'm worried about that too. Liz, you need to let it go. Holding a grudge only hurts you."

Liz shoved the pan of salmon into the oven. "We can eat in about ten minutes. Take off your collar and get comfortable while I finish dinner."

"Liz…"

"Go change. We'll be eating soon."

Lucy sighed in frustration. When Liz didn't want to talk about something, there was no forcing her. Some things had changed, but others definitely hadn't.

# 2

The enormous crane swung each panel off the truck and delicately set it in place on the foundation. There was a distinct thud every time a panel landed. The vibrations shook the office floor. Through the window, Amy watched the architect, wearing a bright yellow hard hat, direct the operator and wave each panel into place. She had come in twice to apologize for the noise. As she'd predicted, the operation was distracting, but Amy didn't need an excuse. Reviewing the files of the patients that she would inherit when she joined the practice was tedious work. Her eyes swam from reading so much detail.

Despite the boring task, she was glad she had decided to spend her vacation as a per diem physician in Hobbs. The waning tourist season had given her a good preview of what practicing medicine in a small resort town would be like. The walk-in cases were usually minor accidents or common, easily treated illnesses like seasonal allergies. The regular patients were mostly older. Statistically, Maine was the grayest state in the union, so that was to be expected. There were some young families, even a few obstetrical cases. Cathy Pelletier, one of the osteopaths, had been trained in OB/GYN.

The range of specialties at Hobbs Family Practice made it exceptionally self-sufficient. One partner was an osteopath who specialized in orthopedics and sports medicine. Liz Stolz was a surgeon. Amy wondered who would extract the fishhooks and close wounds when the senior partner retired. The rest of them would have to brush up on their suturing, something Amy hadn't done since her surgical rotation. Amy's expertise was chronic cardiac care, not exactly a hands-on speciality.

She tried to bring herself back to her task but just couldn't. Watching the architect walk the perimeter of the foundation like a balance beam was far more interesting. Sam McKinnon was in amazingly good shape for a woman in her sixties. Her muscle development suggested she worked out.

Amy had casually asked for the name of her gym, thinking she might join it when she moved, but the woman had laughed. "You think I have time for a gym? I'm always lifting lumber, bags of concrete, and buckets of drywall compound. You can be sure I get plenty of exercise."

Amy watched Sam nimbly move out of the way as another panel approached. It effectively blocked Amy's view. Disappointed, she immersed herself in the case files, but her mind wandered again. She found herself thinking about her dinner date with Liz and her fiancée. She had hoped they would have concluded their negotiations by now. Hopefully, this dinner was to close the deal.

Even without a contract in hand, Amy had felt confident enough to put a deposit on an apartment. Fortunately, she had very little to move. Silently occupying the same house while waiting for it to close, she and her ex-wife had sold or donated much of the common property. Amy's small condo in Mount Kisco, where she'd moved after the divorce, couldn't hold much. After the slow, painful disintegration of her marriage, Amy wasn't into nesting again, so she'd acquired very little. Now, she was eager for a new start. She'd vacationed in Maine as a child and had been scanning the health-care employment sites for opportunities. When she saw that Hobbs Family Practice was looking for a new doctor, she'd sent her resume right away.

The sharp knock on the door made her jump. "That's it for today," said Sam, poking her head into the room. "The guys will set the trusses tomorrow, but that's a quieter operation. Thank you for your patience, Dr. Hsu." The woman's warm brown eyes smiled in a way that seemed like more than professional accommodation.

Amy waved her in. "Please call me Amy, and you don't have to apologize for doing your job."

"I know, but I don't want the noise to keep you from doing yours. When they called yesterday, I could have held them off. Liz wants your office finished, so that you'll have a place to sit when you arrive."

"I'm sure Liz wants her office back, even though she doesn't use it much. She's always running around seeing patients or dealing with something in the practice."

Sam's barely disguised amusement let Amy know she wasn't telling her anything new. "Maybe you'd like to grab lunch today?" asked Sam, her hands clasped together like she was praying. "I know a restaurant on the other side of town the tourists haven't found yet. Their haddock sandwich is the best in town."

Although the invitation surprised Amy, she found herself rationalizing why she should accept. She knew no one in town except the practice staff. Making some social connections seemed like a good idea. Besides, Sam was cute, if fetchingly shy. Amy guessed she'd had to work up the courage to offer the invitation, and she didn't want to hurt her by refusing. "Give me fifteen minutes to finish up."

Sam beamed, but the light in her eyes abruptly faded. "I hope you don't mind riding in my truck."

Amy had lived her entire life in places where only tradesmen owned trucks. Here, everyone seemed to drive one, even women, including her new boss. "I've never ridden in a truck," Amy confessed, "but it sounds like fun."

"Good. Come out when you're ready. Meanwhile, I'm going to talk to my crew, so we can go over the plan for tomorrow."

A few minutes later, Sam came into view outside the window. Her shyness disappeared when she addressed her crew. The attentive posture of the men, leaning in to listen, proved the respect they had for her. Finally, the huddle broke up, and they all headed to their trucks.

While she waited for Sam to return, Amy recalled what Liz had said about her. "Don't be fooled by Sam's humble attitude. She's a world-class, prize-winning architect. Look her up." When Amy googled her, she got page after page of hits. She started with the Wikipedia entry and worked her way down. She discovered that Sam had become internationally famous at a time when few women won high-profile architectural projects. Amy carefully studied the photos of the famous buildings Sam had designed.

Her minimalist architecture showed great strength supported by the least obvious means. The aesthetic was familiar because it had been widely imitated, yet Amy had never heard of Samantha McKinnon before now.

Amy signed out of the system and grabbed her bag. "I'm going out to lunch, Ginny," she said at the check-in desk.

"We're closed until one, Dr. Hsu. No need to rush." Amy glanced at her watch, happy to see she had plenty of time.

Amy found Sam carefully brushing off the passenger seat. "I promise I'm not one of those people who keep a messy truck, but construction materials are dirty. I wouldn't want you to ruin your nice clothes." Amy looked down. The tailored suit was something she would have worn to work in Westchester, but she'd been wondering if she'd been overdressing. The other doctors in the practice wore casual clothes, even shorts. Their clinical coats with the embroidered Hobbs Family Practice logo hung on hooks in the staff room, getting dusty.

"The easiest way to get into a truck with a skirt is to put your backside in first," Sam explained. "Use this hand grip to hike yourself into the seat. Then swing in your legs."

After Amy's eyes measured the height of the seat, she doubted this operation could be achieved gracefully. "Don't look!" she warned. "I'm going to make a fool of myself." Fortunately, there were no wardrobe malfunctions.

"See? You did fine," Sam said, yanking down the seat belt and handing it to Amy before she closed the door.

"This is fun!" Amy said, enjoying the view of the road from truck height on the ride to Route 1. Then they ran smack into bumper-to-bumper traffic. "Oh, my God," murmured Amy. "Is it always this bad?"

"This is nothing. You should see it in the summer. Most of the tourists are gone by Columbus Day—I should say, 'Indigenous People Day'—we got rid of Columbus Day up here. The locals avoid the main roads in the season, but don't worry. I'll show you a shortcut."

Amy found Sam's easy confidence reassuring. "Do you live in town?"

"I do, but I live on the other side of the turnpike. In Hobbs, that's like living on the wrong side of the tracks. Some contractors even have two rates and charge the summer people more."

"Do you?" asked Amy, curious.

"No, I charge what the job is worth. I can't be bothered with all the bookkeeping. Never mind how much it would hurt business if people found out." Looking at Sam's open face, Amy imagined she was honest to a fault.

"I'm looking forward to living up here," said Amy, watching as Sam navigated the country road. "I think I found a rental in Webhanet."

Sam made a little face. "Webhanet is a resort town. They don't even have a school, so they send their kids to ours. We may not be a tourist destination like Webhanet, but Hobbs is a real town. We have schools, a supermarket, two hardware stores, and a movie theater. You'll pay twice as much rent in Webhanet. And the traffic! If you think it's bad in Hobbs…"

"Gee, Sam. I wish I had met you earlier."

"Well, you know me now." Sam smiled in her direction. "I'm no expert on the town. I've only been living in Hobbs full time since last year."

"Where were you living before?"

"New Haven."

"Oh, did you know Liz while she was at Yale?"

"I did. She's the one who encouraged me to move up here."

"Were you a patient of hers?" Amy asked, venturing a guess.

"No, it had nothing to do with her job. She was the president of our woodworking club. She walked into a meeting one day, and a couple of months later, she was running the whole thing. She says she doesn't like being a boss, but always ends up being in charge of everything…the chamber of commerce, the Rotary, the hiking club, the fish and game…"

"Some people are born leaders."

"Not me. I'm an introvert. My firm had to send me for training so that I could supervise the construction of the buildings I designed. Being a boss doesn't come naturally to me."

"I don't know. You looked like you had your crew in line today."

Sam blushed a little, which Amy found endearing. "You were watching?"

"Yes. Do you mind?"

The pink in Sam's cheeks deepened. "The men respect me because I've worked in the trades. I know how to swing a hammer, even though no one uses them anymore, and I do my own tile installations." Amy thought it odd for a Princeton-trained architect to get so involved in the nitty-gritty, but she understood the idea of developing competency. "How about you, Amy? Where are you from?"

"I was born in Manhattan. My father was chief of cardiothoracic surgery at NYU. My mom was a cardiologist. We moved to Westchester when I was five because Dad joined the faculty of New York Medical College. I went to med school there."

"Another Westchester girl."

"You too?"

"No, but Liz is from there."

"Wow, I'm learning more about my new boss from you than from her. Glad I met you, Sam."

Sam turned and winked. "I can be useful sometimes. Plus, I know all the backroads."

❋❋❋

When Liz brought up the prenuptial agreement, Melissa could see Harriet cringe and look in her direction. Confidentiality wasn't an issue since the client had raised it, but Melissa slouched in her chair, trying to make herself small, although her height made it impossible.

"It's all right, Harriet," said Liz with a dismissive wave. "Melissa knows about the engagement, and Lucy announced it to the vestry, which is like taking out an ad in the *Sentinel*. By now, everyone in Hobbs knows."

Harriet regarded her client with a frown. "Liz, you say you don't need a prenup this time, but try to think rationally."

"Rationally," Liz repeated with a snicker. "Harriet, when you got married, was protecting your assets the first thing on your mind?"

"I was twenty-five years old. I didn't do much thinking in those days."

"None of us did, but Harriet, you were already a lawyer, working in a big firm. Why didn't you think of it?"

"Because I didn't want to start the marriage with distrust."

"Exactly," replied Liz, looking pleased that Harriet had made her argument for her. "You know I can be hard-nosed when it comes to business, but this is not business."

"Liz, if you were hard-nosed, you'd sell your practice to Southern Med, take the money, and run."

"It will never happen. I wouldn't do that to my partners. They stuck with me through good times and bad. When no one would come into the office during the lockdown, Bill and Cathy took a reduction in their draw so I wouldn't bankrupt myself. I owe it to them to protect the practice."

"But the prenup is also for your protection," said Harriet patiently. "Someday, you might thank me."

"No, Harriet. I won't thank anyone for encouraging me to plan for this marriage to fail."

Harriet gave her a hard look. "Liz, I'm sure you have the best intentions, but we all know you have an eye for the ladies."

Melissa gripped the arms of the old-fashioned courtroom chair, bracing for a reaction, but Liz smiled proudly, evidently taking the remark as a compliment. Melissa remembered when they'd first met, and Liz had very obviously undressed her with her eyes. Her interest didn't last long. Women usually got the hint when their attention was unwanted, and Liz was no exception.

"All right, Harriet, I'll grant that I like to look at pretty women," Liz admitted affably. "What red-blooded lesbian doesn't? Lucy is trying to teach me to be more respectful, but I'm still a work in progress."

"As are we all," said Harriet with a skeptical look. "You just have a longer way to go than most of us."

Liz glanced at her watch. "Damn! Where the hell is Olivia?"

"Don't worry, Liz. I'm not running the meter. This project is a package deal, and Melissa's part in it is gratis."

"I know, but I have things to do, and Melissa probably needs to get back to work."

Melissa shrugged. "I'm fine. I'm already over my quota of billable hours for the month."

"You're not finding it hard to get work done in that little apartment over my garage?"

"I'm alone for most of the day while Courtney and Kaylee are at school. Courtney's been busy with after-school meetings, and Kaylee made the basketball team. I get most of my work done while they're out."

"Your mother keeps wondering if she'll ever see you again," Harriet said, leaning back in her chair.

"Oh, she's so busy with Jack I'm surprised she even noticed." Since Jack had moved in, the house on the salt marsh no longer felt like home. His male presence had completely changed the atmosphere. After Melissa's father had died, the energy level had noticeably dropped. Now, the air crackled again. Jack's magnetic personality demanded attention. He had a wide range of interests, which made him good company, but Melissa missed having privacy with her mother.

"Sometimes, it's good to have a separate office for work," Harriet said. "Moving your location helps the mental shift into business mode. When I first came up here, I had my office in my home. Then I bought this building for a song. That was in the days when real estate in Maine was still cheap."

"Mom gave me a spare bedroom to use for an office. I guess I could work there. That would probably satisfy her need to see me. Trouble is, it's so comfortable to work in my pajamas. Sometimes, I don't shower or dress until noon."

"Yes, it's easy to get into the habit," Liz said. "During the lockdown, I had all these women walking around my house without bras. It certainly does give you a different perspective on your friends." There was a lewd suggestion in Liz's little smile. Melissa smiled too. Liz might be trying to reform, but that streak of mischief could be entertaining.

The door opened and a harried Olivia flew in. "I'm so sorry to be late. The council meeting turned into a free-for-all."

Liz grunted. "What are your Republican friends complaining about now?"

"It's the masks again. It's just common sense. I don't know what's wrong with these people!"

"I do," said Liz. "It's a proxy fight. They say that making their kids wear a mask in school is infringing on their rights. Well, what about the right of the other kids to stay alive? It's like the gun thing."

"You carry a gun," challenged Olivia.

"That's to defend myself from nuts like them. If they banned guns, I'd be the first to hand mine over."

"Ladies," said Harriet in a patient voice, "let's get to work, so you can all get on with your day." She looked at Olivia to make sure she was settled. "Has everyone reviewed the new documents?" Three heads nodded. "Liz, do you have any questions? This is your last chance. Once you sign, the practice becomes a corporation. It's no longer your personal property. You understand?"

"With you and Melissa explaining everything half a million times, I think I understand. Let's just get this done." Liz opened her bag and took out a fountain pen.

"Wow," said Melissa. "I haven't seen one of those in a long time."

"I like to use a fountain pen to sign important documents. Makes them seem more official. When I went to Catholic school, we had to use a fountain pen when we learned cursive. Damned things leaked into the pockets of my brothers' shirts. Our housekeeper had to use straight bleach to get out the blue stains. Eventually, the fabric disintegrated."

Harriet handed out ballpoints imprinted with "Harriet Keen Associates" to Melissa and Olivia, so they could sign as witnesses. Melissa added her signature to each document, feeling a sense of pride in helping Hobbs Family Practice preserve its independence. Since she'd been working on this project, she felt less like a summer visitor and more like a townie. Hobbs was beginning to feel like home.

***

Olivia hung back while the others pumped Liz's hand and offered their congratulations. The rational part of Olivia's mind acknowledged that Liz had every right to be pleased. It had taken four talented women and months of work to get this deal done.

When Liz offered her hand, her warm smile indicated that she had no idea how much she had offended Olivia by keeping her engagement secret. Lucy's announcement in the vestry meeting had stunned Olivia. She'd thought she had her finger on the pulse of Hobbs. How could something so important happen without her knowing? She was especially hurt that Liz hadn't told her. After Liz had confided some personal matters, Olivia had been lured into thinking they'd become close. Obviously, she'd been mistaken.

Olivia felt crushed like a high-schooler after discovering she hadn't been privy to a secret that had been whispered behind a locker door. In school, the other girls had shunned her and ridiculed her out-of-fashion, thrift-store clothes. Olivia had finally gotten her revenge by becoming a celebrated Wall Street success and fabulously wealthy.

She knew that other women couldn't be trusted, but she studied them to figure out what they cared about to use it for control. That's how she'd kept her female associates and employees in line when she ran the Enright fund. She also used it to manage her lovers, even Sam, but she was no fool. By now, she'd probably figured it out. No wonder she'd started to chafe at the bit.

The meeting was breaking up. Olivia wanted to grab Liz before she disappeared. She needed her support for the mask mandate. More importantly, Olivia needed to share her disappointment that Liz hadn't confided in her. "Liz, would you like to join me for lunch?" Olivia asked, lightly tapping her arm. "I grilled some tuna last night to make salad."

Clearly on a high from the successful conclusion of the project, Liz turned with a smile. "Olivia, your tuna salad is delicious. I'd never turn it down, but I can't stay long. I want to get over to see Erika's father. One of the vestry members lives in his senior residence. Stefan needs to hear about the engagement from me, not one of his cronies."

"I wish you had told me. Did Sam know?" Olivia asked bluntly.

"I haven't told her yet…or Brenda and Cherie. I'm going to meet them at Sláinte tomorrow night for drinks." The Irish pub was the favorite watering hole of the Hobbs police and fire departments. Because they reported to Olivia, she usually avoided the place.

"Do you mind if I stop by the office first?" asked Liz, when they reached the parking lot. "They're installing the insulated panels today. I shouldn't be long. Sam texted me that it's going well."

Olivia forced her face to avoid a reaction at the mention of Sam. Since she'd stormed out the other morning, Sam hadn't responded to any of Olivia's attempts to communicate. "That's fine. I want to pick up fresh rolls for lunch," said Olivia.

At the French bakery, Olivia ordered a pound of fresh fettuccine even though half a pound would be more than enough for her. She kept hoping Sam would show up for dinner. For the same reason, she ordered a full-size Italian bread instead of the half-sized loaf she usually got when she was alone.

Liz hadn't arrived by the time Olivia got home, and she was grateful to get a head start on lunch. As she diced the celery and onion for tuna salad, she recalled making lunch for Sam while she was working on the bathroom renovation that had brought them together. They had gotten off on the wrong foot with an argument over the need for masks. Their relationship had been fraught with tension but that had only added to the sexual excitement when they'd finally consummated it.

Olivia had trusted Sam with some of her darkest secrets. Not that she worried Sam would ever tell—Sam was too decent for that, but Olivia wondered if she'd been a fool for making herself so vulnerable to someone who'd only been in it for the sex.

When the doorbell rang, Olivia's hands were wet, so she let Liz in with the phone app. Liz came into the kitchen with a bag of apples. "I saw these at the farm stand. First of this season's Macouns. I didn't know what else to bring." Liz reached around Olivia and gave her a half hug. "Please don't be angry because I didn't tell you about the engagement."

Olivia shrugged off Liz's arm. "I don't understand why it was such a secret."

"I would have told everyone right away, but Lucy wanted to wait. I assumed it has something to do with her being a priest."

Olivia could partially buy that explanation. As rector of St. Margaret's, Lucy had to maintain an untarnished public profile. Information about her had to be carefully managed, but Liz also had a prominent public role. None of it made sense.

"I'm not mad, Liz. I'm hurt because you didn't trust me."

Now, Liz looked hurt. "Liv, I do trust you. I just went along with what Lucy wanted."

"A first, I bet." Olivia reached up and patted Liz's shoulder. Although she wasn't particularly short, Olivia always felt dwarfed next to her. "I forgive you, Liz, but it would have been nice if one of you had told me."

"Then you would have told Sam, and she would have been hurt that I hadn't told her. No, it was better to tell everyone at the same time."

Olivia nudged Liz aside, so she could get to the fridge. "Make yourself useful and slice the rolls. There's a serrated knife in the block."

Liz pulled out the knives one by one, looking for the bread knife. "That's a hell of a lot of tuna salad you're making. Are you expecting more people?"

"No, I always make extra for Sam to take for lunch."

"You take good care of her. I hope she appreciates it."

"I think she finds it intrusive."

"Hmm," intoned Liz noncommittally, expertly halving two sub rolls. "Sam is the independent type. Probably why her relationships don't last long. I told you not to push her, Liv."

"But I didn't push," protested Olivia indignantly.

Liz made her difference of opinion known with a frank stare.

"All right, I did push her, but I want her to move in with me. My house has a view of the ocean and all this space," Olivia said with an expansive sweep of her hand. "Her house on the pond is as beautiful as you'd expect from an architect, but really, it doesn't compare."

"But Sam likes it there. It's her place. She renovated it, and it's exactly how she wants it."

Olivia spread tuna salad on the rolls. "I think I might have scared her away."

"Well, you have to admit you're pretty scary."

"I don't scare you."

"Not much scares me," said Liz with a shrug. "No, I take that back. Lucy scares me. That priest thing is terrifying."

"It fascinates you. That's why you keep coming back for more. Sit down and eat your sandwich." Olivia put Liz's plate on the kitchen table. "I hope you don't mind the informality. Would you like some wine?"

"I have a lot to do this afternoon, so I'll pass."

"I'm going to have a martini," said Olivia with an enticing note in her voice. She knew how much Liz loved a good martini.

"Well, in that case…"

Olivia took down a glass pitcher. "I'm sure we're both going to regret this, but I know you can hold your liquor."

"I'm kind of out of practice since Erika died. She was my drinking buddy. My German improves with a little alcohol." Liz heaved out a sigh. "We had the best conversations. God, I really miss her."

"I've never had such a close friendship, but I bet you do miss her. I miss her too." Olivia poured a martini from the shaker and handed the glass to Liz.

"Excellent," declared Liz. "You make them even better than my ex."

"Maggie? She doesn't seem like the martini type."

"I meant my ex-ex. You know, Dos Equis. Jenny was a master of the martini."

"I'll have to meet her someday."

"Well, now that Maggie is gone, I'll invite her up. Maggie was never too fond of her. She thought I cheated with her when we first got back together."

"Did you?"

Liz shook her head. "Jenny fell asleep in my bed, and I let her stay. Maggie was in the downstairs bedroom, which was kind of weird. She didn't buy that all Jenny and I did was sleep in the same bed. After I got together with Maggie, I didn't have sex with anyone else."

"What about Lucy?"

Liz stared at her. "Olivia, you sure ask pointed questions."

"That's how I get answers," said Olivia, biting into her sandwich.

"None of your business, but Maggie and I were divorced before Lucy even let me near her."

"Good to know she's not a hypocrite."

Liz frowned as she studied Olivia's face. "I thought you were a Lucy fan."

"Oh, I am. I just like to know who I'm dealing with."

✳✳✳

Cherie heard Sam's distinctive laughter before she saw Dr. Hsu pass the staff room. Cherie glanced at the clock. Five minutes late. She was willing to give Dr. Hsu a pass because she was here as an observer and hadn't officially joined the practice, but she hoped it wasn't a sign that the new doctor couldn't stay on schedule, which would make more work for the assistants and her PA.

"My apologies, Cherie. I completely forgot the time," Dr. Hsu said when Cherie appeared at her door. At least she could admit when she was wrong, which was better than Cherie could say about some doctors.

"Sam is good company," Cherie said. "She's entertaining, and wicked smart. Oh, see? I'm picking up that Maine talk." Cherie laughed at herself.

"From your accent, I'd have guessed you're not from here."

"No, I grew up in Louisiana. Daddy was a Mainer, but he was stationed in New Orleans when he was in the Navy. When he met Mama, it was love at first sight."

"What a sweet story. Now that you told me, I can identify the accent," said Dr. Hsu, tapping her ear. "Moving to Maine must have been a big shock to a Southerner."

"Oh, it is. It's so cold here in the winter. Not only that, Maine is the whitest state in the union."

Dr. Hsu nodded, frowning a little. "When I was considering this job, I was a little worried that I'd be the only non-white in town."

"You're not. I'm black," said Cherie matter-of-factly.

Dr. Hsu stared at Cherie the way everyone did when she told them. Who would expect a blonde with blue-green eyes to be anything but white? The doctor carefully studied Cherie's face, probably seeing the hints of her mixed-race heritage in her perpetual tan and generous lips. "I would never have guessed," Dr. Hsu admitted.

"My mother was black. Mixed race too and very light-skinned. She could pass for white. At least, you look like who you are."

"My family came from China in the nineteenth century. That gives me a better claim to being American than most Europeans, but intermarriage was discouraged in my family. My ex-wife was also Chinese."

Cherie blinked. She hadn't expected the new doctor to come out so casually. "We should get to work," Cherie suggested, "so you can get out of here on time. I hear you have a big dinner tonight."

"I'm meeting Liz and her fiancée at Nathan's."

"Oh, that's a nice place. Pretty fancy."

"Which is why I need some time to put myself together." The woman already looked completely 'put together.' Accessorized, the stylish knit dress she wore could easily be dressy enough for a dinner date. Cherie mentally added some showy jewelry and a scarf to Dr. Hsu's outfit.

"You'll like Mother Lucy," Cherie said. "Everyone adores her."

"When Liz told me she's marrying a priest, I didn't know what to think. I especially didn't know what to think when she told me she has the last word on whether I get hired."

Cherie laughed. "Oh, I don't think you have to worry, but Liz relies on Mother Lucy for advice. She's a licensed therapist."

"You are too, from what I understand."

"I am, and sometimes, I cover for Mother Lucy when she's not available.

She's stretched pretty thin. We don't have enough mental health professionals in this state."

"What made you go back to school to become a PA?" asked Dr. Hsu, leaning back in her chair.

"I figured out that so many mental health issues were rooted in my clients' physical health. Plus, I always secretly wanted to be a doctor."

"So, why didn't you go to medical school?"

"For one thing, I couldn't afford it, and then it was too late. You know how you get to a certain point in your life and realize your options have closed? I always wanted a family too, but never found anyone to settle down with. Now, I finally have someone I love, but it may be too late."

Dr. Hsu's finely tweezed eyebrows shot up nearly to her hairline. "But you must be close to my age."

"I'm fifty-one," Cherie frankly admitted. "Yes, I know. It's really late, but I really want to have a child."

Dr. Hsu composed her face and leaned forward. "It's certainly not ideal, but it's being done all the time now. We used to think forties were the upper limit. You're still fertile, I assume."

"I am, but I'm starting to get symptoms of perimenopause, so it's now or never."

"Obstetrics is not my field, of course, but if there's anything I can do to help, let me know."

"Dr. Pelletier is my doctor. She hasn't been shy about the risks, but it doesn't matter if I can't get my wife to agree."

"Your wife?" she asked, blinking.

"Yes, I'm married to Brenda Harrison, the police chief. I'm sorry. I didn't mean to get into all this personal stuff."

"It's fine. We're just getting to know one another." She glanced up, and Cherie guessed she was checking the clock over the door. "We really should get back to work." But behind her veneer of professionalism, Dr. Hsu looked equally reluctant to let the conversation go.

✳✳✳

The martini had gone straight to Liz's head, but it had also eased the tension. While she drank the coffee she'd accepted to help sober up, she politely listened to her hostess complain about the mask mandate. Liz had never met anyone so single-mindedly devoted to dominating every conversation, but having already gotten on Olivia's bad side, Liz let her go on. By the time Olivia wore out her topic, Liz's head had cleared.

"I need to go," Liz said, getting up. She was glad that her feet felt solid beneath her, which meant she was sober enough to take on Stefan. Erika's father might be ninety-four and stone deaf, but his mind was still razor sharp.

"Would you like to bring some of these lemon bars to Stefan? If you can wait a moment, I'll pack some for you to take."

"That's kind, Olivia." Liz meant it sincerely. That was the paradox of Olivia. She tried to rule everyone with an iron fist, but she had a kind heart. Liz watched Olivia neatly wrap a plate of lemon bars in aluminum foil. "I'm sure Stefan will love them," said Liz. "He has a sweet tooth, and these will remind him of his wife's lemon tart. The perfect sour treat." Liz's mouth puckered at the mere thought. "Erika's mother had a little restaurant at one time. She taught me and Erika how to cook her favorite dishes."

"If you give me her lemon tart recipe, I might forgive you for not telling me about your engagement."

"Deal." Liz put her arm around Olivia and gave her a half hug. "Friends?"

"I thought we were heading there. Then I wasn't sure."

"Be sure," said Liz, giving her shoulders another squeeze.

Olivia slid out from under Liz's arm. "Go on. Explain to Professor Bultmann that you're marrying Lucy. I hope he approves." Olivia's penetrating blue eyes steadily held Liz's gaze.

"You don't?"

"I think you're both rushing into this. I care about Lucy, and I don't want her hurt."

Without blinking, Liz said, "Olivia, I assure you that I would never hurt Lucy."

"I don't want to get into another argument, Liz, but your track record isn't good. There. I've said my piece. Now, go." Olivia urged Liz forward with a little push and handed her the package of lemon bars. "Tell Professor Bultmann I said hello."

Liz parked outside Ocean Terrace Senior Residence and squirreled around in the door compartment for a N95 mask. Usually, visitors were required to sign a guest book, but the receptionist merely waved when Liz entered the lobby. "Hi, Dr. Stolz. Are you here to see a patient today or the professor?"

"Professor Bultmann knows I'm coming."

"Let me ring him to say you're on your way. Rev. Bartlett is already up there." Before Liz could respond, the elevator announced its arrival with a ping. She wondered what Lucy was doing there, but it wasn't unusual for the sly redhead to read her mind, not that Liz actually believed in telepathy.

The door to Stefan's apartment opened just as Liz raised her hand to knock. "Hi, sweetie," said Lucy, pulling her inside. She lowered her mask to give her a quick kiss.

Liz followed her into Stefan's snug living room, where nearly every inch of wall space was covered with shelves containing books of every kind, subject, and vintage. A china tea service had been set out on the table. Stefan struggled to get up from his favorite armchair to greet her.

"Don't get up," Liz said, touching her cheek to his in lieu of a kiss. When she was at a safe distance, she took off her mask.

"What a pleasure to see you," Stefan said, beaming a smile at each of them. "Lovely Lucy, will you pour the tea for me? My hands are shakier than usual today." Liz studied the slight tremor, judging it not to be serious, but she made a mental note to follow up later.

Lucy poured them each a cup of tea. She prepared her father-in-law's the way he liked it with exactly one teaspoon of sugar and a splash of cream. She moved the side table closer so that he could easily reach his cup.

"Thank you, dear." Stefan took a sip of tea. "Good. I can still make tea. That means I will live a little longer." He grinned so everyone would know he was joking. "This must be important for you both to come on the same day," he said, studying them with his pale eyes. "Well, don't keep me in suspense. I hope you came to tell me you're getting married."

Lucy's smile was coy. "And we were hoping to beat the gossip."

"Impossible. Hobbs is a small town like the village outside Berlin where I grew up. Everyone knows everyone else's business." He smiled sweetly in Lucy's direction. "But, Lovely Lucy, you needn't have come to ask for my blessing. Now that my daughter has passed, you are free to marry again."

"Stefan, you've been like a father to me," said Lucy. "I came out of respect."

"I know. And I am touched, but I want you to be happy. You are like a daughter to me. Elizabeth too. She and Erika even looked like sisters."

"Papi, I hope you don't think it's too soon," Lucy said.

"No, no. I know how you loved my Erika, both of you. She loved you too. She, if anyone, should be an example of why life must be lived in the moment. There is no time to lose, especially at your age. There's not as much time as you think. It goes by like that!" He tried to snap his fingers to make his point, but the papery sound was barely audible. Meanwhile, the cup in his other hand was shaking. Liz watched, ready to jump up and catch it, but he stared at it until it was steady. Then he held it carefully in both hands to return it to the saucer.

Relieved, Liz sat back again. "Thank you, Stefan. Not everyone has been so understanding."

He waved his hand dismissively. "*Ach*, don't listen to the naysayers. People don't like change, but as we all know, change is the only constant. It was the one thing that Erika and I could agree on after she left mathematics for philosophy. Of course, we debated its meaning because that was what we were supposed to do. You remember, Elizabeth. You were on my side for a change." When his eyes refocused on the present, he smiled in Lucy's direction. "When the time comes, I would be pleased to give you away."

"That's so kind, but what about Liz?"

"Elizabeth too. It's practical. I shall need both of you to help me get down the aisle. One on each arm should do the trick."

"We'd be honored," Liz said.

"Good," said Stefan decisively. "It's settled."

They caught up on the news. Stefan had been developing a theorem with Lucy's daughter for her doctoral thesis, and they spoke almost daily. He often knew things about Emily before her mother did. Taken up in the pleasant conversation, Liz almost forgot the dinner date with Amy Hsu. Then the old clock on the bookcase chimed the hour. "Stefan, we need to go soon," said Liz, draining her teacup. I'm hiring a new doctor for the practice, and we're meeting her for dinner. We'll come back soon."

"I know you'll be back. Lucy comes every few days and brings me donuts from Congdons." He wagged a finger at Liz. He emphasized the challenge by raising his bushy, white brows. "Don't you dare lecture me, Dr. Stolz. I already know they're bad for me. At my age, why should I care?"

"Well, I brought you some of Olivia's lemon bars, so I'm not exactly practicing what I preach."

"Feed the sweet tooth or it will bite, my mother used to say." Stefan carefully replaced his teacup in its saucer and managed to get to his feet. He blew each of them a kiss. "This virus is a curse. My dear girls, I wish I could really kiss you and give you hugs. Hopefully, soon."

❋❋❋

Lucy enjoyed watching Liz in her professional persona. With Amy Hsu, who was more sophisticated than the other partners, Liz was sharper edged. Tonight, Lucy could easily envision her as the formidable chief of surgery at Yale. Liz had put on makeup and changed into a designer suit, leaving behind the relaxed country doctor look. Lucy was realizing that her fiancée had at least as many facets as her grandmother's big diamond. Lucy had worn her engagement ring because it was a dress-up occasion. While she listened to the conversation, she idly watched the light reflect off the stone.

She had turned off the therapist part of her brain early in the conversation, having already decided that Amy Hsu would be a good addition to Hobbs Family Practice. She had a calm, balanced personality well suited to family medicine. There was nothing showy about her. She was poised and confident, yet she was warm and laughed easily.

Liz was winding down the business conversation. "The contract will be on your desk tomorrow morning," she assured Dr. Hsu.

"Technically, your desk."

"Sam promises to have your office finished soon."

"Meanwhile, I appreciate your hospitality." The woman turned to Lucy and smiled warmly. "So, I guess I passed muster with you, Rev. Bartlett."

"I have confidence in Liz's judgment," Lucy said. "And please call me Lucy."

"And you must call me Amy." She raised her wine glass. "Congratulations on your engagement and my best wishes for your happiness."

After they walked Dr. Hsu to her car, Lucy took Liz's arm and pulled her closer. "Good choice."

"I don't know what I would have done if you hadn't approved."

"You would have hired her and never looked back." Lucy let go of Liz's arm and took a step away, taking in the whole package. "Have I told you how sensational you look tonight?"

"Thank you, but I can't wait to get home and take off this suit."

"Will you stay the night?" asked Lucy, getting into the car.

"I hung some clothes in the car, hoping for an invitation." Liz closed Lucy's door and got in on the other side.

"I called the bishop this afternoon," Lucy said casually, wanting to ease into a topic she knew would be controversial. "I wanted to tell him that we're getting married."

"Was that really necessary?" Liz replied, sounding as irritated as Lucy had expected.

"It's a courtesy I wouldn't dare ignore. He said he'd like to meet you." Lucy leaned forward to see Liz's face. Other than a slight frown, it registered no expression. "You don't have to come along, but I need to see him." Explaining Liz's absence to the bishop would be difficult, but Lucy knew how much Liz would resist being pressured.

There was a long silence before Liz said, "I'll go with you. When is this meeting?"

Lucy, who'd been holding her breath, released it. "I need to set it up. I'll make it for your day off. Okay?"

"Sure," said Liz with an obvious lack of enthusiasm. "Just give me a couple of days' warning."

When they walked in the door of the beach house, Lucy was glad to be home. She'd been awake since dawn and was fading fast. Standing side-by-side with Liz at the double vanity to take off her makeup and brush her teeth, she realized she was seeing a preview of their married life. Their future would be full of such ordinary moments.

Liz, efficient as usual, was in bed first. She looked surprised when Lucy took off her nightgown and got into bed naked. She tugged on Liz's shirt. "Do you think I find your ratty, old T-shirt and men's boxers sexy? Take them off." Liz sat up and discarded her clothing. "That's better," said Lucy. "Sleeping naked encourages intimacy." She snuggled against Liz's breast, enjoying the warmth of her skin and her own familiar scent beneath the cologne she wore. "I miss you when you're not here."

"Living in two houses is getting old. If we lived at my house, we could sleep together every night."

"I don't think moving in together is a good idea just yet, but we do need to decide where we're going to live." Lucy sighed. "I'm not ready to give up the beach house."

Liz's rigid silence indicated she was making an effort to avoid an argument. "Did you make me strip for sex or just to cuddle?"

"Let's talk and see where it leads." Lucy ran her hand over Liz's pubic hair to signal her ultimate intention. "Thank you for inviting me to come tonight. The dinner was delicious, and I enjoyed meeting Dr. Hsu. I think she'll be a good addition to the practice. I like her sense of humor."

"Me too. Thank you for coming. I always value your opinion."

"But you don't really need my advice. Your psychological insights are perceptive. For such an analytic person, you trust your intuition, which is good." Lucy allowed her hand to wander Liz's body. The parts that had been exposed to the sun weren't as soft as the tender places only Lucy saw. Those felt silken under her fingertips. She teased Liz's nipples into hardness.

"You're turning me on," said Liz, making it sound like a complaint.

"That's the idea." Lucy slipped her hand between Liz's legs. "Open up," she whispered into Liz's ear before giving it a wet, probing kiss.

# 3

Brenda's hand searched on her night table where her service phone was dancing. The scanner had gone off twice with calls to respond to a domestic dispute. After the squawking settled down, Brenda had assumed that her officers had things under control, but the vibrating phone was proving her wrong.

Brenda took the phone into the hall. She closed the bedroom door behind her, so that she could speak at a normal volume. "What's up, Moody?"

"Sorry to wake you, Chief. We responded to a domestic call. We have two dead at the scene. Murder-suicide from the looks of it." Brenda was glad that the lieutenant couldn't see her face. Although Hobbs had its share of drug overdoses and suicides, the town hadn't had a homicide since Brenda had become chief. Like most rural towns, Hobbs had plenty of domestic complaints, especially during the long winters when people were shut up together. Alcohol or drugs were almost always involved. Everyone had guns.

"Are the guns secured?" Brenda asked.

"Yes, ma'am. I got photos of their location and packaged them for evidence. I called the staties to send CSI, but they can't come down until tomorrow."

"So, we leave everything like we found it and tape up the place. Any other victims?"

"No, ma'am, but we found two kids in a closet. I was hoping Vachon could get some information out of them, but she can't stop puking."

"What?"

"When you get here, you'll see why. The guy shot the woman at close range with a twelve-gauge. Nothing left of her head, just a flap of skin where her neck was. Big hole in the wall. He shot himself with a 9 mm through the mouth. Much neater, but still a mess."

Even without the graphic details, Brenda could envision the nightmare at the scene. "Did you get the kids out of there?"

"Vachon has them in her cruiser."

"Okay. I'll throw on some clothes and be right there. What's the address?"

"I already texted it to your phone."

Brenda tapped open her text app. "Got it. Thanks."

When Brenda went back into the bedroom, she was surprised to see Cherie sitting up in bed, so she could find her clothes.

"I'm sorry, baby. I tried to be so quiet."

"You were, but I could hear how upset you are in your voice." Having a shrink for a wife was a mixed blessing. Cherie could see through the murky depths of people's feelings better than a fish sonar. "What happened?"

"There's been a murder-suicide in town, and my guys need me." It was an odd turn of phrase, considering that both officers at the scene were female. "I probably won't be back soon. Go to sleep." Brenda switched on the bathroom light.

Cherie got out of bed. "I'll make you some coffee while you dress."

"Oh, baby, you don't need to do that."

"I know, but I want to." Cherie picked up her robe from the chair. Before her wife covered up, Brenda filled her eyes with the sight of her big, dark nipples through the lacy bodice of her nightgown. She liked to assume that her wife dressed for her pleasure, but Cherie was quick to correct her. "Darling, I dress to please myself first. Sexy clothes make me feel sexy. Nice if you like them too, but they're for me." Brenda had felt put in her place, but she admired Cherie's easy confidence and pleasure in her body.

There was no time to take a shower. Brenda put on the same uniform she'd worn to work. Thinking she might get another wearing out of it, she'd carefully hung up the shirt and pants. Her sleeve patches showed her rank, so there was no need for insignia, but at the last minute, she put on her collar pins to look good in case the troopers showed up.

Cherie had Brenda's coffee in a Hobbs Police thermal mug ready to go. Her full lips were deliciously soft when Brenda kissed her. She weighed her warm breast in her hand, wishing she could go back to bed instead of heading out into the dark. "Go to sleep, honey. I'm sorry I woke you."

"Never mind about that. I love you. Please call me and tell me what you find."

Brenda didn't promise to call, but not to spare her wife the gory details. Cherie had done her PA training in a big Houston hospital, where she'd seen plenty of grisly sights. As a homicide detective in New York, Brenda had seen them too. The worst were the decomposed bodies, especially in the summer. The floaters were a close second. The sight of someone pulled out of the river could stay with her for days. In the city, shotgun homicides were uncommon, and Brenda didn't look forward to seeing this one, not that she ever looked forward to seeing a crime scene.

She'd have to talk to Vachon about the vomiting. Police work required seeing things that would disgust most people. Either Vachon would get used to it or she'd need to find another line of work. Then, recalling her own rookie days, Brenda softened her position. As a female cop, she'd endured plenty of hazing, but when she'd vomited at her first messy homicide, the guys looked the other way. Hardening yourself took time, and they'd all been there.

When Brenda arrived, the house was lit up like there was a party going on inside. In the squad car parked in the driveway, the patrol officer was sitting with the kids. Brenda tapped on the window and Vachon rolled it down.

"Where's your mask?" asked Brenda sternly.

"I forgot."

"Put it on," ordered Brenda. "Now!"

"Yes, ma'am!" Vachon dug into her pocket for her regulation mask.

Brenda looked through the back window. "How are the kids?"

"No physical damage, but they're scared to death. The little one won't stop crying." The wailing of the girl in the back made it hard to hear.

"How old are they?" asked Brenda, leaning closer. "Could they say?"

"The older one says he's six. He thinks his little sister is five."

"Did you call CFS?" Brenda asked.

"It went into voice mail. The recorded message said to leave a message and they'd call back during regular business hours."

"Well, that's not very helpful," said Brenda, frowning. "Keep an eye on them until we figure out what to do." She took a deep breath before heading into the house.

"Holy shit," she murmured when she saw the wall behind the female victim. There was blood and shredded flesh everywhere. She glanced at the headless body. Theoretically, she knew a shotgun blast at close range could literally blow someone's head off, but seeing it was shocking.

Moody was busy taking photos with her regulation phone. "I got some good shots, but I'm no expert on homicide investigations."

"You're doing all the right things," said Brenda, carefully stepping around the pool of blood. "Where's the male vic?"

"In the kitchen. Obviously, he shot her and then took himself out."

"I'll go take a look."

"Oh, Chief," said Moody before she got to the door. "The coroner called to say the morgue is completely full of dead COVID patients. They need to find another place to store the bodies, so they might be here for a few days."

Brenda nodded to acknowledge she'd heard. "Who called it in? I didn't see anyone when I drove in. Usually, when people see our flashers, we get a big audience."

"You know how it is with these houses back here in the woods. People don't bother with their neighbors, especially not when there's a lot of screaming and yelling from the house. A woman down the road called it in. She said that gun shots from here were usual. He was always shooting the coyotes. When she heard the second shot, she knew it sounded different."

"Smart woman. Okay. Write it up with as much detail as you can. I'll send Vachon back in here to help you secure the scene. She needs to learn to deal with the blood and guts. I'll take the kids for medical attention."

"Copy that, Chief." Brenda smiled. Jean Moody was an old school cop like Brenda. There weren't many of them left, and Moody was coming up for retirement.

Brenda walked through the house room by room, looking for evidence. Although the furniture was shabby, the house was surprisingly neat. The kids' closet was full of colorful stuffed animals. Brenda was tempted to grab a few and look for clothes for the kids, but she knew she should leave everything exactly as it was for the crime scene investigators.

She headed out to Vachon's patrol car. "I'm taking the kids with me," said Brenda. "Go back inside and help Moody. CSI isn't coming till tomorrow." Terror flooded into the young woman's face. "I'm sorry, Vachon, but it's part of the job."

Vachon reluctantly got out of the car and headed toward the house. When Brenda opened the back door the children cowered in the corner.

"Hi. My name is Brenda. I'm going to take you to the doctor to make sure you're okay." Neither of them moved. The little girl was wailing again. "What's your name," Brenda asked the boy, ignoring her.

"Keith." He turned to the girl. "Come on, Megan. We have to go with the lady." He tugged on her arm, but she wouldn't budge.

"It's okay, Keith," Brenda said. "Let me talk to her. Come on out." Brenda got into the back seat with the girl. "Megan, I need you to come with me."

"I want my mommy!" she screamed.

"I'm sorry, Megan, but you can't see your mommy right now," said Brenda, speaking softly. "I need you to come with me. Can you do that?"

The girl grew quiet except for a few hiccups and stared. Brenda slid out of the backseat, and eventually, the girl followed. She reached up her arms to be carried. When Brenda picked her up, she was surprisingly light. Her small arms clamped onto Brenda's neck. She wouldn't let go when Brenda tried to get her into the truck. She had to pry her legs off her hips.

Brenda telephoned Liz on the way, explaining the situation in the sparsest terms because the kids were in the backseat. That was one thing Brenda knew about kids. They were always listening.

Carefully masked, Liz and Lucy were waiting in the kitchen when they arrived. Lucy's messy hair, carelessly tied back, suggested how they'd been previously occupied. For the first time since Moody's call, Brenda smiled.

"I know these children," said Liz, turning the boy's head to examine his ears. "Their mother is my patient."

"Make that past tense. The husband too." Brenda made a gun of her hand and imitated the firing pin engaging. Brenda seldom saw Liz react in a professional situation, but her shocked look lasted barely a second.

"I'll test our young friends for COVID, and then we can figure out what comes next."

"Liz, I need to call Cherie," said Brenda. "Is there someplace private I can talk?"

"My office. You know where it is."

Brenda had only been in Liz's office a few times and never alone. Curiosity compelled her to inspect the photos and awards that covered the walls. It took a few rings for Cherie to pick up the call. "Brenda…?" asked a sleepy voice. "How did it go?"

"It looks like the man shot his female partner and then himself. Fortunately, their two small children, a boy and a girl, hid in a closet. I brought them to Liz to be checked out. She's testing them for COVID now."

"Oh, my God! Poor babies. Did you call CFS?"

"The recorded message said they'd call back during normal business hours. This is an emergency. What are we supposed to do with traumatized kids? Put them in jail?"

"What are you going to do with the kids?"

Brenda swallowed hard. "Cherie, I know it's a big ask, but can I bring them home?"

"Oh, honey, did you really need to ask? I'll turn down the twin beds in the guest room."

"Do you know how much I love you?"

"I love you too. Finish up there and bring those babies home!"

Brenda returned to the kitchen where the children were having cookies and milk while Lucy sang to them. Brenda leaned in the doorway to listen. Momentarily distracted from their horror, the children looked almost happy. "That's a song from an opera about Hansel and Gretel," Lucy explained when she'd finished. "It's a prayer they sing before going to sleep. Did you like it?"

"Sing more," begged Megan, tugging at Lucy's sleeve.

"Where's Liz?" asked Brenda, looking around.

"She went upstairs to look for clothes for the kids." Lucy stroked Megan's curly, blond hair. "They're beautiful children. They look well cared for. Liz examined them and said they seem healthy and well-fed."

"Keith, is your mom a good cook?" asked Brenda. The boy patted his tummy and nodded. Brenda smiled at his natural response, but she was saddened that the boy would never eat his mother's cooking again. "What did you have for dinner tonight?" Brenda asked as much to distract herself as well as the boy.

"Mom made mac and cheese and chicken nuggets. My favorite. But Dad wanted steak. Mom said steak costs too much, so we can't have it anymore. Then he started to yell and throw things. Mom always tells us to go to the closet when Dad yells. Sometimes, it gets really, really loud, and we put our fingers in our ears." He demonstrated and shut his eyes too.

Brenda pressed the boy's head to her hip. "You're safe now, buddy."

Liz came into the kitchen with a pile of kids' clothes and put them on the counter. "My niece's kids and Maggie's granddaughters are always leaving stuff behind. I'm not going to pay more to ship a bunch of old clothes than they're worth. Trouble is, by the time the kids come back, they've outgrown them." She handed a pink hoodie with printed rainbows to Lucy, who helped Megan into the sleeves. "How about you?" Liz asked Keith.

The boy shook his head.

"You sure? It's pretty cold tonight."

"I'm fine."

The boy was wearing slippers, but the girl wore only socks. Liz handed Lucy a pair of child-size, pink sandals. "Brenda, we could keep them here. God knows, we have plenty of room."

"That's kind of you, but I already told Cherie I'm bringing them home."

"Where's my mommy?" Megan asked. She buried her face in Lucy's polar fleece. "I want to go home to my mommy!"

Brenda bent so that her face was level with the child's. "Megan, you're coming to my house tonight. My wife really likes kids. She'll take good care of you."

"I'm sure Cherie knows how to handle this situation," said Lucy, "but if she needs help breaking the news, I'm available."

Brenda got up from her knees. "How do you even do that? In New York, we had psychologists to handle it. And there, ACS answered their phones. Lucy, maybe you can help us interview the kids tomorrow?"

"Absolutely."

"Let me check on those test results," said Liz, turning to the counter where she had set up the kits. "Well, here's some good news. They're both negative, so you can take off your masks."

"All right, kids," said Brenda. "Let's thank Dr. Stolz and Mother Lucy and head to my house."

"Nooooo!" whined Megan, clinging to Lucy. "I want to stay with her."

"It's okay, Megan," said Lucy, stroking her hair. "Go with Chief Harrison. She has a nice, big house. She'll take good care of you." Lucy kissed her forehead. "I'll see you tomorrow."

With a pout, Megan finally let Lucy go and shuffled toward Brenda.

❋❋❋

When Cherie saw Brenda trudging up the driveway with a golden-haired child in her arms and another one in tow, her heart took a leap of joy. It was a sight she'd only dreamed of seeing. Before they'd married, she and Brenda hadn't talked much about kids. Afterward, Cherie had tried to explain to Brenda why she'd waited so long.

Before they'd met, Cherie hadn't known where she belonged. She was at least half white. Her father's people had lived in French Canada before they'd settled in Maine. The navy sent Jean-Paul Bois to New Orleans to work on ship engines. His funny Northern accent had charmed Cherie's mother, who was light-skinned enough to pass for white. The gentle mechanic had scrubbed his oil-blackened hands nearly raw to clean up for their first date.

Jean-Paul didn't seem to mind that she'd been married before, or that her first husband had been a full-blooded black man. He adopted his wife's daughter from her first marriage and treated her like his own. The two sisters couldn't look more different, but people said they belonged together like the chocolate and vanilla ice cream that came in the same container. In those days, it was considered an innocent remark. People weren't as sensitive then.

Cherie had dated men of both races, but none of them seemed right. After she made love with a woman, she finally understood why. Loving a woman was like coming home. Women were soft and beautiful. They smelled and tasted so good, but by then, Cherie was already in her forties. She'd all but given up the idea of having a family until she married Brenda.

Her wife tenderly held the sleeping child close as she bent to kiss her. "Liz gave us some kids' clothes," Brenda whispered. "They're in the car."

"I'll get them. You should put that little one right to bed."

"Shouldn't we give them a bath or something?"

"After what they've been through, let's let them calm down. We'll deal with the rest in the morning."

"Keith, this is Ms. Bois," Brenda whispered to the boy. Cherie thought the introduction was a bit formal, but she didn't correct her. "Please, help her bring in the bags of clothes. Okay?"

The boy nodded.

"Are you tired, Keith?" Cherie asked, reaching out her hand.

"No," he said. "I need to stay awake for when my parents come."

Cherie knelt beside the boy, so she could speak to his face. "Precious, I'm sorry, but your parents aren't coming for you."

"Yes, they are," he insisted stubbornly, stamping his foot. "And they'll be really mad when they find out we left without telling them. We're not supposed to go outside after dark."

Cherie pulled the bags of clothes out of the front seat. She noticed Keith shivering in the night air. She dug in the bag and found a hoodie about the right size. "Here. Put this on."

"I'm not cold."

"Are you scared?" asked Cherie gently.

"No, I'm not scared," the boy said, lowering the pitch to sound more manly. Cherie guessed he'd learned that trick from his father.

Cherie offered the shirt again. Keith eyed it and finally put it on. "The Bruins are the best." He said, pointing to the yellow-and-black logo.

"Well, I don't know much about hockey," said Cherie. "I hear it's popular up here. Maybe you can tell me why that team is the best."

"That's what my dad told me. They've won a lot of trophies."

"I see," said Cherie, realizing the association with Keith's father made even a hockey team a loaded subject.

After they carried the bags into the house, Cherie asked, "How about something to eat? Are you hungry?"

"The lady with the red hair gave us milk and cookies at her house."

"You mean Mother Lucy? She's very kind."

"She said she'll see us tomorrow. Why will we see her?"

"Maybe she wants to talk to you and your sister. We can all talk together. Okay?"

He thought about it for a moment. "Okay. I like her. She's nice."

Cherie wasn't surprised that the boy was so taken with Lucy. Everyone fell for her. "I'm going to make myself a special treat before I go to bed. It's called 'golden milk.' It makes me feel all warm and cozy, so I can sleep. Want to try it?"

He shook his head.

"You sure? How about I let you taste some of mine?"

"Maybe," he finally said.

In the kitchen, Cherie helped him up to a bar stool at the island. She took out the spices from the cabinet and began measuring them into a saucepan. Brenda, wearing her pajamas and a polar fleece, came into the kitchen and peered into the pot. "Oh, I can really use some of that tonight. What time is it?"

Cherie pointed to the clock over the sink. "Nearly two."

"Hey, Keith," said Brenda, taking the stool beside the boy. "I'm sorry you had such a rough night. Can you tell me what happened?"

"Brenda!" scolded Cherie, hands on hips. "It's late and he's got to be exhausted. Can't this wait until tomorrow?"

"I'm not taking a statement," protested Brenda, putting her hands in her pockets. "Just making conversation."

Cherie rolled her eyes. Being a cop was so ingrained in Brenda that if someone cut her, she'd bleed blue. "Keith, you don't have to talk about it if you don't want to," Cherie assured the boy, but he looked sad enough to cry.

"They were always yelling," he said, wiping his nose on the sleeve of his sweatshirt. "Then they started throwing things. I took Megan to the closet like Mom told us. The one time I stayed to watch, Dad hit me so hard my arms got all red."

"Did you hear anything besides yelling?" asked Brenda.

"I heard the gun go off. Twice. The first shot was really loud. I couldn't hear for a long time after it."

Brenda glanced at Cherie. "That was the shotgun blast, I bet."

"Then I heard another shot, a different gun, I was afraid to come out."

"Did your daddy take you shooting?" Brenda asked. The boy nodded. "So that's how you know that guns can sound different. Smart boy." Brenda patted his back.

"Thank you," he murmured. "When are my parents coming?"

Cherie sighed and exchanged a look with Brenda. "Let me try," she said. "Keith, your mother and father had an accident. They were hurt so bad they went to heaven."

The boy's blue eyes widened. "Only dead people go to heaven. Mom and Dad aren't dead!"

Cherie leaned on the counter and looked directly into his young face. "I'm sorry, baby, but they are."

"Nooooo!" he wailed.

"Yes, Keith. I'm sorry." Keith slithered off the stool and ran from the room.

"I'll get him," said Brenda.

"Leave him for a minute. He needs to absorb the news. He's probably crying in a corner. If you keep an eye on my pot, I'll go. You're so tall, and when you met them, you were wearing your police uniform. You even scare me when you do."

Cherie found Keith trying to figure out how to unlock the front door. "I need to go home," he explained, looking desperate.

"No, Keith," said Cherie, taking his hand off the doorknob. "You need to stay here tonight with us. Tomorrow, we'll look for your family. Do you have a grandma or grandpa?" He shook his head. "How about aunts or uncles?"

"No, I don't think so," he said, staring at his feet.

"Don't worry. If you have family, we'll find them." Cherie gave his hand a squeeze and led him back into the kitchen. "Well, look at this! Our golden milk is all ready to drink!" She took down an espresso cup from the cabinet. "And look here. I have this little cup that's just right for kids. I'll put your milk in here. If you don't like it, you don't have to drink it. Okay?"

He nodded.

"Good boy," said Brenda as Keith picked up the cup. "Careful. It might be hot. I always blow on it a little…like this. Then I take a tiny sip to be sure it won't burn my mouth."

Cherie smiled at the demonstration. "Brenda, you're a natural."

Brenda made a face. "Thanks, I guess."

They drank their golden milk in silence. While Cherie cleared away the cups, Brenda took the boy up to bed. "Make sure he brushes his teeth," Cherie called after them. "I left new toothbrushes in the guest bathroom. They should be soft enough for a child."

Cherie finally turned off the kitchen light. When she came upstairs, she found Brenda sitting on the bed talking to Keith. "This was my teddy when

I was little," she was explaining. "I know he doesn't have eyes anymore, but he has special vision like superman! He can even see in the dark! He'll protect you while you sleep." The boy took the eye-less, battered Teddy and tucked it under his arm. Brenda pulled the covers up and turned off the bedside lamp.

"Leave the door ajar, so we can hear them if they get up during the night," Cherie whispered when Brenda came out of the room.

"I hope they can sleep," said Brenda. "I wish there was something more we could do for them."

"We're making them feel safe. After that trauma, it's what they need most."

Wearily, they got back into bed. Brenda raised her arm, inviting Cherie to cuddle. "I asked Keith about his relatives, but it doesn't sound like he knows of any," Cherie said. "Meantime, we can keep them."

"What?" said Brenda, raising her head from the pillow.

"We can put in an emergency application to be foster parents," Cherie said quickly before Brenda could protest. "With the system overloaded, I bet they'll approve us on the spot."

"Cherie, we need to talk about this."

"We will. Tomorrow. And we're going to have a busy day, so now, go to sleep." Cherie put her hand under Brenda's shirt and gently stroked her soft belly. She began to hum an old Creole lullaby that she knew Brenda especially liked.

✵✵✵

When Courtney first heard the noise, she thought it might be acorns dropping on the metal roof. Sometimes, it sounded like the house was under attack, but the muffled tapping she'd heard was soft and distant. Courtney finally realized it was someone knocking on the door that connected the garage apartment to the main house. She looked through the window into the corridor and saw Lucy Bartlett waiting there. No one ever used the door, and it took Courtney leaning on it with all her weight to get it open.

"Good morning," Lucy said in hushed tones. "I know it's early, but there's something you should know before you leave for school." Lucy's voice was as calm as always, but there was concern in her eyes.

"Come in, Lucy. I'll make you a cup of coffee."

"I don't want to disturb Melissa. Come over to the house, and we can talk."

"Melissa's not here. She's working in Boston today. Kaylee's in the shower." Courtney opened the door wider to encourage Lucy to come inside.

Lucy looked around the living room. "I have fond memories of this place. My wife and I lived here during the lockdown after our refrigerator died." Her gaze fell on the colorful throws on the leather furniture. "I see you've added some personal touches."

"It was supposed to be temporary, but this place is starting to feel like home. And we really like our neighbors," said Courtney with a grin.

"I'm glad it's working out for you."

"We're so grateful you helped us find this place. If not for you, Kaylee and I might be homeless."

"Oh, don't worry. We'd never let that happen."

"Come in and sit down." Courtney gestured toward the small table in the efficiency kitchen. "How do you take your coffee?" Courtney picked up the pot and looked in. "God's looking out for you, Lucy. There's just enough for two cups. I can make more if you like."

"No, thanks. I've already had plenty this morning." Lucy pulled out a chair from the little table. "How are you doing, Courtney?"

Courtney filled Lucy's cup. "Oh, where to start? The first weeks of school are always crazy, but this year, it's over the top. The kids missed so much school last year. They need to be in school. The mask mandate is to keep them safe. Why are the parents fighting us every step of the way?"

"Normally, parents will do anything to protect their kids," said Lucy with a sigh. "Unfortunately, people believe what they hear from their friends or their chosen news source."

"You mean the real fake news? We're only following the state guidelines.

The teachers are so stressed. They expect us to shut down any minute.… Honestly, so do I."

"I'm sorry, Courtney. It must be so hard on you, especially with a new relationship and being a single parent." As she looked into Lucy's sympathetic face, Courtney's eyes began to fill. Lucy put her small, freckled hand over Courtney's. "If you ever need to talk, just knock on the door or give me a call. I'm always happy to listen."

"Thank you, but you and Liz already do so much for us. I don't want to impose."

"Don't worry. If it's not a good time, I'll let you know." Lucy patted Courtney's hand before she reached for the milk. "I'm sorry to add to your worries, but something happened last night that I think you need to know."

Courtney shook her head in discouragement. "Can it really get worse?"

"Yes, I'm afraid it can. Let me try to explain," Lucy said, looking reflective as she stirred her coffee. "The police were called to a domestic dispute last night, which turned out to be a murder-suicide. I'm telling you because the couple's children go to your school."

"Oh, my God! Who are they?"

"Keith and Megan Benoit. The police think Mr. Benoit killed his wife and himself. According to Chief Harrison the scene was grisly, but the children hid in the closet and missed the worst of it. The police couldn't get in touch with the CFS last night, so Brenda took the children home with her."

"That's so incredibly kind," said Courtney.

"In Hobbs, we take care of each other," said Lucy. "The police are keeping it out of the press until we can break the news to the community. And for the sake of the children…"

"Oh, those poor babies," said Courtney as the magnitude of the tragedy began to sink in. "Are they okay?"

"Physically, they're fine. Liz examined them last night. They're in shock, of course. I can tell you more later. Cherie is bringing them to St. Margaret's. We completely sanitized the nursery in the hope of reopening it.

Unfortunately, the Delta surge prevented it. We thought it would be a good place to interview the children."

"Will the police be there? The uniforms may frighten the children," said Courtney.

"Yes, we thought of that. Brenda and the detective assigned to the case will wear their street clothes while Cherie and I interview the children."

"Thank God for you and Ms. Bois. What's wrong with CFS that they didn't respond? I've been following the scandal. I heard the former governor cut back funding for social services."

"I'm sure that's part of it, but they're overwhelmed and short-staffed. Many people are unemployed or working from home, so domestic and child abuse are on the rise. The labor shortage makes it hard to find replacements for the staff that leave. Some are leaving because of the vaccine mandates.  Caregivers are dying at a record rate."

"This is crazy," said Courtney, suddenly seeing her own problems in perspective.

"It's what we have to work with. We'll try to get in touch with CFS again this morning, but for now, we're on our own."

"Mom?" said a young voice, and they both turned in its direction. "Are you going to take me to school soon?" Kaylee came around the divider. "Oh hi, Mother Lucy."

"Good morning, Kaylee," said Lucy. "I need to talk to your mother about something important. Could you give us a couple more minutes?"

"Sure," said the girl, glancing at the clock.

"Don't worry, I won't make you late for school," Lucy assured her with a smile.

They waited until they heard the pocket door to Kaylee's sleeping alcove close before resuming their conversation. "According to the boy, they don't have any close family. Hopefully, we can find someone to take them. Otherwise, they'll be put into the system and sent into foster care."

"Oh, I hope not. That's so hard on children."

"Especially after a trauma like this. The district has a school psychologist, but Cherie and I will make ourselves available, if you need us."

"Thanks. I'll let Ms. Henderson know."

"And now, I'll let you and Kaylee get to school," said Lucy, getting up. "Thanks for the coffee. Don't forget to let me know if I can help."

After Courtney closed the connecting door, she called to her daughter to get ready to leave.

"What did Mother Lucy want?" Kaylee asked when they were in the car. In a way, Courtney was grateful to have a rehearsal before explaining it in school.

"There was an argument last night, and two people died," Courtney told her daughter. "Their children go to Hobbs elementary."

"Did he shoot her?"

Courtney looked at Kaylee with surprise. "Why do you assume that?"

"We have to read the news every day for social studies. Did you know forty-seven percent of Mainers have guns at home? Half of all the murders in our state are caused by domestic violence." For a girl who'd just turned thirteen, Kaylee was remarkably well read, and sometimes, too smart for her own good.

"Yes, the man killed his wife and then himself."

"That's really sad." Kaylee stared straight ahead and let out a long sigh. "What will happen to the kids?"

"The Office of Child and Family Services will look for close relatives, like grandparents or aunts and uncles to see if they will take them."

"What if they don't find any?"

"Then the children will have to go into foster care." Out of the corner of her eye, Courtney watched her daughter's face as she digested the information.

"I'm glad I still have Dad if something ever happened to you," Kaylee finally said.

Courtney had been annoyed when Doug changed his mind and came back from the West Coast. Now, she was glad to have him nearby because it seemed to provide Kaylee with a sense of security.

Her daughter was silent for the remainder of the drive, and Courtney was glad because she was still absorbing the horror. She dropped Kaylee off at her school, then headed to the elementary school. As soon as she walked into the administrative offices, the head admin accosted her "There's a parent waiting for you, Ms. Barnes."

"Is this about the masks again?" asked Courtney in a weary voice. School hadn't even started, and she already felt exhausted.

"Of course, it's about the masks. I've been answering emails since I walked in the door this morning."

"Is Ms. Henderson available?"

"Chief Harrison is in her office now. Can it wait?"

Courtney assumed that the police chief was telling the principal about the shootings. She was glad she didn't have to be the bearer of bad news. "Yes, it can wait. Let me see what the angry parent wants."

"Good luck," said the admin. "He's one of those." She rolled her eyes.

❋❋❋

Lucy felt the anxiety in Cherie's fierce hug. Lucy was a hugger, and the pandemic had been excruciating for her. She didn't worry too much about Cherie because Liz still tested everyone in their group every week to keep up the data for the Yale vaccine study. Their participation meant everyone in the Hobbs study group could get boosters ahead of the CDC's approval. They were lucky, but many others weren't. Many people couldn't always be trusted to tell the truth about their vaccination status. When Lucy waited after a service to greet her parishioners, people tried to embrace her. How could she refuse?

"I'm so glad you're here," Cherie said, finally letting her go. "I want you to take the lead on this interview."

"Sure, but why?"

Cherie stared at the floor. "I've gotten myself emotionally involved. I want to keep the kids. This morning I filed an application to be a foster parent." Cherie had confided her intense desire to be a parent, but this was not how Lucy had expected it to play out.

"How does Brenda feel about this?"

Cherie glanced in the direction of the police chief, standing in the back of the room. "She hasn't said much. She wants to please me, but I keep remembering what she said when I wanted to adopt a rescue dog. She told me, 'We don't know what that animal went through. It's damaged, and I'm not interested in dealing with problems someone else caused.'"

"That's pretty harsh, but she was talking about a dog. These are children."

"I know, but these kids have been traumatized, and they will be a handful."

Lucy put her arm around Cherie's shoulders and gave her a little squeeze. "It may not even be an issue. They could find the kids' relatives, so don't get your hopes up."

"I'm not. But they are so adorable with their golden hair and blue eyes. They look like Brenda, don't you think? I'm hoping she sees the resemblance too."

"Okay, Cherie. This is important, and I promise we will talk about it. For now, let's just get through this interview."

"Have you ever had to tell someone a close relative has been shot?" Cherie asked. "Telling a child has to be the worst. I told Keith last night, but he doesn't seem to believe me."

"It's defensive, of course. His mind can't accept the fact that his parents are gone."

"I know, but hammering home the truth feels so cruel. I had to resort to tales about angels in heaven."

"It's imagery a child that age can understand." Lucy sometimes needed to resort to child-size theology. Many adults couldn't grow up and needed to hear it too.

Brenda waved from the doorway of the nursery. "My wife is telling us we should get started," said Cherie, interpreting Brenda's hand signals. "She wants you to know how much she appreciates being able to use your nursery. I see the kids are enjoying the toys."

"It's the novelty."

"Maybe so, but I think these kids could use their familiar toys. After the CSI goes through the crime scene, Brenda is going back to get some of their stuffed animals and clothes. I'd go with her, but she won't let me."

"She probably doesn't want you to see the mess at the scene."

"I appreciate her wanting to protect me, but I've seen worse."

Lucy patted her arm. "Let Brenda think she's being kind to you. It's sad enough, and you don't need to see the horror to imagine it."

"Isn't that the truth?"

Brenda approached and handed Lucy a sheet of paper. "Here are the questions we'd like you to ask."

"Thanks, Brenda. That's helpful." Lucy scanned the paper, discouraged to see that some of the questions were too complicated for a child to understand. Children simply didn't remember events the way adults did. Yet they could be much more observant about some things, including unfiltered sensory data and raw emotion.

Lucy approached the circle of chairs set up in the play area. The little girl ran to her. "Lucy!" she squealed and crashed into Lucy's leg, hugging it with all her might.

"Obviously, you made a big impression," said Cherie, watching the joyous reunion.

"It's the red hair," Lucy said casually. "Kids remember it."

"Maybe. But kids just love you." Lucy heard the faint note of envy in Cherie's voice and realized that she would need a lot of reassurance on this journey to parenthood.

Although one of the child-size chairs could have supported Lucy's weight, she turned over one of the plastic milk crates used for storing toys. Megan climbed into her lap. "I'm glad you're here," she said, nuzzling against her.

"I promised I would see you today." When Lucy stroked Megan's silken hair, she could smell that it had been freshly washed. Dressed in the second-hand clothes Liz had provided, both children looked fastidiously clean. Lucy reached out to the boy. "Come here, Keith. Sit by me." He pulled a small chair closer and sat down. Keith glanced in the direction of the two police officers. "Don't worry about them. They're just here to listen." Lucy called over her shoulder, "Brenda, you and your detective might want to sit down. It would help."

Brenda, who'd been standing in the corner with her arms folded on her chest, motioned to the detective with a wag of her head.

"Cherie, maybe you can tell Megan what you told Keith last night."

Cherie sat down on one of the adult chairs. "Megan, we heard some sad news last night. Your mom and dad had an accident."

"Noooo," Megan whimpered, hiding her face in Lucy's shoulder.

"Yes, baby," Cherie soothed. "But they're in heaven now, looking down at you."

"They want you to know they love you," Lucy added, stroking Megan's hair. "They sent us to help you."

Lucy felt the girl stiffen in her arms and then wiggle off her lap. She grabbed a stuffed toy and headed to a corner to suck her thumb. Obviously, they wouldn't learn anything from her. They'd have to rely on Keith for information. Lucy methodically went through the list of prepared questions, needing to reword nearly every one into language a child could understand.

Keith told a heartbreaking tale of loud arguments ending in threats of violence, doors slamming, and his father storming out of the house. The boy spoke with unnerving dispassion, as if it had happened to someone else. "Mom always told us to hide in the closet when dad started yelling. She told us to wait until she came to get us to come out." *But last night, she couldn't come back for you,* thought Lucy sadly. "The nice police lady told us to come out, but we told her we had to wait for Mom. The other police lady talked in a loud voice. I was afraid of her, so I came out."

"The police lady was only trying to help," Lucy explained gently.

Megan finally returned to the circle of chairs. She tugged at Lucy's sleeve. "I want my dragon. Can I go home and get it?"

"You have a dragon?" asked Lucy with exaggerated surprise. "Does he breathe fire?"

"Of course! But it's a *she-dragon!*"

Brenda approached. She turned over another milk crate and sat down. "Megan, if you tell me what you want from your house. I'm going back there in a little while, and I'll try to find it." She took a pad and pen out of her pocket and patiently wrote down everything the kids asked for. "I'll do my best. Thank you for telling us what happened in your house. It will really help us."

"Come here, Megan," said Cherie. "I need to wipe your nose before you get it all over Mother Lucy's black shirt." The little girl clung to Lucy's arm, eyeing Cherie. Finally, she allowed her to wipe her snotty nose. "Lucy, I'm going to take them home now. Maybe they'll take a nap. No one got much sleep last night. Good thing Liz took my appointments for the day, or I don't know what I'd do with them."

After Cherie left with the children, Lucy remained to collect her thoughts. She knew that children were amazingly resilient and could recover from horrors that would level an adult. But sometimes, the bad memories could lie buried below the surface for years and had to be excavated like an archeological site.

"You did great with the questions, Lucy," said a voice behind her. Brenda had returned from helping Cherie get the children into the car. "Do you want a job?"

Lucy smiled. "I thought I was doing my job."

"I doubt the CFS people could have done better. It was a great idea to use this place."

Lucy sighed. "Children haven't played in this nursery since the pandemic began. I'm glad we can get some use out of it." Lucy looked over her shoulder to make sure the detective had left the room before she spoke. "Cherie tells me she applied for emergency custody. She says she wants to foster the children if no relatives are found. How do you feel about it?"

Brenda thought for a moment before she answered. "I honestly don't know how I feel. Cherie really wants kids. She was even willing to risk getting pregnant."

"Adoption is an alternative. Do you want kids? You seem to like them."

"I love kids." Brenda stared at her perfectly polished service shoes. Lucy could see she was struggling to articulate what she was feeling. When she looked up, her eyes were bright with tears. "I want Cherie to be happy, but I'm scared, Lucy. I almost had to quit my job because of COVID. I have to work. I have a mortgage. But what if I get sick again? They're just babies, and we're not young."

Lucy reached out for Brenda's hand and rubbed it affectionately. "It's all right to be scared, Brenda. Parenthood is a big responsibility. When I suddenly became a mother again, I was terrified, and my daughter was nearly grown. I can't imagine how I would have handled it if she had been as young as Megan and Keith."

"I'm not opposed to keeping the kids, but it's all happening so fast."

"You and Cherie need to talk," said Lucy, looking directly into Brenda's earnest, blue eyes. "And you know where I am if you need me."

"Thanks, Lucy, and thanks for helping us get the statement."

Lucy watched the tall woman head to the door, seeing the weight of her new burden in every step.

# 4

The water in the harbor was as smooth as glass and reflected the boat hulls like a mirror. There was no wind, which was good because the air had cooled rapidly after the warm day. Liz zipped up her polar fleece. She wished she had worn jeans instead of shorts. She was tired and too lazy to go below to get the quartz heater.

She would have liked company, but Lucy was at the beach house, writing a paper. Liz didn't understand Lucy's big rush to get her degree. She didn't need the credential. She was already ordained and had a license to practice psychotherapy. But Liz knew Lucy's secret. In a moment of vulnerability, she had confessed why being addressed as the Reverend Doctor Lucille Bartlett was so important to her. Surrounded by certifiable geniuses, Lucy felt insecure about her intellect and hoped a PhD would prove that she could hold her own.

But Liz dreaded a crash like the one that had followed Erika's death. In addition to a heavy class schedule and finishing her book, Lucy had a busy psychotherapy practice—as if her main job as the rector of a parish that included two churches wasn't demanding enough. No wonder when she sat down to study, she often fell asleep.

Liz was no stranger to overwork. Years ago, when she had first become chief of surgery at Yale, she'd worked herself to the point of exhaustion. The chief of staff had noticed and ordered her to take two weeks off in a place where no one could find her. Liz had always heard about the beauty of Maine. She'd rented a beach house and fallen in love.

There was nothing like the quiet and beauty of this magical place or the smell of the sea. After a long day at the office, Liz really needed this time on the boat. With Cherie on temporary leave, Liz and Amy were seeing her patients in addition to their own. It was ironic that Liz had hired another doctor so that she'd have more time on her boat and in her workshop. Since Cherie had taken in the Benoit children, Liz hadn't worked on a single project, and this was the first time she'd set foot on The Wet Lady. "Liz, you love being busy," Amy had said when Liz complained. "That's why you haven't retired." Liz didn't like the idea that her new associate had figured her out so quickly, but Amy worked hard and had quickly adapted to the rhythm of the practice. Without her, Liz would be overwhelmed.

Liz never realized how much she depended on Cherie until she'd given her time off to deal with the children. So far, CFS hadn't been able to locate any relatives willing to take them. The mother had a cousin, but she had a record with the police and no job. She said she just couldn't deal with the kids. Meanwhile, Cherie and Brenda were scrambling to set up their home and arrange childcare while CFS expedited their application to become foster parents.

Liz's phone vibrated in her pocket. She pulled it out and glanced at the screen. The caller ID showed Brenda proudly holding the huge striper that had won her first prize in last summer's fish derby.

"I'm at the boat," said Liz, forgoing a greeting, as usual. "Cherie let you off for good behavior?"

"She knows I need a break. The kids are in bed."

"So, come down. I'm here, and I have plenty of that sudsy, red ale you like." Liz didn't know why she was dangling an unnecessary incentive. Brenda never refused a beer since Liz had told her that her heart had recovered enough to drink alcohol. Why the strange damage caused by COVID had reversed itself remained a mystery, but Liz took it at face value, happy to have her fishing buddy back. Now, she was mildly worried that she might lose her again—this time to parenthood.

"I'll be there in ten minutes," Brenda said.

"Don't speed. Those Hobbs cops are everywhere."

Brenda snickered. "Yes, we are. Don't you ever forget it."

After Liz brought up more beer, she remembered the quartz heater and went back down to get it. By the time Brenda climbed into the boat, the glowing coils had created a welcome bubble of warmth that felt good on Liz's bare legs. Brenda plopped down in the neighboring sling chair.

"I'm telling you, Brenda," Liz said, opening a beer for her. 'You need to carve out some alone time when dealing with kids,"

"Yeah, it's hard to do certain things with them around like…you know."

"Brenda, you need to find time for sex. You're newlyweds. But I know, it's hard with kids. My niece's kids and Maggie's grandkids were always getting into bed with us."

"It's easier with grandkids, or nieces or nephews. You can send them home. My brothers' kids are all grown now. It's amazing how quickly you get out of practice. And I'm not a natural parent like Cherie."

"Some people just have that knack. It helps to like kids," said Liz.

"I like them fine, but they still scare me."

Liz dropped her voice an octave, "You're telling me the big, brave Hobbs Police chief is afraid of some little kids?" She grunted a chuckle. "Just think back to what it was like when you were young."

"Liz, I'm fifty-three. Do you think I can remember that far back?"

"Of course, you can. I'm older than you, and I can remember." Liz flipped the cap off another bottle of ale. "How are the kids doing?"

"Megan still cries herself to sleep at night. She keeps asking us when her mother is coming back. Keith seems to have adjusted to the idea, but he looks sad all the time."

"They're grieving. They're at different stages of development, so they will react differently. Some people think young children can't grasp the finality of death." Liz gave that idea another moment's thought. "Some adults can't either. That's probably where the fairy tale of heaven originated, but don't tell Lucy I said so."

"I never tell anyone what we talk about, but I doubt Lucy would be surprised to hear your thoughts on the afterlife. We've talked about it, so I know she doesn't believe that dead people sit on clouds talking to angels."

"Dealing with the living is enough for me," said Liz, raising her beer.

"I'll drink to that. Cheers." She tapped Liz's bottle and took a swig. "Before I get started with my stuff, what's going on with you?"

"It's been really busy. With all the new people moving to Hobbs, the practice has been growing fast. Southern Med realizes their offer to buy us fell flat, so they want to make us an affiliate…as long as we promise a certain number of referrals to their specialists."

"What did you say to them?" asked Brenda, leaning forward to see Liz's face.

"I told them to go fuck themselves."

Brenda laughed. "Good for you."

"But things are crazy in the office. I really miss having Cherie as my backup. Amy came right in time. Good hire."

"Some of my hires lately have been iffy, but it's the candidates. Some of them just aren't tough enough to be cops. Unfortunately, it's what we've got now. How's it going with Lucy?"

"I like being with someone who's not always trying to change me."

"Sure, she is. You just don't see her doing it. I can see how much you've changed."

"Shut up, Brenda."

"I'm not kidding. You have. Cherie doesn't try to change me either, but she has. That's the danger of having a shrink around. They operate on your head without you knowing it."

"Lucy hates to be called a shrink."

"So does Cherie."

"Lucy invited me to her meeting with her bishop. I'm not looking forward to it, but I agreed to go."

"Don't tell me you're worried. Shit. You've met the president. You testified in front of congress!"

"That was different. It was about breast cancer. That was my work, something I felt confident about. I've never met a bishop before except in the fifth grade, when one slapped me at my confirmation."

"I'm sure you'll do fine, Liz. He's just another guy in a collar. Put on your power suit and blow him away."

"I don't think blowing him away will help Lucy. I need to be on good behavior for her sake."

"Oh my God! See? You have changed. I never thought I'd see the day."

"Well, I never thought you'd become a mom."

"Neither did I. When Cherie was talking about having a baby, I just listened. I knew it was a long shot for her to get pregnant. I was worried, of course, that something might happen to her if she did."

"It's not easy to get pregnant when you're in your fifties, and there are a lot of risks to the mother and the fetus. But it's not as unusual as it used to be." Liz took a long drink of beer, then barely stifled a burp.

"I kind of understand. I once thought of having a kid."

"You never told me that," said Liz, giving Brenda her full attention.

"I wasn't really serious. The idea only lasted five minutes."

"But you thought about it," said Liz, wiping the grin off her face. "I did too."

"No! Not you, Liz."

"Yup," she said, compressing her lips and nodding. "As long as I could have a child, it didn't bother me. Now I'm old, so I never think about it anymore."

"Yeah, we're old, aren't we? Fuck. I'll be collecting social security when these kids are in high school," said Brenda, looking up at the sky. "Good thing I have a decent pension."

Liz studied Brenda's youthful face and wondered how she could think of herself as old. She kept herself up by working out at the police gym. She enhanced her refined features with makeup and always wore earrings—studs, because dangling earrings weren't allowed when in uniform. When Liz had first met Brenda, she'd thought she was straight. To her relief, she wasn't.

"There are lots of older parents," said Liz, "...and grandparents, who are raising children because their own kids were messed up by substance abuse."

"Yeah," said Brenda, wiping foam off her lip. "Things are a mess."

Liz looked at her. She hadn't seen Brenda so down since she wanted to quit her job. "What's going on, Brenda? Do you feel forced into taking these kids?"

"A little. I wasn't prepared for an instant family."

"At least, you don't have all the worry that goes along with an elderly prima para."

"I don't think I like the sound of that."

Liz laughed. "It's medical lingo for an older, first-time mother." Liz put her feet up on the deck rail. "Is this going to work for you? If not, now is the time to speak up."

"I kind of like it. Keith follows me around like a puppy when I do work around the house. Megan falls asleep in my lap when I read them a story. It feels good, but I'm worried about what happens if we don't get approved as foster parents."

"Why wouldn't you?"

"Because we're gay."

"This is Maine, Brenda. I don't think they can deny you for that. Besides you're both model citizens. You're the police chief for god's sake. Cherie is a physician's assistant. You both make good money. You own your own home. You got recommendations from the town manager and the Episcopal rector."

"And you."

"You don't know what I said in my recommendation," said Liz, giving her the side eye.

"You didn't."

Liz laughed. "Of course, I didn't."

"The home visit is the day after tomorrow. We fixed up the house to show them how much we want these kids. Cherie gave up her little office, so Megan can have her own room. Cherie washed all of the kids' toys. Some of them disintegrated in the washing machine."

"I could have told you that you can't put some stuffed toys through the washer. I found out the hard way. It helps to read the tags."

"See all the things we don't know."

"No one knows. Kids don't come with an owner's manual."

"If this foster thing works out, Cherie wants to adopt them. And I support the idea. I know, Liz. Don't look so shocked. These kids have been through so much, and I want them to feel secure."

Liz's phone vibrated noisily. "Must be Lucy wondering if I'm ever coming home," she said, digging it out of her pocket. But the caller was Sam. Liz swiped open the call. "I'm on the boat."

"I know. I came by the house, and Lucy told me you're there."

"Brenda's here too." Brenda turned at the sound of her name and looked curious, so Liz held up the phone so she could see Sam's picture. "Come down and have a beer with us."

There was a moment of hesitation. "Liz, I need to talk to you."

"So, come down and talk. We're all friends, Sam. Is it that private?" Brenda started to get up, but Liz patted the air to indicate she should stay seated.

"I'll be right down," Sam said.

While they waited for Sam, Liz went below to bring up more beer. She rummaged in the galley for salty snacks and came up with peanuts and chips. She found another sling chair and opened it for Sam.

"That was fast," said Brenda, looking suspicious when Sam climbed into the boat.

"I didn't speed," replied Sam in a testy voice. "It doesn't take long to get here from Liz's house."

Liz uncapped a bottle of ale for Sam. "To the *tres amigas!*" Liz proposed, raising her glass. They all clicked bottles.

"Liz, your Spanish accent sucks," Brenda said, "but I should talk. I took it in high school and almost failed. My Hispanic cops were always laughing at me. Once I tried to tell them to get to work but ended up telling them to go to hell." After a few good natured jabs at Brenda, the laughter finally settled down.

"So, what's up, Sam?" Liz asked and took a swig of beer.

"I broke up with Olivia."

"Holy shit!" Liz took her feet off the deck wall and sat up straight. "What brought that on?"

"I couldn't stand it anymore. She wanted me there all the time. I have my own house. She even complained when I had to go home to cut the grass."

"I get it," said Liz. "Lucy and I are having this same discussion. She doesn't want to give up the beach house, and I don't want to move." She gave Sam a hard look. "But this debate between you and Olivia has been going on since you got together. What brought it to a head?"

"I'm seeing someone."

"Oh." Liz and Brenda exchanged a look. "Who?" they asked in unison.

"I don't know if I should tell you, especially you, Liz."

Liz shrugged. "Okay, then don't."

"Oh, Liz, don't even try that 'as if I care' crap on me."

"Why not? Works every time."

"All right, I'll tell you. I'm seeing your new doctor, Amy Hsu."

"Oh, for fuck's sake, Sam! You're kidding me!"

Sam shook her head. "We've been having lunch together while I'm working on your renovation. I really like her."

"That was fast," Brenda said in a neutral voice.

"Sam! Olivia will blame me, even though I had nothing to do with it," said Liz. "How did she take it? Was she furious?"

"No, it was weird," said Sam. "She was as cold as ice."

"You didn't tell her you're seeing Amy?" Liz asked.

"No. I'm not that stupid. And she's not the reason we're breaking up, so why bring her into it?"

"Well, Sam," said Brenda, stretching out her legs, "a woman's gotta do what she's gotta do."

Sam raised her beer bottle in salute. "That's right. Doesn't make it any easier, though."

❁❁❁

Olivia had gone downstairs while Sam packed because she couldn't watch. Everything that Sam had brought to the house fit into one duffle bag with room to spare. Transience had been the operating principle of their relationship. "I'll stay as long as it works," Sam had said, when she'd brought over underwear, a few pairs of socks, and some jeans. The drawers Olivia had cleared for her had remained mostly empty. She'd set aside a section of her closet, but only a few shirts had ever hung there. As long as they had remained, there had been reason for hope.

*What a stupid word!* Olivia thought with contempt. *Hope is for people who can't get what they want.* That certainly didn't describe Olivia Enright, once known as "the female wolf of Wall Street." If people didn't give her what she wanted, she took it. If she set her sights on someone, she got her, one way or the other. Since that vile man had walked out on her, she was the one who did the leaving—when she became bored with them, or they became too needy. Part of Sam's appeal was her independence, even when it was annoying.

After she heard Sam close the front door, Olivia went into the kitchen to mix a pitcher of martinis. Liz liked her martinis. Maybe she'd be interested in coming over for a drink. No, that would be admitting that Olivia needed company, which she didn't. She was absolutely fine alone. Besides, Sam would probably run straight to Liz. Sam looked up to Liz and needed her approval. Everyone in that annoying little cabal needed Liz's approval.

Olivia put her martini pitcher on a tray and took it out to the deck. She needed the view of the ocean to remind her that her grand house with its perfect location provided all the comfort she needed. People were strictly optional. The night air was chilly, so Olivia turned on the gas fire pit for both the heat and ambience and stretched out on the chaise lounge to listen to the waves. Usually, the rhythmic sound soothed her, but she cringed as she imagined Sam telling the whole story to Liz—her side of it. "I never wanted a commitment," Sam had said, flinging her socks into her bag. "We said we'd be together as long as we were both enjoying it, but it's not fun anymore."

It was hard to believe that Sam only wanted sex. She was too smart and too complicated for that, and she wasn't a user like those other women Olivia had been involved with. She suspected there might be another woman involved, but she had no idea who. All the other women in their little group were coupled.

Olivia felt an odd little pressure pain in her chest. She wrote it off to the broccoli rabe she'd eaten at dinner and went back to savoring her martini. It was excellent because she only used the best gin. When gin made up ninety-eight percent of the drink, only the best would do. The olives were imported from a remote Greek island known for its small, bitter fruit. All the food magazines had raved about them.

Why waste time on second-best when you could afford premium products? It had taken Olivia years to cultivate the tastes that came naturally to those born to wealth. She'd come from nothing, but she had taught herself to move smoothly in upper-crust social circles. That was before the scandal. After her son's insider trading was exposed, the New York elite shunned her. She remembered walking into a museum benefit and watching her former so-called "friends" melt away. *The lesbian network of Hobbs will probably do the same*, Olivia thought bitterly. *They'll side with Sam, and I'll be persona non grata again.*

"To hell with them," Olivia shouted to the moon rising over the water. "I don't need them. I don't need anyone!" She finished her martini and poured another.

Over the sound of the crashing surf, she heard the warble of her phone. "Oh, go away! I'm not interested!" But the phone continued to ring. The hope that it might be Sam calling finally motivated Olivia to get up and look for her phone, which she found under a throw pillow on the sofa. By that time, the call had gone into voice mail.

Her caller had been Lucy Bartlett. It was hard to resist Lucy, the one person in the group who had been consistently decent.

"Hello, Lucy. I saw that you called," Olivia said, enunciating carefully because the martini was starting to go to her head.

"We haven't talked much lately. I don't like to disturb you in the evening, but Sam was just here, so I figured you might be alone."

The timing of the call made Olivia instantly suspicious. She wondered if Sam was already spreading dirt about them. "Did you sense that I needed a call? What did Sam tell you?"

"Nothing. She was looking for Liz, but she's down at the boat."

"Sam didn't tell you the news?"

"What news?" asked Lucy in an innocent voice. Lucy had been on the operatic stage, but Olivia could tell this wasn't acting.

"We broke up," said Olivia in a bitter voice.

"Oh, no! Oh, Olivia. I'm so sorry."

"Thank you," said Olivia with a sigh. "So, Liz is down at the boat. Are you looking for company? Would you like to come over?"

"Oh, I would love to, but I can't. I'm writing a paper. I just took a break to rest my eyes."

"Are you sure Sam didn't say something? Tell the truth, Lucy. I need to know if Sam is blabbing my business all over town."

"She looked upset. When I asked what was wrong, she said she needed to talk to Liz."

"She'll probably tell her."

"I'm sure she will. They go back a long time. Sam's become her confidante, now that Erika is gone."

"Doesn't it bother you that Liz may be telling Sam things you'd rather be kept private?"

There was an extended silence. "Everyone needs someone to talk to when they're troubled," said Lucy diplomatically. "Oh, Olivia. I'm so sorry. How do you feel?"

While Olivia took an inventory of her emotions, she sipped her martini. "It's what I expected, but I'm not used to being left, not since my husband ran out on me, but that was decades ago." Olivia had already told her life's story to Lucy when she was in therapy and didn't feel like recapping it now.

As if she were reading her thoughts, Lucy said, "You decided to quit counseling after you'd reconciled with your granddaughters. Maybe you should come in and have a little check up."

"Are you looking for business, Mother Lucy?" Olivia asked suspiciously.

"No, of course not," protested Lucy, sounding hurt. "In fact, I have more business than I can possibly handle. This pandemic has caused so much depression and family strife. I can't keep up."

"Lucy, you're trying to do too much. Look at you. You take a break and end up counseling me. You're so dedicated, Lucy, and we all love you for it, but you need to pace yourself or you'll burn out."

"I know. Liz lectures me all the time."

"I hope she takes care of you."

"Oh, she does. She feeds me well and makes me rest."

"I'm jealous," Olivia said in a light tone, but it was the truth.

"Don't be jealous, Olivia. You're a strong, extremely competent woman, who takes good care of herself. And if Sam isn't a good match, maybe there's someone else for you. Someone who wants what you want out of a relationship. Were you hoping for a commitment from Sam?"

"A commitment would be nice. I'm not a big believer in marriage after my husband left me. It was a long time ago, but it made me leery of saying, 'I do.'"

"That's a big topic. We should talk about it."

"All right, Lucy," Olivia said impatiently. "I'll make an appointment. I'll call tomorrow."

"But you're okay…for now?"

"No, but I'm numbing myself with some excellent gin."

"Take it easy. When you wake up from the buzz, you might feel worse."

"I am familiar with that particular misery, but compared to the pain I'm feeling now…"

"Oh, Olivia. Let me throw on some clothes, and I'll come right over."

"No, Lucy. You're working, and I'm a grown woman. In the grand scheme of things, this counts as a minor disaster. You stay put."

"Are you sure?"

Olivia forced a smile, so that she sounded intact when she said, "Absolutely. Go back to work. I'll be fine."

"Okay, Olivia. I'm sorry things didn't work out with Sam. Your friends are here for you. Try to have a good night."

"Good night, Lucy, and thank you for the call."

Olivia put down the phone and burst into tears.

❋❋❋

Sam had said that the restaurant was a "nice place, a step up from the usual tourist fare." Amy had decided to wear a dress because it was the most formal thing she'd brought to Maine. Fortunately, the maroon knit could be dressed up or down. She'd worn it the night she'd gone out to dinner with Liz. Afterward, Amy was glad she'd made a little fuss, especially after meeting Liz's fiancée who looked every bit as glamorous as you'd expect from an opera star.

When Amy had packed for this trip, she was supposed to be on vacation. She hadn't expected the deal with Hobbs Family Practice to be concluded so quickly. Once she got a weekend off, she needed to get back to New York to get more clothes and pack up her Mt. Kisco studio. There wasn't much left—a minimal amount of furniture from Ikea, her clothes, and some family memorabilia. The kitchen had barely enough pots and pans to cook a meal. Jill had taken most of the kitchen utensils because she was a gourmet cook. Amy let everything go because she didn't want the reminders. Now, she wished she'd held on to some things. Her new apartment was larger and looked bare. She hadn't had time to check out the secondhand furniture shops along Route 1 that Liz had recommended.

When she'd applied for this job, the last thing Amy had expected was to meet another woman, especially not so soon. When Jill moved out, Amy had resolved to stay single for at least a year. At first, she hadn't known what to say when Sam sauntered into her office and invited her to dinner. She'd been enjoying their walks at lunchtime. They seldom went to a restaurant because there wasn't enough time. With COVID surging again, Amy was fine doing takeout. She had to wear a mask all day in the office and needed to breathe unfiltered air, so they often sat on a bench overlooking Hobbs Beach. Usually, they split a sandwich or treated themselves to lobster rolls. While they talked, they ignored the people around them. The seagulls eyeing their sandwiches were harder to ignore.

When she realized that Sam was inviting her on what was obviously meant to be their first date, Amy had hedged her bets. She said she'd think about it. The internal debate was brief. Sam McKinnon intrigued her, and she wanted to get to know her better.

She'd run the usual background check she always did on potential partners. As a physician, she couldn't risk a scandal, so she liked to be extra careful. For the same reason, she never used dating apps, preferring to meet people through a personal introduction. In Sam's case, Liz was the connection. It was hard to beat a reference from your employer.

Amy had been cagily asking Liz for information about Sam, spacing out her questions so it didn't seem too obvious. "With Sam, what you see is what you get," Liz responded offhandedly. When Amy continued to probe, Liz added, "She's a trust fund baby who rebelled against her Junior League upbringing and succeeded because she's wicked smart." Amy was learning that "wicked" was a surprisingly useful Maine qualifier that could apply to everything from the weather to intelligence.

Amy tried on one necklace and exchanged it for a simple gold chain. You could never go wrong with the real thing. If Sam came from old money, she probably wouldn't approve of ostentatious jewelry. Her building designs, inspired by mid-century modern architecture, had simple lines, but she used glass much differently from the architects who'd inspired her. Light was still a big factor, but unlike the architecture of some of her contemporaries, her buildings didn't look like a pile of ice cubes.

Architectural appreciation was an esoteric niche, but Amy's younger brother was an architect. During their weekly call, she'd picked his brain trying to find out more about Sam. "After she got the Grayson commission, her career took off. She was in all the design magazines. She was even interviewed on *Sixty Minutes*. Samantha McKinnon is one of the most talented female architects of her generation." Remembering that he was talking to his sister, Vincent corrected himself. "Yes, I know. I shouldn't be describing professionals by gender."

"That's right, little brother." Amy adored Vincent, so the warning was gentle.

Amy had asked her brother why Sam McKinnon left corporate architecture. "The tastemakers are so fickle. Once she wasn't a shiny, new toy anymore, they dropped her." Liz had a different take: "Sam didn't want to become a parody of herself, so she quit while she was ahead."

Sam's past fame interested Amy less than her quiet intelligence. Her shyness and modesty about her work were also attractive. Amy had never liked women who came on too strong. Persistence was more appealing than bravado. Although Sam swaggered on the job site, Amy had perceived that it was to fit in with the guys. Otherwise, Sam was gentle and attentive—courteous rather than gallant.

Amy wondered if Sam had any idea that she'd been analyzed to that degree. Of course, maybe Sam had done a similar dive into Amy's background, but she didn't think so. Sam struck her as a basically trusting person, almost naïve in her approach to people.

Amy went downstairs to wait for her date. She was ten minutes early, but she always liked to be on time. The doorbell rang. Amy opened the door to a smartly dressed, tall woman with engaging brown eyes.

"You look wonderful," said Amy, admiring Sam's outfit. The classic olive suit was understated and timeless, probably a left-over from Sam's days as a corporate architect.

"I wanted you to know that I can look like a grown-up when I need to. Are you ready?"

Amy stepped out of the door of her rented condo and looked around for a truck but saw a Subaru sedan parked in the visitor's space. Sam's eyes followed the direction of her gaze. "I keep that for scooting around town, especially now that gas has gotten expensive again. I bought it when I used to come up to Hobbs from New Haven on the train." She grinned. "I'm not completely uncivilized."

"I never thought so. What made you say that?"

"My former girlfriend told me I should live in a cave. She made it her goal to civilize me. I don't like people trying to change me." Sam probably didn't intend to reveal all that statement had implied. In fact, she seemed perfectly civilized, although like many WASPs who'd attended boarding school, there were some unexpected rough edges. Sam had once picked lobster out of her teeth in public, which had completely shocked Amy.

Sam gestured in the direction of the Subaru. "Shall we?" Amy was relieved that Sam clicked open the locks but expected her to find her own way into the passenger seat. Role play was all right, but Amy would resist a man displaying old-fashioned manners. Why would she accept it from a woman? So far, Sam was doing all the right things.

"Where are we going for dinner?" Amy asked.

"There's a five-star restaurant in Kennebunkport that specializes in using local ingredients."

"That's a big thing up here, I gather."

"It is. We're proud to support our local food producers." Sam studied her briefly. "After what you've seen so far, are you still glad you moved up here?"

"I am. I'm learning new things all the time."

"At least, you don't sound like a New Yorker. Brenda slips sometimes, and you can hear her Brooklyn accent. Liz's Brooklyn accent only comes out when she's excited about something. Like you, she was young when she moved out of the city. You should know that people up here don't always like people 'from away,' especially New Yorkers."

"Thanks for the warning. I'll keep that part to myself. Although my medical degrees and certifications kind of give it away."

Sam shrugged. "That doesn't mean anything. People go to medical school where they can get in." Sam smiled. "I don't hold it against you, but I'm 'from away' too. Most of the people in Southern Maine are."

"Tell me about your ex," said Amy, changing the subject.

"Why?"

"Because I'm curious."

"We literally just broke up. I was heading there for a while, but I don't like confrontation, so I avoided saying so. But I'm not one of those people who start an affair to get out of a relationship. I like to make a clean break."

"How long ago did you break up?" asked Amy, feeling faintly anxious.

"Last night."

"Oh," said Amy, facing forward. "You weren't kidding about it being recent."

"I needed to tell her. I didn't want any misunderstandings in case she runs into us in town."

"So, she lives here."

"Yes, she's the town manager."

"I hope it wasn't an acrimonious break-up. I don't need to watch out for repercussions, do I? Some woman coming after me with an axe or whatever Mainers do when they break up?"

Sam laughed. "No, Olivia is not like that. She's very classy."

"Good. I hate dyke drama."

"Me too," said Sam.

At dinner, Amy enjoyed Sam's relaxed conversation. The meal was superb, with a focus on late-season harvest—curried squash soup, pork medallions with sauteed apples, hydroponic microgreens. They skipped dessert because the meal was more than satisfying, but the pies on the dessert menu sounded scrumptious.

When Sam dropped Amy off after what had been a perfect evening, she stopped the engine of her car and waited. Amy realized she was working up the courage to kiss her. Of course, that's where things had been leading, the end goal of Sam's careful courting, but Amy's body tensed when she leaned in her direction. Sam's smile was as sweet as ever, but the intensity of the look in her eyes made Amy pull away.

"I'm sorry, Sam. I'm not ready."

"Oh," said Sam, flinching like she'd been pinched. "I'm sorry too. I thought…"

"I can understand why you might think I'm interested in a romantic relationship. We've been spending a lot of time together. Please understand that It has nothing to do with you. I just came out of a bad marriage, and I need to be single for a while to figure out what I did wrong."

"Why do you assume that you're the one at fault?" asked Sam, sitting back in her seat. The intense look had faded from her eyes. She'd resumed the role of supportive friend.

"I stayed in the relationship too long, hoping things would change, but they never did, so I blame myself." Sam's sympathetic expression made Amy want to talk about it. "She was abusive, not physically, but her words hurt even more. She was constantly putting me down. She's an extremely talented and accomplished neurosurgeon, very famous in some circles. She used every opportunity to remind me that I'm just a lowly internist. She was so damned arrogant, not at all like Liz."

"You didn't know Liz Stolz in the old days," said Sam with a little smile.

"Arrogance seems to be common among surgeons, and you need to be exceptionally confident to do the things they do. Many of them go overboard. They seem to thrive on the adrenalin rush and see their abilities as some kind of superpower. In the beginning, I was drawn to Jill's confidence and cool head. I'm attracted to ice queens. You're the complete opposite—warm and considerate." Sam began to blush at being praised so obviously. "I thought seeing you would be a good way to learn how to relate to a normal person."

"You're being generous by calling me normal," said Sam, "but I think I understand what you're trying to say."

Amy took Sam's hand. "Please don't misunderstand. I like you very much, Sam, but I'm just not ready to get involved."

"Okay," said Sam slowly. "It's not what I'd hoped for, but we can be friends for now and see where it leads."

Amy pulled her closer and gave her a quick peck on the lips. "Thank you, Sam. You're very special, you know."

Despite the fading light, Amy could see Sam blushing.

# 5

"Honey, your phone is ringing." Lucy finally recognized the voice. She'd been dreaming about Erika, but the soft lips pressing against her temple belonged to the living woman who loved her in the present.

Lucy slowly opened her eyes. "What time is it?"

"Around three-thirty, I think," Liz whispered into her ear. Her breath was warm and sexy. Liz liked to make love in the middle of the night, especially when she couldn't fall asleep again after getting up. Lucy wished for that possibility instead of answering what she knew would be a sick call. She groaned and raised herself on her elbow.

The flashing of the phone was lighting up the entire room. Lucy saw that the call had passed through the church forwarding system. "Oh, why do they always wait until the last minute?" Lucy sat up and cleared her throat. "St. Margaret's Church. Rev. Bartlett speaking." She listened to the woman at the other end of the call breathlessly explaining that her mother wanted to see a priest.

"I'm sorry to call so late, Mother Lucy," said Mrs. Dyer. "I offered to call you weeks ago, but Mom kept resisting. I think she thought delaying would forestall the inevitable. A few minutes ago, she suddenly opened her eyes and said, 'I want to make my peace with God.'"

"It's fine, Mrs. Dyer. Many people wait. What's your address?" Lucy opened the GPS app to key in the information. "Can your mother take communion?"

"It's too late for that. She's barely conscious."

"I'll be there in a few minutes." Lucy ended the call and got out of bed. She was surprised to see Liz get up too.

"I'm coming with you." Liz pulled on her T-shirt and headed toward the bathroom.

"But I might not be back for hours," Lucy called after her. "We have a busy day ahead. We're going to Portland to see the bishop this afternoon."

"It's my day off. I can take a nap later." Liz closed the bathroom door. Lucy stared at it, wondering if this gesture was the result of the warm feelings engendered by their new romance. Knowing Liz, she'd probably considered it one of her "duties" and would make it permanent. Taking care of people was in Liz's genes, but Lucy had been going out on sick calls since she'd been ordained. Sometimes, the calls led her to rough Boston neighborhoods, where she'd prayed for her own safety. If her prayers didn't protect her, she always had her martial arts training as back up. As much as she loved Liz for wanting to take care of her, she could take care of herself.

Fortunately, they'd spent the night at the beach house, where Lucy had access to her clerical clothes and her sick call kit. She put on black dress pants and a fresh clerical blouse out of respect. Liz came out of the bathroom and began to dress, putting on the office clothes she'd worn the day before. Within minutes, they were in Liz's car, heading to the Dyer house.

"Not that I don't appreciate you coming along, but Erika always trusted me to find my way in the dark," Lucy said, patting Liz's thigh.

"I wouldn't have been able to go back to sleep until you got back safely. It's been a long time since I've had to get up in the middle of the night to answer a call, but I'm not completely out of practice."

"I hope you don't think you're going to sleep in the car while I do the work. I expect your full participation. You can say the responses."

"Lucy, I didn't sign up for that part."

"Yes, you did. You're marrying a priest. That will make you a pastor's wife, which comes with certain responsibilities."

"Such as?"

"Well, you need to be nice to my parishioners. No glaring at them after a service because you need to wait while I greet them. You can't smirk during my sermons, no matter how much you hate them."

"I never hate them, but I sometimes wonder when you're going to get to the point."

Lucy raised an indignant brow in Liz's direction, but her eyes were focused on the road, so the gesture was wasted. "I'm sure there are duties that come with being a doctor's wife."

"They're mostly the same. Smile when we meet my patients. Don't complain when I'm late, or our family time is interrupted. Listen sympathetically when I lose a patient. But you already do all those things." Liz turned into the Dyer's driveway. "When I was a surgeon, I sometimes had to tell relatives when a patient didn't survive. Surgical deaths are usually quick. Watching someone linger and die slowly is hard. Fortunately, the nurses handled those."

"Then you missed a special opportunity. Witnessing someone leave this life is one of the most moving experiences I have as a priest."

"Because you think the person is going to their eternal reward?"

"No, because the separation of the soul from the body is one of the great mysteries of life."

"The process is fairly well documented. The heart stops bringing oxygen to the brain, which shuts down the other systems, the cells begin to break down, and the resident bacteria…"

"Liz, that's a description of the physical changes. It's only part of the story."

"Lucy, it's not even four in the morning. I am not going to debate the afterlife."

"It's not a debate, Liz. It's not always about winning. We're just talking," said Lucy in a weary voice.

She rang the doorbell. The porch light came on, and a middle-aged woman opened the door. Mrs. Dyer hadn't attended church services for months. The need to care for her mother and the fear of bringing the virus home to a vulnerable, elderly woman had kept her away. She occasionally joined a service on ZOOM, but seeing her in-person was shocking. The poor woman had gained a significant amount of weight, and yet her face looked haggard.

"Thank you so much for coming, Mother Lucy," said Mrs. Dyer, offering a weak smile.

"Of course, I'd come. I hope you don't mind that I brought Dr. Stolz along. She's going to say the responses."

"Hello, Dr. Stolz," said Mrs. Dyer. "Thank you for coming."

Lucy glanced at Liz, merely to acknowledge her, and met a fierce frown. When Mrs. Dyer turned to go into the house, Lucy nudged Liz with her hip. "Don't frown. You volunteered," she whispered.

The scent of imminent death permeated the house. It wasn't anything specific—not the smell of stale urine that clung to the commode, or the odor of an elderly body too fragile to wash properly. It was an indefinable quality of the air, the uneasy anticipation of something that had been long-awaited, but dreaded too.

Lucy watched Liz's observant eyes taking in every detail—the piles of bed pads, wet wipes, lotion for preventing bedsores, a sippy cup to provide hydration. The many items needed for the care of a bedridden patient had been staged on the dining room table. The business of dying seemed to have taken over the whole house.

"Hospice was here yesterday and said it will be soon, probably today or tomorrow," Mrs. Dyer said in a hushed tone. "Maybe you can tell us, Dr. Stolz."

Liz looked surprised, but she nodded. "I'm not here as a physician. I only came to assist Rev. Bartlett, but I'll tell you what I can."

They went into a room lined with bookshelves, which Lucy guessed had once been a study. All the furniture had been pushed to one side of the room to make space for a hospital bed. On its rigid surface lay an elderly woman, so fragile and shrunken that she looked like she would blow away if someone sneezed.

Lucy pushed down her natural revulsion to look at the dying woman's face. Beneath the skin, so pale and thin that the blue veins showed, was the bone structure of a woman who had once been beautiful. A woman who'd made love and conceived children. "To everything there is a season…" Lucy thought, recalling the famous verse from Ecclesiastes. Annoyingly, the tune of the 1960s song began to play in her head.

Liz took the woman's wrist and looked at her watch. She raised an eyelid and touched her bare feet. "What hospice told you seems right. It will be soon."

The woman sighed and nodded. "I've been giving her the morphine like they told me."

"That's good," said Liz. "It helps with the pain and the hallucinations. Has she been conscious today?"

"In and out," the woman replied. Liz nodded knowingly.

"What's your mother's name?" Lucy asked, gently touching Mrs. Dyer's arm.

"Diane."

Lucy took the items out of her zippered bag—a small vial of blessed oil, a miniature stole, a compact *Book of Common Prayer,* and a vigil holder with a tea light. Lucy lit the candle and centered her mind.

"Peace be to this house, and to all who dwell in it!" After the opening prayer, Lucy read Psalm 23, followed by the general confession and absolution. She laid her hand on the woman's matted hair and felt, as always, a perceptible connection that went beyond touch. When she anointed the pale forehead with the blessed oil, the old woman startled her by responding, "Amen!" in a loud, clear voice. Some memories went so deep they could never be forgotten. Because Liz was present, Lucy added the prayer for doctors and nurses. "That's the end of the prayers for the sick," Lucy explained to Mrs. Dyer. "If you feel your mother is about to pass, we can continue."

Mrs. Dyer turned around to look at Liz.

"When was the last time you gave your mother morphine?"

"Just before you arrived."

Liz glanced at her watch. "You could give her another dose."

"She's not suffering. She looks peaceful."

"It's up to you," Liz said neutrally, withdrawing again.

The woman left and returned with a syringe. She tried to offer it to Liz to administer, but she shook her head. "You do it." All eyes were trained on the syringe as it emptied.

Lucy asked Liz to say the responses to the prayers for the dying. When the ritual was complete, she said, "Let's sit for a while and keep Diane company." Without prompting, Liz brought in additional chairs from the dining room table, and they sat at the bedside, holding hands.

The candle went out just as the light of the rising sun cast a golden glow on the blanket. The woman's breaths grew shallower until it seemed she was barely breathing. Finally, there was a long, final gasp.

Liz got up and felt for a pulse in her neck. "She's gone." She looked at her watch. "Time of death. Seven-forty-three. Did the hospice service leave any paperwork?" While Mrs. Dyer looked for the papers, Liz carefully closed the deceased woman's eyes and arranged her limbs. Lucy was moved by the tenderness with which Liz handled the elderly woman's body.

Mrs. Dyer began to weep silently. "There are so many people I have to call." She took a deep breath, brushed away her tears, and tried to put on a brave face.

"Shh," Lucy soothed, putting her arms around her. "There will be time for that later. There's no rush. Your mother is still here. Let's honor her spirit with our silence."

No one made a sound as the minutes passed. Mrs. Dyer held her mother's hand. Finally, Lucy got up to say the prayer for a departed soul. After it was concluded, she collected the items used for the ritual.

"Mother Lucy, will you and Dr. Stolz stay for a cup of tea?" asked Mrs. Dyer, looking suddenly lost.

"That's very kind," said Lucy, ignoring Liz's look of impatience. "Thank you."

Liz accepted a cup of tea, which she drank while she went through the papers from hospice. "I can call them to collect their equipment and the remaining drugs. I know the director of the funeral home from the chamber of commerce. Would you like me to give him a call?"

While Liz was in the other room on the phone, Lucy and Mrs. Dyer discussed the service for her mother. Finally, after a flurry of thanks at the front door, Mrs. Dyer finally let go of Lucy's hand.

The door closed behind them, and Lucy breathed a sigh of relief. Liz looked up at the sky, where the sun had fully risen and shone brightly. "'This was not judgment day—only morning,'" Liz quoted in a theatrical voice. "'Morning: excellent and fair.'"

"That sounds familiar."

"William Styron. *Sophie's Choice.*"

"Another end. Another beginning." Lucy studied Liz, leaning against the porch post. "Did you suggest the morphine to move things along?"

Liz shrugged. "One way or the other, it was only a matter of hours. This way her daughter wasn't alone when her mother died, and I was there to pronounce the death. It all worked out."

"I should take you along all the time." Lucy squinted at the sun, peeking through the tree branches. "There's no hope of us going back to sleep now."

"There never was. Let's take a quick walk on the beach. Then I'll drop you off and go home to get dressed for our meeting with your bishop." She gazed at Lucy thoughtfully. "What if you'd had to miss the meeting with the bishop to pray for that dying woman?"

"Then I would have missed the meeting."

"Glad you have the right priorities."

When Liz returned from getting changed, she wore one of her best suits and looked as scrubbed and polished as a child on the first day of school. Lucy realized that some things still impressed Liz. Meeting the bishop was evidently one of them. Lucy had dressed carefully too. She put on a real linen collar. She seldom wore them since Erika had died. Her wife knew how to press them so that they curved perfectly but never puckered. Ellie, the cleaner, ironed them now. She did a fine job, but it wasn't the way Erika had pressed them.

Lucy had been dreading this meeting but hadn't understood why. Her relationship with Bishop Greene was warm. He was an exceptionally handsome and completely out gay man in his late forties with progressive views. Like most Episcopal bishops, he saw his role as primarily pastoral rather than administrative. He tended to stay out of the local parishes' business, which Lucy and her fellow rectors appreciated.

As they drove north on I95, Lucy finally realized her anxiety had nothing to do with the bishop. Her real worry was Liz. In her effort to reform, she had cut back on her diatribes about religion, but Lucy never knew what would come out of her mouth.

Singing always helped Lucy relax, so she decided to practice some pieces she was considering for the Webhanet Playhouse benefit. Tony Roselli had been nagging her for months, but things with Maggie Fitzgerald, her singing partner, were still strained, and Lucy was reluctant to do a solo show. Then Tony came up with the idea of teaming up with Denise. Her tastes were more classical. They'd agreed to do some Broadway tunes because that's what the playhouse audience expected, but also some popular arias from opera and operettas, including one of Lucy's favorites, "Csárdás" from *Die Fledermaus.*

When Lucy finished singing, Liz clapped one hand against her thigh because she couldn't take her other hand off the steering wheel.

"I wish you would sing with me sometimes," Lucy said. "You used to sing with Maggie."

"Maggie sang folk music and Broadway tunes. You sing opera. I'd be embarrassed to sing with you."

"Why? You have a nice voice. You always sing on key. You have good breath control, and you know all the tenor parts even though you're really a contralto. The other morning, I heard you singing the drinking song from *La Traviata* in the shower. Come on. Sing it with me. I won't judge you."

Liz didn't respond. Lucy shook her head and started the accompaniment, fully expecting to sing alone, but at the cue for the tenor, Liz joined in.

"You were great," said Lucy when the duet ended. Liz blushed all the way to crimson. Lucy knew that Liz hated to do things at which she didn't feel completely competent. Agreeing to sing was a big stretch for her. "Thanks for singing with me," said Lucy, patting her thigh. "We could sing more."

"You sing if you want. I'll listen."

Lucy's anxiety returned as soon as they sat in the reception room outside the bishop's office. She prayed for divine guidance. She also prayed that Liz would behave herself.

Finally, the bishop emerged, wearing a mask embroidered with the white, blue, and red Episcopal shield. After embracing Lucy, he extended his hand to Liz. "Dr. Stolz! Lucy has told me so much about you!" Liz's eyes narrowed skeptically, and she wasn't subtle about sizing him up. In flat shoes, she would already be a few inches taller. Today, she was wearing heels. She stood straight, obviously to emphasize their difference in their height. Lucy tensed. *Oh, Liz, please don't get into a pissing contest with my bishop!*" "I hope you don't mind if I keep Lucy for a few minutes," Bishop Greene said affably. "We have a few business items to discuss."

"Take all the time you need," Liz replied coolly.

After the bishop closed the door, he gestured to a visitors' chair. Once they were both seated, he took off his mask, so Lucy did the same. "Oh, Lucy, it's so good to see your smile. Forgive the cliché, but your smile lights up the entire room. You are well named."

"I'm afraid my parents had no idea what my name meant. They were fans of the 1950s TV show."

"Well, I love Lucy too!" said the bishop. "I'm not supposed to have favorites among my clergy, but Lucy, you're certainly high on my list!" He continued to smile warmly. "How are you? You've been very much on my mind since you lost your wife."

"I appreciate every one of your calls and emails. They've been a real comfort to me. I'm doing well, considering. My book has been accepted by a publisher. I hope to graduate next June. St. Margaret's is growing with all the new people moving into Hobbs. My therapy practice is flourishing…"

"…and you're engaged." Lucy had already talked to him extensively about the engagement, but his expectant pause seemed to indicate he wanted to hear more. She didn't know what else to say. "We'll get to that later," he said, smoothly moving on. "Lucy, the pandemic is putting so much stress on our clergy. It's especially important to practice self-care. Despite your beautiful smile, you look tired. Are you getting enough rest?"

"If I look tired, it's probably because I was called to the bedside of a dying woman at three this morning."

"Yes, it's impossible to go back to sleep after those calls. You could have rescheduled for another day. I would have understood."

"I made this appointment because Liz has Mondays off. Besides her medical practice, she's involved in so many community activities. It's not easy to find time on her calendar."

The bishop looked sympathetic and nodded. He steepled his hands, indicating he was about to broach a topic that could cause discomfort. "Lucy, I'll be honest. I've had a call from one of your vestry members who's extremely concerned about you."

Lucy mentally reviewed the vestry members to identify who might have gone to the bishop. Her associate rector had been gently urging her to get more rest, but Tom was an experienced churchman, astute when it came to diocesan politics. Unless the situation were truly dire, he would never go over her head. Abbie, the senior warden, had come up through the ranks in a large corporation. Her first choice would be to work laterally or from below to remedy a problem. It had to be someone used to getting their way. That described some of the small business owners in the vestry, but she doubted any of them would bother going to the bishop. That left one person—Olivia. "Let me guess," said Lucy. "Olivia Enright."

The bishop nodded. "She insisted that I speak to you. Since she's been so generous in providing an endowment for St. Margaret's, I had to listen to what she had to say. You understand."

"Yes, but I hope you're not taking it seriously."

"Lucy, you collapsed in your churchyard after last year's Christmas service."

"That was because Erika's death was so sudden. I was in shock."

His blue eyes were sympathetic. "I can't even imagine it. A healthy woman in her sixties dying suddenly…and you'd been married little more than a year. If my husband were to drop dead tomorrow, I'd be completely devastated."

"Fortunately, I had my friends to help me keep body and soul together."

"You are lucky to have the support of your community. And please don't be angry with Ms. Enright. She means well."

"Maybe, but Olivia is the kind who likes to be in control."

"But is there any basis for her concern? You have so much on your plate. Why are you so determined to graduate next year?"

"Part of it is the rivalry I have with my daughter, who's working on her doctorate at Yale. I'm not going to let my eighteen-year-old get her PhD before me!" The bishop smiled. "Seriously, I want to finish because school is taking so much away from other things I want to do. Traveling to New York is exhausting. Because of the Delta surge, the residency requirements have been relaxed again. I want to take advantage of the online classes before they force us back to the classroom."

"You couldn't take a break?"

"But I'm so close now."

"What about your therapy practice?"

"I've limited my practice to those who come in through pastoral care. Unfortunately, that's still more than I can handle. There's a long waiting list. Fortunately, one of the other licensed therapists in town needs to arrange her schedule around childcare. We've talked about her joining me on a part-time basis."

"That sounds like a good solution. Very creative."

"Thank you."

"There's one last thing before we get on to the next subject. I know how proud you are of the work you've done at St. Margaret's, and you should be. The parish was in decline, but you built it back into a vibrant, growing faith community. You've done a great job in every way, including getting Ms. Enright on board as a donor."

"To be clear. That was her idea. I didn't cultivate her as a donor."

"Yes, I know, but you inspired her, which she is the first to say." He gave her a coy look, which meant she wouldn't like what he was about to say next. "Lucy, you're very lucky to have an experienced rector in Tom

Simmons. While you're finishing your degree, you could appoint him interim-rector to take some of the burden off you." Lucy gritted her teeth to stop the words from flying out of her mouth. The bishop stared at her cautiously. "You don't like that idea."

"Would you?"

"No," he admitted.

"It's like saying I'm not doing my job, which I am, even though it's been a challenge. I agreed to let Tom fill in for me after my wife's death, but I'm not moving over for him now." As a man, the bishop probably wouldn't understand why she felt so strongly, but he nodded. "Have you already talked to Tom about this idea?" Lucy asked. "I'd be surprised if he went along with it. He came up to Maine because he wanted less responsibility after being rector at Trinity for all those years."

"No, I haven't talked to him. I wanted to run it by you first. I'm sorry. I only suggested it because I'm trying to find ways to ease your burden. And please, there was no implication that you've been neglecting your duties. On the contrary, you've been trying too hard to prove that you aren't neglecting them."

"Is that what Ms. Enright said?"

"Not in so many words. Lucy, she called me out of concern. Not to tell on you."

"I appreciate that my friends look after me so well, but sometimes, it gets a little overbearing."

"Then let's forget I said any of those things. I'll leave it to you to find your own solutions."

"I'd appreciate it."

He gave her a quick, anxious look. "Which brings us to the next item. Thank you for bringing Dr. Stolz up here to meet me. When you told me you were engaged, I was surprised. It seemed very soon after the death of your wife. I want to make sure this relationship is on sound footing. Again, Lucy, don't take this as criticism. I only raise it out of concern for you."

"Jim, I appreciate your concern, and maybe it does seem soon. As I told you, Liz and Erika were the closest of friends. Erika asked Liz to look after me if anything happened to her. It wasn't a sudden thing. The relationship grew out of our friendship."

"There's quite an age difference between you and Dr. Stolz. How much? Nine years? That may not seem like a lot now while you're both healthy and young, but have you considered what it will mean as you age?"

"When people talk about growing old together, it sounds very romantic, but I've seen the burden age places on a family. At my pastoral care visit this morning, the poor daughter looked exhausted. Aging is difficult under the best conditions. But one thing I learned from Erika's death is that life is short and every moment should be lived. I love Liz Stolz, and I want to spend my life with her, long or short, easy or difficult. There are no "happily ever afters" in real life. It all ends, and it all ends the same way." Lucy sighed and wiped the tear that was threatening to fall. The lack of sleep was taking its toll. She never would have spoken so openly if she weren't exhausted.

The bishop's practiced smile had faded while she'd been talking. Now, he looked grave. Maybe she'd offended him. "Lucy, I try to give you pastoral advice because it's my role as your bishop, but it's clear that, of the two of us, you are the wiser."

Lucy managed a weak smile. "Thank you. It comes with age… sometimes."

"I pray for such wisdom." He rose. "Now, if you don't mind, I'm going to invite Dr. Stolz to join us."

✳✳✳

Liz was reading the medical news on her phone when the door finally opened. She checked her watch. The annoying little man had kept Lucy in his office for almost forty minutes. He approached, smiling the glib smile of an experienced administrator. Whenever Liz saw people smile so unctuously, she felt like punching them.

"Dr. Stolz, would you like to join us?"

Liz stowed her phone in her pocket and got up. He backed up to the door as she approached. She forced a smile for Lucy's benefit and followed him into the room. Lucy's pale face instantly told her that the first part of the meeting had been stressful. As Liz sat down beside her, she reached out for her hand.

"Dr. Stolz, I understand that today is your day off. Thank you for giving up your time to meet me. Tell me. What would you be doing today if you hadn't come up to Portland?"

Liz recognized the trick of trying to put her at ease before getting down to business. She despised small talk. "I hardly ever make a plan for my days off. Isn't that the point of having free time?"

He laughed nervously. "You're right. It is. But what would you be doing today if you weren't here talking to me?"

"Well, let's see." Liz sat back and crossed her legs. "I might be working in my shop or on my boat. I might take her out if the stripers are running. If I can convince Lucy to meet me for lunch, we might go out for a bite. That kind of thing."

"I understand you're involved in many community service activities," said the bishop. Liz recognized the leading statement.

"That's true, but I've cut back, so I have more time for myself…and for Lucy."

Lucy smiled at her warmly.

"Speaking of Lucy, how do you feel about being married to a priest? It will mean sharing her with her congregation."

Liz shrugged. "She will be sharing me with my patients. It's one of the things we have in common, the fact that our lives are not completely our own."

"We pray for doctors during our liturgy."

"I find that touching," Liz said, "and that's not sarcasm."

He gave Liz a long measuring look. "When I asked Lucy if you were a member of her congregation, she told me that you're a 'proud atheist.' What does that mean exactly?"

"She said that?" Liz turned to Lucy, who gave her a guilty smile. "Maybe Lucy should explain what she means."

"Liz, you've told me how you hate religious hypocrisy. You said that you would never forgive the Church for how it has treated women and gays."

"I won't. Will you?"

"I despise the evil done in God's name," said Lucy evenly. "But I can't take it back. The only thing I can do is to work from within to make things better."

"Which is why I respect your faith, even though I don't follow it." Liz leveled her eyes on the bishop. "Is it a requirement that I believe in God to marry one of your priests? My friend, Erika, who was Lucy's first wife, was an agnostic."

"Yes, but as you know, Dr. Stolz, an agnostic allows that God could exist."

Liz was tempted to respond with a filthy look to his condescending explanation, but for Lucy's sake, she kept a straight face. "Yes, Bishop, I understand. I have more than a passing interest in theology. I suppose by your definition, I qualify as an agnostic. There are many unproven things that could exist. Alternate universes, other dimensions, yet undiscovered sub-atomic particles. Human knowledge has limits." In her peripheral vision, Liz noticed Lucy's white-knuckled grip on the arms of her chair.

"So, you're not an atheist?" asked the bishop with a growing smile.

"You know how they say: 'there are no atheists in foxholes?' There are no atheists in the OR either. When you're a surgeon, literally holding someone's life in your hands, you ask for help when you need it."

"Who do you ask for help?" he asked, looking curious.

Liz thought for a moment. "A higher power, which sometimes I believe in, although most of the time, I don't."

The bishop studied her thoughtfully before turning to Lucy. "Lucy, it sounds like you two have more in common than you think, and much to talk about." He turned back to Liz. "Thank you for your honesty, Dr. Stolz. That was very enlightening. You're a unique couple. I'm happy to make myself available to either or both of you to continue this conversation. And if you would like me to officiate at your wedding, I would be honored."

Liz turned to Lucy, waiting for her to protest that they'd already chosen Tom Simmons, but she said, "Thank you, Jim. That's very generous."

"Have you set a date yet?"

"We haven't," Liz replied, "but we'd like it to be soon."

"Let me know as soon as you decide, so I can get it on my calendar." The bishop put on his mask and rose, indicating the interview was over. "Ladies, I've already taken up enough of your time today. Thanks for coming up here. It's been a pleasure meeting you, Dr. Stolz. I look forward to seeing you again." *What does that mean?* Liz wondered.

Lucy let out an enormous sigh when the door closed behind them.

"Tough meeting?" asked Liz as they walked down the stairs to the lobby.

"Yes, it was. In many ways."

"I want to hear all about it, but would you like to have lunch up here? I know some good restaurants."

"Let's go home. I'm exhausted." Lucy did look beyond tired. Liz took her arm as they headed to the parking lot. While they drove back to Hobbs, Lucy seemed quieter than usual. Liz was lost in her own thoughts about the meeting. She remained troubled by Lucy's silence when the bishop offered to officiate at their wedding.

"Why didn't you defend our decision to have Tom marry us?" Liz finally asked.

"Having the bishop officiate is an honor. One that's hard to refuse."

"But we agreed to be married by Tom."

"Tom is used to church politics. He'll understand."

"But Tom's been my friend for a long time. I know him. I don't know your bishop from Adam."

When Lucy turned, her eyes were flashing with an emotion Liz couldn't quite identify—a blend of anger, confusion, and hurt. "Why didn't you tell me about there being no atheists in the OR?"

"What?"

"You knew it would be important to me, but you didn't say a word!"

"Why is this such a big thing? You know now."

"It's how I know!" said Lucy shrilly. "You let me believe your propaganda about being a 'proud atheist.' Those are your words. You didn't tell me the truth until someone forced it out of you!"

Liz was shocked to see Lucy's effortless self-control replaced by tense anger. She usually expressed her disapproval gently, like a mother correcting a child. On rare occasions, she overflowed with righteous anger, like when the vestry had balked at hiring a trans music director, but Liz seldom saw it unleashed on her. The one exception was when Lucy fended off her unwanted advance with a Jiu Jitsu move.

"No one forced it out of me," Liz said defensively. "You think I would allow myself to be forced by someone wearing a magenta shirt and a dog collar? I revealed it voluntarily. Why are you so angry?"

"I'm not angry. I'm hurt! I'm the woman you say you love. Your faith, or lack of it, is important to me. Why couldn't you just tell me?"

Liz needed a few minutes to compose a reasonable explanation. In fact, there was none except that it was difficult to give up a position she had so carefully cultivated and defended. For years, she had worn her atheism as a badge of honor. "I didn't want to give you an opening to exploit," she finally said. "I didn't want you to see me as a possible convert."

"Exploit! Liz, I love you! I don't see you as someone I can't wait to convert. My faith is something I'd like to share with you, but you declared it off limits. Now, I have to reevaluate everything I assumed about you."

"No, you don't. I'm still the same. Now I'm sorry I told your fucking bishop."

"No, you're not. You're relieved. You've been sitting on this, afraid of what might happen when I found out."

Liz glanced cautiously in Lucy's direction. "I wanted to tell you. I didn't know how. But don't get the wrong idea. I'm not a believer. I'm a curious skeptic."

Lucy reached over and patted Liz's thigh. "Oh, Liz, I forgive you. And wherever you are on your journey is all right with me. It just came at the wrong time. The bishop had a lot to say before you came in."

"Want to tell me about it?"

"No, but I will. Olivia went over my head to the bishop. She's worried I'm working too hard. I know she means well, but someone needs to talk to her about boundaries, and it looks like that's going to be me."

"That's incredible. Who the hell does she think she is?" Liz said, relieved to have Lucy's anger directed at someone else. "That's crossing a line, and she shouldn't be allowed to get away with it."

"No, she can't, but I'm not looking forward to the confrontation. I don't want to offend her and drive her back into her shell. She's come a long way since we first met."

"I'm sure you'll figure out how to tell her. You always know what to say. I'm always putting my foot in my mouth."

"You're not the only one. I think I was too direct with the bishop when he suggested we install Tom as the interim rector, as if I'm not doing my job!"

"You've got to be kidding! That's outrageous, but men just don't get it. Their authority is unquestioned. Women have to prove themselves every day."

"There was more. He suggested I take time off from school."

Liz slowed down to get off the exit for Hobbs. "Well, you could take a little break from school." Lucy's icy silence indicated she'd expected sympathy instead of agreement with the bishop. "Okay, Lucy. I won't tell you what to do. It sounds like you've had enough of that for one day. Let's go to my house. I'll make us some lunch and then we can have a little nap."

"A nap?" asked Lucy, turning in her direction. "You just want to get me back in bed."

Liz merely smiled.

"Okay, but you need to feed me first. I'm starving."

"Oh, I will. You'll need energy for what I have planned for you," said Liz with a wink.

# 6

While Keith sleepily munched his Cheerios, Brenda finished the braid in Megan's hair. She took the rainbow scrunchie off her wrist to secure the end. Doing hair wasn't Brenda's favorite thing, which was why she wore her blond hair tied back. On formal occasions, she put it in a tidy bun because the dress uniform code prohibited hair on the shoulders. Otherwise, she couldn't be bothered. With a girl child in the house, she might have to learn some new tricks.

Cherie was upstairs dressing. Today was her first day back at the office. She'd been worried that she had let Liz down by cutting her hours, but with characteristic practicality, her boss had already started looking for a part-time nurse practitioner. Meanwhile, Lucy had taken Cherie into her counseling practice to make up for the lost income.

Everything was falling into place for Brenda and Cherie to make the transition from a couple to a family. The home visit for permanent authorization to be the kids' foster parents was scheduled. Cherie had been fixing up the kids' rooms to get ready. She'd let them pick the paint colors. The neon purple Megan had chosen hurt Brenda's eyes, but she grudgingly carried the can to the paint station for mixing. When she'd grumbled that they'd never get rid of the color, the helpful associate explained that they sold effective block-out paint.

In Brenda's opinion, people pandered too much to kids. Cherie had once told her that people learned parenting from the people who raised them. Brenda's father, a by-the-book New York City detective, would never have allowed Brenda and her sister to paint their bedroom a garish color. He was a strict man, given to uncontrolled rages, especially when he'd been drinking. He'd once beaten her brother black and blue with a piece of garden hose. Brenda didn't believe in corporal punishment, but she thought discipline was good for children. Early signs indicated that she and Cherie would disagree on this subject.

Cherie breezed into the kitchen, looking elegant in a dark orange dress that complimented her unique coloring. To Brenda, she was the most beautiful woman she'd ever seen. Only Mother Lucy gave her competition in that department. Brenda only wished that Cherie wasn't always so exhausted and could stay awake when they were finally alone in their bedroom. She missed the sweetness of Cherie's mouth on her body and the delicious smell and taste of her.

"All right, babies," Cherie said. "Mama C is going to work today. Mama B is going to drive you to school in her truck." Keith perked up at the mention of the truck. Brenda guessed it reminded him of the F-250 his father used to drive. It was on auction along with the house to be put in a trust for the kids. Cherie inspected Megan's braids. "Mama B, you did a perfect job. Maybe there's hope for you." She winked to let Brenda know she was teasing.

The titles Cherie had come up with made Brenda smile. Keith, who was a sharp kid, had asked why there was a Mama B and a Mama C, but no Mama A. "That's because your birth mama, who went to heaven, is Mama A," Cherie had explained without missing a beat. Cherie always came up with the right things to tell the kids. They naturally went to her for comfort when they bruised a knee or to cuddle, but they clung to Brenda when they awoke from a nightmare. She found it interesting that the kids had already assigned them roles, but she didn't like the idea that the kids might be trying to reproduce their birth parents. More likely it was the kids gravitating to Cherie's natural warmth, whereas Brenda's uniform had mixed associations—protective but dangerous. Keith always stared warily whenever Brenda wore her service pistol.

But she loved how Keith followed her around, asking her questions about everything. She'd bought him some child-sized gardening tools, so he could help her with the yard work. When they watched a movie together, the kids piled on her like puppies. Megan usually fell asleep in her lap and had to be carried up to bed. Brenda hadn't chosen this motherhood thing, but it was growing on her.

Cherie kissed each of the children and reached up to get a kiss from her wife. "Have a good day, sweetie-pie. I'll be home in time to meet their school bus."

Watching Cherie head to the door, Brenda felt a flutter of anxiety. This was the first time she'd be solo with the kids. Usually, Cherie was nearby to rescue her. Brenda reassured herself by replaying Cherie's words in her head: "Don't worry, precious. Trust your instincts." The idea that Brenda had maternal instinct had shaken up her ideas about herself, yet she was discovering that certain behaviors came naturally.

"Listen up!" Brenda said, clapping. "Finish your breakfast, and let's head out!" The kids stared at her until Brenda realized she'd addressed them like new police recruits. She spoke in a lighter tone generously laced with enthusiasm. "Eat your cereal and then we'll take a ride in the truck!"

When they approached the school, Brenda saw a crowd of protestors gathering in the parking lot. Few looked young enough to be parents of elementary school students or even grandparents. *Old farts with nothing better to do*, thought Brenda with contempt as she drove by. Since school had opened, people had gathered outside the building to advertise their politics with posters and chants.

"Kids, put on your masks," Brenda ordered. Distracted by the protestors, she was pleased that the children obeyed without an argument.

Brenda was helping Megan out of her booster seat when she heard a female voice behind her. "That was fast. I just called it in." Brenda turned around to see Courtney Barnes, the assistant principal standing behind her.

"Oh, I'm not responding to a call. It's my turn to drop off the kids." Brenda's radio began to squawk, and she leaned into the cab to listen. "That's the dispatch. They'll be here soon."

"I wish those people would get out of the parking lot," said Courtney, watching the protestors with a frown. "The buses will be arriving any minute. I don't want anyone to get hurt."

"I'll ask them to move," Brenda said. "They shouldn't be blocking the buses. That's a bigger crowd than usual. What brought them out this morning?"

"We had to send home one of the second-grade classes because three children tested positive for COVID. I realize it's a burden on parents who work, but what can we do? I don't want the other students to get sick."

"Are you on your own today?"

"The principal had to go to the hospital with her mother. She fell and hurt herself. She's in her nineties." Brenda looked closer and saw that the young woman appeared calm on the surface, but she was hugging herself. It wasn't that cold this morning.

"Let me push these people back from the parking lot. Where's your crossing guard?"

"Out sick with COVID."

The kids were still waiting on the sidewalk. "Ms. Barnes, will you take in my kids while I take care of things out here?" asked Brenda, putting on her hat.

"Of course."

Brenda watched the principal escort Keith and Megan into the building. Once they were inside, she put on her service belt and headed toward the knot of people. A woman shouted as she approached, "You can't do anything, Chief Harrison! We have a constitutional right to be here! It's freedom of speech!" Technically, it was freedom of assembly, but Brenda knew better than to reason with crazies.

"You don't have a right to block traffic," she replied evenly. "Get back on the sidewalk."

"The school is public property."

"The school is only open to authorized personnel. Now, get back!" It became a staring match between Brenda and the woman, who'd shouted at her. No one moved an inch. Brenda hooked her fingers in her service belt. "If you don't move, I can and will arrest you." Out of the corner of her eye, she spotted the flashing blue lights of a patrol car speeding up the street. She tapped her radio to call for more back up before stepping toward the protestors. To Brenda's relief, the people in the rear began to fall back. Eventually, all of them retreated to the sidewalk. The mouthy woman responded with a menacing glare, but finally, she followed the others to the curb.

Brenda waited for the second cruiser to arrive. "Don't make any moves unless threatened," Brenda cautioned her officers. "For now, just keep an eye on them."

She shook her head as she headed into the school. This was not how she'd expected to start her day. She knew her way to the administrative office because she'd been in the school for town events and assemblies on safety. Twice, she'd come to supervise school shooting drills. How had it become so dangerous to come to school? In her Brooklyn public school, things could be rough at times, but she'd never feared coming to school because of protests or gunmen.

"Where's Ms. Barnes?" she asked at the admins' desk. One of them pointed to the assistant principal's office. "She said to go right in. Dr. Stolz is in there with her."

When Brenda stood in the doorway, Liz looked up. "Welcome to the situation room. Don't you love it?"

"What are you doing here, Liz?"

"The school board sent me over to help them figure out a testing program for the kids."

"Ms. Barnes, aren't you lucky to be in charge while the boss is away?"

"It's good practice for me," said Courtney. "Barbara is training me to take over when she retires."

"Nice of her to throw you into the deep end of the pool," Liz said. "Her mother's getting frail. She may retire sooner than she expects. Of course, she probably didn't expect you to deal with this today."

"You really have to wonder why these people don't have something better to do," Brenda said, taking the seat next to Liz. "Now that the extended unemployment has ended, maybe they'll get jobs."

"Brenda, sometimes, you sound like Olivia," said Liz.

"Well, it's true. Why work when you're making more money on unemployment?"

Courtney watched them with a little frown. Brenda doubted she wanted to listen to them argue about politics. "How can I help you, Ms. Barnes?"

"Can you leave your officers here until school lets out?"

Brenda tried to remember the schedule for the day. Some of her patrol officers had taken vacation now that most of the summer people had left. "I can leave one, but I'll send out an alert to drive by more frequently. When is your crossing guard coming back?"

"He's in the ICU at Southern Med."

"So, not soon." Brenda pulled out her note pad and scribbled out her personal phone number. "Call me directly if there's any trouble. I'll come right away."

"Thanks, Chief. I appreciate it."

"Just keep my kids safe." Brenda leaned on her knees to get up. "I'll go out and talk to them. Of course, all their Blue Lives Matter flags mean squat when you push back on them."

"I'll go with you," said Liz, getting up. When Brenda gave her a questioning look, Liz smiled. "Reinforcements." Liz was probably packing, but her gun would never be as useful as the authority of her words. People in Hobbs looked up to Liz Stolz.

❋❋❋

Lucy surveyed the plants on the stand near her window. People were always giving her plants because they were neutral gifts for the rector of an Episcopal church. The poor souls had no way of knowing that Lucy used to be a notorious plant murderer. Erika, who was a natural gardener, had taught her how to care for houseplants. Now, the greenery at her window flourished. Two of the Halloween cactuses had put out buds. Lucy took one of the plants and headed to the small office they had set up for Cherie.

Living things always made a room more cheerful. The spare office had served as a storage space for old records before they'd reclaimed it. They'd found some upholstered chairs in good condition and a sofa. With a side table to hold the ubiquitous box of tissues, and now a plant on the coffee table, the space looked perfect for holding counseling sessions. Lucy had no doubt that Cherie would excel in this new role. Her warm personality naturally made people want to talk to her about their troubles. Just listening to her honeyed Louisiana accent was comforting.

"I thought I might find you in here," said a carefully modulated female voice.

Lucy turned around to see Denise Chantal standing in the doorway. As always, she was beautifully dressed. Women in Maine dressed informally. Denise had paid dearly to become a woman, so she never missed the opportunity to flaunt her new assets. She usually wore form-fitting dresses and tight skirts. Lucy almost never saw her in pants. The only hint that Denise was not a natural-born woman was her extraordinary height.

"Hello, Denise. You're just in time. Can you help me move this sofa?" Denise put her hands on her hips and stared at her. "Oh, come on, Denise. Women move furniture all the time. We just do it differently. We use our legs and leverage our body weight."

"Which in your case, can't be much."

"It's not, but I use it strategically. I learned how when I took martial arts classes."

"I heard you have a brown belt in Jiu Jitsu, and you're deadly."

"You heard right." Lucy smiled and wagged a finger. "So, don't mess with me!"

"I wouldn't dare," said Denise, drawing back with mock dread.

Together they pushed the sofa closer to the wall.

"This way, the clients can observe social distancing and don't have to wear masks." Lucy explained, glancing around to make sure everything was ready. "Would you mind opening the window a bit for air circulation?" Again, Denise looked indignant, but she opened the window. The room finally met Lucy's approval. "Thanks for your help, but you came in here for another reason."

"Yes, Mother Lucy, I want to discuss a few things with you."

Lucy glanced at the fancy smartwatch Liz had given her as a birthday gift. It had so many features that Lucy never used, but at least, it was good for telling time. "I have a counseling appointment in ten minutes."

"I'll be quick."

"All right," said Lucy, reluctantly. Her previous sessions had been rough, and she needed to reserve some emotional energy for her talk with Olivia. To underscore that she didn't have much time, Lucy continued to stand after Denise sat down.

Denise carefully arranged herself for modesty, tightly holding her legs together. She folded her hands in her lap. "Let me start by saying that I love my job as music director of St. Margaret's."

Lucy was impatient with the preamble, but she played along. "And we love having you here. Filling Maggie Fitzgerald's shoes was challenging, but you've done a spectacular job."

"Thank you. I've been introducing more classics. I hope people don't mind."

"I haven't heard any complaints. Every music director leaves their own stamp." Lucy tried to be discreet about glancing at her watch.

"Mother Lucy, your voice lessons have been helpful, but I can only practice so much before I get hoarse. In short, I don't have enough to do, so I came up with an idea." Denise paused for effect. "Wouldn't it be wonderful to have a children's choir? You may remember that I have enough credits in education to be a teacher. That was my backup in case my vocal career didn't take off. The real goal of this choir is to teach kids about music, real music. If we get a working choir out of the deal, great, but music education is the goal," said Denise, barely taking a breath. "And! If you need more ammo for the vestry, choir practice would provide a place for working parents to park their children after school. The buses could drop them off here."

Lucy tried to keep the skeptical look off her face, but she was finding it difficult.

"What's the matter?" asked Denise, sitting back to interpret Lucy's expression. "You don't think I'm capable of managing children? I got an A in classroom management."

"Denise, I'm sure you'd be great at keeping the kids in line."

"You're worried people will object to me being with their kids…because I'm trans?"

Lucy offered a kind smile. "Denise, I don't want you to set yourself up for rejection."

"Mother Lucy, if I hide, I'm rejecting myself." The truth of Denise's statement hit Lucy like a punch. "Please support me, and I promise to do the rest."

"All right. Send me the particulars by email. I'll make an announcement in the vestry meeting that this is what you plan. We'll spin it as after-school enrichment. And I'll lobby our allies for support before the meeting."

"Oh, thank you!"

"No promises," Lucy said with a firm look. "I'll do my best, but be prepared for disappointment. Now, what's the other thing you wanted to talk to me about?"

"Maybe you should sit down for this one," said Denise in an ominous tone.

Reluctantly, Lucy took a seat in one of the armchairs. She was glad to find that, despite their age, they were comfortable. She folded her hands in her lap and sat back to indicate she was ready to listen.

Denise nervously rearranged her position. She crossed her legs, then uncrossed them. "This one is harder to talk about. I don't want to get on your wrong side or offend you in any way."

"With that buildup, you're guaranteeing I won't like what you're going to say, but let's hear it."

Denise looked directly into her eyes. "You may know that I've been in communication with your daughter."

"Yes, Emily told me how delighted she was to find a friend who knows so much about music."

Denise stared at the floor in front of her. "I'm afraid it's become more than that. We really care about one another."

"What?" Usually, Lucy was better at controlling her reactions, but this was her child they were talking about. She forced the look of disapproval off her face and said, "Tell me more."

"Please understand that it's not my intention to throw Emily out of the closet, but because I work for you and I'm older than your daughter, I thought I should ask your permission before this goes any further."

"Remind me how old you are, Denise."

"I'm twenty-seven."

"Emily is eighteen, but she's a very young eighteen because of her upbringing in a conservative, religious family. She's had little experience with romantic relationships." When her daughter had reappeared in her life, Lucy had discovered that the Jehovah's Witnesses who'd adopted Emily had told her almost nothing about sex. Then, Emily was only sixteen, and her awkwardness made the possibility of a sexual relationship remote, but Lucy insisted on having a frank discussion. Emily looked disgusted when Lucy had described the mechanics. As someone on the spectrum, Emily sometimes had an aversion to touch.

"I haven't encouraged a romance because of the age difference and her disability."

"Thank you. That's very sensitive of you."

"I care about your daughter, and I care about my relationship with you, which is why I'm trying to do the right thing here. Has Emily said anything about this to you?"

"No, but Emily has difficulty expressing her feelings. Once she's finished analyzing it, she'll probably tell me. I like to think we have a good relationship."

"Emily adores you," Denise said fervently.

Lucy sighed but didn't say what she usually did when someone said she was adored, namely, 'I don't want to be adored, just loved.'

"Nine years is not a big age difference," added Denise in a hopeful voice. It didn't escape Lucy's notice that she and Liz had the same age gap. She remembered what she'd said to the bishop when he'd brought up this point. The situation couldn't be more different. Lucy and Liz weren't young. Time was running out for them, but Emily had her entire life ahead of her.

"It's not a big age gap for most adults," said Lucy, "but there are times when age differences mean more. Early adulthood is one of those periods."

"Emily seems very mature, despite being on the spectrum," said Denise. "Her range of reactions has increased since she's been at Yale. She told me that she studies other people's behavior and practices in the mirror. When we video chat, I can see how much she's improved."

"I'm glad you've been talking, Denise, but this is a very complicated situation."

"A lesbian relationship between an autistic woman and a trans woman? Yes, I know it's odd, but maybe we are attracted to one another because we're not like other people."

"Denise, I want my daughter to have a complete and full life. I hope she finds a loving, sexual relationship, but my first instinct as a mother is to protect her. I hope you understand."

"Maybe it will help to know that my first instinct is also to protect her."

Lucy studied Denise's earnest face. "You didn't have to tell me about your rleationship with Emily."

"Coming out as trans liberated me from hiding. Now, transparency is my policy."

"That's good, Denise. But not everyone will hear your truth with an open mind."

"Believe me, Mother Lucy, I am well versed on that subject."

Again, the truth of the statement slammed Lucy. She took a moment to compose a response. "Thank you for sharing your plans. I can't stop you from exploring a relationship with Emily, but please be sensitive and kind. I feel silly saying it because I have never known you to be anything but sensitive and kind. You put other people to shame."

"For obvious reasons, I've become more attuned to the feelings of others. You don't know me well, but I am a decent person."

"Telling me about your friendship with my daughter confirms how ethical you are." Lucy's watch vibrated, the five-minute reminder of her appointment with Olivia. "I'm sorry, Denise, but I have a counseling session. Is there anything else you wanted to talk about?"

"That's not enough?"

Lucy chuckled. "Yes, I think that's more than enough."

Before Denise left, she gave Lucy a crushing hug. She wished she had more time to process the conversation, but she knew that Olivia, who was always punctual, would be waiting outside her door.

"Come in, Olivia," said Lucy cheerfully. Olivia gave her a cautious look. She was perceptive. Of course, she knew she had overstepped by going to the bishop. Once Lucy opened her office door, Olivia quickly slipped by her and retreated to a visitors' chair. After opening the window for ventilation, Lucy took off her mask.

"I'm so disappointed that we're back here with masks," Olivia complained.

"I know what you mean. Liz was hoping to resume our weekly get togethers. Now, it doesn't look like we can."

"I miss our Thirsty Thursdays on Liz's deck, even with the weekly probing. Of course, that assumes I'll still be invited." Lucy recognized the ploy for her to intervene, but she didn't respond to it. "I could use some social activity now that Samantha has abandoned me."

"What do you think went wrong?" Lucy asked, sitting down.

"Samantha says I'm overbearing. Too bossy and directive."

"Is it true?

"All right. It's true, but someone has to call the shots."

"Isn't it better to get consensus?"

"How well do you know Samantha?" asked Olivia, raising her brows. "She could write the book on passive aggressive behavior."

"Sam's quiet. That's not the same." Lucy studied Olivia's face and saw how pale and pinched it was. She hoped the breakup wasn't affecting her health.

"It's not all Samantha's fault," Olivia said with a sigh. "I wanted more from the relationship than she was willing to give."

"You didn't talk about your expectations?"

"We did, and she was clear that our relationship was about sex. Nothing more."

"But you wanted more."

"Yes, but I'm not going to let this get me down. It's time to move on. Now that I have more time, I'm going to get involved in politics again and grow my financial advisor clientele."

"How about your other relationships? How's it going with your grandchildren?"

"We video chat several times a week. Thanks to you, I have a civil relationship with my ex-daughter-in-law."

"I'm glad I was able to help."

"You're very good at helping people, Lucy, but not at pacing yourself. Last winter you were a basket case, but as soon as you recovered, you jumped right back in with both feet. Now, you're running yourself ragged again. You need to pace yourself, Lucy, or..."

Lucy let Olivia go on with this unwanted advice until she took a breath. "Is that why you went over my head to the bishop?"

Olivia visibly flinched. Then she stared defiantly. "You're a public figure. You belong to the people of our church. You have a duty to look after yourself."

"Olivia, I know you take your role in the vestry seriously, but it's not your place to decide when I'm overburdened. Going behind my back to the bishop is a serious breach of trust. There are appropriate channels for dealing with your concerns. You should have come to me first."

"But you don't listen, Lucy. You're too generous with your time. You give your energy to people so freely. You can't stop. I thought the bishop would order you to cut back. He's your boss, isn't he?"

"Yes, but the church is not like a corporation where the CEO gives an order, and either you obey it, or you're fired. It's more nuanced than that. What did he say when you told him your concerns?"

"He said that I should talk to you directly."

"Which was the right thing to say, and for you to do."

Olivia raised her pointed chin and looked defiant. "You resent my intrusion."

"Of course, I do. I'm an adult and I'm responsible for myself."

"Then why did you fall apart and waste away to nearly nothing because you wouldn't eat?"

"Olivia, my wife died suddenly. My reaction might seem dramatic to you, but it wasn't abnormal. I needed to experience my grief, but I'm recovered now."

"You always look tired."

"Sometimes, I am tired. I live a busy life, but it's my life, which I don't have to defend to you, and I certainly don't want to be forced to defend it to my bishop."

"That hit a nerve," Olivia said with a wary look.

"Yes, it did. You can't interfere in the lives of other adults and expect them to say, 'thank you.' When I was a singer, I was always being managed… by my mother, my agent, the directors, the heads of the opera companies…. I don't need to be managed! I can take care of myself." The words had flown out of Lucy's mouth before she could stop them. As the penetrating blue eyes scrutinized her, Lucy remembered her client describing how she preyed on other people's weaknesses. By telling her how she hated being managed, Lucy had just handed her powerful leverage.

"Let's get back to you, Olivia. I've made my point."

"You did. And I understand better now." Olivia sat back with a thoughtful frown. "Is this how I went wrong with Samantha, by interfering?"

"Possibly. Maybe we can discuss it and figure it out together. I'm sure it will take more time than we have today."

Olivia's face looked stony. "You'll say anything to get me back into therapy."

"That's your choice, Olivia. Unfortunately, we've wasted a good portion of your time talking about you going to the bishop. We can extend this session to make up for it."

"See? There you are being overly generous again."

Lucy struggled to find patience. This woman literally had an answer for everything. "Fine, Olivia. We'll end on time."

"I'm sorry I stuck my nose in your business, Lucy, but I'm fond of you, and I do care."

"I know, but next time, please come to me first."

After Olivia left, Lucy packed up for the day. On her way out, she waved through the small window in Cherie's office door to let her know she was leaving.

She stopped at the beach house to get a change of clothes. While she was there, she went from room to room, looking around wistfully. She'd been spending so much time at Liz's place that her own house no longer seemed like home. When she'd been an opera singer and constantly traveled, she'd never considered a particular place home, not even the Manhattan apartment, where she crashed between engagements. Since she'd been ordained, wherever she lived was temporary. The beach house was the closest thing to a home since she'd lived with her parents as a child.

The porch lights were lit, and the front door was open when Lucy arrived at Liz's house. The tantalizing aroma that greeted her meant Liz was in the kitchen making dinner.

"Oh, my! What smells so good?"

"A Moroccan chicken stew recipe I found in the *New York Times*," said Liz, frowning at a small bottle, "but they always call for some weird ingredient I don't have. I'm trying to figure out what spices to substitute." Liz wiped her hands on a towel and pulled Lucy into a hug. Lucy allowed herself to fall into Liz's body with a grateful sigh. The cooking smells absorbed by her T-shirt reminded Lucy how hungry she was. She hadn't eaten since wolfing down some cinnamon raisin toast at breakfast.

"I invited our neighbors for dinner," said Liz, affectionately rubbing Lucy's back. "Courtney had a really bad day. Her boss is dealing with a family issue, which meant Courtney had to handle the protesters. It got so bad that Brenda left a patrol car there the whole day."

Lucy tightened her embrace. She didn't want company tonight. She wanted Liz all to herself. Liz tried to move away, but Lucy hung on. "Don't go," Lucy murmured. "I had a bad day too."

"Oh, baby, I'm sorry. I can uninvite the kids. I'll bring over a care package for their dinner."

"No, don't do that," said Lucy, still clinging to Liz. "They need us. Just hold me for a minute. Then I'll go up and change."

***

Melissa rolled over to cuddle her lover but found the space where she slept empty. Courtney's phone had been playing ridiculously cheerful music on and off for at least a half hour. Finally, she had gotten up to get ready for school.

Because Melissa was working remotely, she could sleep later. It was such a struggle to get up in the dark, but it would be this way until the time changed. The reprieve would be brief. The days would continue to grow shorter until they reached the longest night. As much as Melissa hated to wake up to darkness, she liked the change of seasons, something she'd missed when she'd stayed with her mother in Florida. Autumn in Maine brought vibrant colors and crisp air, just right for spending the evening in front of the propane stove to watch the flames.

Already showered, Courtney came into the room. She dropped the towel and stepped into her underpants. Her skin was pale, and her figure ideally proportioned. Such objectively perfect beauty was meant to be savored in the moment. It didn't last long, which Melissa had been thinking about lately because her birthday was fast approaching.

The prospect of aging looked less frightening when she looked at their neighbors. Lucy was in the last blush of female perfection. Liz was older. Her throat had the texture of fine crepe. Yet her sculptural face and shaggy gray hair had its own beauty. Neither of them seemed especially concerned about their fading looks, and both made the most of what remained, especially Lucy. In fact, they seemed more at home in their skin than most of Melissa's contemporaries. They already seemed as settled as an old married couple. Was that a gift of age or the sign of a good match?

Courtney, evidently aware that Melissa had been watching her, turned around as she hooked her bra. "How long have you been awake?"

"Oh, not long."

"Getting in a little voyeurism before you get up?"

"Yes. And thinking."

"I should have guessed. You have that pensive look. Are you preparing a brilliant legal argument for some big case?"

"No, I was thinking about time passing. During this pandemic, with everyone shut up inside, it seemed to stand still, but it hasn't. Look how much Kaylee has grown in just a few months."

"She's at that age when kids grow like weeds," said Courtney, zipping up her slacks. "Someone's getting worried about her birthday, isn't she? Don't worry, Melissa. Forty-two isn't any worse than forty-one. Take it from someone who knows." Courtney pulled a cotton sweater over her head. "We should go out for your birthday," she said when her head popped through.

"Aren't you worried about the surge? The numbers keep going up."

"With all the exposure I have at school, I'm less worried about eating in a restaurant. How about sushi? You liked that place in Portsmouth." Courtney sat down on the bed and pulled down the covers. She appreciatively ran her hand over Melissa's bare skin, ending the tour of her body at her right nipple. "You were amazing last night. Sooooo sexy!"

"It turns me on to be with other queer women, especially when they have the hots for each other like Liz and Lucy do. With them, you don't mind PDAs."

"You were cute last night. If Liz put her arm around Lucy, you put your arm around me. If she held her hand, you held mine. It was like watching ourselves in a mirror."

"I like seeing ourselves reflected in another couple. Usually, when I'm in a new relationship, I want to be alone with my lover as much as I can. Of course, with Kaylee in the house, I've had to adjust, especially because we share such a small space. But I like being part of our little community. For the first time in my life, I don't feel so lonely."

Courtney gently stroked her arm, raising the hair. "You feel lonely? Even when you're with me?"

"Sometimes," Melissa admitted.

"That's sad. I have so many people around me all the time I don't have time to feel lonely. I often find myself wishing everyone would go away and give me a few minutes of peace!"

Melissa sat up in bed. "If Barbara doesn't come back to work, and you become principal, it's going to get worse."

"Tell me about it. I can really use the bump in pay, but I'm not looking forward to all the responsibility."

"Yesterday was a bad day. They won't all be like that."

"I know, but it makes me wonder if climbing the ladder is all that people say it is. In a small school district the principal does a lot, including personnel evaluations all the way down to the custodians."

"You'll do fine," said Melissa confidently. "How about I get up and have a cup of coffee with you before Kaylee gets up?"

"I'd love it!"

Melissa slipped out of bed and put on the nightshirt that had landed on the floor during the night. "I'll put on the coffee," she volunteered. "You'd think Liz, who's such a tech head, would have one of those programmable coffee pots in this apartment."

"But her mother probably wasn't tech savvy, and Liz built the place for her. We should take my coffee pot out of storage, except I don't remember which box I put it in."

"I can help you look for it when I get back from my mother's."

Courtney put down the hairbrush and turned around. "Are you sure working over there is a good idea?"

"It gets me out of the house, and my mother gets to see my face. Besides, I have more room over there."

"Liz offered you space in her house."

"I think we're already taking too much advantage of Liz, and my mother always complains she never sees me. Don't worry. I'll be back by the time Kaylee gets off the bus."

"She has soccer tonight. I should be home by then too."

Courtney went into the bathroom to put on her makeup. Melissa put on the coffee to brew. From the window, she watched Liz and Lucy heading out for their beach walk.

Courtney came into the kitchen and put two English muffins in the toaster. She leaned against the counter while she waited. Melissa admired her. She liked how Courtney put herself together. Today, she wore a smart suit with a sheer scarf of fall colors highlighted by gold metallic.

"I love this little apartment, but I think we should start looking for a bigger place," Courtney said. "The trouble is finding one I can afford."

"I can help with the rent."

"I don't want to be dependent on your contribution."

"But I'm sharing the space. Why shouldn't I contribute?"

"You don't actually live here. I appreciate that you chip in for groceries."

"I eat with you most of the time. It's the least I can do."

"When I find a place I can afford, we can talk about how to share the expenses."

Melissa was tempted to argue, but she knew how sensitive Courtney was on this subject. She was trying to prove that she could make it on her own after years of being married to a man. Melissa tried a different tack. "I admire your independence. Some of my girlfriends thought it was great to live with a high-salaried lawyer and never thought twice about taking advantage of me." Melissa could see from Courtney's little frown that her mind had already moved on to another topic. "What's the matter?"

"I don't know if I can face another day like yesterday. I'm glad Liz was there, and Brenda. Otherwise, I don't know what I would have done."

Melissa gave Courtney a little hug. "Take some deep breaths. It will be okay."

Courtney clung to her. "I used to have panic attacks when I was young. I finally got them under control. I don't want to start having them again."

"I've never had them, but I've heard they can be pretty awful. What can I do to help?"

"Please, don't pressure me. I'm already under enough pressure."

"Okay. No pressure. What else?"

Courtney was trembling. "Just hold me. It really helps."

# 7

The sudden change from the warm, tropical air brought north by the hurricanes to the chilly nights of early October made Amy glad to have her warm clothes. A friend had helped her pack up the Westchester apartment over the weekend. She'd shipped a few boxes by UPS, but almost everything else fit in the back of her SUV. She was happy to have more than the bare necessities in the Hobbs condo Sam had helped her find. The landlord in Webhanet had been happy to return her deposit because he could instantly find another tenant at an even higher rent. The TV news was full of stories about the housing shortage, which was making the local homeless problem even worse.

Life in Maine was proving to be more complicated than Amy had expected. Sam had given her a crash course in the problems the summer tourists never saw. Some of Amy's elderly patients were unhealthily thin, but they were too proud to admit they didn't have enough to eat. Prescriptions for nutritional supplements helped a little, but it was a systemic problem. Lack of childcare had forced women to give up their jobs, crashing their family budgets. Hobbs might be considered an affluent town by Maine standards, but Amy was beginning to see how the year-round residents struggled.

"Dr. Hsu?" asked Cherie, knocking on her open door. "Do you have a minute?"

"Sure, Cherie. Come in."

Looking distraught, Cherie came in and shut the door. "I need you to see one of Cathy's patients. She's camped out in the waiting room and won't leave. I explained that Cathy doesn't come in until nine, but she insists on waiting. She really wants to see Liz, but she's not coming in until this afternoon."

"Whoa! Slow down. Who's her doctor? Cathy or Liz?"

"Well, neither really. She moved out of town and transferred to another practice."

"So, why is she here? I'm not following."

Cherie looked perplexed and frustrated. "Maybe I should back up a little." She took a deep breath and began again. "This patient had stage one breast cancer years ago. It was removed by lumpectomy. Her prognosis looked excellent until she tested positive for the BRCA2 gene. She had a prophylactic salpingo-oophorectomy and has been on tamoxifen ever since. Liz made sure she got all her screenings until she moved to Scarborough. Between COVID and moving, it took a while for her to find a new doctor, who finally ordered the screening for tumor markers."

"…and they're elevated," said Amy, shaking her head. "So much testing and treatment is falling through the cracks with COVID. But what does she expect Liz to do?"

"Liz was managing her breast cancer."

"If I had breast cancer, I'd want one of the world's leading experts to manage my case too," said Amy. "So, I get it now, but will she even talk to me?"

"I hope so. At least, you could try to calm her down. I know her pretty well, but I can't."

Amy glanced at the clock over the door. "I have a patient in five minutes."

"I know. I can take your patient. It's just a routine review of blood work and prescriptions, right?"

"Okay. Give my apologies to…" Amy checked her appointments list. "…Mr. Daniels, and tell him I'll see him the next time he comes in. Give me a little time to review the case file. What's her name?"

"Maggie Fitzgerald."

"The Broadway actress?"

"Yes, and Liz's ex-wife."

"Oh," said Amy, connecting the dots.

"Yes, it's a dicey situation, but she's in a bad way. Please help."

"Okay. I'll do my best but let me take a look at the history before she comes in."

As soon as Cherie left, Amy navigated to the patient's file. She glanced at the DOB at the top of the file and calculated the woman's age—sixty-eight. She scrolled through page after page of notes, trying to find the end of the file. Finally, she let out a long, exasperated breath, realizing it would take hours to review this case. She skipped down to the most recent entries. The last note in the file was a cover letter from a Beverly Birnbaum, an oncologist associated with Yale New Haven. She was retiring and had transferred her files on the case to Liz.

When Amy had read enough to give her a basic understanding, she picked up the office phone to call the front desk. "Ginny, please send Ms. Fitzgerald down to Liz's office. I assume she knows where it is."

At the knock on the door, Amy opened it to an attractive woman with long, white hair, artfully arranged and pinned back. The style effectively showed her good bone structure. Beneath carefully applied makeup, she looked pale. Her hazel eyes were bloodshot and glassy. She was still attractive, but at the age when sleep deprivation did her no favors.

"What are you doing in Liz's office?" the woman demanded, narrowing her eyes.

"Dr. Stolz and I have worked out a timeshare until the new offices are ready." Amy had gotten out of the habit of shaking hands since the pandemic, but this woman looked like she desperately needed human contact. "It's nice to meet you, Ms. Fitzgerald." The woman's hand was cool to the touch. Obviously, she was anxious. "Why don't you have a seat and tell me what brought you in today?"

"I want to see Dr. Stolz."

"So I understand, but she doesn't have office hours until after lunch. Please sit down."

"I want to see her," the woman insisted, reluctantly taking a seat.

"Why don't you call her? Maybe she can come in earlier."

The woman's cheeks flamed. "Liz isn't taking my calls."

"Oh," said Amy, beginning to wonder what she had gotten herself into.

"Would you like me to call her and tell her you're here?"

"Yes. Please. I tried to get Ginny to call Liz, but she won't." If the scrupulously professional practice manager wouldn't call Liz, there must be a good reason. Amy peered at Ms. Fitzgerald, hoping she would say more. Finally, she admitted the truth. "Liz and I had an argument, and she's blocked my calls. Not very adult of a woman in her sixties!"

Amy carefully navigated around the statement like it was a tire in the middle of the road. "Tell me, Ms. Fitzgerald. Why can't your regular doctor help you?"

"She's just a GP. Liz is an expert. And she knows everything there is to know about my cancer. She was with me through all my treatments."

"I saw in the file that your oncologist recently retired. Is that one of your concerns?"

"Yes, Liz and Bev are personal friends. She would know how to contact her."

Amy shifted uncomfortably in her chair. The idea that the patient would insist on consulting a retired physician felt invasive. "Ms. Fitzgerald, there are other oncologists."

"Yes, I know. My daughter is one."

"Then why don't you ask her for a referral?"

The woman gave her a sharp look. "I don't want Sophia involved. She loses her head over anything to do with my health."

Amy released a long sigh. There was no reasoning with this woman, but facing a recurrence of cancer could make people irrational. Amy drummed her fingers lightly on the desk while she considered what to do. "I'm going to send Liz a text message and tell her that you're here. Maybe you could find a place to meet outside the office. It might be more comfortable," said Amy, offering the hint with a large dose of enthusiasm.

"I used to have some friends in town, but I haven't kept in touch with them since I left."

"It's a nice day. The benches overlooking the beach are…"

"You've gotten to know Hobbs very well, Dr. Hsu," said Ms. Fitzgerald in a challenging tone that made Amy sit back.

"Let me text Dr. Stolz, and you two can figure out where to talk. Meanwhile, I have other patients to see."

"I'll sit in the waiting room until Liz gets here." The woman's voice was resolute. She intended to park herself until Liz showed up.

"Okay. I'll let Ginny know if I get a reply." Amy picked up her phone to compose a text.

"Thanks, Doctor. And I'm not usually this rude or impatient. I just want to see Liz."

"I know," said Amy in a kind voice. "A cancer recurrence is frightening. I'll let you know as soon as I hear anything from Dr. Stolz."

"Thank you for seeing me," Ms. Fitzgerald said. "Really." When the hazel eyes engaged Amy's, she could see the raw fear in them.

✳✳✳

The message from Amy was brief: *Your ex-wife is at the office. Her tumor markers are high. She wants to see you ASAP.*

"Oh, my God," muttered Liz.

"What's the matter?" asked Olivia, looking up from the financial reports they'd been reviewing.

"I need to go to the office." Liz got up. "I'm sorry, Olivia, but we need to do this another time."

"I hope it's nothing serious," Olivia said, following her to the door. "Let me know if there's anything I can do."

Liz started the engine of the truck, but before she took off, she texted a reply to Amy: *On my way. Thanks for running interference.* She appreciated Amy stepping in to handle the situation, but now her new hire had seen how badly her boss had botched her personal life. Of course, Liz's embarrassment was inconsequential compared to her worry about the rise in Maggie's tumor markers. She called her practice manager through the dashboard Bluetooth. "Ginny, can you put Maggie in an exam room and call her doctor to get her tumor markers?"

"On it," said Ginny. Liz heard rapid typing in the background.

Liz ended the call and called Maggie. While she waited for her to answer, she eyed the white Hobbs police car hiding in a driveway and reduced her speed. She watched in the rear-view mirror to make sure she wasn't being followed.

A familiar voice, sounding shaky and surprisingly young, came on the line. "Oh, Liz. Thank God!"

"Maggie, I'll be there in a few minutes. Ginny will put you in an exam room to wait for me. Don't worry. Everything will be all right."

"Please get here soon."

Heading down Route 1, Liz realized she could have asked Maggie to meet her at home. After the divorce, Maggie had been in and out of the house to finish her packing. Their conversations hadn't always been friendly, but Liz never even considered asking her to return her keys.

That was before Maggie found out about the engagement. When she called to let Liz know exactly how she felt about it, her voice was loud and shrill. Liz left the room so Lucy wouldn't overhear the disgusting names she was being called: bitch, cheat, liar, slut, cunt. Liz despised that word and couldn't believe it had come out of Maggie's mouth. She hated bad language. Afterward, the calls wouldn't stop, or the texts. Finally, Liz decided to block Maggie's number until she came to her senses. "What if there's an emergency, and she really needs you?" Lucy had asked, but Liz had shrugged off the question.

When Liz parked next to Maggie's Subaru, she noticed a new dent in the fender. Maggie had always been a careful driver, but Liz knew a major life change like a divorce could make someone less attentive. She told herself not to read too much into it.

"We put her in room three," Ginny explained when Liz came through the door. That was the place where they stuck the screaming pediatric patients because it was at the end of the hall and separated from the other rooms by a closet. "She's very upset," Ginny said with a look that made Liz wonder how much drama had already transpired.

"Did her results come in?"

"Yes. They gave me an argument because she hadn't designated anyone to receive her medical information, not even her daughters, but when I said it was for you, they sent it."

"Sometimes, it pays to be famous." Liz tapped the counter in front of the reception window. "Thanks. Don't let anyone know I'm here. This may take a while."

"Good luck," said Ginny as Liz headed down the hall.

Liz steeled herself before knocking on the door. "Hello, Maggie," she said cheerfully as she came into the room. Maggie threw herself into her arms. Awkwardly, Liz patted her back, but Maggie held on until she gave her a real hug. "Why don't you have a seat?" Liz suggested. Maggie retreated to the patient chair, where she looked Liz over from head to toe.

"You look good, Liz."

Liz glanced down. She was wearing her usual cool-weather office attire—dress slacks, a button-down shirt, and a blazer—nothing special, but Maggie had always preferred the more professional look to the shorts and polo shirts Liz wore in the summer.

"Thanks," muttered Liz. She couldn't honestly return the compliment because Maggie looked like hell. As always, her hair and makeup looked professional, but it was obvious she hadn't had any sleep. "When did you get the results?" asked Liz, pulling the office laptop on an articulating arm closer. She sat down on a rolling stool and logged into the system.

"Last night. My doctor called."

Liz opened Maggie's file and read the numbers. They weren't exceptionally high, but with Maggie's history, any change was cause for concern. "They're elevated," Liz said calmly. "What did your doctor say?"

"That I should have a mammogram. Maybe other tests."

"She's right. I'd say the same."

Maggie stared at her with wide eyes, looking expectant.

"That's what you wanted to hear, isn't it?"

"Liz! I need you now. I need you!"

The stool squeaked as Liz shifted her weight. She studied the numbers again. "What would you like me to do?"

"Show some concern!"

Liz struggled to remain composed. "We don't really know anything yet. Let's wait, get some imaging, and then—"

"There you go, sounding like a doctor!"

"Which is why you should be talking to your doctor, not me."

"She's a nice woman, but she's not you. It was really hard to get someone to take me as a patient. Do you know how hard it is for people on Medicare to find a primary care doctor?"

"I'm afraid I do."

"And you know the people who can help me. Dr. Birnbaum retired last year."

Liz released her breath slowly to prevent an audible sigh. "Maybe it's time to find providers closer to home."

"That's not what you said last time. Then, you wanted only the best doctors for me."

"If you need extensive treatment, you'll want to have access to local providers, not scramble to find them at the last minute." What Liz was saying was completely reasonable. She was giving Maggie the same advice she would give any patient. She could see from Maggie's expression that she wasn't impressed. "Why don't you talk to Sophia about it?" Liz suggested. "She's at Dana-Farber now. I'm sure she knows many good people who can help you."

"I don't want Sophia involved. I don't even want her to know."

"Maggie…you have to tell the girls. They have a right to know."

"You know that Alina and Sophia never recovered from that Romanian orphanage. They become hysterical when they think something might happen to me."

"They're adults now, and they need to know. They're your family."

"You used to be my family."

Liz felt her patience was growing thin. "Maggie, you know why I can't be involved in your case."

"No, why?"

"Well, for starters, you're my ex-wife. And you're still angry with me."

"I'm over that now."

"You are? The last time we talked, you were screaming at me and calling Lucy names."

"Lucy," said Maggie, making a face like she'd bitten into a lemon.

"See?"

"See what? She destroyed our relationship."

Liz got up. "Talk to your doctor. I can't help you." She headed to the door.

"Liz, wait! I'll stop."

Liz sat down again.

"Please, help me. Please!" begged Maggie.

Liz looked at her. Once, she had been desperately in love with this woman. Now, she felt only pity. "What would you like me to do?" she asked in a flat voice.

"You know what I want you to do, what I need you to do."

Liz crossed her arms on her chest. "You should be asking your doctor for referrals. If I get involved, you either need to keep her in the loop or transfer back to Cathy. I can't be your doctor."

"All right. I'll transfer back to Cathy."

"Okay. Let Ginny know. Meanwhile, I'll work on getting you some imaging. I'll call Alyson at Southern Med and see what she can set up. I'll push her as much as I can."

"Will you call Dr. Birnbaum too?"

"Bev is retired, but I can ask for a referral. Are you sure you want to go all the way to Yale for treatment?"

"Your protégée is still there, right?"

"Ellen Connelly? Yes."

"Then, that's where I want to go." Maggie's face was resolute. It was becoming clear that this was exactly the outcome she had planned. The drama had only been for show.

"Do you mind waiting outside while I call Alyson? I shouldn't be long."

Maggie looked around for her purse and got up to leave.

***

The crew seemed to have things under control, so Sam decided to quit early. It was one of those High October days when it was warm enough to go without a jacket. The renovation of Liz's office had scuttled her plans to get in more fishing since she'd split from Olivia. This afternoon, she intended to remedy that.

She headed across the parking lot and noticed a familiar Subaru parked next to Liz's truck. Looking more closely, she saw a woman hunched over the steering wheel. Sam knocked softly on the window. "Are are you okay?" she called through the glass.

Maggie looked up and rolled down the window. "Yes, Sam. I'm fine." She managed a brave smile, but her cheeks were streaked with tears. Her damaged eye-makeup formed dark circles around her eyes, making her look fragile and old.

"You don't look fine," said Sam, leaning on her knees so her face was at Maggie's eye level. "Did you and Liz have a fight?"

Maggie shook her head.

"Then what's going on?"

"The cancer's back."

"Oh, shit! I'm so sorry, Maggie!" Sam glanced back at the office. "Did you come to see Cathy?"

"No, Liz."

Sam stood straight. "Oh! How did that go?"

"Not well, but better than I expected. She has a lot of connections. She can pull strings no one else can."

"Liz is a good friend. She won't let you down." Sam knew that she couldn't just leave Maggie crying in a parking lot. She sighed as she saw her hope for a free afternoon dissolve. That big bass she'd been chasing all summer could happily swim around the pond for another day. "Maggie, I'm heading home for lunch. Want to join me? I made some chili in the Crockpot. Should be ready to eat by now."

"Oh, Sam, I love your chili, but the beans give me gas."

Sam grinned. "Me too, but I won't tell if you won't." Sam gently elbowed Maggie's shoulder. "After lunch, you can keep me company while I fish. What do you say?"

"Okay. I'll follow you to your house."

As Sam hauled herself into her truck, she tried to imagine how Maggie felt facing cancer again. Sam had once had a scare in the days when they still took mammograms with x-ray film. Most of the women in Sam's office had signed up for the mobile unit that parked right in front of the building. A week later, Sam had gotten a letter urging her to schedule a follow-up ultrasound and mammogram. "What am I supposed to be looking for?" asked the puzzled technician, sliding the cold, slippery wand over Sam's breast. Later, Sam heard women in the break room talking about similar notices. It turned out that the mobile camera had been damaged in a traffic accident and afterward gave everyone suspicious results. Those few days of worry were enough to give Sam a tiny peek at the terror that Maggie must be feeling.

Sam drove the back roads, enjoying the festive look of the trees in their bright autumn colors. Her house on Jimson Pond was her favorite place on earth. Erika, who had a way with words and whose slight British accent always made ordinary things seem grander, had once pronounced the setting "idyllic." The renovated cabin looked like an old Maine camp on the outside, but on the inside, it was an architectural marvel of sleek lines combined with warm, natural materials and custom details.

A savory smell greeted Sam when she opened the door. Coming home to the aroma of her chili, rich with green peppers, ground turkey, white beans, and salsa verde always made her smile.

Maggie came in behind her. "Smells good in here."

"It does, doesn't it?" Sam opened a cabinet and took down two handled bowls, shaped like oversized coffee cups and two porcelain Chinese restaurant spoons.

"What can I do to help?" asked Maggie at her elbow.

"Nothing," said Sam. "Have a seat." She waved toward the stools at the island. "I've been using this whole-milk Greek yogurt instead of sour cream. I hope you don't mind."

"No, I'll have to try that," said Maggie, turning the container to read the label.

"I'm not a fancy cook like you, Maggie. I cook to eat."

"You're a good cook, Sam. I always enjoy your food."

Sam ladled out the chili and put everything on a tray she'd made in her workshop. "Come on, Maggie. Let's sit on the porch. We can look at the pond while we eat. The trees are starting to change."

On the enclosed porch, Sam repositioned the table so that they could both look out at the pond. The trees were shyly showing their first blush of color. The yellows and reds reflected on the surface of the water. A breeze had come up, which made successful fishing less likely. Sam was sorry now that she'd even mentioned it. At the end of her marriage, Maggie had frequently complained that Liz spent too much time fishing with her friends. She probably hated it.

Maggie waited until Sam sat down beside her before picking up her spoon. Sam, raised by a Junior League mother, recognized the polite gesture. "Go on. Dig in," Sam urged. "We don't stand on formality in this house."

"That's why I like being here. I enjoyed skinny dipping in the pond."

"You did? You were always so shy."

"I thought everyone would be staring at the dimple from my lumpectomy."

Sam shrugged. "No one cared."

"But Lucy has perfect breasts."

Lucy was a dangerous subject. Sam ignored the remark and dug into her lunch. She always ate too fast when she was hungry, but she slowed down because she'd noticed that Maggie had eaten next to nothing.

"I thought you said you liked it," said Sam, frowning.

"I love it, but I don't have much of an appetite. I'm trying to eat more because I don't want to hurt your feelings."

"I understand. You can take it home if you want."

"Thank you. I promise to bring back the bowl when I see you again."

"Which I hope is soon," said Sam, continuing to eat. "Since you and Liz split up, I never see you." Sam tried for a light tone. She hated guilt trips, especially after being with Olivia, but it still came out sounding like an accusation.

"Maybe I'll be in Hobbs more often because of this…thing." Maggie gestured toward her breasts.

"It's hard to say, isn't it?"

"Cancer is an ugly word. If you've had it, it's the scariest word in the world."

"Well, I hate to think being sick is the only reason you'd come to town. We've missed you, Maggie."  Sam grinned. "I've especially missed your cooking."

Maggie attempted to look modest, but Sam could see she was pleased. "Olivia is a good cook."

Sam stared into her nearly empty bowl. "We broke up."

"Oh, Sam," said Maggie with a sympathetic look. "I'm so sorry."

"No, it's a good thing. At least, for me. We had fun, but she's so bossy. She always wants me to be there with her. I need my space. I have things to do."

"Like fishing?"

"Well, yes, but actually, Olivia likes to fish. She often said she'd like to go out with us, but you know how it is with the *tres amigas*."

"Yes, I do. You're like a bunch of guys. My husband played cards with his friends. No women allowed."

"It's similar," said Sam thoughtfully, "but not the same." She finished her chili but decided to forego scraping the bottom of the bowl because she had company. "I wasn't looking for a relationship when I met Olivia. And it was pretty good in the beginning. The sex was great." To Sam's surprise, Maggie blushed a little. "Too much information?"

"No," said Maggie, obviously lying.

"I'm glad it's over," Sam continued. "When I was with Olivia, I never had any time. I missed working in my shop. I've been doing architectural designs again. Just for fun, of course. These days, no one really cares about my work."

"Oh, don't give up so easily, Sam. You're brilliant. You have all those awards to prove it."

"Proves how fleeting fame can be," said Sam, gazing at the pond.

"Don't I know it. I wish I had stuck with acting, but Barry wanted me at home, playing the good, little housewife and entertaining his corporate cronies. Then I became obsessed with having children. At least, all the fertility treatments gave me a sense of purpose. Well, you know that story."

"But even though you had to adopt, you ended up with two wonderful daughters who love you. It's all good." Sam pushed Maggie's bowl closer. "Won't you eat just a little more? Please, so I know you like it?" Sam knew it was a form of blackmail. She watched Maggie force down a few more mouthfuls to please her. Finally, she put down her spoon. "I'll wrap it up and put it in the fridge," said Sam, ready to launch herself from her seat.

"There's no hurry," Maggie said, touching her arm. "It's cool out here. It will keep."

Sam settled back in her chair. "You're the food expert, so I'll take your word for it. Do you cook for your gang up there in Scarborough?"

"Every night. I do most of the housecleaning. I miss having Ellie clean the house when I lived with Liz."

"Yeah, it must be nice to have a cleaner," said Sam, glancing around. She had picked up on the porch that morning, so it wasn't as bad as it could be. "You can see I don't have an Ellie to clean up after me."

"I miss a lot of the things I had when I was married. Liz is a great cook. I get tired of cooking all the time. I enjoyed her company…when she was around. She looked after things for me…my car, my insurance, my finances. Olivia looks after my investments now."

"She's very good at it. I bought shares in the Enright fund. It does really well." Sam looked at Maggie cautiously. "You know you didn't have to leave Liz. She was trying to make it work."

"No, she wasn't," Maggie instantly snapped.

"Liz talked to me about it," said Sam in a gentle tone. "She was really trying. That's why she gave up some of the things she loved but you didn't enjoy, like the hiking club and going on mineral digs. She resigned from the chamber of commerce. She wanted to make more time for you. And she was trying to stay away from Lucy."

"But she couldn't."

"Maggie, they had to work together. They both have important roles in the town."

"Maybe, but she couldn't stay away from Lucy in her heart. I knew our marriage was over the minute Liz laid eyes on that woman. Liz is an opera fanatic. All that gorgeous redhead had to do was open her mouth and sing, and Liz was a goner."

"That's not true," Sam protested to defend her friend. "Liz loved you." Sam wasn't about to tell Maggie what Liz had shared with her—that Maggie had pushed her away with her jealousy and by withholding sex. "I'm sorry it didn't work out for you. I hope you and Liz can still be friends."

"Well," Maggie said, carefully folding her napkin. "I guess I'm about to find out."

Sam patted her shoulder. "Maggie, you're already stressed. Let's talk about something else."

"Thank you, Sam. You're one of the kindest people I know."

❋❋❋

The only thing Lucy had eaten since breakfast was the apple that Liz had tucked into her pocket before she headed out the door. An emergency counseling session had taken up the time Lucy usually reserved for lunch. The sandwich Liz had made for her was still in the refrigerator at the rectory. Now, Lucy was ravenous and salivating in anticipation of the dinner Liz would be cooking.

The sight of Liz's truck in the driveway brought an instant smile to her face. Having someone waiting for her at home was one of the many things she'd missed since Erika had died. Lucy dragged her bags into the house, surprised to find everything dark. Usually, the house would be blazing with light and emanating delicious aromas. Instead, it was cold and silent. The only sound was the humming of the refrigerator. Lucy dropped her bags on the couch and called through the house. When she got to the back of the house, a voice called, "Out on the deck!"

Lucy looked through the back window. There was Liz, sitting at the table with a bottle of that horrible brown liquor she used to drink with Erika.

"I hope you don't mind that I helped myself," she said when Lucy opened the door.

"You gave it to Erika. No one else drinks it, so it's yours now." Lucy made a face to show just how vile she found Liz's favorite single-malt scotch. "What are you doing out here? It's getting cold."

"I was watching the sunset."

"But it's getting dark. Come in. It's too cold out here."

Liz grabbed the bottle of Lagavulin and her glass, and they went into the house.

"We're not eating tonight?" asked Lucy.

"Oh, we are," said Liz. "Just broiled fish and veggies. It's fast."

"I hope so. I'm starving."

"Poor baby," Liz murmured, bending to kiss her. "I'll feed you right away." The kiss tasted like scotch. Lucy wrinkled up her nose when Liz turned to hang her blazer on the back of a chair. Usually, the first thing she did when she came home was to change into casual clothes. Something was clearly off.

"Late appointment at the office?" ventured Lucy, watching Liz take Erika's apron off the back of the pantry door.

"No, I've been here for a while." Liz rolled up her sleeves and began fiercely ripping lettuce into the salad spinner. Lucy wondered who she was shredding in her mind.

"Hard day?" asked Lucy, fishing for information.

"Yes."

"Do you want to talk about it?"

"Not yet."

"Okay, tell me when you're ready. I'll go up and change."

"Good idea. There's a lot of butter in this dish. You don't want grease stains on your black shirt. They're hard to get out."

From the kitchen door, Lucy watched Liz assemble her cooking ingredients. Usually, when they got home, each did a quick download of the day's news. Liz's silence was puzzling, but Lucy knew better than to keep asking the reason for it. She sighed and headed upstairs to take off her work clothes.

By the time she returned to the kitchen, it was filled with enticing aromas.

"Sit down," said Liz. "Your dinner is ready."

"Wow. That was fast," said Lucy as Liz put a plate in front of her.

"There's nothing to broiled haddock with beurre noisette and capers. I'll teach you how to make it if you want." She turned to the stove to serve herself. "Go on, eat."

Lucy put some of the fish in her mouth. "Oh, my word! This is so good!"

Liz pointed to the components of the meal. "Baked potato with butter. Steamed broccoli with lemon butter. Basically, everything has butter on it except the salad. As Julia Child would say, 'you can never have enough butter.'"

"Isn't all that butter bad for you?"

"Not really, and it tastes good. It won't hurt you. You're too thin. We need to fatten you up."

"That's what Erika used to say."

"I remember, and I promised her I'd take care of you."

Lucy was relieved to see Liz smile because it meant the cloud that she'd been under hadn't completely engulfed her. After such a busy day of her own, Lucy didn't mind the silence while they ate.

While Liz changed her clothes, Lucy surveyed the kitchen to strategize how to clean up. Like Erika, Liz was a tidy cook. The preparation bowls had already been washed and sat drying on the drainboard. When Lucy cooked, the kitchen looked like a bomb had exploded, but Liz cleaned up and never complained.

Lucy emerged from the kitchen to find Liz frowning at her tablet. "Something wrong?"

"Nope," said Liz dismissively. Since Liz began reading all those theology books to help Lucy with her schoolwork, she often frowned. Lucy took it as a sign that she was thinking about what she read instead of just vacuuming up the information into that big brain of hers.

Lucy leaned into Liz's warm body and settled down to study, but when she looked up to rest her eyes, she noticed that Liz, who read incredibly fast, hadn't even turned the page.

"Okay, Liz. What's going on?" asked Lucy, putting down her tablet.

"Nothing."

"Yes, there is. Now tell me."

"It's privileged." That was an ironclad excuse. A physician and a priest, who was also a therapist, often had to keep things confidential.

"Then tell me in general, not specifically. How does it affect you?"

"A person came to my office who may have a recurrence of cancer. I don't want to be involved, but I don't know how I can refuse."

There was only one person who fit this description and could cause so much upset. "Maggie has cancer again?" Lucy guessed. Liz's refusal to look at her confirmed it. "Liz, I don't expect you to tell me the details, but isn't it a serious breach of ethics for you to treat Maggie?"

"Yes, but I don't intend to treat her. I'll only hook her up with the right providers. But that's not the problem."

"What's the problem?"

"I'm angry she expects me to help her." Liz put her tablet down and crossed her arms.

"You helped her before. It's not an unreasonable expectation."

"After what she did, I certainly think so. And you didn't hear the names she called you."

"Don't tell me. It would only make me sad." Lucy thought she was stroking Liz's arm to console her when she was really consoling herself.

"What's wrong with that woman?" Liz asked in a frustrated voice.

It was a rhetorical question, but Lucy decided to answer. "Somewhere along the line, Maggie got the idea that she only has worth if she pleases other people. No matter how hard she tries, it always backfires. People reject her, cheat on her, leave her. It creates an endless loop of trying to win approval, getting it for a short time, and then being rejected."

Liz listened thoughtfully. "But why does she get rejected?"

"In trying to be the perfect woman, she's scrubbed away all of the things that make her who she really is. She probably doesn't even remember. I'd guess that's why she became an actress, so that she could express emotions, even though they're not her own."

"But that's her baggage. What am I supposed to do?"

"You help her as far as you are able. Support her as much as you can without compromising yourself."

"But I'm still so angry with her, sometimes I could just..."

Lucy could guess what Liz was about to say, but she was glad she didn't have to hear it. "You need to get past that. Liz, she came to you because she's frightened and desperate. To her, you are the one person who can save her. She always told me that you're her rock."

Liz groaned and rolled her eyes.

"Don't make faces at me, Liz. You set it up that way. You're the white knight who always rushes in to save the damsel in distress, the brilliant surgeon who snatches life out of the jaws of death. You get a high from saving people. Maggie's just supplying you with your drug of choice."

Liz scowled at her. "Lucy, do you always have to be so fucking direct?"

"Why not? You are."

"Maybe that's why we get along."

"Maybe it is." Lucy took Liz's arm to pull her closer. "You're my rock too. You probably saved my life after Erika died."

"I don't know about that. You're pretty tough, Lucy, but fainting over your wife's grave wasn't one of your finest moments."

"But very operatic."

Liz chuckled. "Yes, brilliantly choreographed and executed." Liz sighed. "I seem to be attracted to drama queens."

"That's because your Teutonic personality and your profession require such discipline and self-control. You need us to channel your feelings, so you can experience them vicariously…like when you listen to music." Liz's scornful look made Lucy think she should dial back on the analysis. Liz was upset and probably wouldn't like being so exposed.

"What a mess. I don't want to be involved, but I can't let her down. Her daughter is an oncologist. She should be talking to her, not me."

"Sophia can't be involved in her treatment any more than you can be."

"But she needs to know her mother may have a recurrence. Alina too."

"Then Maggie needs to tell them, not you, no matter how good a relationship you think you have with them."

In a huff of frustration, Liz jumped up and headed to the kitchen. Lucy heard the door of a cabinet open and the clink of ice filling a glass. The hateful brown liquor was returning to the conversation. Liz sat down across from her and pulled the cork out of the bottle. "Don't say anything," she warned.

"I don't have to. You know what I think."

Impatiently, Liz stuffed the cork back in the bottle. "Damnit, Lucy! Why do you always crawl into my head like this?"

"Because you ask me to." Lucy got up. "Obviously, I'm not going to get any studying done tonight. Why don't we go up to bed?"

"For a mercy fuck?"

"No, Liz. I just want to hold you. You're too upset, and I'm not going to let you use sex to blot out your feelings. That's making it a drug, like your nasty scotch." Lucy reached out her hand. "Come on. Give me the glass. I'll get rid of the ice. Then I'll meet you upstairs."

Glaring at her, Liz handed over the glass.

"The bottle too."

Lucy went into the kitchen. She stowed the bottle in the cabinet and dumped the ice cubes into the sink. She was relieved to hear Liz's feet going up the stairs. She was already in bed when Lucy came in and didn't look up from her tablet.

Lucy's exhaustion finally hit her when she began to take off her makeup, but she needed to find the energy to deal with Liz. Fortunately, when she got into bed, she didn't have to encourage Liz to turn off the light. Lucy stretched out her arm to invite her to snuggle against her breast. Lucy stroked Liz's soft curls, imagining she could feel the storms raging in her active mind. Her heart ached for her, but for now, offering her the comfort of her body was the best she could do.

# 8

Liz finally noticed Cathy Pelletier standing in the doorway. The bright light from the hall threw her prominent cheekbones, a legacy from her Native American ancestors, into high relief. The concern in her dark eyes was immediately evident. Liz closed her laptop to show that she had her attention, and Cathy stepped into the room.

"Did you find anything?" asked Liz.

Cathy shook her head. "No, but my fingers aren't as experienced as yours. I wish you would examine her."

"Cathy, you've been doing this for a long time. If there's anything large enough to feel, you would find it. I don't know why she insisted on a breast exam. She has a mammogram this afternoon."

"You know why. The uncertainty is driving her crazy. You were lucky that Alyson was able to get you in right away."

"What did she say when you told her you didn't find anything? Did it calm her down?"

Cathy shook her head. "She wants to hear it from you, but obviously, you don't want to be involved."

"It's not that I don't want to be involved!" Liz stifled her annoyance. She waved Cathy into the office and pointed to a visitors' chair. "It's a matter of ethics."

Cathy gave her a skeptical look. "Rationalize it any way you want, but where Maggie is concerned, you've always bent the rules. I might have been her doctor, but you were managing her cancer."

"Fair enough, but what if I examine Maggie and find nothing? That doesn't mean she doesn't have cancer. It could be anywhere. As you know, this mutation makes her more susceptible to melanoma. Maggie's so fair, she was already at high risk. There could be lesions in the pancreas. We can only hope that wherever it is, it hasn't metastasized. I'm just glad she already had her ovaries removed."

Cathy's sympathetic gaze was unnerving. Since Maggie had returned as a patient to the practice, the staff had been tiptoeing around Liz. To avoid Cathy's dark eyes, Liz stared at the surface of her desk. Now that she was sharing it with Amy, she'd had to keep it neater. She'd even put away her family photos, including the one of Alina and the girls. She still considered Maggie's daughters family. She'd helped Alina get back on her feet after her ex-husband nearly bankrupted her. Sophia owed her position in the oncology department at Dana-Farber to Liz's network of connections.

"I can see how hard this is for you, Liz. Can't someone else take her for the imaging?"

"I promised I would take her. Maggie won't tell her daughters. They have a right to know, but Lucy says it's not my place to tell them."

Cathy's brows shot up. "You needed Lucy to tell you that?"

"No, of course not, but they should know. If it is a recurrence, she'll need their support." Liz suddenly wondered if she was pushing to tell them because she didn't want to bear the burden alone.

"Maggie is still trying to undo the trauma of that Romanian orphanage and ease their abandonment anxiety. Alina tried to get off Zoloft, but she couldn't. I'll talk to Maggie and encourage her to tell them." Cathy glanced at her watch. "What time are you supposed to meet Alyson?"

"Two o'clock."

"You should probably go soon. Give me a call later and let me know what they find."

"Thanks for examining her."

Cathy got up and gave Liz's shoulder an affectionate squeeze. "Good luck at Southern Med."

Reluctantly, Liz walked down the hall to the patient waiting area. Maggie was staring vacantly at the floorboards. Today, she was wearing her long, white hair in a braid. Liz guessed it was to make it easier to position herself during the scans. After being treated for infertility for years as a young wife and later for breast cancer, Maggie had become an expert at accommodating medical examinations. Liz had always suspected that the hormones they'd pumped into her to help her get pregnant had contributed to the breast cancer. The unlucky genetic mutation had all but guaranteed it.

Maggie's eyes were glittering with anxiety when she looked up. "Time to go?"

"Yes, are you ready?"

"As I'll ever be," said Maggie, pulling on her sweater.

Liz held the door open for her. On the way to the car, Liz's hand found its way to the small of Maggie's back, gently guiding her in the right direction. These little gestures were instinctive after seven years of marriage. Liz wondered if she would ever unlearn them.

"I was kind of hoping Alyson could take us earlier," Maggie said when Liz slid into the driver's seat. "It would be fun to have a Cuban sandwich like we used to. Since I quit therapy, I haven't been to Portsmouth much."

"You quit therapy?" said Liz with surprise.

"I wasn't getting anything out of it."

Maggie had been seeing a therapist to decide what to do about the marriage. Once she'd decided to sleep with that young actor, it was a foregone conclusion—at least from Liz's point of view. Why Maggie had confessed her infidelity still made no sense, especially knowing how confrontation frightened her. Not that her husband had been a violent man, but he'd threatened her with his fists. "Did you ever tell Barry that you'd slept with Katherine Gleason?"

Maggie looked surprised by the question. "I told him I had an affair. I didn't tell him it was with a woman."

"How did he react?"

"He lost his mind, just like you did when I told you I slept with Brad."

"I'd already agreed to the divorce. Why did you need to tell me? You knew it would only bring back bad memories from when you dated men in college. Did you do it to hurt me?"

"No, you started to talk about trying again, and I wanted you to know the relationship was over." The extended silence while Liz chewed on the information apparently made Maggie uncomfortable. "You could talk to me, you know," she said. "I could use the distraction. I'm really scared."

"I'm sure you are."

"Did you always know the cancer would come back?"

"The law of averages predicted it, but people aren't statistics. Sometimes, cancer doesn't recur. It depends on the type of cancer, the stage, the pathological profile."

"Why do you always sound like a doctor?"

"Because I am one!" said Liz, frustrated by having to state the obvious.

"That was a big part of your appeal in the beginning. My mother always wanted me to marry up."

"I doubt your mother, if she were alive, would ever have approved of me. Look at how hard she worked to break us up."

Maggie stared ahead. "She didn't have to work hard. I wanted to break up with you. The guilt about what we were doing was awful. That's why I told my parents."

"Maggie, why are we revisiting this old stuff?"

"You brought it up."

"I did, didn't I?"

"I've been thinking about it too. I've had time on my hands to think about the past. I'm alone most of the day now that the kids have gone back to school. Don't you ever wonder how your life could have been different if we'd stayed together the first time? I often regret not being stronger. At least, you had the courage to come out."

Liz had long ago exhausted that what-if scenario. They'd talked about it so much after they'd first gotten back together. No matter what Maggie said, Liz couldn't imagine her choosing to be anything other than a man's dutiful wife. Catholic girls of that era were filled with guilt. Even Liz wasn't immune to it, but she'd solved her dilemma by turning her back on the Church. Maggie had taken the path of least resistance.

Liz changed the subject to the protests at the schools, an upsetting, but in this case, relatively neutral topic. It was a relief to finally arrive at Southern Med.

"Why don't you go in and ask for Alyson?" Liz said, pulling up to the entrance to the Women's Imaging Center. "I'll look for a place to park."

"I'll wait and go in with you. You're the one who knows Alyson."

Liz had already broken up with the radiologist by the time Maggie came on the scene, but they had remained good friends. Liz suddenly wondered if she and Maggie could ever get past all the anger and get to friendship. Liz prided herself in maintaining good relationships with her exes.

She found a space in the doctors' lot, and they walked back to the entrance. When the clerk took Maggie inside the admissions office, Liz found a seat in the waiting room and sat down to text Lucy: *Pray for me. This is really hard.*

Lucy instantly texted back an emoji of hands praying. *Stay calm.* She followed the message with a string of red hearts.

In her peripheral vision, Liz saw Alyson's strawberry-blond hair and turned in her direction. Alyson wore it loose over her shoulders today. Radiologists almost never touched a patient, so she didn't need to tie back her hair for hygiene. Alyson gave Liz a sweet kiss on the mouth. She might be married now, but she was as flirtatious as ever. "Hey, stranger. Missed you."

"Missed you too," Liz murmured, giving her a half hug.

"I can't say I'm happy about the reason you came down here today. I've been reviewing Maggie's original imaging and subsequent scans. She's been lucky so far. Let's hope her luck holds." Alyson raised her crossed fingers. She led Liz to the imaging booth, where they waited while the technician reviewed the process with Maggie. "How do you feel about being back here with her?"

"Well, obviously it sucks that she may have a recurrence."

"I meant being involved in her treatment after your divorce, but you said you parted on good terms."

"The financial part went fine, but she's been a real bitch since she found out Lucy and I are engaged."

Alyson's pale eyebrows shot up. "You're getting married again?" Liz had meant to tell her and many others, but she just hadn't found the time. "Isn't it a little soon? Didn't Lucy's wife die around Christmas?"

"Yes, but we haven't set a date yet," said Liz, deflecting. She was too anxious about the mammogram to mount a full-bore defense of their plans. The technician came into the imaging booth. "Are you ladies ready?"

Alyson took a seat in front of the console with Liz looking over her shoulder. "And let the games begin!" Alyson said with a grand flourish. Liz was accustomed to black humor in medical situations, but she prickled with annoyance, subconsciously defending Maggie's dignity. Fortunately, Alyson became all business once the images started coming in. There was no sign of cancer in the breast where it had originally appeared. The technician switched to the other breast. And there it was—a tiny bright spot, but clearly visible. From the pattern and density, it was almost certainly cancer.

❋❋❋

Sam emptied a bag of pellets into the stove. The day had been warm, but her house cooled quickly after the sun went down. That was a downside of living at the water's edge, but given the choice, Sam wouldn't live anywhere else. She sat down on the sofa with a glass of cabernet and watched the sparks dance in the crucible. Mesmerized by the flames, she almost forgot she had a pot heating on the stove.

As she stirred the beef stew, the savory smell made her hungry. This recipe had been passed down from her grandmother. It was the hearty, old-fashioned version. Olivia had always made Julia Child's classic boeuf bourguignon. The memory made Sam wonder what Olivia might be cooking tonight, but she was glad she didn't have to report for dinner. The pressure had often made even the most skillfully prepared meals taste like dust in her mouth.

The stew was sticking a little at the bottom of the pot, so Sam lowered the flame. When she was setting the timer to remind her to check later, the phone startled her by ringing in her hand. The image of an attractive, white-haired woman with hazel eyes appeared on her screen.

"Hey, Maggie," said Sam, surprised to hear from her. She couldn't remember the last time Maggie had called her. Before the divorce, she'd let Liz handle all the communication with her friends.

"I hope I'm not bothering you." There was a distinct edge in Maggie's voice.

"Are you okay?" she asked anxiously.

"No."

"What's wrong?"

"I went for the scans today to find out if I have cancer."

The long pause forced Sam to ask, "…And?"

"It looks like I do."

"Oh, Maggie. I'm so sorry. Do you want to come over?"

After another long silence, Maggie said, "I don't want to intrude on your evening, but I had to tell someone. Someone who might care. Obviously, Liz doesn't."

"Of course, she does, but you did the right thing to call me. I'm here for you."

"Thank you, Sam." Maggie sounded like she was on the verge of tears.

"Come over. I only have leftover stew to offer, but there's enough for the two of us."

"Thank you, Sam. I'll be there in a few minutes."

When Maggie arrived, the only evidence that she'd been crying was her reddened eyes. Her eyeliner and mascara were perfect. Her lipstick was vibrantly red. Sam guessed Maggie had probably put on a fresh coat in the car. They'd known each other for years, but Sam had never seen her without makeup, not even on a camping trip.

She took Maggie's coat and hung it on the coat tree she'd made from the old choke cherry she'd taken down in front of the barn. She opened her arms for a hug, and Maggie fell into them. "I'm so sorry," Sam murmured into her hair.

"I knew I could count on you, Sam. I didn't know where else to go."

"Didn't Liz go with you for the scans?"

"Oh, she did, but there's a barbecue over there tonight. She invited me, but I couldn't face seeing all those happy people, especially the Reverend Lucille Bartlett. I'm surprised you weren't invited."

Sam had known about the barbecue but hadn't felt slighted until Maggie had mentioned it. "Liz has so many friends she can't fit them all in at once, even in her big house," Sam said, defending her friend. "If you're looking for privacy, you came to the right place. There's no one here except me and the loons."

"That sounds perfect." Maggie came into the living room and looked around. "Your fire is toasty. I miss a fire."

"Your house in Scarborough doesn't have a fireplace?"

"It does, but we haven't bothered getting firewood. Alina is so busy with her job at the news station, and with the children…"

"I have a cord of wood left over. I was going to burn it for campfires on cold nights, but it was so rainy this summer. I could bring some up and stack it in your yard."

"I'll ask Alina, but who knows what shape I'll be in after treatment."

Sam patted her shoulder. "You'll be just fine!"

"I know it's good to be positive, but sometimes, it's really hard." Maggie's voice was thick with tears. "I wish I could be so optimistic."

"I always try to be optimistic. When you're designing multimillion dollar high rises, you have to be…and a little crazy."

"You're not crazy, Sam."

"Our dinner is ready. We can sit down and eat, or I can leave the stew on warm, and we can have a drink first."

"No, let's eat. I'm hungrier than I thought. I felt nauseous imagining what they would find, so I skipped lunch."

Usually, Sam ate at the island in the kitchen while she read her emails and listened to the news on her laptop. For her guest, she'd set the dining room table with coordinating placemats and cloth napkins. She used the fancy, stemmed wine glasses, and set the bread on a cutting board she'd made from scraps of wood from her shop.

"Your table is lovely," Maggie said, "but you didn't need to make a fuss for me, Sam."

"You didn't have a good day, so I wanted to make your evening better."

"You're so sweet." Maggie gave her a kiss on the cheek.

Sam felt herself blushing. She never would have imagined a famous actress like Maggie even looking at her. When they'd first met, Sam thought Maggie was judging her like her mother's upper-crust bridge partners. They'd looked down on her boyish clothes, and Sam wished she could disappear into the floor. Sam had felt the same under Maggie's critical gaze. But things had changed, and Maggie needed her now, which had leveled the playing field.

"Sit down," said Sam, pulling out the chair for her. "Let me get the stew. Help yourself to bread." Sam returned with bowls of steaming stew. "I love one pot meals. Fewer dishes."

"I'll do the dishes.

"No, you won't. You're my guest tonight."

"Smells delicious," said Maggie.

Sam watched anxiously while Maggie, who was a professionally trained cook, tasted the stew. "Is it okay?"

"Perfect. Just the right amount of tarragon. Did you glaze the vegetables?"

"No, I cheated. And I put in some ketchup. My grandmother's secret ingredient."

"Don't tell but I do too," Maggie confided behind her hand. "More bread for you?" She picked up the bread knife shaped like a fiddle bow. "This is very clever. Did you make it?"

"Yes. I make the blades from pieces of snapped bandsaw blades."

"I love it. Will you make one for me?"

"I always make extras. I'll give you one," said Sam, positioning the wine bottle to replenish Maggie's glass.

"Take it easy," said Maggie, covering her glass with her hand. "I have to drive, and Scarborough isn't exactly down the street."

"I have a guest room if you drink too much."

"That's a sweet offer, but I have to get the kids ready for school in the morning. However," purred Maggie, "I might take a rain check." She gave Sam a positively flirtatious look.

Sam's ears burned like they were on fire. She didn't dare look at Maggie, so she took her time buttering her bread.

❊❊❊

"Come on, babies. Time to go home," Cherie called into the room. The children ran to her. Megan hugged her around the legs, almost tripping her. The tall woman who'd been playing the piano rose from the bench. She was wearing a 'treble maker' face mask like Lucy often wore. "I'm sorry to be so late," Cherie apologized. "My session ran a little long."

"It's not a problem," Denise said. "We're learning about chords. The children are picking up music theory quickly."

Cherie patted her arm. "I don't know what I would do without your music classes. The schools don't teach music anymore, and it's so helpful to the parents to have a place for the kids to go after school."

Denise's blue eyes lit up with pleasure, but her delight quickly faded. "I just wish other parents felt the same."

"I'm spreading the word as fast as I can. You're doing good work, Denise. We're all proud of you."

"Thank you, Ms. Bois. Encouragement is always welcome."

"Oh, Denise, please call me Cherie." Megan was tugging on her skirt. Cherie stroked the girl's hair to buy herself another minute to talk. "What can I do to help?"

"What you're doing. Encourage other parents to bring their kids." Over the mask, Denise's eyes smiled again. "Tell them I don't bite."

"Are you ready to go, Cherie?" said a sweet voice from the doorway.

"Mother Lucy!" said Keith, running to her for a hug.

Cherie turned back to Denise. "I'm sorry, but I have to go. Brenda got a great buy on spareribs at Market Basket, so she's making our last barbecue before it gets too cold. Liz is the only one with a place big enough to host it."

"Sounds like fun. It's been years since I had good barbecue."

"Do you have dinner plans?"

"Alas," said Denise with a dramatic flourish, "I have a date with Lean Cuisine."

"Well, we can't have that." Cherie turned around. "Lucy, do you think Liz would mind one more?"

"You know what Liz thinks—the more, the merrier. Come with us, Denise. I should have thought of inviting you earlier."

"I don't want to impose," said Denise shyly.

"You're not imposing," Lucy assured her. "Liz enjoys entertaining, and she'll love to see you. Get your coat. I'll call Liz and warn her to put out another plate."

"And I need to get my biscuits and cornbread in the oven," Cherie said. "I'll see you there."

Lucy helped herd the children into the car. Keith could snap himself into his booster seat, but Megan still needed help.

"Lucy, you are a natural mama," said Cherie, watching her unwind the seat belt and pull it down around the girl.

"I missed out on all those years when Emily was growing up. I guess I keep trying to make up for it with other children." Cherie looked at her with a pang of sympathy. She couldn't imagine giving away a child she'd carried for nine months, but Lucy was lucky enough to have her baby back, even if she was all grown up now.

Megan began whining when Lucy closed the door and walked away. Cherie had learned that the one sure thing to quiet them was music. She began singing an old hymn she'd learned from her mother, and the soft crying from the backseat instantly stopped.

When they arrived at Liz's place, the kitchen was a flurry of activity. Huge bowls of potato salad and bean salad sat on the counter. Somehow, Liz had found time to make them, which didn't surprise Cherie. Her boss was amazingly efficient. Brenda had brought over the coleslaw Cherie had made the night before and the parboiled ribs.

"Where's my honey?" Cherie asked, looking around.

Liz looked up from folding paper napkins. "Out at the grill, watching the ribs. We'll be ready to eat soon."

"Thanks for letting Denise come."

"It's fine. I'm sure we'll be seeing a lot more of her." Cherie gave her a quizzical look. "She's seeing Lucy's daughter."

"Oh," said Cherie in surprise.

"Yeah. Oh."

"I need some mixing bowls," said Cherie.

Liz pointed to the pantry. "Second shelf, right-hand side." Cherie located the bowl and the cooler Brenda had used to bring over their dinner contributions. She got down to work at an empty counter. Working shoulder to shoulder with the other women in the kitchen made it feel like Thanksgiving, but Liz never needed an excuse for a communal meal. Soon, the bread and biscuits were in the oven.

"I'm going outside to say hello to my Brenda," said Cherie.

"Go ahead," said Liz. "I'm just waiting on our neighbors. Lucy will keep an eye on the kids."

Cherie found Brenda, proudly wearing her apron from the chili cook-off between the police and fire departments. When Brenda bent to kiss her wife, Cherie instantly sensed something off. "Hey, babe. What's going on?"

"I heard from the lawyer today about the adoption. The kid's aunt or cousin, or whatever the hell she is, heard there might be money involved and resurfaced. The lawyer says it's going to be expensive to fight her."

"Oh, shit."

"Exactly." Brenda glanced up. Courtney and Melissa were coming out on the deck. "Let's talk about this later," she said under her breath.

Cherie put her hand on Brenda's arm. "Melissa is a lawyer. Maybe she knows what we can do."

Brenda gave her a sharp look. "This is our business."

Melissa smiled. "I heard the word 'lawyer.'" She looked from Cherie to Brenda. "What's up? Someone in trouble?"

Cherie quickly explained how the state had looked for relatives of the children but had only found the mother's cousin.

"At first, she said she wasn't interested," said Brenda. "Now that she smells money, I guess she is."

Melissa raised a brow. "First of all, the court will put the parents' assets into a trust until they're of age, so I can't imagine what this woman expects she'll get."

"According to the lawyer, she wants to stop the sale of the house and move in there with the kids," said Brenda. "The place is a mess after the shooting. Just cleaning it up enough to sell will cost big bucks."

"Well, if she thinks she can move in there, that's fantasy on her part. The children are the default heirs. The court will appoint someone to manage their assets, and it will probably be a disinterested party, not a distant relative."

"She wants to adopt them," said Brenda. "So do we. We've already filed papers."

"Ah, I see," said Melissa with a frown. "A cousin is not a close relative. It will come down to who will make better parents." Melissa patted Cherie's arm. "This probably isn't as big a problem as it sounds. Give me a call tomorrow and we'll set up a time to talk. I'll help you."

"I don't know," said Brenda uncertainly. "It's already cost us a lot of money." Cherie turned sharply. She hoped Brenda wasn't going to give up on adopting the kids because of money.

"Brenda!"

"Well, it has been expensive."

"Don't worry about the cost," Melissa said in a reassuring tone. "We'll figure it out."

❋❋❋

Courtney slipped into bed beside Melissa, who was writing something on her laptop. It seemed like the woman worked nonstop. Courtney often woke up in the middle of the night to see Melissa's face illuminated by the screen and realized she was responding to emails. People seemed to have no boundaries when it came to those who worked remotely.

"Lights out," ordered Courtney.

"I just need to answer this. It won't take long." Melissa reached out and switched off the bedside lamp, but she continued to pound on the keys.

"Come on, Melissa. I have an early morning tomorrow, but it's Friday. Thank God!"

"I'm sorry I kept us out late, but I was enjoying myself."

"You kept asking them to sing. They could have said, no. It's obvious how much Denise and Lucy enjoy performing. It's a shame they don't have more opportunity."

"That's why it's our duty to ask them to share their talent whenever we can. It was cool hearing about how Liz's ex organized entertainment for the town during the lockdown," said Melissa, finally closing her computer. She shoved it into its neoprene sleeve and got up to stow it in her bag. "I wonder what really happened between them."

"When you see the way Liz looks at Lucy, I think you can guess. They were all living here together. They probably got into mischief that broke up the party. I bet if you sit up drinking that awful single-malt scotch with Liz one night, you'll get the whole story out of her."

Melissa got back into bed and pulled up the covers. "I hate hangovers, and that stuff can give you a real skull banger. Besides, it's none of our business."

Courtney reached under Melissa's nightshirt and gently stroked the springy pubic hair, but her legs were shut tight, so she had to be content with stroking her like a cat. "I was so proud of you tonight."

"You were? Why?"

"You jumped right in to offer help to Brenda and Cherie with the adoption."

Courtney, happily settled against Melissa's breast, felt her shrug. "It's not a big thing. I doubt the court will consider a distant cousin with a shady background a plausible guardian. I wonder what kind of shyster lawyer thinks she has a case, but these nuisance suits can drag on and be expensive."

"I hope you give them a good deal."

"I wasn't going to charge them anything. I was going to do it pro bono. I like them, and they'll be wonderful parents."

"You helped Hobbs Family Practice too. You're so generous." The compliment had earned Courtney an opening. Melissa's legs parted a little. Courtney wasted no time in taking advantage of it and caressed the soft skin on the inside of her thigh.

"It's a mitzvah," Melissa explained, "a good deed. Jews are supposed to do good works for the glory of God. That's how I was raised. My father always did pro bono work."

"I didn't know it was a religious thing."

"It's what we would now call paying it forward."

Courtney slipped down in bed. Now they were eye-to-eye. "I heard something good today," she said in a tantalizing voice. "I'm not supposed to spread it around, but I'm allowed to tell you."

"Attorneys are good at keeping secrets. Tell me," said Melissa, mirroring Courtney's excitement.

"Lucy thinks she might know of a house for rent. She asked how much rent I can afford. She's not sure when, or even if, it will be available, but I told her to keep me posted."

"That is good news," Melissa agreed. She rolled her hips so that she could open her legs wider. "Stop teasing and do something!"

Courtney reached in until she felt the slick wetness. "Is that better?" she asked, even though she could see the answer in Melissa's eyes.

"Yes. Don't stop."

Courtney pushed deeper into Melissa's body and shivered as the delicious warmth enclosed her fingers.

# 9

The door to the media room opened. Bundled in a workout suit, Liz trudged in with her coffee cup. Lucy looked up from scanning her phone for the accompaniment to the next selection. "Anything special you'd like to hear this morning?"

Liz took a sip of her coffee and shook her head. "I just want to hear you sing, especially because I'll be gone for a few days."

"While you're in New Haven with Maggie, I'll be back in my garret studio like Mimi." Lucy sighed theatrically and touched the back of her hand to her forehead. She knew that Liz, who knew all the operas in the standard repertoire, would catch the reference to *La Bohème.*

"Poor you," said Liz unsympathetically. "After Sam and I built you that nice space over Erika's garage."

"It's wonderful, but when you built it, you were more concerned about keeping my voice from annoying the neighbors than the sound quality. I love to sing in here." Lucy tapped a piano key, and the rich tone of the Steinway grand reverberated in the enormous room. "The acoustics are superb."

"I'm glad you think so." Liz gazed up at the ceiling. "I paid a ton of money to that engineer to make sure. Does that mean you could live here with me?"

"Maybe," said Lucy, "but why don't I ever hear you consider moving into the beach house?" Liz made a sour face. "I see. My wishes aren't as important as yours."

"That's not true!" Liz protested, sitting up straight. "Your wishes are just as important. But we can't live in two places, and I'm tired of dragging my clothes to your house."

"How do you think I feel? We live here most of the time. I feel like when I traveled the opera circuit and never slept in my own bed."

"Lucy, I can't deal with an argument before my second cup of coffee.

Come on, woman, sing! I have to go to work and so do you. What's on the program this morning?"

"'Senza Mamma' from *Suor Angelica.*"

"An unwed mother is forced to give up her baby for adoption. Hmm. That sounds familiar and pretty sad."

"Sad fits my mood this morning. You're leaving for days to do something difficult. But at least, you get to see my daughter. I won't see her until Thanksgiving break."

"She sounds excited to go out for dinner. ...as excited as Emily gets."

"Oh, she told me she's really looking forward to it."

"Good, so am I." Liz put her feet up on the hassock. "All right, Madame Bartlett, let's hear your sad aria."

Lucy cued up the accompaniment and began to sing. She loved watching Liz's face when she sang for her. Sometimes, Liz conducted, which she did quite well, or anticipated her favorite passages by closing her eyes. When Lucy was still singing professionally, she often sang to one especially attentive member of the audience. In Liz, she had that perfect listener, someone who completely understood the music and what Lucy invested in her performance.

She concluded the aria. There was a long interval before Liz put down her coffee cup to clap. "Sublime," she pronounced and stopped clapping to wipe her cheeks with her sweatshirt sleeve. Liz might be stubborn and uncommunicative, but Lucy could always reach her with music.

The heavy mood stayed with Lucy while they walked on the beach. Usually, the sight of the sun rising over the ocean filled her heart with a burst of energy and hope. Today, the sky was leaden, and the only sign of the sun was a puddle of red leaking across the horizon like blood.

Liz pulled Lucy's hand into her pocket. The warmth was welcome, but the gentle pressure even more so. Lucy knew Liz was dreading this trip to New Haven. Now that they were sharing a bed nearly every night, the separation would be more difficult. She would miss Liz's warmth and the communication that went beyond words. Liz had been teaching Lucy's body to experience sensations she'd never dared to imagine. There were moments when they ceased to be two individuals and seemed to merge, a profane but apt metaphor for communion.

Liz abruptly halted their march across the sand, forcing Lucy to stop too. "Let's get married!"

"What?" Lucy studied Liz's face. "We are getting married."

"I mean, let's elope," said Liz. "Today."

"Liz, you know why I can't. I'm a priest. I have to play by the rules." Lucy took back her hand and touched Liz's cheek with her fingertips. "Sweetheart, where is this coming from?"

"I want everyone to know that we belong to each other."

"Everyone already knows we're a couple." Lucy gave Liz a hard look. "I think you want everything settled because you're anxious about spending time with Maggie. You have all these unresolved issues with her and want confirmation of our relationship."

"Fuck! Why did I ever think it was a good idea to fall in love with a shrink?" asked Liz in a prickly voice.

Lucy reached out her hand. Liz looked at it for a long moment before she took it and put it back in her pocket. She tugged gently at Lucy's arm to indicate they should resume their walk. "I don't want to go to New Haven with Maggie. I promised I would be there for her surgery, but I wish I hadn't. Being thrown back together again for such an emotional reason is really messing with my head. I would have liked more time to get used to being divorced before dealing with her cancer."

"Of course, you would, but that's not how it happened. My father always said, 'you have to play the hand you're dealt.' Why do you think being married to me would make it any easier?"

Liz glowered at a fat, gray-speckled seagull that came up to beg. She stomped her foot, which made it scurry off.

"Don't take it out on the gulls, Liz. It's not their fault."

In her pocket, Liz squeezed Lucy's hand. "I want you to know there's no threat from Maggie."

"I never thought there was, but I know you're still angry. Being angry means you still care. You know how they say, 'the opposite of love isn't hate; it's indifference.' A part of you still loves Maggie."

"I want you to know there will only be two people in our marriage."

Lucy stopped walking, so that she could study Liz's face. "A ceremony won't change anything. Maggie will be in our marriage, Erika…and Susan. Everyone who's deeply affected us will be in our marriage—our parents, our friends, our enemies…. Every person who's made us who we are will be in our marriage." Liz raised a brow, which meant she was skeptical but mulling over the idea. "Maybe we should suspend our engagement while you work through your issues with Maggie."

"No," Liz said without a second of hesitation. The clear, unconsidered response was reassuring.

"Sweetheart, I want to marry you, but it will be at a time we both agree works for us, not to prove a point. You jumped into marriage with Maggie and look what happened. If you need more time to figure out your feelings about the divorce, I'm willing to give it to you. And you might want to talk to someone about it besides me." Lucy expected Liz's usual response—an abrupt dismissal of counseling, but instead, she looked thoughtful.

"Maybe I'll talk to Tom," she said.

Lucy pulled her face down and kissed her. "Oh, I'm so proud of you!"

"Lucy, don't get all excited. I said, maybe."

Lucy was buoyant as they headed back to the beach house. The little victory had dispelled the gloom. As if to agree, the sky had begun to clear, and the sun broke through the clouds and shined brightly.

❈❈❈

It was ridiculous at this stage of her career, but Amy felt proud that Liz had left her in charge. "Why not Cathy or Bill?" she'd wondered aloud.

"You're my successor, and you need the practice. But call me any time. I don't have an official role on this trip. I'm just the support person." Liz's compressed lips, combined with a frown, clearly conveyed her reluctance. Amy understood. Who ever wants to help a friend deal with cancer?

After Maggie Fitzgerald had barged into the office, Amy had taken some time to review her case. Officially, she was Cathy's patient, but the connection to Liz interested Amy. Liz had told her she'd discovered the cancer when they'd spent a romantic weekend in Acadia. Amy tried to imagine the horror of it—discovering a lump in your partner's breast after being apart for forty years. The twist of fate was unimaginably cruel, but who better to manage the case than Liz?

When the head doctor from Hobbs Family Practice had first called Amy to arrange an interview, she hadn't realized at first that she was Elizabeth A. Stolz, one of the world's leading experts on breast cancer. Amy had read Liz's book when it first came out, but once she knew she was going to join the practice, she'd bought the latest version and reread it. The book had gone through ten editions and scores of printings, being updated over the years to cover genetic testing and advancements in biologic treatments. It was remarkably complete, containing enough technical information to satisfy a physician while still being understandable to a lay person.

Sam went by Amy's office door, interrupting her thoughts. Sam had been working on the bathroom in the new wing. All morning long, she'd trudged down the hall, lugging five-gallon buckets.

"Sam!" called Amy, getting up to call after her.

Sam walked backwards and grinned. "Hey," she said softly. "How are you doing?"

"Okay, but we haven't had lunch together in a while."

Sam looked both ways to see if anyone was listening, but Amy was the only person who'd moved into the new wing.

"I thought when you said you wanted to step back from a relationship, you weren't interested in having lunch with me."

"I said I'm not ready for a relationship, but I was enjoying our friendship and our lunch dates."

Sam glanced down at her dusty clothes. "I'm filthy."

"It's a nice day. We can eat outside. I'll pick up some sandwiches."

Sam's face instantly brightened. "Okay, but I need to use this mortar before it sets up. Can you wait twenty minutes?"

Amy took a quick look at her schedule. "Sure. I'm free until two. Meanwhile, I'll get the sandwiches."

"Sounds like a plan."

When Amy returned from the deli, she saw Maggie Fitzgerald in the waiting room. Fortunately, she was absorbed in a book and didn't look up. Amy rushed by with her bag of sandwiches. She wasn't purposely trying to avoid Maggie, but she'd rather not have to make small talk with a woman who was obviously under so much stress.

A few minutes later, Sam showed up at Amy's door, all clean. "I showered, so I'm not filthy while we eat. I think you'll enjoy that new bathroom."

"Won't you have to get dirty again?"

"Not today. I finished the last section of the floor. Tomorrow, I'll grout it."

"Let's go out the back way," Amy encouraged.

"Okay," said Sam, frowning slightly, but she didn't ask why.

They settled at the new picnic table in the little park Sam had created from the vacant lot where the overgrown shrubs had once stood. "I felt guilty ripping out the sumac," Sam said, trying to wind her long legs over the bench. "The monarch butterflies really like it. I planted some milkweed to make up for it. They like that too."

The nature talk meant little to Amy, who'd never understood the appeal of the great outdoors. She preferred to appreciate the beauty of nature from a car window.

Sam unwrapped her sandwich. She grinned when she discovered it was a turkey club with bacon and cranberry sauce. "Thanks for remembering."

"Thanks for accepting my lunch invitation," said Amy. "I've missed our lunch dates."

"I wasn't too sure what you wanted me to do, so I've been keeping my distance."

"Just be yourself, Sam. I'm the one who's not ready."

"Maybe, sometime, you'll tell me more. No pressure." Sam bit into her sandwich with gusto.

Amy enjoyed Sam's look pleasure as she chewed. "Hungry?"

Sam nodded. "Starving. Thanks for lunch. I'll buy next time."

Amy liked the idea that there would be a next time. While Sam inhaled her sandwich, Amy watched her fondly. She was saddened that Sam thought she wasn't interested in her friendship. She never wanted to hurt Sam, who was so kind. "Liz recommended Olivia Enright as a financial advisor. Will that be a problem?"

"Not for me. You should talk to her. She's very good."

"I imagine she would be after running the Enright Fund for all those years, but it must be boring to deal with small investors like me."

"Oh, I wouldn't say so. I think she's happy to have something to do. Being the town manager doesn't keep her busy enough."

"You promise it won't be awkward for you?"

"Hell no. I'm used to rearrangements in our little community. It's important to adjust quickly and not encourage bad blood."

"You mean like with Liz and Maggie?"

Sam gave her a sharp look, which Amy took as a warning. "It's not as black and white as it might seem," Sam explained.

"It never is. What goes on inside a relationship is really known only to the people in it. Things change. Sometimes, relationships don't work for them anymore."

"Sounds like you speak from experience."

"I do. Sounds like you do, too."

"It's my policy not to hang around past the 'best by' date." Sam grinned. "I suppose I should have told you that from the beginning."

"Wow, we certainly had a short shelf life," quipped Amy, riffing on Sam's metaphor.

Sam laughed. "We hadn't even gotten started, so expiration dates don't count for us."

"I like to think we started a wonderful friendship. Does that count?"

"Of course," said Sam, opening her mouth wide to take another bite of the overstuffed sandwich. She ended up with cranberry sauce on her cheek, which she wiped away with the back of her fist.

"I feel lucky to know you," said Amy. "It's not easy to make friends as an adult. Where do you even start? I'm not a big fan of mixing business and pleasure."

"It's almost impossible in a small town like Hobbs. If you're the town doctor like Liz, or a pastor, like Lucy, you know everyone. Your social and business lives will cross frequently. You can't help it."

"I'm beginning to see that the rules don't always apply up here."

"We have our own rules," Sam said conclusively. "You have to pay attention to figure them out, or you'll end up stubbing your toe without even knowing it."

"Thank you for telling me that. Do you have any advice regarding Olivia? Is she a straight-shooter?"

Sam was clearly struggling to suppress a smile, but she ended up grinning anyway. "How's that toe feel? Hurt yet?"

***

Sam stopped at the check-in desk to say she was leaving and noticed Maggie sitting in the staff area. Ginny, the practice manager, knew the backstory. Clearly, she was trying to shield Maggie from the curious stares of the patients in the waiting room.

It had to be so hard for Maggie to return in such changed circumstances. Many people in Hobbs knew her because she'd been the drama coach at the high school and taught at the community college after retiring from UNE. She was on the board of the Webhanet Playhouse and the State Theater and had a starring role in their productions. Her life had been so busy. Then everything had changed. Not long after her daughter arrived, wrecked by an abusive marriage and penniless, Maggie had retired from one activity after another. That's when Sam had first noticed a change in the relationship between Maggie and Liz. In the beginning, the difference was subtle, but it became more pronounced as time passed.

"Is Liz tied up with a patient?" Sam quietly asked Ginny.

"Yes, and it always seems to happen when she has to go somewhere. They were supposed to leave twenty minutes ago."

Sam nodded, recognizing a familiar refrain. "Hey, Maggie," called Sam at an audible volume. "Want to come outside with me? We can catch up while you're waiting."

Maggie's face instantly brightened. She stowed her book in her bag and came to the door. "But I don't want to sit on the bench out front where everyone can see me," she said in a confidential tone.

"That's fine. We can sit in my truck. Ginny can tell Liz where to find you. Right, Ginny?"

"You bet."

Maggie smiled graciously at Ginny. "Thank you. You're all being so kind."

"Good luck down at Yale," Ginny called after them. "I'll tell Liz when she comes out."

Clicking open the doors to her truck, Sam watched Maggie's eyes scan the surrounding cars to make sure they were empty. "I know. It's weird sitting in a truck in a parking lot."

"No, I think it's sweet of you to invite me." Maggie climbed into the passenger side. "You have no idea how humiliating it is to sit in that waiting room with all the patients staring. Everyone in Hobbs knows the story by now. That's the main reason I moved out of town."

Sam opened the windows a little so they could get some air. The tide was out. The salt marsh smelled tangy but not unpleasant. "You also moved away from all your friends."

Maggie raised her chin a little. Sam's eyes fell on the slight cleft. "They knew where to find me."

Sam looked out at the multicolored seagrass in the marsh. "I know I've been remiss, but I've been working like crazy. With all the building up here, contractors are overwhelmed."

"And you had Olivia demanding your free time."

"Well, that's done now."

"She wasn't right for you, Sam."

"I know, but it was fun while it lasted." She grinned and raised a brow lewdly.

"At least, you're not a kiss and tell like Liz."

Talking about her friend made Sam uncomfortable, so she changed the subject. "How do you spend your time now that you're retired?"

"While the schools were shut down, I was busy homeschooling the girls. Now that they're back at school, I don't know what to do with myself. Being a full-time grandma was not what I had in mind when I retired. Oh, don't get me wrong. I love the kids, but I need adult company. Alina is so tired when she drags herself home from work, I can barely get two words out of her. Tony wants me to come back to the Playhouse board. And the college needs adjuncts. Maybe I should go back to work."

"If that's what you want to do, it's not a bad idea."

"First, I have to recover from this surgery."

"So, you're going through with the double mastectomy?"

Maggie heaved out a long sigh. "I don't want to lose my breasts. I let Liz talk me out of it last time because I didn't want to deprive her. She's really into breasts. But I can't live with the fear anymore. Every time my tumor marker test is due, I can't sleep for weeks. I had my ovaries and uterus removed. Why not my breasts?"

"No one sees your ovaries or uterus," Sam said, as if that weren't obvious.

"No one sees my breasts either unless I'm naked, and that's only in the shower or when I get undressed." Maggie made it sound like she had given up on having a lover again, which made Sam sad. She reached out and took Maggie's hand.

"Maggie, you're a beautiful woman. After the mastectomies, you'll still be beautiful."

"Oh, Sam, where have you been all my life?" Maggie quipped with a sad smile. She squeezed Sam's hand before letting it go. "Unfortunately, having the mastectomies meant I had to tell the girls. Alina was relatively calm. Sophia was furious, which I understand, but I know it's mostly fear. She wanted me to go to Dana-Farber, but the last thing I need is my oncologist-daughter harassing my doctors."

"So, instead, your ex-wife can do it."

Maggie shook her head. "Liz has always been more level-headed about my case than my daughter, but I hear Sophia is a good doctor. She's taking time off to pick me up from the hospital, so Liz can come back to Maine."

"Sounds like everyone's pitching in to help. I can too, you know."

"Oh, Sam, you're such a good person," said Maggie, leaning over to kiss her on the cheek. "Thanks for offering."

"Seriously, tell me what I can do." Sam mentally reviewed her schedule. The renovation project was at the point where it was mostly interior surfaces, which she'd hired contractors to do. She could afford to take some time off. "Do you need me to run errands? Take you to appointments? Name it, and I'll be there."

"In a couple of weeks, the leaves will be at their peak. Maybe you can take me out for a drive to see the colors. High October is still one of my favorite times of year."

"No camping trip this year, I guess."

"No. Too many memories, and everything's been rearranged…" Maggie's voice trailing off into a note of sadness pulled at a tender place in Sam's heart. "Things change," added Maggie in a philosophical tone.

A knock made Sam jump. She turned around to see Liz standing there and rolled down the window.

"Sorry to be so late. Thanks for keeping her company, Sam." Liz looked through the half-open window to get Maggie's attention. "You ready to go?"

Maggie reached over and gave Sam's hand a gentle pat. "Thank you, Sam. You're a gem."

Sam's eyes followed them as they walked to Liz's car. She could see the tension hanging over them like a storm rolling in.

❋❋❋

The playlist was winding to a close. Lucy had advised listening to music in the car to maintain calm. "Nothing too emotional. Light classics. Easy jazz. Nothing with ties to your past or to me." The simple advice seemed to be working. The conversation so far had been relatively pleasant. Maggie hadn't complained that Liz was driving too fast, not even once. They talked about a subject of common interest—whether the Playhouse would have a normal season next year after being disrupted by the pandemic. It felt like the old days, when their conversations were relaxed and easy. Liz was optimistic they might get to New Haven without an argument. Then Maggie asked, "When are you going to set a date for your wedding?"

The question landed like a brick through the windshield.

"Soon," said Liz, trying to sound casual, but this topic made her instantly tense. She volunteered information to underscore that she wasn't hiding anything. "We've met with Lucy's bishop. He's offered to officiate."

"That's quite an honor."

"That's what Lucy says, but I'd rather have Tom."

"What are you going to do about it?"

"I don't know. Lucy says it's political, and we don't have much choice."

"She's not in a position to refuse, but you could probably explain to the bishop why you'd rather have Tom officiate."

Liz glanced at Maggie, wondering what had changed. The memory of her screeching into the phone and calling Lucy nasty names was still vivid. "Why are you being so helpful? Now you're okay with me marrying Lucy?"

"I didn't say that, but there's nothing I can do about it," replied Maggie, folding her arms on her chest.

"You make it sound like you're a victim. Like you had no agency."

"Listen to you," Maggie said in a disparaging voice. "Did you pick up that word from Lucy?"

Liz thought for a moment. "I suppose I did. It's a shrink word, isn't it?"

"Yes. And probably a priest word. Yes, I had agency, but there was nothing I could do. After you laid eyes on Lucy, that was it. I let you get away with too much. All that teasing and flirting. I thought it was in good fun. Then you had to kiss her."

"Okay. I was tempted for a moment, but you made such a big deal out of it. It was just a kiss for God's sake, but you never let me forget it. You were always walking around with that wounded dog look on your face…glaring at me with resentment. I said I was sorry, and I was. You kept pushing me away!!!"

"You didn't fight for our marriage."

"I did! You're the one who gave up on it. I never kissed Lucy again, but you had to fuck that Brad what's-his-name. Couldn't wait to get a dick back inside you, could you?" asked Liz in a furious voice.

"Because you couldn't wait to stick your tongue down Lucy's throat!"

"If you hadn't been such a jealous bitch, we might still be together!"

The ring of a call through the dashboard Bluetooth made them both jump. "Lucy Bartlett calling," the device announced in a pleasant voice. "Should I answer it?"

"What the hell?" Maggie said in disgust. "Can she smell that we're having a fight?"

Liz rolled her eyes and pressed the call answer button on the steering wheel. "We're still on the road."

"Oh, no!" Lucy replied. "I was hoping you'd be at Jenny's by now."

"There was a big tie-up outside of Hartford. Orange cones everywhere."

"Hello, Lucy," Maggie interjected. "You have perfect timing. You just interrupted a fight." Liz shot her an irritated look. Maggie cocked a shoulder at her.

On the other end of the call, there was a moment of tense hesitation. "Maybe I should give you two some privacy."

"No," said Maggie. "It was a good thing you called, Lucy. Things were getting pretty hot in here. Say a prayer that we arrive in one piece."

"I will," said Lucy in a kind voice, "but it would be better if you both tried to lower the temperature."

"We will. I'll send you a text when we get there," Liz said to end the conversation quickly. She pushed the button on the steering wheel. The music resumed, meaning the call had ended.

"So, Lucy keeps tabs on you too," Maggie said.

Liz shot her a hostile look. "What didn't you understand about 'lowering the temperature?'"

Maggie gazed out the window, and Liz was grateful for a few moments of silence. Finally, Maggie spoke. "Liz, I'm scared. At least, an argument is a distraction. I wish you hadn't accepted Jenny's invitation to stay with her and Laura."

"I almost never see them anymore. You'll only be there one night."

"Yes. Tomorrow, I get to sleep in the hospital. Lucky me."

Liz glanced at Maggie, wondering when she had become so cranky. People called Liz a grump, which she cultivated by playing to their expectations, but Maggie had become downright negative. The slide predated the infamous kiss, but pinpointing when things fell apart was difficult. Maggie had become distant and uncommunicative. She ate like a bird and lost weight, not that she had an ounce to spare. The sex became sporadic until one day, it stopped. Looking back, Liz felt like an idiot for not recognizing the classic symptoms of depression. If she'd only been paying more attention, maybe she could have done something to help.

"Great," said Maggie. "Now, you're mute." In seconds, all the sympathy engendered by Liz's retrospection vanished. Maggie stared at her with narrowed eyes. "Liz, don't you have an ounce of compassion?"

Liz began counting so she wouldn't explode. When she got to ten, she said in the calmest voice she could muster: "Why don't we stop talking for a while? It's enough for me to deal with this fucking traffic." Liz could feel Maggie glaring at her, but she got the message. She sulked for the remainder of the trip. Liz turned off the happy music and was grateful for the silence.

Maggie slipped into full-fledged actress mode when she greeted Liz's former partner. Maggie's exaggerated pleasure in their reunion was totally fake. Liz knew how much Maggie disliked Jenny. There were times when Liz didn't like Jenny either, but they'd parted as friends, and she had a standing invitation to stay in the showplace house on Long Island Sound they'd once owned together.

"Go bring your things in from the car, and I'll mix some martinis," said Jenny, giving Liz a bone-crushing hug. She turned to Maggie and clucked her tongue. "None for you, girlfriend. You have surgery tomorrow."

"Maggie hates martinis," Liz reminded her.

Jenny snapped her fingers. "That's right! I forgot."

"But I'm dying for a glass of wine," Maggie said.

Jenny turned to Liz. "What do you think? Can we give her a tiny glass?" She measured a small quantity with her fingers.

"Just one," said Liz in a firm voice.

"The boss says you can have one." Jenny took Maggie's arm and led her into the kitchen, "Don't worry. I'll slip you a glass when she's not looking. Liz can be ridiculously rigid." Liz shook her head. Jenny never missed an opportunity to make trouble.

Liz opened the trunk of the Audi and surveyed the luggage to figure out what to bring in first. She'd learned from years of attending conferences that efficient packing made all the difference, but Maggie had brought a large suitcase and a makeup kit that weighed almost as much.

"I put Maggie in the front room," Jenny called after Liz as she trudged up the stairs with their bags. Liz was grateful that Jenny had considered the sleeping arrangements. Liz hadn't given them a single thought.

Before she went downstairs, Liz texted Lucy to let her know they'd arrived. When she returned, she found Jenny and Maggie parked in the huge living room with its spectacular view of Long Island Sound.

"I didn't pour your martini because I wanted it to be cold," said Jenny. "Help yourself." Liz took the shaker out of the chiller and poured her drink into a glass with three olives. Jenny knew exactly how Liz liked her martinis.

When she took a seat on the opposite sofa, Liz perceived the irony of facing two exes. She took a gulp of martini for fortification.

"Laura apologizes for being late," Jenny said, evidently feeling the need to explain her wife's absence. "Her practice is holding an after-hours staff meeting, but she promised to be here in time for dinner."

As they ate the salmon that Jenny had prepared—one of her half dozen signature dishes—the conversation was relaxed and friendly. It almost seemed like nothing had changed since they'd last visited as a married couple. The difference hit home when they went up to bed, and Maggie headed down the hall to a room on the other side of the house.

Liz got ready for bed and sat down to call Lucy, whose voice was sleepy when she answered. "I thought you'd forgotten me." Liz imagined Lucy's little pout and smiled.

"You know how it is when you're with old friends you haven't seen in a long time. I haven't been down here since the pandemic began. It was good to catch up with Jenny and Laura. They're good company and wonderful hosts. I think it was a good distraction for Maggie."

"How is she doing?"

"She seems fine, but it's hard to tell with her. She's always 'on'. I'm sure she's anxious about tomorrow."

"She's lucky to have you there as her support person."

"I'd rather be home with you, but I'm looking forward to having dinner with Emily tomorrow."

"She is too."

"Honey, I'll let you go back to sleep. You sound too tired for phone sex."

"Who said that?"

"All right. I'm projecting. I'm too tired for phone sex. Go back to sleep. I'll text you in the morning."

After some silly lover talk, Liz ended the call. She checked her work emails, relieved to find that Amy was keeping the office under control. With that thought in mind, Liz turned off the light. Utterly exhausted by the day, she soon fell into a stupor.

When she heard a shaky voice in the dark, Liz was instantly alert. Trained by years of hospital work, she could be completely awake at a moment's notice. She glanced at the bedside clock and saw it was past two. "Liz?" the voice repeated. She could make out Maggie's face in the glow of the digital numerals.

"Maggie, what's wrong? Are you okay?"

"I can't sleep."

"Do you need a tranquilizer?" Liz asked, sitting up.

"No, I just want you to hold me. You know. Like the last time I had surgery. Please."

Liz was too groggy to explain why that was a bad idea, although she vaguely knew it was. It was easier to move over. "All right. Get in," she said, holding up the covers. She could feel Maggie trembling, so she spooned her. "Maggie, there's nothing to worry about. Ellen is one of the best. I know. I trained her. By this time tomorrow, it will all be over." Maggie pulled Liz's arm around her waist closer. Eventually, she stopped shaking, and Liz fell sleep.

She woke to pleasurable stroking between her legs. She smiled because she'd been dreaming of Lucy and repositioned herself to get more of her sexy touch. Then she opened her eyes and realized that Lucy was at home, and she was in Guilford, hundreds of miles away. She flinched away from Maggie's fingers and sat up. "What are you doing?"

"Please, Liz. You know sex is the only thing that stops the anxiety."

"Are you crazy? I'm engaged to Lucy."

"You're not married yet."

Liz scrambled out of bed. "You need to leave. Now."

"After tomorrow, I might have no feeling in my breasts. One last time… before they're gone forever."

Liz raked her fingers through her hair as she considered what to do. "You need to go, Maggie. Right now."

"No, please," begged Maggie and began to whimper like an injured dog. "Please, let me stay."

"You need to get out." Liz opened the door and pointed to the hall. "Out!"

After Maggie left, Liz locked the door, but she could hear her outside, crying. Liz leaned against the door, although listening to the pitiful sound was pure torture. Finally, the soft weeping stopped.

Liz was heading back to bed when there was a sharp knock at the door.

"Go to sleep, Maggie!" called Liz, getting back into bed.

"It's Jenny!" Liz got up and unlocked the door. "What the hell is going on?" asked Jenny with an angry scowl. "If you two can't fight quietly, take it downstairs."

"Go back to bed. The show's over," said Liz, ready to close the door.

Jenny pushed past her into the room. "What happened? Is she okay?"

Liz shrugged. "How the hell should I know, but I'm not going down to her room to find out."

"Oh," said Jenny. "Do you want me to go?"

"No. Leave her alone. She needs to learn there are boundaries now."

Jenny's dark brows shot up. "Sounds like a good story. I can't wait to hear it but tell me tomorrow. Now, I need to get some sleep."

"Me too. Sorry about the noise."

After Jenny left, Liz turned off the lights. The failed seduction had rattled her. Although she'd done nothing to feel guilty about, Liz felt the impulse to call Lucy and confess. As much as she longed to hear Lucy's soothing voice tell her she was forgiven, Liz knew she should let her sleep. Tuesday was Lucy's busy day with a full slate of therapy appointments.

Liz stared at the ceiling for a half hour before she got up and located the pill case in her bag. She broke a tablet of alprazolam in two and gulped down half.

# 10

The tension in Liz's voice was like a violin string stretched to the point of breaking. Lucy's vocal training had taught her to hear the subtlest nuances in voices. As soon as Liz spoke, Lucy instantly sensed that something was wrong.

"You can't talk now," Lucy ventured cautiously.

"Jenny and I are talking while Maggie's in the shower."

"Oh, I'm sorry I interrupted."

"No, it's fine. I'll call you later. When are you free?"

"After three, but we have that prep for the adoption hearing at three thirty, so I don't have a lot of time."

"Forgot about that meeting. I'm sorry I'm missing it. By three Maggie should be in recovery. I'll call you then."

"Have you decided if you're going into the OR?"

"I'm going to watch from the observation room. I can't stand all the attention focused on me when it should be on the patient. I've been gone for over a decade, but the old timers still watch me as if I were still chief." Liz's audible sigh sounded like pure despair. "Let me talk to you later."

"Okay, sweetie. I love you."

"Me too," said Liz and hung up.

Lucy wrote off the curt dismissal to the presence of Liz's ex, but she was worried about the odd tone in her voice. Unfortunately, she'd have to wait until later to discover its cause.

The day turned out to be so busy that Liz's three o'clock call went into voice mail. Before returning it, Lucy got up to close the office door—not that she ever suspected Jodi of eavesdropping. It was a habit because people shared their deepest confidences with her. Lucy's head was so full of secrets that she sometimes felt it would explode. Thankfully, confiding in the seagulls during her morning walks relieved some of the pressure.

Lucy listened to the phone ring on the other end, hoping she hadn't missed her window of opportunity. The call opened without a greeting, as usual. "I'm heading to Bev's for a visit. Good timing."

"Do you have time to talk now?"

"For you, I always have time to talk. Let me pull over. Meanwhile, tell me about your day."

"It was long and busy."

"What else is new?" Lucy was glad to hear the amused sarcasm in Liz's voice.

"Oh, Liz. I miss you so much! It's cold in bed without you. I want my heater back!"

"I'll be home tomorrow, after I hand off the baton to Maggie's daughter. She said she's coming around noon, so that should get me home by dinner time. Let's go out to dinner."

"Yes! That sounds like fun." The sound of the tires on the roadway ended and the car engine went off. Liz had found a place to park. "How's the patient?" Lucy asked.

"She's recovering as well as can be expected. Maggie has trouble shaking off anesthesia. Fortunately, Ellen was quick and didn't keep her under long. Anesthesia is a risk factor for dementia in older patients. The plastic surgeon seemed competent, so the cosmetic results should be satisfactory."

Lucy strained to hear the emotions below Liz's succinct summary. Liz had to have feelings about watching another surgeon cut into the body of a woman she'd loved. Imagining the medical details made Lucy queasy, so she focused on the emotional connection instead.

"How's it going between you and Maggie?"

Liz's voice went up a quarter octave in pitch. "I was going to wait until I got home to talk to you about it."

"Talk to me now," Lucy urged gently. "Maybe I can help." There was an extended silence. Lucy felt frustrated because she couldn't see Liz's face, so she tapped the button for a video chat. It rang on the other end for a long time before it opened. "Liz, talk to me," Lucy urged.

"It hasn't been easy." Lucy recognized the statement as a form of linguistic throat clearing, Liz warming up to her topic. "She really knows how to get to me."

"She's known you for a very long time. And Maggie is an actress and stage director. She knows how to read people. You were in an intimate relationship for years. Of course, she knows how to get to you."

"We had a big argument last night. I had to apologize to Jenny this morning. That's why I couldn't talk when you called. Jenny never had a high opinion of Maggie, so there was a lot of smoothing over to do."

"What were you arguing about?"

"I'll tell you when I get home, but it got loud enough to wake up Jenny. She got up to tell us to keep it down."

"I bet that was embarrassing. How was Maggie this morning?"

"She acted like nothing ever happened. Not even an apology."

"I'm sure she was worried about the surgery."

"Maggie panics before surgery. She's especially worried about losing sensation in her nipples. When a double mastectomy was on the table years ago, we discussed that subject quite a bit."

"Is it a realistic worry?" asked Lucy.

"Unfortunately, it is. Thinking back, I wonder if I only talked her out of the surgery because I didn't want her to lose her breasts."

"You really like breasts."

"You know I do." Liz grinned and craned her neck as if that would allow her to see below the camera window. "Don't you need to get to your meeting?"

Lucy glanced at the time on her computer. Liz was right. Lucy blew her a quick kiss before she tapped off the call.

❋❋❋

Melissa reviewed her notes while waiting for the small group to find seats. It had been a long time since she'd prepared witnesses to appear before a judge. Trust work didn't usually lend itself to courtroom settings. Occasionally, a trust came under legal scrutiny, and she found herself called as a witness, but seldom as lead counsel.

She suddenly thought of her father, who regularly did pro-bono work. Raised by a rabbi and a devout mother, he took living a godly life seriously. It wasn't surprising that Melissa's sister, who'd adored their grandfather, had followed in his footsteps. Soon, Rebecca would be living nearby. The reform synagogue in Portland had chosen her to be their rabbi. Ruth, Melissa's mother, was delighted, of course, to have her daughter close to home. Lucy, who'd worked with Rebecca on LGBTQ youth advocacy, was overjoyed to have her friend and ally in Maine. Surrounded by so much religion, Melissa, who considered herself an agnostic, wondered where she could hide.

Her eyes lighted on Lucy, who was wearing her black blouse open at the neck, which reminded Melissa that they needed to talk about whether the priest should wear her collar in the hearing. Distinctive clothing indicating the wearer's profession could subtly influence a decision either way. Melissa had already decided that Brenda should wear street clothes instead of her police uniform. Her role as police chief would come up in testimony.

Seemingly aware that Melissa was scrutinizing her, Lucy smiled. Melissa realized she was encouraging her to get the meeting underway. She clapped her hands to get everyone's attention. "All right! Let's get started." The murmur of female voices fell silent, and all eyes turned in her direction. "Thank you all for coming. I'm sure everyone's had a busy day, so I want to get you out of here quickly. The hearing is next Thursday at eleven. Please make sure you've got it on your calendar." While everyone checked their phones, Melissa continued her preamble. "The purpose of the hearing is to decide whether the adoption application made by Cherie and Brenda can proceed. A cousin of the Benoit children has applied for legal guardianship. Granting it isn't automatic because she's not a close blood relative. This case will be decided on which party will make better parents, and that's where you character witnesses come in."

Courtney raised her hand. "Where are the children now? They can't hear us, can they?"

"Denise has them in choir practice in the church basement. That's why we chose this time," Cherie explained

"Okay," said Melissa. "Let's begin by thinking of a time when you personally witnessed Brenda or Cherie displaying good character. Then we'll listen to the stories and decide which to share in court. Situations that involve children get bonus points."

The door opened at the back of the room, and everyone turned around. A tall, heavy-set man stood in the doorway.

"Can I help you?" asked Melissa.

"I heard you need character witnesses for Chief Harrison."

"Yes, we do. Are you here to speak for her?"

"I'm Paul Duvaney, the fire chief. I've known Brenda for years and can tell lots of stories about her." His grin suggested that some of his stories might not be fit for everyone's ears, never mind a courtroom. The big man took a chair from the stack against the wall and sat down next to Brenda.

She patted his shoulder and murmured, "Thanks for coming, Paul."

The door opened again, and Sam McKinnon poked her head into the room. "Am I too late?"

"No, come on in. We're just getting started. Pull up a chair." Sam conspicuously chose a position far from where Olivia sat.

Melissa repeated the instructions and gave everyone a few more minutes to think of positive stories about Brenda and Cherie. "Okay. Let's see what you came up with. Who wants to go first?" Several hands shot up. Melissa pointed with her dry-erase marker. "Go ahead, Lucy."

"Cherie has been volunteering for the youth suicide hotline since she came to Maine. I know for a fact that she has saved the lives of at least two Hobbs teens."

"Perfect," said Melissa in an encouraging voice and wrote down "suicide hotline" under the column for Cherie. "How about Brenda?"

"Brenda showed extraordinary sensitivity in dealing with a member of the clergy when she discovered she was wanted for a traffic incident in another state. She made sure there were appropriate consequences, but always allowed the priest to maintain her dignity."

"Excellent. Thanks, Lucy." Melissa pointed to the fire chief.

"I saw Brenda climb under an overturned car to rescue a baby at an accident scene. The gas tank was leaking, so there was a real fire risk, but she never hesitated. I don't know Cherie as well, but she took care of my mother-in-law before she died, and she kept saying how kind she was."

"That's good. I'll take it," said Melissa writing it down. "Maybe you can think of something else to say about Cherie."

Melissa went around the group collecting the stories. Then, Sam's hand went up. "We were at a Black Lives Matter demonstration and there was a young, mentally disabled man shouting at the police. The local police handled him roughly, but Brenda showed her police badge and got them to back off."

"Which almost cost Brenda her job," Olivia piped in. "It was caught on tape and broadcast all over the state."

"She was defending an innocent person who didn't understand," said Sam with a challenging stare.

"It embarrassed the town," Olivia countered.

Melissa could feel the tension rising. "Maybe we could stay away from politics," she suggested. "Depending on the judge's leanings that could go either way."

Sam sat back in her seat and folded her arms on her chest. "Let me think about it." She sent a hate dart in Olivia's direction.

Courtney described how Brenda, who was off duty, calmed the protestors at the school. Melissa reviewed the list on the board. The stories were compelling, and she couldn't ask for a better group of witnesses: a school principal, the town manager, a member of the clergy, an award-winning architect, and the fire chief. Brenda and Cherie were married, owned their own home, and had stable jobs. It seemed like an open and shut case against an unemployed woman, who lived in a rented trailer with her boyfriend. The cousin had a sketchy background and several arrests for pot possession before Maine had changed its laws.

*This is too easy*, Melissa thought, and wondered if there was something she was missing.

❆❆❆

Olivia watched Sam make a hasty exit as soon as the meeting was over. She had no way of knowing whether Sam had to be somewhere or was trying to avoid a confrontation, but she certainly seemed to be in a hurry. Olivia's eyes followed her as she wove through the chatting women on her way to the door.

The others were talking about meeting at Dockside for a drink. Olivia associated the restaurant with chamber of commerce meetings, so the idea of socializing there was unappealing. It didn't matter. No one in the group seemed to have noticed her standing alone at the back. She resolved to ignore them and turned to leave.

"Olivia, would you like to join us?" asked Lucy, suddenly at her side.

"I want to get home and make dinner." This explanation had the virtue of being the truth.

"Oh, do you have company coming?" asked Lucy, looking surprised.

"No, but I bought some lovely veal cutlets from the butcher, and I don't want them to go to waste." Sam had always lectured her on the cruelty to veal calves. Olivia looked forward to enjoying a veal piccata without guilt. The idea to invite Lucy for dinner suddenly popped up into her mind. "There's enough for two, if you'd like to join me."

Lucy looked back at the group of younger women. They'd clearly been energized by the meeting and were looking forward to continuing the discussion at the bar. Olivia could see how much Lucy longed to go with them, but she surprised her by saying, "Thanks, Olivia. It will be good to catch up."

Olivia studied Lucy's face to see if there was a hidden agenda. "I know you're disappointed that I didn't sign up for therapy again."

Lucy looked directly into her eyes. "You know where I am if you need me."

"So, can we agree this evening will be strictly social?"

"Oh, please. It's been a long, busy day. I'm looking forward to some downtime."

"And you'll have someone to cook dinner for you while Liz is away."

"Liz left me a dish to heat up," Lucy said casually. "I'll put it in the freezer for another time."

"Sounds like Liz looks after you better than I expected, given her busy schedule."

Lucy ignored the ploy to extract information. "I'll meet you there. I want to go home and change first." She waved to the others and headed out.

Denise brought her young charges to join Brenda and Cherie. The joyous reunion with their foster parents reinforced Olivia's decision to involve herself in the lawsuit. After the Feds had gotten into her son's business, she'd had enough of lawyers, but this was for a good cause. Besides, she was fond of Melissa, who'd impressed her with her smarts and practicality in dealing with Liz's case. She wasn't too sure about Courtney yet. She'd handled the parent protests well, but she'd had Brenda and Liz at her back. With more experience, Courtney might be an excellent principal, but Olivia wasn't convinced she was ready yet.

Before Lucy arrived, Olivia prepared a snack tray with cheeses and garlic-stuffed olives from the Webhanet Deli. Neither of them was expecting a bed partner tonight, so a whiff of garlic wouldn't offend anyone. She sat down with a glass of pinot grigio, which she'd chosen because she knew Lucy liked white wine.

When the doorbell rang, Olivia went to the door to greet her guest. Olivia liked the formality of the collar when Lucy was in her role as rector, but she also liked seeing the imaginative way she put herself together when off duty. Tonight, she wore an outfit straight out of the L. L. Bean catalog— olive cords and a long, open cardigan over a Vee-neck low enough to show a hint of cleavage.

Lucy's glamor always seemed so effortless. When Olivia had asked if it was the result of being an opera star, Lucy had explained that she'd learned it from her mother, a fashion model and a classical singer like herself. Olivia had learned nothing from her mother. God knows, her mother had been a mess, especially after she started drinking.

"Lucy, I'm so glad you dressed warmly. We can have our appetizers outside. It's a lovely evening."

"It's so warm for October. It feels strange. By this time of year, I expect a little crispness in the air."

"It is unnatural," Olivia agreed. "Climate change, they say. Go out to the deck. I'll bring out the snacks and wine."

Lucy was admiring the seascape when Olivia joined her on the deck. "I'm sad that it gets dark so early now," Lucy said. "And it's so dark in the morning when I go for my walk."

"Wait until the time changes."

"Don't remind me. I know I should embrace the lessons the dark offers, but I still find it difficult. In the summer, eight o'clock seems early. Now, it's a time to curl up in bed with a book."

"Speaking of books. How's yours coming along?" asked Olivia, handing Lucy a glass of wine.

"It's almost finished."

"And your studies?"

"I'm still on target to graduate in June."

"The bishop couldn't persuade you to take a break?"

Lucy stared at her.

"I'm sorry. Out of bounds again, but I worry about you, Lucy. Your parish needs you."

"I thought we were done with this topic."

Olivia saw a flash of Lucy's fire. She knew her priest wasn't always the sweet, accepting person everyone thought she was. Out of curiosity, Olivia had watched some of Lucy's taped opera performances. That kind of passion was totally authentic. Olivia had a momentary vision of Lucy as a lover, but the image shocked her, so she instantly dismissed it.

Lucy helped herself to a piece of cheese. "To answer your original question, I'm enjoying my courses. Next semester, I'll have all the heavy-duty classes behind me, and I can take some for fun."

"Studying theology for fun? I can't even imagine it. I admire your determination, Lucy. I could never see myself going back to school at this age."

"Neither could I, but when I started talking about writing a book, Erika encouraged me. She thought having my doctorate would give the book more credibility."

"Being a professor, Erika would think so. Is that why you're doing it?" Olivia offered the plate of garlic-stuffed olives. "Go on. Have one. I'm not going to kiss you, and Liz isn't coming home until tomorrow." She gave Lucy the side eye to let her know she was teasing.

"Credibility is important. It's not easy being a female priest, even in a progressive denomination. And sex is always a controversial topic."

"I'm looking forward to reading it. Are there pointers in it?"

Lucy arched an auburn brow. "You mean about physical relationships? Yes, some. Most of it is a deconstruction of purity culture and an exploration of the misogyny of the patriarchal religions."

"That means nothing to me, Lucy. Speak English."

"To get to a positive view of sexuality, I had to cut through a lot of bullshit." Olivia couldn't stop her eyes from blinking. She had never heard Lucy use profanity. "These garlic olives are addictive," Lucy said, reaching for another.

"Your fiancée likes them too."

"So that's why she comes home from your house smelling like a kosher pickle."

"Sorry. I won't offer them to her again."

"Go ahead. I like garlic. And it's supposed to keep vampires away," Lucy said dryly.

"You believe in vampires?" asked Olivia, surprised.

"Only the emotional kind who suck your energy and leave you drained."

"I've known a few of those."

"Good to keep your distance from such people or approach them cautiously," said Lucy.

"That must be difficult in your position."

"You mean because I'm a pastor?" Lucy helped herself to another olive. "Sometimes, it's hard. That's why it's important to have clear boundaries."

Olivia rolled her eyes. "You won't ever let me forget that, will you?"

"I didn't say it for your benefit, and it goes both ways. If you tell me, you don't want more therapy, I must respect your wishes. If I tell you, don't manage me, you need to listen."

"All right, Lucy," said Olivia in an excessively patient voice. "I get it."

"I thought you would. You're very observant and good at reading between the lines."

"But not in matters of the heart. I should have expected that Sam would leave. She's so independent. She doesn't want a big commitment."

"But you couldn't resist pushing for one because that's what you want," said Lucy.

Olivia gazed out at the surf. "Maybe if I hadn't pushed so hard, we'd still be together."

"Maybe. Or Sam may need to walk another path…or you. Be open to new possibilities. Let the Spirit guide you. Who knows what you might learn?"

"Is that what you told yourself when you got involved with Liz?"

"Not exactly. It just sort of happened. Sometimes, I felt like I didn't have much choice, like I was caught in a tractor beam."

Olivia smiled at the space opera metaphor. "I didn't know you like sci-fi movies, Lucy."

"I don't especially, but Liz does, so I watch them with her." Lucy responded to Olivia's curious look with a smile. "You make sacrifices when you're in a relationship."

"Sacrifice," Olivia repeated. "What an interesting concept."

❋❋❋

Liz glanced at her watch. She should get this visit over with, so she'd be on time to pick up Emily. She steeled herself before walking into Maggie's room. Watching the procedure from the gallery had been much harder than she'd expected. Over the course of her career, she had performed hundreds of double mastectomies, but her ability to detach herself had eroded since she'd put down her scalpel. Watching the breasts that she'd once caressed be carted away as medical waste had been extremely difficult.

Maggie was dozing, despite the sound of her roommate talking rather loudly on the phone. Liz's fingers instinctively went to Maggie's wrist. No one counted pulse beats anymore. There were gadgets with sensors to do that now, but Liz believed in the healing power of touch. It was one of the reasons she still did physical exams, even though medical associations had written them off as mostly useless. They were a point of connection with the patient that she couldn't get from merely reviewing blood tests.

Maggie stirred and opened her eyes, trying to focus on Liz's face. "Hey, you," she said softly. "How long have you been here?"

"I just came. I wanted to see how you are before I pick up Emily for dinner." Liz brushed a stray strand of hair out of Maggie's face. "How do you feel?"

"Tired. My chest feels like it's been dragged on the road."

"Do you need something for the pain?"

"In a little while. I'm okay for now."

Liz looked under the white cotton hospital blanket. "Your drains are full. I'll call the nurse to empty them."

"Don't call her yet. Talk to me." Maggie smiled tenderly the way she used to when they had first become lovers. Had she forgotten that she hated her? Maybe it was the happy drugs the anesthesiologist had pumped into her. "Thank you for being here for me," Maggie murmured.

"You're welcome," said Liz. She wanted to say that it was her duty as a friend, but she didn't because it wasn't the entire truth. Part of her still cared, just as Lucy had said.

Maggie's hand crawled across the blanket searching for Liz's. Liz took it and found it was cold. She pulled up the other blanket from the foot of the bed.

"I'm sorry about last night. I was scared," Maggie said. "I just wanted to blot out the fear."

"I know. I'm sorry I reacted so harshly."

"No, you were right. I was way out of line. I just wanted you to love me like you used to and make it all go away." Maggie sighed, wincing because taking a deep breath obviously caused her pain. "Jenny and Laura must think I'm crazy."

"Well, you are." She grinned to let Maggie know she was kidding.

Maggie pinched Liz's hand. "Don't be a shit, Liz. I'm in a compromised position and can't defend myself." She grimaced as she tried to move higher on the pillow. "Can you help me sit up?"

"You shouldn't. I'll raise the bed instead." Liz looked around until she located the button. "Is that better?"

"Yes, much."

Liz placed the control in easy reach. "I can't stay. I promised Emily that I would pick her up at seven." Maggie pouted. "I'll call the nurse to empty the drains," She found the call button. "I'll be back tomorrow to look in on you. Around ten. I'll call first in case you need something."

"Okay," said Maggie, looking sad.

"Get some rest now."

Liz headed to the door, but Maggie called her back. She had tears in her eyes. "Liz, I want you to know that I love you."

The declaration startled Liz, but she said, "I love you too." She bent and gently kissed Maggie's foreheads. The nurse had come in behind her. She began fussing with the drains, muttering to herself that she should have checked earlier. Liz used the distraction to cover her escape, but as she rode down to the lobby in the glacially slow elevator, Liz couldn't shake off the odd, little conversation. In the lobby, a former colleague called to her, which briefly distracted her. Heading to the parking garage, she found herself thinking about Maggie again. The idea that Maggie still loved her confused her. Even more confusing was her response.

She knew this wasn't something she could talk about with Lucy. Maybe she should call Tom and set a time to talk. After Liz started the car, she asked Siri to set a reminder to call Tom in the morning. That settled, Liz focused on the happy prospect of seeing Emily again.

Obviously, Emily was excited too. When Liz pulled up, she was waiting on the sidewalk outside the Yale graduate student residence. She was wearing only a thin sweater.

"Why are you waiting out here?" Liz asked when Emily got into the car.

"I know how hard it is to find parking," Emily replied, hugging herself.

"Thank you for thinking of me, but the next time, dress more warmly," said Liz, leaning over to kiss her. "How are you?"

"Fine, except for being cold and hungry," Emily reported in her usual direct tone.

Liz reached in the back for the polar fleece throw she kept in the car for emergencies. "Here, put this around you until you warm up." Her eyes gave the young woman a quick once over.

Whenever she saw her after an absence she was struck by the resemblance to her mother. Seeing her was like a time machine to the past where Liz could see young Lucy, perhaps in her student days at Juilliard. There were differences. Emily's eyes were blue, not green like her mother's, and she was now nearly as tall as Liz. Most importantly, Lucy's personality shined through her smile and her eyes. Emily's was veiled.

"The Guilford Bistro okay with you?" Liz asked, "I thought we'd go somewhere with better parking."

"I wouldn't mind getting out of New Haven. I'm stuck here most of the time."

"You have Erika's car. You should take a ride and enjoy the scenery. It's good for the soul."

"Now, you sound like Mom."

"I'm sure she would put it more poetically," said Liz. "How's school?"

"Okay. They're going to give me a bachelor's degree in January."

"Woohoo. Congratulations."

"It's a formality," replied Emily matter-of-factly.

"Must be nice to be so smart they hand you a degree for doing nothing."

"You should know."

"But I had to study to get into medical school…and when I got there."

"When you went to medical school, you needed to memorize a lot of information. I bet it's different now. It's so easy to access data," said Emily. "I read an article in Fortune that put doctors on a list of dying professions. Supposedly, AI is better at diagnosis than a human. But it won't happen in your lifetime, so you don't have to worry, Aunt Liz." Emily turned in her seat. Liz felt herself being studied curiously. "Do you still want me to call you Aunt Liz after you marry my mother?"

"Call me whatever feels comfortable. Just Liz is fine."

"I called Erika 'Mom.' She seemed okay with it."

Liz knew that Erika had been much more than okay with the idea. The cerebral, controlled woman had been moved to tears when she'd told Liz about it. "As I said, call me whatever works for you. Just don't call me any nasty names in front of your mother." Liz grinned, so Emily would know she was joking. With her emotional deficit, Emily sometimes needed blatant cues to interpret people's communication.

Emily looked thoughtful. "I think I'll still call you Aunt Liz. Not because I won't see you as a stepmother, but because everyone should have an Aunt Liz. Someone who is always there for you, no questions asked. Someone who always tells you the truth."

"Sounds like me," said Liz, happily owning the assessment. "You're a pretty good judge of character, Emily."

"I pay attention. I don't always know why people do things, but I observe them to figure it out. If you watch carefully, you can learn a lot. But you already know that, being a doctor."

"As a matter of fact, I do."

"See? That's why you're a good doctor and won't be replaced by AI." Emily's observations were pointed, but her admiration was almost childlike. Lucy always said that her daughter was young for her age. Emily made up for it by paying scrupulous attention to detail and researching everything exhaustively. Her observations could be savagely accurate, but they were always insightful.

The talk at dinner was mostly about Emily's studies and the revolutionary theorem she had developed with Stefan Bultmann. He was emeritus in the math department at Yale and revered by his former colleagues. The female faculty and graduate assistants kept a close eye on Emily. Their subtle but attentive care was one of the reasons that Lucy had blessed her daughter's plan to move to New Haven.

While they were waiting for their dessert, Emily suddenly asked, "Did Mom tell you I'm seeing Denise?"

Liz merely smiled, not wanting to confirm it. "I can see why you're attracted. You have music in common. How is it going?"

"Good, but we haven't had sex yet," Emily announced loudly enough to worry Liz that someone might overhear. "Is sex as good as they say it is?"

Liz suppressed the urge to chuckle, but she never wanted Emily to think she wasn't taking her seriously. "I think so, but it's especially good with someone you really like."

Emily eyed her carefully. "That's what Mom says. She seems really worried about this."

"Look at it from her point of view. It must be hard to think of her little girl being grown up enough to have sex."

"She didn't know me as a little girl. I was only a baby when she gave me up for adoption."

"True." Liz studied the young woman's freckled face. "Have you had sex with anyone?"

"No, I don't really like people touching me, but I like to touch myself."

This time, Liz tried to be more subtle about looking around to see if anyone had heard. Fortunately, no one seemed to be paying attention. "Emily, are you sure you like girls?" Liz asked, leaning forward.

"No, but I guess I'll find out. Denise is different. She's kind of both, even though she wants to be a woman. She banked her sperm before the operation…in case she wanted kids."

"That was good planning," Liz said.

"I thought so too. Denise is very practical." Emily focused her eyes on Liz's. Making eye contact involved a deliberate effort on her part, so Liz knew something important was coming. "Did you ever want kids?" Emily asked.

Liz heard the hidden question. She wanted to answer honestly but also to reassure Emily that she was wanted. "I love kids, and I've been lucky to have them in my life, but I never saw myself having children of my own. It didn't fit with my career plans."

"But you don't mind having me around?"

"I like having you around. It's fun to talk to such a smart person. That's one reason I miss Erika so much."

Emily's gaze was locked on Liz's eyes again. Another important message was on the way. "Are we having Thanksgiving at your house?" Emily asked.

"Yes."

"Can you invite Denise?"

Liz smiled. "Of course."

# 11

Liz admired the perfectly book-matched chestnut panels in Lucy's closed door. Chestnut trees were virtually extinct in North America. Wide lumber of any type was nearly impossible to find, which was why Sam had started buying up old furniture to reclaim the wood. She said that it was a metaphor for what she was doing at this stage in her life—taking apart the old to build something new.

"Dr. Stolz, can I get you a cup of coffee while you're waiting?" Jodi asked, interrupting Liz's ruminations on the demise of a venerable American species.

"No, thanks, Jodi. I'm awake enough, even though I may not look it."

"Did you run into a lot of traffic coming up from Connecticut?" It was a good guess, but Liz's fatigue came from lack of sleep. She'd awakened in the middle of the night and pondered her conversation with Maggie. They'd never really talked about why the marriage had failed. Once Liz started thinking about it, there was no hope she'd get back to sleep.

"Father Tom should be back any minute now," Jodi assured her in a cheerful, professional tone. She returned to her computer screen, and Liz went back to studying the architecture. Finally, the door opened, and a middle-aged woman emerged, followed by Lucy. They headed to the admin's desk to discuss the next appointment.

Today, Lucy wore black slacks and a gray heather cardigan over her clerical blouse. Her red hair was in a ponytail. She'd been auditioning a more casual look on the days she saw clients to put them at ease.

Jodi pointed in Liz's direction, and Lucy finally turned around.

"Liz! I didn't expect you so soon!" She threw herself into Liz's arms, nearly knocking her down.

"Maggie's daughter showed up early," Liz explained. "I escaped while no one was looking."

"But I have a client at four o'clock," said Lucy with a sad face.

"I know. Jodi told me, but I'm here to see Tom."

Lucy's eyes brightened. "An official visit?"

"Yes, I called him from the road. He said he had time to talk at four."

"Come in for a minute," said Lucy, tugging on Liz's hand. "I have a little time before my next appointment."

"Don't you need a bathroom break or something?"

"No, Doctor, I'm fine," said Lucy, rolling her eyes. "And I've been hydrating like you recommended." Once they were inside her office, Lucy closed the door. "Thought you could get away without giving me a kiss?" She took off her mask and turned up her face. Liz looked down at Lucy's lips, lush with dark lipstick, and needed no further invitation. As soon as their mouths touched, Lucy's lips parted. She backed up to the door for support while Liz explored her warm mouth with her tongue. Finally, Lucy gave her a little nudge to indicate that it needed to end. "Oh, sweetie," she moaned, leaning against her. "You don't know how much I missed you! I wish we could go home right now!"

"Me too. Are you still okay about going out to dinner?"

"Maybe we can do take out, so we can go home…and maybe do other things." Lucy raised an auburn brow suggestively.

"Even better," Liz said.

"Why are you here to see Tom?" Lucy's green eyes were wide with curiosity.

"You know why."

"Oh, Liz, yes! I'm so proud of you!"

"But, Luce, if you're too close to shrink me, why is Tom okay? He's been my friend for years."

"There's a big difference between an old friend and your intimate partner." Lucy pulled Liz into another kiss. "Oh, sweetie, I hate to let you go, but my four o'clock will be waiting." She opened the door a crack, and Liz could see a couple chatting with Jodi. While they were distracted, Liz stole a quick kiss. "I'll see you in an hour," whispered Lucy and pushed her out the door.

Liz was just about to sit down again when Tom came down the hall. His polo shirt and carefully pressed slacks indicated he was coming directly from the golf course. He'd told Liz he'd like to get in a game before their meeting.

"Enjoy your game?" said Liz, getting up to greet him.

"You should try it some time," he said, giving her a half hug. "I'll teach you."

"Nah, golf is too slow for me."

"But you fish."

"Completely different."

Liz felt Lucy's eyes on her while she spoke to Tom and saw her subtly approving look. It inexplicably ignited a spark of childish rebellion. She had the impulse to thank Tom for interrupting his afternoon and leave. Then a memory flashed into her mind—slapping away her grandmother's hand when she tried to teach her to tie her shoes. "No, don't help me!" she'd screamed. She'd invented her own method, using double loops, and stubbornly resisted learning the conventional way, even though her shoes always came untied.

"Come in, Liz," said Tom, opening the door of the office next to Lucy's.

Liz cautiously entered the room, noting the small items Tom had added to the space to make it his own—a photo of the historic church in New Haven that he'd led for decades, some Byzantine religious art, and shelves full of exegetical books and gospel commentaries. "Can she hear us in here?" Liz asked anxiously.

Tom glanced at the wall separating his office from Lucy's. "I can't imagine she could. These old buildings were built right."

"Keeping God's secrets?"

"No, the ordinary human kind." He pointed to an armchair that appeared to be the same vintage as the rectory. "Make yourself comfortable."

Liz sat down, noting that the chairs were placed at a strategically safe distance, so she took off her mask. "I thought we were past the masks," said Liz, pulling hers taut to neaten the folds.

Tom sighed. "So did I. I hope we're not heading for another winter like the last."

"So do I." Liz smiled. "I appreciate you making time for me, Tom."

"Of course, I would make time for you." Tom sat down opposite her. "I'm flattered that you would choose me for counseling. I know how stubborn you are about psychotherapy."

"Professionally, I believe in it. I often recommend it for my patients. Some people really benefit."

"But not Liz Stolz, superhero." Tom's warm smile made it impossible to take offense at the jab.

"In fact, I tried it once."

"Really? You never told me."

"It was long after we lost touch…before we discovered you were living right around the corner from Erika's father."

"One of life's many ironies," Tom agreed.

"I had a rough patch after the malpractice lawsuit was decided in my favor. I was so relieved that I'd been cleared that I was walking on air. Then the balloon deflated, and I fell flat." Liz smacked her hands together.

"When we build something up and have so much expectation, it's often a disappointment. Or we're left without something to look forward to, and there's a void."

"The abyss looking back…"

"Now, there's a man who could have used therapy!"

"Some people think Nietzsche was syphilitic," said Liz, steepling her hands. "In that case, antibiotics were what he really needed, but penicillin wasn't discovered until 1928, and it couldn't be produced in useful quantities until World War Two. Sulfa drugs were relatively effective, but…" Tom gave her an impatient look, which Liz knew she entirely deserved. She was being an encyclopedia of useless information again. Reluctantly, she returned to the original subject. "Unfortunately, the therapist I chose was a dim bulb, and I could run circles around her. She never seemed to recognize that I was playing her."

"Maybe she did, but she was letting you go on to see if it would bring up something useful."

Liz shook her head. "No, I'm quite sure she didn't get it. After I realized as much, I intentionally obfuscated for the pleasure of seeing her puzzled face."

Tom clucked his tongue. "You're bad."

"I thought counselors weren't supposed to judge their clients."

"I'm not counseling you. We're talking as friends. If I think you need more, I'll probably refer you to someone, but let's see how it goes."

"At least, I don't have to tell you my entire life story. You already know a lot about me."

"I do, but there's a lot about you I don't know. There were all those missing years."

Liz shrugged. "You didn't miss much. I was busy impersonating a successful career woman."

"The success was genuine."

"Yes, but playing the game to get there wasn't."

"That sounds like a big topic. Do you want to talk about it?"

"Not today. I resolved the problem by quitting my job and coming up to Maine. I still haven't completely made the transition, but maybe I will by the time I retire."

"You're not alone. I haven't figured out what I want to be when I grow up."

Liz gave herself a moment to figure out how to begin. On the way up from New Haven, she'd been rehearsing what she wanted to say to Tom. Now that she sat across from one of her oldest friends, the words sounded contrived.

"When you called, you mentioned unfinished business with Maggie," said Tom, offering her an opening.

"Maybe that was misleading. The business is finished, at least in terms of the marriage."

Tom nodded but didn't look convinced.

Liz stared at the golden image on Tom's desk. "That's a beautiful icon. Who is it?"

"Thomas, the apostle. Better known as Doubting Thomas. I keep it near, not only because he's my namesake, but to remind me that healthy skepticism is good." Tom gave her a firm look. He was not having the diversion. "Is supporting Maggie through her cancer treatments bringing up uncomfortable feelings?"

"Well, of course. I'm upset that the cancer has recurred, even though I knew it was more or less inevitable."

"You knew it, and yet you married her."

"That's why I married her. To assure her that I wouldn't run out on her because of the cancer. In fact, if Maggie hadn't asked for a divorce, I think I would have stayed in the marriage. I believe in keeping my word."

"That doesn't surprise me. You were raised with a strong sense of responsibility, but when I first met you, you used to brag about your conquests."

"That was then. When I was in my twenties, I prided myself on being a heartbreaker. After Maggie left me in college, I spent the next decade seducing women and leaving them to get back at her."

"You used other women to get revenge on her? How did that work?"

"It didn't really. She had no way of knowing because she wasn't speaking to me. And it only made me feel bad about myself. I don't do that anymore. I've grown up."

"Have you? Was all that flirting with Lucy just for fun?"

"Yes, at first."

"But then it became serious. If you'd stayed in your marriage, how would you have handled the powerful attraction to Lucy?"

"I don't know. We tried to stay away from one another, but we couldn't. It wasn't a matter of will power. That didn't even come into play. It was like being drunk all the time. I had no idea what I was doing."

"But you did know what you were doing," said Tom, raising his chin in challenge.

"Yes, I could see myself doing it, but I couldn't stop it."

"How did it make you feel to be so out of control?"

Liz thought for a moment. "It was terrifying, especially because I'd been trained to keep my emotions under control and to myself. But it's impossible when I hear Lucy sing."

"So, it was her voice that attracted you."

"And her radiance. Although, in the beginning, I really didn't pay much attention to her. She was beautiful and entertaining, but she was Maggie's friend. I had no interest in the girlie things they shared. Then Erika gave me some copies of Lucy's recordings. When I work in my shop, I listen to music through Bluetooth hearing protectors, but Lucy's voice can never be background music. Whenever I play one of her recordings, I turn off the machinery, so I can really listen. More often than not, I end up standing at my table saw, crying like a baby."

"Oh, Liz, you do love your divas. The absurd amounts of money you and Erika paid to hear your favorites sing."

"One of my biggest regrets is that I only heard Lucy sing at the Met once. By the time I'd discovered her, my surgical career had become demanding, and I had no time to go to the opera. When I finally did, Lucy's singing career was nearly over. It's criminal that she was forced out of the Met because that bastard raped her and then lied about it. If we didn't have those recordings, her talent would have been forgotten."

"Her singing touches the emotions you usually keep hidden, so you're drawn to her. But she was married to your best friend."

"Yes, which is why I stayed away. Then Erika and Lucy came to live with us because their refrigerator died. We had a houseful of talented musicians, so it made perfect sense for us to entertain ourselves with music. That's when Lucy began to sing at my request, and I fell more deeply in love with her. I also got to know her and discovered that she was intelligent and funny. She didn't push her religion on me, which I appreciated, even though she was broadcasting her services from my house."

"Which was a gift to the community."

"Glad you think so. I'll never see my media room the same way again. One night while they were living there, I told Lucy that I loved her. She was flustered but she let me down gently. She gave me a little speech about Philos, Agape, and Caritas, speaking in theological babytalk because she thought I wouldn't understand. I did, of course. You'll be happy to know I resisted the impulse to lecture her on the subject."

"I'm surprised, Liz. You never turn down an argument. What stopped you?"

"Lucy was explaining to me with such kindness why we couldn't be lovers. It wasn't a game like when I argued with you or Erika. I didn't have to win. In her dear, sweet Lucy way, she was telling me how much she loved me."

"But how can you respect Lucy if you have such low regard for her intelligence?"

"As I got to know her, I perceived that her intelligence is different. It isn't sharp and brittle like ours. It's round and lush—feminine, if you will. She's every bit as intelligent as we are, but she expresses herself differently. It's as if she speaks another language that I'm just beginning to understand."

"Lucy has strong emotional intelligence. That's why she makes such a good counselor and priest."

"She never lets me get away with anything, but she doesn't nail me. She looks at me with those big green eyes, patiently waiting for me to tell her the truth, and I tell her because I can't stop myself."

"She sees you."

"Yes."

"But what happened after Lucy's little talk about the different kinds of love?"

"She tried to convince me to go back to a little game we played. She was my lady; I was her knight. Very romantic and operatic." Liz sang the opening bars of Lohengrin's "Grail Song." "Not innocent by any means, but mostly harmless."

"And Maggie? Did she know this was going on?"

"Of course, it was very public, but she must have sensed the change. She became much more interested in sex, which had to be deliberate because her libido is depressed by anti-hormone drugs. I think she was trying to give Lucy competition. Fortunately, Erika's refrigerator turned up, and they moved out. Just in time."

Tom nodded thoughtfully as he reflected. "You could have left it there, but you didn't."

"No, unfortunately not. Once the spark was ignited, I couldn't put it out."

"That's the past, and we'll get back to it, but what about now? I'm sure it isn't easy to support Maggie through her cancer with all these conflicting emotions swirling inside you, especially your anger. That was my biggest concern when Lucy told me you intended to marry."

"It was easier when I thought I hated Maggie. Now, I'm not so sure. When she was coming out of anesthesia, she told me that she loved me. It might have been the drugs. Sometimes, they cause euphoria and make people suddenly generous."

"How did you respond?"

"I told her that I loved her too, and I do. I love her deeply."

"It sounds like you still have strong feelings for her. Are you sure there's no possibility of a reconciliation?"

Liz shook her head. "By the time Maggie asked for a divorce, our communication had completely broken down. We did the information exchange, but otherwise we barely talked. After she forced Lucy to confess that I'd kissed her, Maggie gave me the silent treatment. She wouldn't let go of her jealousy, no matter how many times I apologized, or what I did or didn't do. She became suspicious of everyone and asked me to account for my whereabouts. It was so annoying that I told her where I was going before she even asked. One day, I became sick of it and stopped telling her anything at all. Then she complained that I never talked to her."

"Because you didn't."

"I had nothing more to say. When she told me about fucking her boy toy, knowing it was a red line for me, the marriage was over. Even now, when I think about her marrying that idiot, Barry Krusick, I become insanely jealous. I go into a rage about something that happened in 1975!"

Liz looked up to see that Tom was regarding her warily. "At least, you know it's irrational. Fortunately, you have good impulse control, especially with all those guns you keep in your house."

"I would never hurt anyone, least of all Maggie," said Liz quickly to reassure him.

He still looked concerned, but his frown had lessened. "Your anger with Maggie goes back a long time. I remember you talking about it when we met forty-five years ago."

"Then, it was still fresh in my mind. I was in a bad way when Maggie left me in college. It took me a long time to let it go."

"If it still causes such strong feelings all these years later, you haven't let it go. It sounds like your anger is a response to the pain of rejection. I'm guessing the pattern goes deeper than your college experience with Maggie." Tom gazed thoughtfully out the window. "This isn't something that can be solved in an hour's talk with me. I can ask Lucy to suggest a referral, but I doubt you have the patience for long-term therapy."

"You can be sure I don't," said Liz with a challenging stare. "I only came to you because of this mess with Maggie. I didn't want to be involved again, but the cancer gave me no choice."

"Well, Liz, you did have a choice. You could have said no, but your strong sense of loyalty and responsibility won't allow it, so in that sense, you didn't."

"Soft determinism?"

"Let's save that debate for another time. For now, we need to figure out how to deal with your problem. If we can chip away at the anger that consumes you, it might help you deal with Maggie. How does that sound?"

Liz didn't look forward to more of this torture, but she agreed.

***

Lucy glanced at her watch, surprised to see Tom's door was still closed.

His session with Liz should have ended by now. She wondered how much longer it would go on. Although she was the one who'd encouraged Liz to seek counseling, she now felt prickles of embarrassment over what Liz might be telling Tom. Liz could speak more openly about sex than her feelings. The idea that she might be talking about their sex life to a man she worked with left Lucy feeling exposed.

She avoided thinking about Liz and Tom by turning her mind to her last appointment. She'd been counseling a couple who were both divorced, which had caused her to reread the bishop's guidance on remarriage. It advised waiting a year after the divorce filing. Lucy didn't mind waiting. Hopefully by then, she'd have had more time to grieve, and Liz would have sorted out her feelings about Maggie. But the other part of the guidance made her uncomfortable. Could she honestly say she hadn't caused the divorce? Her response to that unsolicited kiss had lasted only a few seconds. Liz and Lucy had dutifully stayed in their marriages. Technically, they had done the right thing, but Lucy couldn't dismiss it as being that simple.

Instead of interrupting the therapy session, Lucy sent a text message to let Liz know she would pick up dinner. The idea that she could choose what they were going to eat gave her a little thrill. Sometimes, she missed the complete independence of single life. The thought of a comforting Pad Thai made her mouth water. Her lunch had been a wolfed-down tuna sandwich from the prepared food case in the supermarket, tasteless compared to the lunches Liz packed for her.

Before heading to the Thai restaurant, Lucy stopped by the beach house to pick up clothes for the next day. While she was waiting for their food order, a text message from Liz came in: *Thank you for picking up dinner. Mine with shrimp.* Another text instantly followed, Liz remembering her manners: *Please.*

Lucy smiled because she'd gotten the order right—not that she could change it now. It was easy to guess what Liz wanted for dinner. Despite her wide culinary repertoire, she had favorites at local restaurants. Unless a special was compelling, she always ordered the same thing.

The phone rang, and Lucy stepped back from the hostess' desk to answer it. "Hello, Sweetie. Did you have a good session with Tom?"

"I guess so."

"Well, do you feel better?"

"No, but I have a lot to think about."

A little finger of anxiety poked Lucy as she wondered what had been discussed. She could hear the engine and roadway in the background. "Where are you?"

"On the way home. Almost there."

The hostess brought out the paper bag with their takeout order. "Our dinner is here," said Lucy. "I'll be there in a few minutes."

Liz, dressed in jeans and a hoodie, came out to help Lucy in with her bags. She waited until they were inside to kiss her. "No need to entertain our young neighbors." Liz's kiss was a quick, dry peck. Not what Lucy had expected after days of separation. She tried to read into its cool temperature, then decided she was overlaying it with her own concerns. "I'll bring your bag upstairs," Liz offered.

"It can wait. Let's eat first."

Liz took out dinner plates from the cabinet. Despite her informality, she still liked to eat takeout food on real plates. The one exception was lobster rolls.

"Thank you for bringing this," said Liz, digging into the fragrant mass of noodles. Lucy took a moment to give thanks before picking up her chopsticks. Knowing Liz's aversion to prayer, she never asked Liz to participate and only formally prayed before meals when they had company.

"I told Tom I'd rather have him marry us than your bishop," said Liz casually.

"What did he say?"

"That it was an enormous honor to be married by the bishop, and I should accept it graciously."

"I knew he would understand."

"He might understand, but I don't. And why didn't you tell me we needed to wait a year after the divorce was filed?" Although Liz's challenging tone was mild, Lucy tensed.

"I didn't think it would matter to you. It's not as if we were waiting until marriage to have sex."

Lucy watched Liz's face, waiting for her to argue, but she nodded and returned to eating her dinner.

"How is Sophia?" asked Lucy, trying to keep the conversation going. "Was she friendly?"

"Fortunately, the girls are smart enough not to take sides."

"They're not girls, Liz. They're in their thirties."

"They're girls to me," Liz answered. "Do you want some wine? I think there's a bottle of white open in the fridge."

"Sure," said Lucy, staring at Liz's backside while she rummaged in the refrigerator, but she wasn't thinking it was attractive, even though it was. She was wondering why she needed to yank conversation out of Liz. The rest of dinner went much the same way—Lucy feeling forced to extract information while Liz inhaled her Pad Thai.

As usual, Lucy couldn't finish. "I'll pack your leftovers for your lunch tomorrow," Liz offered. "Go study while I clean up the kitchen."

Listening to the clatter of dishes in the kitchen, which sounded louder than usual, Lucy wondered if she should have stayed home and given Liz an opportunity to process her counseling session. The wish was partially selfish because she was tired and needed to prepare for a class that one of her professors had asked her to lead. Usually, such assignments went to students who needed to develop confidence in front of an audience. After years on the stage and in the pulpit, Lucy had no lack of confidence. She'd only agreed to do this project because the professor had confided he wanted to use her as a role model.

Liz flopped on the sofa beside her, startling her. "Feet, here," she instructed, patting her thigh. Lucy smiled in anticipation of a foot massage and the little game to see how long she could concentrate on her work while Liz skillfully kneaded the muscles and bones in her feet. Mesmerized, Lucy put down her book and enjoyed the pleasure. When she opened her eyes, she saw Liz's hands were working independently of her mind.

"Liz, what are you thinking about?"

"My conversation with Tom."

Lucy waited, hoping Liz would say more, but she didn't. "I don't expect you to share what you talk about with Tom," said Lucy, knowing lack of interest would get her further than overt curiosity. "But if you need to talk about anything—in general, I mean—I'll listen."

"Let's go on a trip," Liz suddenly said.

"What?" asked Lucy, startled by the sharp diversion from the topic.

"The whole cancer thing is depressing. I'm so done with this pandemic. I need to get out of here. Let's go camping this weekend."

Lucy heard the urgency in Liz's voice and hated to disappoint her. "Oh, Liz, I can't. The church harvest fair is on Saturday." It was obvious from the look on Liz's face that she'd forgotten all about it. "I could really use your help. Plus, you'll be expected to be there."

"But I would like to get in one last trip up North before winter sets in. It's probably too late to book a cabin at Moosehead unless it's one of those rustic hunting cabins, where the only heat is a wood stove, and the plumbing is iffy. Last time I stayed in one of those places, the toilet backed up."

Lucy wrinkled her nose.

"Yeah, not really your style." Inspiration suddenly dawned on Liz's face. "But we could take the boat up to Casco Bay. If it's too cold to sleep on the boat, I'm sure we can find a room somewhere."

"I like that idea better," Lucy said. "I don't know about sleeping on the boat, but it might be fun."

"That's what I love about you. You'll try anything."

"Liz, I don't see myself getting any work done tonight. Let's go to bed." Liz raised her hand to look at her watch. "I know it's still early, but I missed you," explained Lucy.

In anticipation of a passionate reunion, she had brought a fancy nightgown, but now she sat in bed, chin on her knees, hugging herself while the shower water beat against the wall. Despite the obvious sign of Liz's presence, she felt alone. She'd seen Liz retreat into her mind before. It was a place Lucy couldn't reach with words or even touch with her body. Sometimes, she simply had to wait for the door to open again and let her in. Lucy thought she had learned the value of patience in countless therapy sessions, but when it came to the woman she loved, it was different.

The water cut off and the hair dryer went on. Liz never came to bed with wet hair.

Instead of getting under the covers, Liz sat at the end of the bed. "Lucy, you look beautiful, and all I want to do is make love to you, but there's something I need to tell you." The tone in Liz's voice, along with an extended pause, filled Lucy with dread. Finally, Liz continued. "The night before the surgery, Maggie came into my room." Lucy blinked. This wasn't what she'd expected. "She wanted me to hold her because she was frightened. I was exhausted from the drive, so I didn't argue and let her get into bed with me."

Lucy drew on all her skills as a therapist to maintain a neutral expression. "Did you have sex?" she asked. She held her breath while she waited for the answer.

"No, but she tried. I woke up with her hand between my legs." Hearing it stated so bluntly shocked Lucy more than she might have expected. She quickly ejected the image that formed in her mind.

"How did you handle that?"

"I threw her out, but she stood outside my door crying. I felt bad for being so mean."

"You weren't mean, Liz. You were setting boundaries. Maybe you could have been kinder, but you were probably shocked and angry that she dared to test them in that way."

"Hell, yeah. Especially because we hadn't had sex for such a long time before we broke up."

Despite the tension, Lucy laughed. "Liz, for you, a long time is a day!"

Liz frowned as she studied Lucy's face. "You're angry."

Lucy threw off the control she'd learned as a therapist and examined her feelings. "Yes, actually, I am."

"You don't look angry."

"Not everyone screams and yells when they're angry. It's still sinking in. I'm shocked that you didn't know better."

"I thought it was harmless. She only asked me to hold her."

"For someone who's had so many female lovers, you don't know much about women, do you?"

"What do you mean?"

"Obviously, Maggie was manipulating you, and you were stupid enough to fall for it."

"Lucy..."

"Don't 'Lucy' me! You know what you did was wrong. You never should have let her into your bed in the first place. What were you thinking?"

"I don't know. Yes, I should have known better. After I discovered the cancer, sex was the only thing that could block Maggie's anxiety."

"Then you certainly should have known better. Liz, you say you love me. You asked me to marry you. That means making a commitment to me and only me. I am not going to put up with your antics with other women. I understand why you need to support Maggie through the cancer, but I feel angry and hurt that you let her into your bed. From now on, there is only one woman in your bed, and that's me. Do you understand?"

"Yes, Lucy, and I'm sorry, really and truly sorry."

"I'm not kidding you, Liz. I'm not going to watch you flirt with other women. If that's your plan, tell me now, and we'll end it here."

"No, Lucy. I love you, only you. And I am so sorry this happened."

Lucy gave Liz a hard look. "You didn't have to tell me about this. I'll give you some credit for that."

"Oh, I did have to tell you. I never wanted you to find out from Jenny, who likes to make trouble, or Maggie, who would love to break us up. And...I felt guilty because I knew it was stupid."

Lucy let out a long sigh. She lifted the quilt. "Get in."

# 12

Megan had awakened in a sulky mood, scowling under her blond brows at anyone who came near. She contrarily held up the wrong foot when Cherie tried to help her into her shoes and squirmed in her seat when she tried to brush her hair.

Cherie wondered if the children sensed their worry about the hearing. She knew that kids were like satellite dishes, picking up remote signals from the adults orbiting around them. Cherie's instincts told her to avoid mentioning the possibility that a distant relative might take them away. Lucy had concurred when Cherie had asked her advice. "Don't worry them before the fact. Have faith. Say a prayer for the best outcome." Without any prompting from her pastor, Cherie had been praying fervently.

"Good morning, everyone," Brenda said, coming into the kitchen. She looked smart in a blazer and dress slacks, but not as impressive as in her uniform.

"Are you still okay with dropping off the kids at school?" Cherie asked. "We could put them on the bus."

"No, it's okay. I told Melissa we would meet them at the diner for coffee. The timing works out just right." Brenda's warm lips on the back of her neck made Cherie wish they could stay home instead. Since the kids had come into their lives, opportunities for sex were less frequent. Their busy jobs and adjusting to being full-time parents left them exhausted at the end of the day. Most nights, their heads hit the pillow, and they went out cold.

"I wasn't so sure about Melissa when Liz first introduced her," said Brenda, "but I like her. She certainly is saving us a ton of money handling our case."

"Hopefully, she gets the job done. She admits she doesn't have much experience in family law. Maybe we should have found a lawyer who does."

Brenda put her arms around Cherie. "Honey, sometimes, you worry too much. Look at all the people who are testifying for us. With all those heavy hitters, we've got it made!" Cherie gave her a skeptical look. "Yeah, I know. I'm worried too."

"I liked it better when you were optimistic."

"Me too."

Cherie sighed. "All we can do is hope for the best."

The adults were silent as they drove to the school, determined not to infect the children with their fears. In the back seat, the kids were playing a game—trying to find the most beautiful tree among the brilliant orange and scarlet maples.

"Mama C, which tree do you like best?" asked Megan, inviting Cherie to play.

"They're all pretty. I never get enough of seeing the fall colors here in the North."

"Why do the trees change color?" Keith asked.

"Because the trees are getting ready to sleep for the winter. Before they say goodbye, they have one last, big party. All summer long, they made food in the green part of the leaf. But when summer's over, the trees stop making green chlorophyll. Hiding under it, like the crayons in the back of the box you save for special occasions, are those yellows and oranges and reds, just waiting to come out!"

Brenda, who was driving, glanced in Cherie's direction. "What a great explanation. Even I understood it."

Cherie reached out and patted her thigh. "Thank you, sweetie pie."

When they dropped the children off at school, Cherie held them longer and tighter than usual. "I just want this to be over," she murmured, watching the children head into the building.

"I know, baby," Brenda said. "Me too."

The anxious silence resumed as they drove to the diner. Cherie felt a little better when she saw Lucy's car parked next to Courtney's old Subaru. She felt even more confident when they found their friends seated at Liz's usual table in the back.

"Where's Liz?" Brenda asked, looking around.

"At the office," explained Lucy. "She's talking to Amy about the vaccine rollout for young children. She says approval is close, and this time, they're going to use primary care offices to distribute it."

"They should have done that right from the beginning," said Cherie. "There would have been a lot more compliance. When your doctor tells you that you need something, it has a lot more impact than when the government tells you."

Melissa moved over to make room for them. "Have a seat and let's review our strategy." She waved to Lois, the morning waitress, to bring more coffee. "I spoke to Liz last night to prep her. I'm going to lead with her testimony. She's had experience testifying in court as an expert witness and, unfortunately, defending herself against that malpractice suit. She has roots in this state and knows you two the longest."

"When I was working homicide in New York, I had to take the stand many times," Brenda said. "Every situation is different, depending on the prosecutor and the judge."

"I did a little research on this judge," Melissa said. "Although she keeps her party affiliation quiet—as she should—she came in under a Republican administration, She's a strong advocate for the rights of fathers in custody battles. I'm guessing she leans conservative."

"Maybe I should have worn my uniform," said Brenda. "You know. 'Blue Lives Matter.'"

"The fact that you are the police chief won't hurt. As a potential parent, you check all the right boxes—employed in a good job, homeowner, married…all the things the plaintiff is not."

"Part of me feels sad for this woman," said Lucy. "Going through all this effort for such a small amount of money."

"To some people, fourteen thousand dollars is a lot of money!" Courtney said, looking offended. "Especially if you have student loan debt like me."

"I'm sorry, Courtney," said Lucy, reaching across the table to pat Courtney's hand. "I didn't mean it the way it sounded."

Cherie gave Courtney a sympathetic look. They'd both gone back to school for advanced degrees long after college, and Cherie was still paying back student loans for her PA training. Sometimes, it seemed she would be making loan payments until she died.

"The irony is, the mother's cousin won't even get the money," said Melissa. "It will be in trust for the kids. I'm guessing her lawyer thinks she'll get her client appointed the trustee, but that's a long shot. Usually, the trustee is a disinterested party."

"Do you think she really wants the children?" asked Lucy.

Melissa raised her shoulders. "It's possible. I haven't met her. She may feel some family obligation to look after them. Who knows?" She glanced at her watch. "We should head up to the courthouse soon. I don't know what's keeping Liz." She glanced anxiously at the door.

"I'll give her a call on the way," offered Lucy.

***

"Thanks for holding down the fort while I was in New Haven," said Liz, getting up from the visitor's chair in Amy's office. "I hate to ask you for another favor, but I want to take my boat up to Casco Bay for a couple of days before it gets too cold. Do you mind covering for me?"

"No, just give me the dates. I think you could use a little vacation after dealing with your ex-wife's cancer."

"The timing sucked, but there's never a good time for cancer. Sometimes, I think I shouldn't have discouraged her from having the double mastectomy years ago. A lot of BRCA women are opting for it now."

"Stop second-guessing yourself, Liz. You know as well as I do, the most drastic solution isn't necessarily the right one."

Liz was surprised to be lectured by her junior partner, especially someone so new, but it felt comfortable. It had been a long time since she'd openly discussed her professional regrets with another physician—not since she'd lived with Jenny. "Thank you for listening…and for covering for me."

"Just wait. I'm saving up the favors. Christmas is coming, and I haven't had a vacation in a year." Amy tapped Liz's arm. "Only kidding, and I don't mind keeping an eye on things here."

Liz's phone vibrated in her pocket. She took it out and saw Lucy's face with one of her solar-flare smiles. "I've got to take this," she said to Amy. "I'm leaving right now," she said into the phone.

"Liz, you can't be late. Melissa intends to call you first."

"I know. I'm on my way out the door, but thanks for the reminder." As she hung up, Liz realized that Lucy's gentle prodding didn't bother her the way Maggie's had. "I'm an adult," she'd snap in a surly voice. "I don't need you to tell me what to do." There had been a time when Liz appreciated how well Maggie took care of her—packing lunch, insisting that she rest when she had a cold, covering her with an afghan when she fell asleep on the sofa after dinner. When had she begun to perceive it as intrusive?

Liz got distracted listening to her messages when she went back to her office to get her bag. Sam appeared at her door, wearing an outfit appropriate to giving testimony in court—a sleek pantsuit and dress shoes.

"Sam. What are you doing here?" Liz asked, looking up.

"I wanted to check on the furniture they delivered yesterday. I was glad you were gone a few days, so I could get your office done. How do you like it?" asked Sam, casually inspecting the work.

"Looks beautiful. I'm sure my patients will appreciate those new chairs. The others were literally a pain in the ass." Sam smiled. Liz guessed she was thinking, "I told you so."

"Do you mind if I ride with you? I don't know where this place is." Liz wondered why she didn't just use her GPS until she realized Sam was looking for an opportunity to spend time with her.

"Sure. Why not? I can drop you off here when we get back." Liz opened the safe where she kept her gun purse. She took the pistol out of its holster, knowing they wouldn't let her take it into the courthouse.

"Good idea," said Sam, watching her. "You don't want the guard to take it away at the door."

"No, that would be embarrassing."

Before she got into her car, Liz exchanged her heels for flats. "Can't drive in these fucking things," she complained to Sam. "Never mind that I can barely walk."

"But that power suit needs heels. Plus, being taller than anyone in the room intimidates people."

"That's the idea," said Liz, looking Sam over. "You look pretty spiffy yourself. Did you come to the office to show Amy how well you clean up?"

Sam laughed. "No. She's seen me in my grown-up clothes. And we're not seeing each other anymore."

Liz yanked down her seat belt. "When did this happen?"

"A few weeks ago. We agreed that friendship is better for now."

"That was fast," said Liz. "I hadn't seen you two going out to lunch in a while and wondered why. Thanks for keeping me in the loop."

Sam evidently heard the sarcasm. "I don't have to tell you everything," she replied in a slightly belligerent voice. "You didn't tell me when you got engaged to Lucy."

Liz looked over her shoulder to back up, ignoring the video feed on the dashboard. "That was her idea. She thought we should tell everyone at the same time, so no one's feelings got hurt. So instead, everyone was pissed off. Can't win."

"Pissed off? Really? I think people were just surprised it all happened so fast. Not me. You told me when you kissed Lucy on the boat because there was no one else to tell."

"Sam, that's not true! I told you because you're my friend, and I needed someone to confide in. Obviously, I couldn't tell Erika."

"She was your wingman. I'm just the alt."

Liz glanced at Sam to gauge how big an issue this was. Fortunately, she didn't seem particularly upset.

"When is Maggie coming back from New Haven?" asked Sam. "If we didn't have this damned hearing, I would have gone down to visit her."

"That's kind of you, but she should be coming home tomorrow. Going to New Haven is beyond the call of duty." An uncomfortable idea occurred to Liz. "Sam, you're not interested in Maggie, are you?"

"What if I am? Is that any of your business?"

"No. We're divorced. She can do whatever she wants now," Liz declared with bravado, but she felt a twinge of jealousy. "Are you? Interested, I mean?"

"I've always found Maggie attractive, but when she was married to you, she was off-limits."

Liz knew Sam preferred feminine women and Liz could see why she would find Maggie, with her carefully crafted glamor, attractive. "Is that why you were around so much when you came up on vacation? And I thought it was to hang out with me."

"It was…and for Maggie's gourmet dinners." Liz felt Sam's eyes boring into the side of her face. "Please say it doesn't matter to you."

"I can't, because it does matter. I care about both of you, and I don't want to see anyone get hurt. This mess has caused enough pain."

"It sure has."

"But watch out, Sam. Maggie's really needy right now. If you think Olivia was demanding, wait until you meet the real Maggie."

"It's different. Olivia wanted to run my life. Maggie appreciates my attention, but she doesn't expect it."

Liz bit her tongue. Anything she said would sound like sour grapes. "Just keep your eyes open, Sam. Don't jump in too fast."

"Considering the source, I'll take that advice with a mountain of salt."

❊❊❊

Lucy glanced at the clock over the courtroom door. She rubbed her hands to bring back the circulation because she'd been gripping her seat. The hard wooden benches reminded her of unyielding church pews. The association was strong enough to incline her fellow witnesses to speak softly while they waited, except Olivia, who was completely silent and sat apart from the others. She looked prim in a fitted suit that could have come out of their mothers' era. All she needed was a hat and white gloves to complete the look.

*Five minutes to go.* Lucy silently prayed that Liz would get there in time. A moment later, an extremely tall woman appeared in the doorway. Few women could rock a power suit like Liz Stolz. Sam, standing behind her, was nearly as tall as her friend, but somehow, she seemed small beside her. Lucy knew it had nothing to do with height. 'It's attitude, not altitude,' as Liz liked to say. No matter how much Liz tried to deny her female power, when she chose to summon it, she simply radiated authority and control.

"You look terrific," Lucy whispered as Liz sat down beside her.

"So do you," Liz whispered back, "but you always do."

Lucy watched Sam take a seat two benches back, obviously to avoid Olivia, who kept her eyes focused straight ahead. Clearly, they were aware of one another but purposely creating distance. The thought saddened Lucy. In their small community, any animosity could be felt by everyone. It was the one reason Lucy was glad when Maggie had decided to leave Hobbs after the divorce.

Cherie turned around and waved. She was smiling bravely. Lucy was tempted to go up to the counsel's table to offer Cherie and Brenda some words of encouragement, but the hearing would begin any minute.

"Sam came up with you?" Lucy asked, leaning toward Liz.

"Yes, she wanted to talk. I'll tell you about it later." Liz eyed Olivia, who seemed to be ignoring them, but she was probably close enough to hear.

The door behind the judge's bench opened. "All rise," called the bailiff.

Lucy scrutinized the judge. The careful attention she'd given her appearance went beyond being well groomed. Her dark eyebrows had been emphasized with pencil. Her cheekbones had been sculpted with blush. Her mouth had been enhanced with dark red lipstick. Her face was like a mask, allowing her expressions, or in this case, the lack of them, to be seen all the way to the back of the courtroom.

"Good morning, everyone. Today, we will hear arguments regarding the adoption of Keith and Megan Benoit. Counsel for the plaintiffs, you may proceed."

The cousin seeking custody lived in the northern part of the state, where the children's mother had grown up. She wore too much makeup, and her glittery outfit was more appropriate for a wedding than a courtroom. Her lawyer, a young woman, was fashionably dressed. "Ms. Papin, can you tell the court why you want custody of your cousin's children?" she asked with a pronounced Maine accent.

The witness began speaking in a soft, thin voice. "I was raised to believe that blood is thicker than water. I can't let Linda's kids go to strangers." She glared at Brenda and Cherie. Her voice grew stronger as she seemed to remember her lines. "I think kids should be raised in a normal home. Boys, especially, need a man around." She gazed lovingly at a scruffy man, whose beard overflowed his shirt collar.

"Can you describe the provisions you've made for the children?"

"We sold the trailer, so we can rent a little house. Each child will have a room of their own. I got a full-time job at CVS. I wanted to become a pharmacy tech, but they told me I couldn't because of the drug charge."

Her attorney gave her a sharp look. Obviously, that hadn't been in the script. "Your honor, move to strike that from the record."

The court recorder looked up expectantly.

"I'll allow it. Proceed."

Finally, it was Melissa's turn to examine the witness. She looked sophisticated and confident compared to the opposing counsel. "Ms. Papin, when was the last time you saw Keith and Megan?"

"I was at Keith's christening."

"That was when…six years ago?"

"Yes, Linda and Mike still lived in the county."

"By the county, you mean Aroostook County?"

The woman smiled. "Is there any other?"

There was a murmur of laughter. "We know that people who live there think it's special," Melissa said with a smile. "How about Megan? When was the last time you saw her?"

"We've never met," the woman admitted, pulling up her shoulders protectively.

"No further questions," said Melissa, looking satisfied that she'd made her point.

The burly man who'd been sitting beside Ms. Papin took the stand. He looked stiff and awkward wearing a tie, which he kept adjusting. The creases of his button-down shirt showed it was straight out of the package. Obviously, he had been cleaned up for the hearing. He shifted uncomfortably in the witness chair as he described his job as a motorcycle and snowmobile mechanic.

After he stepped down, the plaintiff's attorney called an older woman. Her testimony was frequently interrupted by a bronchial cough, and her wrinkled, yellow skin identified her as a long-time smoker. She stated that she was the boyfriend's mother and promised to make herself available to babysit after school.

Lucy admired how the lawyer, despite having little to work with, had methodically built her case. She began to worry that the outcome might not be as certain as Melissa had expected.

Now, it was Brenda's turn. She took the stand and answered Melissa's questions about her background as a police officer, her decorations for heroism in New York, and her financial standing. "You own your own home?"

"I do. And my mortgage will be paid off in two years," Brenda said proudly.

"Congratulations," said Melissa. "I'm sure you're looking forward to that."

"You have no idea."

There was a murmur of sympathetic laughter.

Cherie was next. She explained that she was a licensed therapist in addition to being a physician's assistant. If someone had been keeping score, there were certainly more points in Brenda and Cherie's column than the plaintiffs'.

"Your honor, if it please the court, I would like to call some character witnesses to testify regarding the couple's fitness to be parents." The judge signaled her permission with a gesture. "I call Dr. Elizabeth Stolz to the stand."

"Good luck," Lucy whispered.

Liz smoothed down her skirt and strode toward the witness stand. After she was sworn in, Melissa approached.

"Dr. Stolz, please state your full name for the record."

"Elizabeth Anne Stolz."

"You are a physician and surgeon by profession?"

"I am a board-certified surgeon, but I now practice family medicine in Hobbs."

"How long have you known the parties who wish to adopt the Benoit children?"

"Chief Harrison and I have known one another since I bought Hobbs Family Practice ten years ago. We regularly work together, but we know one another socially as well."

"So, you would say you know Brenda Harrison well?"

"Yes, I would say we are close friends."

"And Cherie Bois. How do you know her?"

"Ms. Bois is my physician's assistant. She has been employed by our practice for more than two years."

"Tell us why you think these two women would make good parents."

"Chief Harrison and Ms. Bois are responsible, quiet living people. I have personally observed how the chief disciplines her officers. She is always kind but gets her point across. Rather than being punitive, she uses the opportunity for improvement. Ms. Bois is highly rated by her patients for caring and listening to their needs. She is one of the kindest people I have ever known."

"Thank you, Dr. Stolz. Is there anything you'd like to add?"

"Separately or together, these two women would make exceptionally good parents."

Melissa glanced at the table where the opposing attorney sat. "Do you have questions for this witness?"

"As a matter of fact, I do," said the woman, rising.

Melissa's brow furrowed. Apparently, she hadn't expected cross-examination of the character witnesses.

"Dr. Stolz, are you aware that Ms. Harrison and Ms. Bois are in a same-sex relationship?"

Liz blinked but didn't flinch. "I think their marriage is a matter of public record. The fact speaks to the stability of their relationship. Unlike your client, who is unmarried." Lucy saw Melissa wince. She'd specifically advised against mentioning the other side's deficits. Of course, Liz hadn't been at that meeting, so how would she know?

"Are you aware that studies show being raised by same-sex parents is detrimental to the well-being of children?"

Liz glowered at the opposing counsel. "Those studies have no scientific basis and have since been discredited. Legitimate studies have found that there is no difference in the well-being of children raised by same-sex couples. In fact, one study showed that children fare better when raised by two mothers."

"Dr. Stolz, is it true that you are a lesbian?"

Liz turned to the judge. "Your honor, must I answer this question? This is Maine, and my rights are protected."

The judge took a moment to consider the question. "I'll allow it for now. In family court, social context is relevant."

"Yes," said Liz with a deadly stare. "I am a lesbian. Are you attempting to discredit my testimony with this fact?"

"I'm asking the questions, Dr. Stolz," replied the young woman sternly. "I just want to acknowledge the elephant in the room." She pointed to the section of the courtroom, where the character witnesses sat. "In fact, all of the plaintiffs' witnesses are lesbians."

"I'm not a lesbian!" Chief Duvaney shot up from his seat like a rocket. "I've been married for almost thirty years. To a woman!"

"Your honor…!" protested Melissa, getting to her feet.

The judge slammed her gavel. "Sit down, Ms. Morgenstern. Counsel has made her point. Do you have further questions for Dr. Stolz?"

"No," said the attorneys in stereo.

"You may step down, Dr. Stolz," the judge said.

When Liz returned to her seat, Lucy took her hand and held it. "You were great."

"What the fuck was that about?" Liz whispered angrily.

"It's all they've got."

The rest of the testimony proceeded as planned. Lucy rose to tell the court how Cherie had adjusted her schedule to accommodate the children. She praised her skills as a counselor.

"Reverend Bartlett, as a licensed family counselor, and someone who's served in the capacity of guardian *ad litem*, would you judge Ms. Harrison and Ms. Bois suitable as parents?" Melissa asked.

"Absolutely and without reservation."

The last witness for their side was Olivia, who gave a polished evaluation of Brenda's performance as police chief and said complimentary things about Cherie as a physician's assistant.

Finally, the opposing counsel got up to deliver her closing argument. She reviewed the adjustments her client was willing to make to become the children's guardian. "And they even have a plan for childcare while they are working, instead of leaving them with a choir director who's a transsexual!" Obviously, the other lawyer had been saving this sensational information for the climax. Lucy scrutinized the judge for a reaction, but her expression was inscrutable. The lawyer finally wrapped up her speech and sat down, looking confident that the damaging information had done its evil work.

"Why don't we take a brief recess before we hear the defendants' closing arguments?" the judge suggested. "Fifteen minutes." She gaveled the session closed. Both sides retreated to the hall outside the courtroom, speaking softly because the cavernous hall echoed.

"Why didn't the judge shut down the questioning about being gay?" Liz asked, glaring angrily at the courtroom door. "It seems so prejudicial."

"Honestly, I'm surprised she let it go as far as she did," Melissa admitted. "Maine has laws protecting the rights of gay people. And that question was an invasion of your privacy. You called it right. It was meant to undermine your credibility."

"Will it succeed?"

Melissa raised her shoulders. "If the judge decides against Brenda and Cherie on that basis, they have a serious case for appeal."

"Will you respond to the gay-bashing in your closing remarks?" Cherie asked.

"No, responding to questions about sexual orientation suggests it's a deficit. You're legally married in this state. That makes your relationship more stable than your opponent's and should be a point in your favor. Let's see what happens."

Melissa took the opportunity to use the ladies' room and Courtney went with her. Cherie and Brenda looked like they needed some privacy, so Lucy encouraged Liz to walk down the hall with her.

"When you were staring down the other lawyer, I got a glimpse of what a bad ass you used to be. You scared the hell out of me!"

"Are you kidding me? That was mild, compared to the old days."

Lucy reached for Liz's hand and gave it a squeeze. A few minutes later, Melissa approached, gathering up her troops. When they returned to the courtroom, the fire chief was chatting with Brenda. Melissa shooed him back to his seat just in time.

"All rise!" intoned the bailiff.

The judge gazed over the courtroom. Her eyes finally rested on Melissa. "Counsel, you may begin your closing arguments."

"Your honor, Ms. Bois and Chief Harrison sincerely wish to adopt the Benoit children. Their home was the children's first refuge when tragedy took their young parents away from them. They never hesitated to shelter and comfort them." Melissa was speaking in a quiet voice, which was especially effective. The judge's eyes were locked on her.

"These women are solid people, who have proven themselves through a lifetime of service to their communities. Undoubtedly, the trauma of loss in such a violent way will have a long-term impact on these children. Cherie Bois has special training to help them cope, especially because she herself was a victim of gun violence." Melissa pointed to the area where the character witnesses sat. "All these people took time out of their busy lives to come here today. Their support for Chief Harrison and Ms. Bois shows they won't be alone in parenting Keith and Megan. The more support parents have, the better the outcome. Reliable studies have proven this fact. It has become a cliché, but it does take a village. It is my hope that you will allow Ms. Harrison and Ms. Bois to continue the adoption process they've initiated."

After Melissa sat down, the extended silence was broken only by a few coughs and sniffles. The judge looked thoughtful. Finally, she said, "I always try to keep a child with the family when I can, but a distant cousin, while technically family, is not a close relative. By Ms. Papin's own admission, she hardly knows these children. In initiating an adoption, Ms. Harrison and Ms. Bois have shown how serious they are about becoming parents. Their testimony and that of the character witnesses has demonstrated how well-qualified they are to be parents. Sadly, Ms. Papin, despite your efforts to show that you can provide for the children, you are struggling financially and lack the stability to give them a good home. It is my judgment that the Bois-Harrison adoption may go forward. This court is adjourned."

Tears of relief streamed down Cherie's face. When Lucy approached, she fell into her arms. When it was Brenda's turn, she hugged Lucy so hard she squeezed the breath of her. The others were approaching to congratulate Cherie and Brenda, so Lucy stepped back.

She noticed that the lawyer for the other side had already abandoned her client. The boyfriend and the older woman had also left the courtroom. Only the woman who'd brought the suit remained. She looked dazed and didn't seem to notice Lucy's approach.

"I'm sorry it didn't turn out as you hoped," Lucy said gently to get her attention.

"No, you're not. Those women are your friends."

"They are, but they'll be good parents to your cousins."

"They only got the kids because they have money," the young woman said bitterly. "I would have been a good mother."

"It's a big responsibility. Those children will have many challenges."

"Expensive too. That lawyer already cost me a shitload of money," she said, then gave Lucy's collar a guilty look. "She'll be looking to be paid, now that we didn't win."

"Legal action is expensive," said Lucy. "I'm sorry."

"No, you're not. You're a priest. You're supposed to say nice things." The woman turned and walked away.

***

"Thank you for taking time off to be a witness," said Melissa as she drove Courtney back to school. "That was great testimony you gave."

"I admire those women for taking in those kids. After that trauma, throwing them into the foster care system would only make things worse, especially if they got separated."

"How are they doing in school?"

"I haven't heard any complaints from their teachers. One said the girl has been exceptionally quiet, which doesn't surprise me. She's probably still in shock. If the violence was an established pattern in their home, being taken away from it will be a good thing for the kids. I'm sure they miss their parents, but many people think young children don't have a clear concept of death."

Melissa listened thoughtfully. Before she'd been involved with Courtney, she'd never given child development much thought. Of course, she'd noted the changes in her twin nieces, but she seldom saw them, so it was like watching child actors grow up in a television series.

"I've always marveled that some women really want to be a mother," said Melissa. "Did you feel that way?"

"No, not at first, but after I ended up pregnant, it became the center of my life. I read everything I could get my hands on. I stopped drinking… even coffee. For the first time, I realized all the sacrifices women make to have children."

"Some women don't and give birth to defective children," said Melissa.

"The Benoit children will be scarred too…not physically, but it will be a handicap. With good parents and the right therapy, they can recover. That's why Cherie is such a perfect mother for them." Melissa felt Courtney studying her. "Did you ever want to be a mother?"

"Never. I wasn't interested in playing with dolls either. My parents thought I was strange. I learned to read early and preferred books."

"I went through a period where I really liked my dolls," said Courtney. "By the time I was ten, I'd lost interest in them. Then I was into My Little Pony. They still make them, believe it or not. Kaylee loved mine to death, so I had to buy her new ones. We threw them out when we moved to Maine, and I had to get rid of her little-girl toys."

"My mother threw out all my toys, except the dolls. She still has the dolls. What does that say?"

"The dolls were about her, not you."

Melissa nodded. "You're right. Everything is about her."

"Are you finding it hard working over there?"

"Sometimes. My mother gets chatty when Jack's off doing something and won't leave me alone. I've taken to putting a 'do not disturb' sign on my door to keep her out during my conference calls."

Courtney emitted an audible sigh. "I wish we had a bigger place where you could have your own office."

"Has Lucy said any more about the rental that might become available?"

"No, she hasn't mentioned it again. After the holidays, we should start looking for a bigger place."

"Are you sure?" asked Melissa. "You seem pretty content in Liz's garage. You're saving a ton of money."

"I know, but Kaylee needs a real room of her own, not a sleeping nook with a sliding door."

Melissa entered the school zone and slowed down. Only two protesters stood on the sidewalk in front of the school today, and they looked beleaguered and cold. The principal had come back to work, but there were persistent rumors that she might announce her retirement soon. Since dealing with the protestors, Courtney was on the fence about applying for the position.

Melissa parked in front of the school entrance and leaned over to offer a kiss. Courtney twisted away. "Melissa! Not in front of the school!" Melissa gazed out the window to avoid showing her hurt. Courtney had to tug at her arm to make her face her. "I'm sorry. Please understand. I need this job."

"I know. I just wish we could be like other couples and show affection."

"I'm sorry, sweetie." Courtney stroked Melissa's thigh. "I'll make it up to you tonight. I promise."

In a cloud of discouragement, Melissa watched her walk into the school.

# 13

"Dammit!" Lucy muttered, glaring at the flap of dough clinging to the rolling pin.

"Mother Lucy! The language!" Liz gave Lucy a head-to-toe inspection. "You do realize you're covered in flour?" Lucy looked down at the mess she'd created. There was flour everywhere—on the tabletop, the floor where she stood, her bare arms, even her shoes. Meanwhile, Liz had kept all her flour neatly on the pastry board. Next to it stood five plates of perfectly rolled-out, tear-free pastry waiting for filling.

"Liz, stop gloating. You know what you're doing! You could help me!"

"If you can't roll pie crusts, what are you doing here?"

"Showing solidarity with the pie committee."

"The pie committee," Liz repeated with disdain. "Only an Episcopal church would have a pie committee! And a flower committee, and a mittens committee. If you were a male rector, would you be here making pies?"

"No, probably not. The rector's wife would be working with the ladies."

"That's why I'm here, practicing for my new job. I will prove to you, Rev. Lucille Bartlett, that where pies are concerned, I have it covered."

"Liz, keep your voice down. People shouldn't hear us arguing." Lucy anxiously glanced around the parish hall, where a dozen women were making pies. The folding tables had been carefully spaced for safety, so the volume was louder than usual because people had to call across the room to be heard. The only person in the vicinity was Cherie, but she was focused on rolling out pastry.

"We're not arguing, Lucy. Even if we were, your church ladies know that everyone argues with their partner. Even you."

"Erika never argued with me like you do."

"Erika was a saint," said Liz. "I'm not."

Impatiently, Lucy leaned the rolling pin into the dough and tore up another flap. "I'll never get this right!" she said, trying to blow a strand of red hair out of her eyes because her hands were sticky with dough.

"Don't press down so hard. It's like sex, a lighter touch sometimes works better," Liz advised before walking away to the kitchen, where the pie fillings were being doled out.

Cherie came over to the table. "Let me show you, Lucy. Liz is right. You're pressing too hard. You want to roll out the dough gradually, like this." Cherie demonstrated and the dough effortlessly stretched into a round shape. "The texture will be better if you roll lightly. Working the dough too much makes the crust tough." She pinched off a knob of dough and repeated the process for Lucy's benefit.

"Now, why can't I do that?" Lucy allowed her lower lip to slip over the upper.

Cherie laughed. "Don't be discouraged, Lucy. It takes practice. Try again." Cherie stepped aside and handed Lucy the rolling pin.

"At least, you're patient. Liz demonstrates once and expects me to be an expert. My mother never taught me to make pies. My grandmother always baked them. After she died, all our Thanksgiving pies came from the bakery."

"It's never too late to learn. My Aunt Simone was my teacher. She made the flakiest pie crust on the planet. My mama was a wonderful cook, but she left the baking to her sister. I'm hoping Aunt Simone will come for Thanksgiving, but with the COVID numbers still rising, I'm afraid to encourage her."

"I'm sorry, Cherie. I know how fond you are of her. When you saw her face on the screen at your wedding, you just glowed with happiness."

"She's my favorite aunt. My cousin says she might fly down from Atlanta and drive her up, but it's a long way from Louisiana." Cherie nudged Lucy with her hip. "Come on. Let's show Liz you can do it. I'll stay here to give you pointers."

Lucy picked up the rolling pin. She'd never expected something that looked so simple to be this hard.

"Good job," Cherie encouraged, watching. "We'll make a pastry chef of you yet!" She glanced across the room to where Liz was lined up with an enormous measuring cup to get fillings for her pies. "I can't believe you talked your honey into coming to help. This is the last place I'd expect her."

"Liz is a good baker, and she volunteered without my asking. She's trying to prove she'll make a worthy pastor's wife."

"That's an old joke in church communities. Pay for one but get two. The unpaid labor of church wives is immeasurable."

While Cherie was talking, Lucy produced a pie crust with only a small tear. "Seal it back together with your fingertips, like this," Cherie said, showing how with an expert touch. Lucy gingerly lifted the dough into the waiting pan. "You're doing great."

"Is Brenda watching the kids?"

"She really wanted to come. She's a good baker."

"How are you adapting to being tied down by the children?"

Cherie shrugged. "We'll get there. It's such a big change."

"I hope it's not affecting your relationship," said Lucy gently.

"It's a challenge, but we try to find time for each other."

Lucy spoke directly into Cherie's ear. "Find time. Intimacy is important."

"I know," said Cherie with a guilty look. "I try, but sometimes I just can't stay awake. The kids are older, so we don't have to get up for midnight feedings. Of course, we have two right away, but I wouldn't trade them for anything. Hopefully, we'll hear about the adoption soon."

Liz came back with the enormous measuring cup full of a mixture that smelled delicious. "I've never understood why people are so wild about pork pies up here," she said. "What's so great about a pie filled with what's basically hamburger?"

"Don't say that to a French Canadian! Tourtière is a special treat at Christmas. My papa brought his mother's recipe to Louisiana. That was the one pie mama had to master. You come over after the midnight service and taste one made from scratch."

Liz glanced at Lucy, looking to her to respond to the invitation. She knew that religious holidays were Lucy's busiest times. Cherie was waiting hopefully, and Lucy couldn't bear to disappoint her. "Thank you for the invitation, Cherie. We'll be there."

After some practice, Lucy's pie crusts weren't perfect, but they had fewer holes. The committee had assigned her the mixed berry pie, so she joined the line to get the filling. Although she wasn't a baker, she enjoyed working with the women of the parish. Men knew to stay away from what had been a female-only event for generations. Tom was disappointed because he prided himself on his pastry crust, but he made his pies at home.

There were dozens of pies already in the freezer, prepared over the last months on the weekly "pie night." Tonight, the pie committee was baking for the people who preferred to buy a freshly baked pie.

Finally, the industrial-sized oven was baking the last batch. While the clean-up crew shooed the piemakers out of the hall, Lucy stood at the church door to thank people for coming. She shivered when they stepped out into the chilly, night air. "I'm going to need the services of my private bed warmer tonight," she said, taking Liz's arm. "Thank you for agreeing to stay at the beach house."

"It's closer to the church, and you have all your stuff there. Tomorrow's going to be a busy day for you."

Lucy couldn't wait to slip off her shoes and head up to bed. She did her nightly chores while Liz took a shower. Lucy almost fell asleep waiting. Once her lover crept into bed, still steamy and hot, she decided she wasn't too tired for sex after all.

When she awakened many hours later, the amber glow of dawn streamed through the window. Lucy murmured a prayer of thanksgiving for the good weather. With the pandemic still going on, Lucy had been against holding the fair, but the committee assured her they could do it safely. She hoped for their sakes that it was a success, especially because last year's fair had to be cancelled.

She slipped out of bed quietly to avoid waking Liz. As much as she loved to have Liz's company on her walks, there were mornings when Lucy needed solitude to pray and recharge her spiritual batteries.

On the beach, she greeted her seagull friends. She never fed them, but they always seemed to be there when she arrived. Sometimes, they sang to her. Sometimes, she sang to them.

By the time Lucy had returned from her walk, Liz was already dressed and had baked popovers for their breakfast. She leaned against the counter while waiting for Lucy's coffee to brew.

"Okay if I dress casually?" Liz asked. She was wearing dress jeans and a turtleneck. A classic tweed blazer hung on the back of her chair.

"You look fine. Better than fine, actually."

"Are you going to wear your collar today?"

"I usually do at official church events. That way people who don't belong to the church will know who's who."

"And know you're the boss."

"That's important sometimes."

"Yes, it is."

After breakfast, Liz headed to the office because Amy was on solo weekend duty for the first time. Lucy hurried to the church to see how the setup was going. The committee had put up a big sign under the enormous maple in front of the church. Hopefully, the tourists, who would soon be jamming the roads of Hobbs, would be tempted to observe what they'd no doubt consider to be a quaint, Maine custom. The older ladies, the ones who bragged about being baptized, confirmed, and married in St. Margaret's Church, liked to reminisce about the harvest fairs of their childhood, pointing out their parents, and grandparents, and even great grandparents in the fading photos in the parish hall.

The big maple in front of the church was weeping bright red leaves that spread across the green lawn like a colorful carpet. As Lucy stepped into the roped path, a leaf floated down, circling like a ballerina as it spiraled to the ground.

She was pleased to hear Liz reciting the approved formula: "Welcome to St. Margaret's. Thanks for coming." She dutifully distributed the flyers listing the offerings at the booths: crafts, second-hand costume jewelry, used books, personalized Christmas ornaments, the pumpkin carving area for the children being supervised by Cherie, the cookie table and the ultimate destination—the pie booth. A separate area had been set up for people who'd reserved the fresh pies. The frozen pies were being dispensed from a fleet of tailgate coolers.

"You're doing great," Lucy said, patting Liz's arm. "Keep up the good work."

Tom, who was supervising the ring toss game, came over to where Lucy stood. "So far, so good," he said, raising his fingers in a Vee. "We've been blessed with a spectacular day, and the leaf peepers are here in droves."

"As long as they have a good time and spend lots of money, I'm happy."

By lunchtime, Lucy's feet were beginning to hurt. She switched with Tom and invited Liz to the food booth for a bowl of homemade fish chowder. Liz handed the volunteer a twenty and told her to keep the change.

"You're one of the workers," Lucy said as they carried their trays to a picnic table. "You don't need to pay for your lunch. It's on the house."

"That's why St. Margaret's always needs money. You give away all the profits. Besides, it's for a good cause," Liz said, dipping her plastic spoon into her soup.

"How's it going on your end? I saw a bunch of people laughing with you."

"I've been entertaining the patrons with dirty jokes," Liz said dryly.

"No!"

Liz laughed. "Not really. I was telling them how I woke up with a throbbing headache in Acadia and found half the campground in front of our cabin with you celebrating Holy Communion Rite II. They were Episcopalians, so they got the picture." Lucy got the picture too. Liz understood more about church rituals than she was willing to admit.

"That experience should have taught you to be more moderate with your awful scotch."

"It didn't," said Liz, scooping up the last bit of soup from her cup.

By one-thirty, all the pies had been sold. The people in charge of the pie booth were packing up. Lucy glanced over to where Liz had been stationed and saw that she'd been replaced by Abby, the senior warden. Lucy waved to Tom, who headed in her direction.

"Have you seen Liz?" she asked.

He looked around. "She said she needed a break. She headed thataway." He pointed in the direction of the churchyard. Lucy squinted and saw a figure seated on the stone bench placed by Erika's Colby students. The memorial was carefully located near her grave to provide a restful place for meditation. "Tom, do you mind taking over here for a few minutes?"

He glanced at his watch. "It's almost over. I can take it from here."

"I just want to see what's going on with Liz. She's new to this."

"Lucky her," Tom said with a grunt. "Go on. I'll hold down the fort."

As Lucy approached, she caught a whiff of cigarette smoke, one of the vices Liz and Erika liked to indulge in when they wanted to be especially naughty. Liz was speaking aloud in German: "*Sie glaubt, dass sie mich erziehen kann, aber da irrt sie sich gewaltig.*"

"Complaining to Erika?" Lucy asked, sitting down beside Liz. "Of course, I don't think I can train you. I know you're incorrigible." She patted Liz's thigh. "Being a pastor's wife too much for you?"

"Making pies last night. Chatting up fairgoers today. I don't know if I'm cut out for this. I could really use a drink." Liz reached into her coat and produced a flask. She unscrewed the top and offered it to Lucy, who made a face.

"You know I hate that stuff. It's vile."

"Just being polite," replied Liz with a shrug. "Can't commune with the dead without a proper libation." She leaned forward to pour a few drops on the grave, then raised the flask in salute. "To you, Erika, wherever you are." She took a swig from the flask and returned it to her pocket. "Don't worry. I haven't had much. It's medicinal—to ward off the chill."

"It's hard for you, isn't it?"

Liz thought for a moment. "Which part? Standing in the cold all day? Practicing being the pastor's wife? Missing Erika?"

"All of the above." Lucy reached for Liz's hand. "Liz, you don't need to prove you love me. I know you do. I hope you know I love you too…exactly as you are." Lucy tugged on Liz's hand to pull her closer. Just as their lips were about to touch, Lucy heard a voice.

"There they are!"

Lucy turned around to see Sam heading their way with Maggie right behind her.

***

"No!" said Maggie, pulling on Sam's arm. "They're talking. Let's go."

Sam could see that Maggie was right. She was torn for a moment between wanting to make sure Liz and Lucy knew they had shown up to support the church fair and Maggie's obvious discomfort. "We'll just say hello. We won't stay long. I promise."

Maggie gave her a stricken look. "I'm not sure I'm up for it."

"Are you in pain?"

"No, physically, I feel fine. It's just hard to see them together."

"Come on. You're Maggie Fitzgerald. Show them what a trooper you are!" Sam hated to give Maggie a pep talk, especially because this was her first outing since the surgery.

Since Sam had been visiting Maggie in Scarborough, she'd seen another side of her. She'd listened to her fears about the return of the cancer and watched her cry over losing her breasts. Maggie's tears had shocked her at first. She'd never seen Maggie as anything but completely poised. On the surface, that's how Maggie looked today, but Sam knew better.

When she'd arrived, Maggie had asked her to empty the drains, explaining there was no one else to help because Alina wasn't home. Sam had cringed at the idea, thinking she'd have to see the scars in Maggie's breasts. Fortunately, the only thing she'd seen was the white mastectomy bra. Pinned to it was a collection of small plastic bottles collecting the pale liquid still seeping out. To look at Maggie now, no one would ever guess that's what was hidden under her loose blouse and artisan-weave shawl.

Sam didn't tug hard on Maggie's arm because she was afraid of hurting her, but she could feel her resistance. The cartoon image of pulling a stubborn mule suddenly popped into Sam's mind. Then she realized she was the stubborn one and released her. "If you really don't want to talk to them, we can leave."

Maggie sighed. "Too late now. They've seen us."

Lucy had gotten up from the bench and was approaching. Liz was frowning. Eventually, she followed Lucy but stood a few feet behind her with her hands in her pockets.

"Maggie! Thanks so much for coming," said Lucy, putting on her mask before giving her a hug.

"Easy. I'm still tender," Maggie warned gently.

Lucy stepped back and gave her a sympathetic look. "I'm sorry. I forgot. But you look absolutely great!"

"I still can't drive. Sam brought me down."

"Thank you, Sam," said Lucy, taking Maggie's arm. She led her back to the fair. "I think there's still some fish chowder and mac and cheese. And we have homemade baked beans and steamed hot dogs. And pie, of course."

"Thanks, Lucy," said Maggie. "We've eaten."

"Then take some home, and you won't have to make dinner tonight. I'll ask them to pack some up for you."

One of the choir members spotted Maggie and waved. "This is one of the reasons I was reluctant to come," Maggie said.

"You shouldn't be. We're all so happy to see you! Come on. Let's see what we can find at the food booth."

Sam turned to Liz. "We're sidelined, I see."

"Lucy's really glad to see her. She misses her, but she doesn't want to push too hard."

Sam thrust her hands into her pockets, mirroring Liz's stance. "It's awkward for everyone."

"It is," Liz agreed. "But I'm glad you came."

"Maggie told me she misses St. Margaret's."

"No one is keeping her away," replied Liz with an annoying shrug.

Sam felt her shoulders tense. She consciously opened her hands to keep them from clenching into fists. "You know why she's staying away. She feels humiliated. You're engaged to her rival. She's been replaced as music director by a classical singer. All of us who knew you as a couple avoid her because we're afraid of offending you. What's left for her here?"

"Anything else you'd like to say, Sam?" asked Liz, standing at her full height. Usually, Sam would back up, but she raised her chin and stepped forward.

"Be kind, Liz. She's fragile now."

"You think I don't know it? I was there for the surgery. I've treated thousands of women with breast cancer, including Maggie."

"I know, Liz. You're such an expert on everything."

"Whoa! Sam, have I done something to offend you?"

"No, not exactly," said Sam, turning her gaze to where Maggie stood. "I'm just seeing things from a different perspective…which isn't always yours."

"So, she's been pissing in your ear." Liz crossed her arms on her chest. "Look, Sam, I didn't leave her. She left me."

"She needs you right now. She thinks you're the only person who can help her."

"That's irrational. Her prognosis is good, and I'm doing the best I can. I promised the surgeon I would look after the surgical wounds and remove the drains. It's inappropriate for me to do more."

"You could listen to her concerns."

"Sam, I do listen," Liz said, sounding frustrated. "There's nothing I can say or do that will magically take away the anxiety. For some people, it's unbearable. Maybe she should go back to that shrink she was seeing."

"You don't get it, do you?"

"No, Sam. Enlighten me."

Sam shook her head. "You won't listen to me. You already know everything." She could see the fury in Liz's eyes. Her temple was pulsing, which meant she was working hard to keep her temper in check. At this point,

Sam would usually say something conciliatory. Not this time.

Maggie and Lucy returned, weighed down by a reusable shopping bag.

"Let me get that," Sam offered. She found the bag even heavier than it looked.

"She wouldn't take no for an answer," Maggie explained. "We have enough food for a week! The girls will love the mac and cheese."

"We're still making your recipe," said Lucy. "People love it! I'm surprised there's any left to take home, but they said they were making extra."

Maggie reached for Sam's arm. "I'm getting tired. Do you mind taking me home?"

"I'll be up after church to check the wounds," said Liz, approaching. Sam studied her face. Her anger had either passed or she'd gotten control of it. "Maybe I can take out the drains tomorrow."

"Oh, that would be wonderful!" said Maggie. "They're so annoying, especially when I sleep."

Lucy gave Sam and Maggie hugs. "Thank you so much for coming,"

"Bye, Liz," said Sam warily.

"Thanks for coming, Sam."

On their way to the parking lot, Sam could feel their eyes on her back and wondered what they were saying. Knowing Lucy, she would be complimenting Maggie on how good she looked so soon after the surgery. Liz would still be sulking over the words they'd exchanged. Sam had surprised herself. Usually, she didn't argue with Liz because she always won anyway, but it had felt good to stand up to her.

"I hope you plan to stay for dinner," Maggie said after Sam arranged her seat belt so it wouldn't bind. "Lucy gave us too much food."

"Sure. I'll stay even though I bet their mac and cheese isn't nearly as good as when you make it.

Maggie smiled. "You certainly know how to charm a woman, Sam. I've never understood why you're not taken."

"Many have tried," said Sam, smiling to herself as she slid into the driver's seat.

"You just haven't found the right woman. Olivia was too overbearing.

Liz was like that. She wasn't as obvious about it as Olivia, but she always had to have the last word."

Sam was surprised by the perception, especially because it seemed that Maggie had ruled that household. "Let's not talk about them," Sam said.

"You're right. Let's not."

"I was dating someone else for a while," Sam volunteered.

"Who?"

"Amy Hsu, the new doc in Liz's practice. We met when I was working on the renovation."

"But you're not together now?"

Sam had a funny feeling that it was more than a casual question. Maggie was adding things up in her mind, and there was some self-interest involved in her calculations.

"We decided we're better off as friends."

Out of the corner of her eye, Sam caught Maggie smiling. "Dr. Hsu seems like a nice woman. Very attractive too." Maggie turned in her seat. "Sam, what do you find attractive in a woman?"

"Well, let's see. I like women who look and act like women. Beyond that, I don't really have a list of qualities I look for." She glanced shyly at Maggie. "How about you?"

"Hmm." Maggie thought for a moment. "I think kindness. Kindness is really sexy. Common decency is important. Honesty. After that, I look for steadiness—someone who's solid."

"That certainly describes someone we agreed not to talk about."

"It also describes you." Sam's breath caught. Maggie was telling her that she found her attractive. "You're one of the kindest people I know," Maggie continued in her delicious actress voice that caressed Sam's ears like gentle fingertips. "You were so sweet that day to come over to the car because you saw I was crying. I'll never forget it. Then you were kind enough to invite me home. You don't know how much that meant to me."

Sam squirmed in her seat, and her cheeks were heating up. "Oh, Sam, you're blushing. How adorable!" Now, Sam's cheeks flamed. She wanted to sink into her seat. "You probably think I'm too old for you," said Maggie with a sigh.

"No, I don't," Sam instantly replied.

Sam wanted to turn to see Maggie's reaction, but she felt it in the sudden silence. She didn't know what else to say, so she looked at the view of the trees along the highway, blazing with oranges and reds so brilliant they nearly hurt her eyes.

"The tourists won't be disappointed this year," Maggie said, taking the cue. "They're really getting a good show. Thank you for taking me out today, Sam. I really appreciate it."

Sam parked in the paved area set off from the driveway and yanked up the parking brake. "Let me get the food out of the back," she offered. "I'll be right in."

She found Maggie struggling to get out of her coat. "Here. Let me help," Sam said, carefully slipping the coat off Maggie's shoulders and hanging it on the hook by the door.

When she turned around, she saw Maggie gazing at her intently before her hands reached up to cup her cheeks. She squeezed them gently as she pulled her face closer. Sam found Maggie's mouth soft and open, and she allowed herself to be drawn deeply into the kiss. When they parted, Maggie's hazel eyes searched hers, and she smiled. "You liked that. How about another?"

# 14

Liz wagged her foot while she waited for Lucy to get to the point. Since she'd been editing Lucy's doctoral dissertation, she'd been trying to teach her how to think in an orderly, clear, and linear manner. Obviously, none of those lessons had found their way into Lucy's sermons. She was a lateral thinker and often wandered before her lesson became clear.

Now that she'd been faithfully attending Lucy's services, Liz recognized a pattern. Lucy still wrote her sermons every Wednesday and memorized the text. The only notes she used were the scripture passages to make sure she didn't misquote them. She usually opened and closed with the same passage.

Whatever Liz thought about Lucy's preaching style, her parishioners seemed to like it. "Down to earth," people called it. Lucy always brought experiences from her week and interjected a little self-deprecating humor. Today, she told the story of how her pie crusts kept getting holes until she let up on the rolling pin. She used the incident to illustrate why it's important to be gentle to yourself and others.

The sunlight suddenly broke into the sacristy through the side window. In the natural spotlight, Lucy was brilliantly illuminated, and her red hair seemed to glow. Liz was transfixed by the sight until she reminded herself that the church had been sited to focus the light in the sanctuary. As the seasons changed, the morning sun streamed in from different windows. Stage lighting could not be more effective.

Lucy finally concluded the sermon and asked the congregation to stand to recite the Nicene Creed. Liz still considered bodies rising from the dead and virgin births complete nonsense. She knew that the repetition of the words one Sunday after another was a form of subtle brainwashing. Even so, she recited the text along with the others. While Denise sang "*Panis Angelicus*," Liz followed the people in her row to the communion rail. Now that everyone knew she and Lucy were engaged, any lack of participation in the rituals might start rumors. Liz was caught in a trap of her own making, but she no longer struggled to escape.

At the end of the service, Liz waited in the background while Lucy greeted her parishioners. When she touched Lucy's shoulder to get her attention, she felt the fine silk of the chasuble slick under her fingers. "Honey, I'm going to the office to pick up what I need before heading up to Maggie's," she whispered into her ear. "I'll be home by one, and then we'll leave."

"Okay." Lucy's pinky reached out and entwined with Liz's. Usually, they avoided public displays of affection, but this was innocent enough. "Drive carefully."

At the office, Liz searched the shelves for a suture removal kit. The new nurse practitioner they'd hired to backfill for Cherie had taken it upon herself to reorganize the supply closet. Liz growled until her hand found the right bin, carefully labeled and staring her right in the face.

Passing Amy's office, Liz noticed the light on under the door, so she knocked.

"Come in," Amy sang out.

"I wanted you to know no one's stealing drugs, It's only me rummaging around in the supply closet. What are you doing here on your day off?" Liz glanced at the laptop screen and saw columns of numbers.

"I'm organizing my financial files for Olivia Enright. We're meeting this afternoon." Liz had almost forgotten that she'd referred Amy to Olivia for financial advice.

"Liv is really gifted. That's why the Enright Fund was the hottest thing on Wall Street…at least, for a while."

"She invited me to dinner after the meeting."

That came as a surprise, but Liz nodded approvingly. "Olivia is an amazing cook. I'm sure you'll enjoy the meal. And thanks again for looking after things while I'm up in Casco Bay."

"Don't forget. I expect full reciprocity."

"Oh, I remember." Liz closed the door behind her, pleased by the idea of Olivia and Amy having dinner. It showed that Amy was putting down roots in Hobbs.

As Liz drove to Scarborough, she wondered if Alina and the children would be there. She missed seeing the girls, who were growing up so fast. Katrina was nearly as tall as her tiny mother. The girl's hair had suddenly darkened, which Liz recognized as an early sign of puberty.

The girls tackled Liz when Alina opened the front door. "Grandma!" They squealed, hugging Liz while she planted a kiss on the top of each head. She leaned over Nicki to accept a kiss from their mother.

"Thanks for coming up, Mo…" Alina started to say. "…Liz," she said, correcting herself.

Liz wanted to say, *it's all right. You can still call me Mom if you want to,* but she didn't because their relationship had changed. Sophia had been awkward too, when Liz had handed off Maggie's care to her oncologist daughter.

"All right, kids. Let's give Grandma Liz a chance to get in the door."

"Where's your mother?" Liz asked quietly.

"In her apartment." Alina pointed to the lower level. Liz was surprised that Maggie had taken the smaller space. Her money had paid for the house, but it made sense. Alina and her daughters made three. Maggie was only one.

"I won't be long. I'm sure you have plans for the day."

"Take all the time you need." Alina gave Liz's arm a little squeeze. "It's so nice to see you."

Liz went down the stairs and knocked on the apartment door. Maggie looked sleepy when she opened it. "Liz! I didn't expect you so early. I would have fixed myself up a little." Maggie was wearing makeup. The only sign that she might have been napping were a few strands of white hair that had escaped from her braid.

"I've seen you every which way, Maggie. You don't have to fix yourself up for me."

"Thanks. I love you too," Maggie replied in a tart voice, but she reached up to offer Liz a kiss on the cheek. "Come in."

The basement apartment reminded Liz of Maggie's cramped

one-bedroom in Greenwich Village. Photos of family and Broadway shows in which Maggie had appeared covered the walls. Liz recognized the furniture from the New York apartment, some of which had been in storage in the space above Liz's workshop for years.

"Are you comfortable here?" asked Liz. "It's kind of small."

Maggie shrugged. "It's what it is."

"Well, let me get rid of those drains, and you can get back to what you were doing."

"You mean, taking a nap?"

Liz frowned and gave Maggie a closer look. "Still feeling fatigued?"

"No, the kids wear me out. But I love them."

Liz glanced around looking for a place to set up the suture kit. "Where will you be most comfortable?"

"How's the bed?"

Liz looked through the door to the small bedroom. "Sure. Can I turn up the heat, so you don't get chilled?" Her eyes looked around for a thermostat. She wasn't surprised when Maggie read her mind.

"In the kitchenette."

While Liz was in the kitchen, she used the sink to wash her hands. "Do you cook in here much?"

"Almost never. I cook for all of us in the main kitchen. Sometimes, I make myself a cup of tea down here when the kids are in school. It's nice to have."

When Liz returned from the kitchen, she found Maggie in the bedroom, struggling to open the mastectomy bra. Liz reached down to help her.

"Thank you," murmured Maggie. "It's so awkward not being able to raise my arms."

Liz snapped on surgical gloves. "Ellen certainly went overboard on these drains. Six is a little extreme, but you know how fussy she is. She puts me to shame. When did you last empty them?"

"Early this morning." Maggie handed Liz the drain volume chart. She scanned it, noting Maggie's careful round penmanship, beneath it, her daughter's angular letters, and a couple of entries in another familiar hand-writing that Liz recognized as Sam's.

"I needed help," Maggie volunteered. "It wasn't easy emptying them." The statement was merely factual, not a complaint.

"It's awkward." Liz opened the sterile suture removal kit. She carefully traced the first tube and snipped the suture holding it in place. "You'll feel a little pulling. It shouldn't hurt. Let me know if it does." Maggie flinched slightly as Liz pulled out the tube. She deposited the drain in the red medical waste bag she'd brought from the office. "One down. Five to go."

"Does this mean I can drive now?"

"You can drive when you can lift your arms without pain. But that doesn't mean you should go back to everything you were doing."

"I know. No lifting anything heavier than a gallon of milk."

"Do you have any sensation in your nipples?"

"A little."

"That's a good sign. Ellen helped me develop that technique for nipple conservation."

"Were you watching the whole time?" Maggie asked, looking curious.

"Yes. I wanted to make sure everyone was doing their job." Liz removed the next drain. She dabbed the small amount of fluid that escaped with some sterile gauze. "That's why you wanted me there, wasn't it?"

"Yes. I trust you to make good decisions for me."

"Since we're no longer married, I really couldn't make any decisions."

"You're still my medical proxy," Maggie said, "and if it's all right with you, I'm not going to change it."

Liz was glad to be busy removing the drains, so Maggie couldn't see her face. "That's fine. I'm just surprised."

"Liz, look at me." Liz dumped the plastic tubing in the red bag and looked up. "I need to know that you forgive me. I'm so sorry I came on to you the night before the surgery."

"You already apologized for that, and I forgave you."

"I'm sorry for all of it, especially for being so angry and jealous."

"I can understand. I would be angry and jealous if you'd kissed someone while we were married."

"Well, I did. Brad wasn't the first one."

"What?" asked Liz, freezing with the forceps and suture scissors poised in the air. "You had other affairs?"

"No. I only slept with Brad, but I kissed other people and flirted a lot. You know. It's how theater people are, always hugging and kissing. Affairs are rampant."

Liz focused on steadying her hands as she snipped a suture. She carefully pulled out the last drain and swabbed the area with antiseptic.

"Now, I've made you angry," Maggie observed, scrutinizing her face.

"Actually, I was cursing Ellen for putting in all these fucking drains," said Liz, deflecting. Of course, she was angry. Furious, in fact. "How long was this going on?"

"Before you and Lucy went out on the boat. I figured you'd given me permission by openly flirting with her."

"That wasn't my intention, and I now regret that behavior." Liz applied steri-strips to the drain wounds. "It was disrespectful to both of you, especially to you."

"Never mind to your best friend."

Liz shrugged. "Erika was cool. She only got married because that's what Lucy wanted, but she was never a huge fan of marriage or monogamy."

"Neither were you, but you asked me to marry you." Maggie touched Liz's cheek to make her look up. "Liz, I need you to forgive me. I don't want you to hate me."

Liz moved her head away from Maggie's hand. "I don't hate you."

"You're still so angry."

"Telling me about your flirtations didn't help." Liz pulled off her gloves and deposited them in the red bag.

Maggie pulled down her shirt. "Oh, that's so much better."

"I bet."

"Liz, I'm trying to clear the air. No more secrets. I want us to be friends. I don't want to have to avoid people because we broke up."

"You mean like Sam?" asked Liz, cleaning up the debris from removing the drains. She added it to the medical waste bag and sealed it.

"Sam. Brenda. Cherie. Even that bitch, Olivia. I suppose that's harsh. I should be more charitable. I had a long talk with Lucy last night."

"So, you were the one who had her ear for hours."

"It wasn't hours," Maggie protested. She stared. "Did you hear the whole conversation?"

"No, of course not. Lucy went into her office and closed the door. I didn't hear a word. Sam soundproofed that house well."

"Please, Liz. I need peace, especially with this going on." Maggie gestured to her breasts, which caused Liz to give them another look. Now that the swelling had gone down, it was evident that Maggie's new breasts would closely match the originals. The scars would hardly be visible once the incisions had healed completely. In all, an excellent cosmetic result.

"Do you mind if I take a couple of quick photos for Ellen? She asked me, since she won't see you for a few weeks."

"Liz! I'm talking to you about something important!"

"I understand, but can I take the photos?"

"Go ahead," said Maggie with a sigh.

✳✳✳

Driving up the turnpike, Sam thought about the kiss. Since yesterday, she'd thought about nothing else. Revisiting it had kept her awake for most of the night. Today, she was paying for it. Her eyes were sticky, and she was tired. She forced herself to pay closer attention to the road. The highway was still crowded with tourists.

As she approached Maggie's driveway, Liz was coming out of the house. She hugged Alina and the girls at the door but remained to talk. Finally, she picked up her medical bag and headed to her car. She stood, shading her eyes against the sun, while Sam pulled in next to her truck.

"Hey, Liz," Sam said, sliding out of her SUV. "Did you take out the drains?" She tried to sound cheerful to avoid any suggestion of animosity, especially after their last conversation.

"All done." Her tone was factual, but friendly. Sam felt at ease enough to smile.

Liz put her bag in the back seat of her truck. She leaned on the door with narrowed eyes. Sam knew she was sizing her up to see where things stood.

"About yesterday…" Sam started to say.

"I'm sorry too," said Liz, completing her sentence. "It always gets confusing with lesbians. So many of us stay friends with our exes. Sometimes our exes get involved with our friends. I just try to avoid dyke drama as much as I can."

"Me too."

Liz gave her a direct look. "Are you seeing Maggie?"

Sam shrugged. "Not officially."

"Come on, Sam. I know you are. But you've known her for years. What's the sudden attraction?"

"She's beautiful," said Sam.

Liz turned around and looked at the house. "Yes, she is, isn't she?" Liz patted Sam's shoulder. "I wish you all the best."

"That's it?"

"What else should I say? Good luck? Don't fuck it up like I did?"

"Liz…." Sam looked at her feet. She was wearing her dress sneakers, the dark ones with the laces that matched exactly. She'd put on her best hoodie and nearly new jeans, which counted as dressing up on a Sunday afternoon.

"I'll see you, Sam. I have to get home. Lucy and I are taking the boat up to Casco Bay this afternoon."

"Nice day for it. The weather's supposed to be warm all weekend."

"I hope so, but it's unnatural for it to be this warm so late in October." Liz gazed up at the sky. "But if we're going to do this, best to do it while the ocean's still warm and before the time changes. Winter's coming."

"Still want me to plow for you?" Sam asked.

"Sure. If you don't mind. Can't beat the price." Sam plowed Liz's driveway for nothing to make it worth putting on the plow. She plowed Lucy's driveway too. Liz smacked Sam's shoulder again. "Let's get together for beers when I get back from my trip."

Sam watched Liz drive down the road before reaching into the car for the gifts she'd brought. The bright yellow, potted chrysanthemum was not very romantic, but it would be cheerful in Maggie's dark, little apartment. There was also a tin of chocolate-chip cookies that Sam had baked for the girls. She wasn't much of a baker, but she excelled at cookies. Despite the bribe, Katrina and Nicki hung back, regarding her suspiciously.

"Mom's in her apartment," Alina explained. "You know the way."

Sam noticed that she'd left the price tag on the potted mum. She peeled it off and stuffed it into her pocket on the way down the stairs. She found it hard to imagine how Maggie could stand living in such cramped quarters after living in Liz's spacious house. The Scarborough house was only a three-bedroom raised ranch with an apartment in the lower living space— the kind of conventional 1980s architecture that Sam hated.

Maggie looked freshly made-up when she came to the door. Her cologne was fresh too. Sam inhaled a light, floral scent that reminded her of her mother's generation, but Maggie wore it well. Everything about her recalled the elegance of an earlier time. Maggie Fitzgerald was a classic.

"Come in, Sam. Liz just left."

"I know. I saw her in the driveway."

Maggie's perfectly arched brow twitched up. "Oh? That go okay?"

"It was fine. Liz and I have known each other for a long time."

"I'm sorry to cause friction between friends," said Maggie, but she sounded almost disappointed. Sam wondered if she found the idea of two women fighting over her romantic.

"I brought you a mum," said Sam shyly, thrusting forward the little pot. "It looked healthy."

"Thank you. You're so sweet." Maggie put the bright flowers on the table in the kitchenette.

"How are you?" Sam asked. "You look tired."

"The kids won't leave me alone. I think they're worried about me. They come down here to watch TV, even though they have their own TV in the family room. They stare at me as if they expect me to vanish."

Sam hesitated to say what she was thinking because it seemed forward, but Maggie looked so tired. Sam decided to just put it out there. "You could stay at my house." Maggie's eyes widened. "Maggie, I promise I'm not coming on to you. You can stay in the big guest room facing the pond."

"I don't know…. Someone needs to be here to meet the kids from the school bus."

"What did Alina do before you moved up here?"

"After-school daycare. She signed them up again while I was in the hospital."

"There you go. Problem solved. Now, pack a bag and we'll go. It's a nice day. We can sit by the pond." Sam watched Maggie struggle with the suggestion. The little permanent furrow between her brows grew deeper. "Maggie, you've been through a lot. You need to rest. Come home with me, and I'll take care of you." She reached out her hand. Maggie stared at it a moment before she took it.

"I need to pack."

"Do you want me to help you?"

"If you could take down the small suitcase from the top of the closet…" Sam watched Maggie carefully fold slacks and tops into her bag, but she modestly turned away when Maggie added fancy nightgowns and underwear. "I need my mastectomy bras. Alina hung them in the bathroom. I can't raise my arms over my head yet, so I'm not sure I can reach them."

"I'll get them," Sam offered. She found the sturdy bras hanging on the shower rod. Despite washing, the white cotton still showed faint stains.

"Those bras hold my fake boobs in place until everything heals," Maggie explained when Sam returned. "Unfortunately, you can't bleach them." She looked up into Sam's face, clearly scrutinizing it for signs of revulsion. "Are you sure you're up for this, Sam?"

"It will be fine."

"Can you get my makeup bag down from the top shelf of the closet?" Maggie returned from the bathroom with plastic bags filled with an incredible number of jars and tubes. Sam, who seldom wore makeup these days, stared. "Believe it or not, I've cut down," Maggie said. "At some point, no matter how much cream you put on your face, it doesn't matter. Too much makeup makes you just look like an old call girl."

"Oh, Maggie, you're still so beautiful," Sam said ardently. "Don't let anyone make you feel otherwise."

"You're being kind, Sam." Maggie switched to a Southern accent, reprising her signature role from *A Streetcar Named Desire*. "Whoever you are, I have always depended on the kindness of strangers."

"I'm not a stranger. I'm your friend," Sam insisted, but she'd been charmed by the little performance.

Maggie zipped closed the suitcase. "I think that's it. I'm sorry I have to impose again, but I'm not supposed to carry anything heavy."

"I was going to get the bags anyway." Sam picked them up and carried them to the stairs. "Don't forget the chrysanthemum. It was a gift."

As they ascended the stairs, Alina came out from the kitchen. Her dark eyes widened, first with surprise, then alarm. "What's this? Where are you going, Mom?"

Maggie stood on the landing. "Sam has invited me to stay with her for a few days…so I can get some rest."

"I knew the girls were bothering you too much."

"They don't bother me. They just want attention, and I'm not up for it."

Alina's dark brows bent toward her nose. "I knew I should have taken time off."

"You need your job, dear. I'm sorry, but the kids will need to go back to after-school daycare. I'll pay for it."

"It's not the money, Mom. They'll miss you." She called into the kitchen: "Katrina! Nicki! Come say goodbye to your grandmother."

The girls shot out of the kitchen. Nicki's face was sticky with chocolate from Sam's cookies. Maggie wiped it away with her thumb, then blotted it on a tissue from her cardigan pocket. The girls took turns offering hugs.

"Bye, Grandma," Nicki said sadly. Sam could see how difficult it would be for Maggie to get away, so she called out her own goodbyes and carried the bags to her car.

"You must have planned on kidnapping me," said Maggie as she climbed into Sam's Subaru. "You brought your car instead of the truck."

"The idea didn't occur to me until I saw how tired you are." Sam arranged the seat belt around Maggie, so it wouldn't bind where she was still tender and climbed into the driver's seat. "Ready?"

Maggie stared at the house. "I can't believe I'm doing this. It feels so irresponsible to just leave, but I wasn't really doing much."

"Taking care of yourself should be your first priority. And you are doing something. You're recovering from surgery."

Maggie began to direct her to the highway, but Sam turned and said gently, "Thank you, Maggie. I know the way."

"Of course, you do. You have a good sense of direction, like…" Maggie cut herself off. Sam deflected the little poke of jealousy, knowing that comparison to Maggie's ex was inevitable. There were worse things than being in the same league with Liz Stolz.

Sam took the backroads to Jimson Pond to avoid the traffic. It was a little longer, but more scenic. Everywhere, the trees blazed with color.

"Thanks for forcing me out of my basement today…and yesterday. If you hadn't come along, I would have missed the fall colors."

"Maybe we can take a drive up to Sebago this week. Except for checking on the painters at Hobbs Family Practice, I don't have much to do, and I'm not starting another job for a while. Consider me your personal chauffeur and assistant."

"How long do you expect me to stay?" asked Maggie with surprise.

"As long as you want. No one's using that room. I won't bother you."

"You know, that's how Liz seduced me. She held me captive for two months while my broken leg healed."

"You think that's what I'm trying to do? Seduce you?" Sam glanced at her shyly.

Maggie sighed. "I don't know why you would. Currently, I'm incapable of doing anything useful in that department."

"You could let me do all the work." Sam gave Maggie a sexy side-eye.

"Never mind that, Samantha McKinnon! I'll consider it when I can take a real shower."

"Can you take a bath? I have a really nice bathroom. I even tiled the bath surround."

"You don't give up, do you? If I had known, I would have stayed home."

Sam grinned. "Don't worry. I don't have any naughty designs on you. All I want is for you to rest and get better." She could feel Maggie's eyes studying her.

"In that case, maybe I will take you up on that hot bath. It would feel so good to be clean! But you might have to help me out of the bathtub."

"I don't mind."

❋❋❋

"Lucy! Are you ready to go?" Liz called from downstairs.

Lucy scanned the cover email one last time. Deciding it looked good, she closed her eyes and pressed send. The last installment of her book was now on its way to the publisher. Lucy said a little prayer that the critics wouldn't crucify her.

"Lucy!" Liz called impatiently.

"My bag is by the door!" Lucy called back.

"I'll put it in the truck."

Lucy closed her laptop but left it charging. She'd promised Liz she wouldn't work during their little vacation. She'd brought along her tablet to read for pleasure and receive emails, but schoolwork and anything relating to church business was off limits. Tom and Cherie had volunteered to cover for her in the event of an emergency. Lucy grabbed her purse and hurried down the stairs.

Liz had returned from putting her bag in the truck. When she bent to offer a kiss, she tasted like a brisk wind and sea air, offering a tantalizing harbinger of what it would be like living on the boat for five days. That was the romantic part. It would also be cold and scary.

"I was beginning to think you'd left without me," Lucy teased, taking her parka down from the coat stand. "It's already so late. I thought you might have decided to wait until tomorrow."

"It took longer than I expected, but we have about four hours of daylight left. I have a list of all the marinas along the navigation route. If we don't make it all the way to Portland by sundown, we'll put in wherever we find ourselves."

When they reached the marina, Liz idled the engine to warm it up. The deck rumbled under their feet as they made ready to cast off. Lucy had spent enough time on the boat to know the drill, but when she overreached and leaned too far over the side, Liz yanked her back by her waistband. "Be careful. That water is cold."

"You're very protective today," said Lucy, hands on hips. "What's going on?"

"I'll tell you once we get underway."

Lucy scrutinized Liz's face. "Things go okay with Maggie?"

"Lucy, I said I'll tell you later. Now, *sit down*." Surprised by the sharp tone, Lucy stared in annoyance, but Liz was busy trying to get underway and not paying attention. Lucy decided to let it go and hiked herself into the chair next to the pilot's. It was high enough to see the water from the window. *This must be the perspective tall women have,* Lucy thought with delight as Liz steered out of the berth. There was no traffic in the channel, but it felt like the boat was going too fast. It rocked when the wake slapped against the jetty.

"Are you trying to make me seasick?" Lucy asked, winding her hair over her ears so she could hear better over the engine noise.

"I'm sorry." Liz cut back on the throttle. "I'm annoyed that we're getting such a late start. I forgot that Ellen put in all those drains."

Lucy stroked Liz's shoulder. "We'll get there. This is supposed to be a vacation. There's no need to rush."

"Most people have their boats in dry dock already. This is the longest trip I've ever taken this late in the season. There won't be as many boats on the water if we get into trouble. We're crazy to do this."

"I know."

"If you know it's crazy, why are you coming with me?"

"Because you wanted to do it, and it sounded like fun. I know you're too sensible to put us in real danger."

"When the Coast Guard shows up to rescue us, I'll remind you that you said that." Once they were out of the channel, Liz turned up the throttle again. "I packed sandwiches for dinner. If we're near civilization at dusk, we can put in and go to a restaurant."

"Sandwiches are okay too."

"That's what I love about you, Lucy. You're game for anything and you're not fussy."

"About some things, I am."

"Name one."

Lucy thought for a moment. "Underwear. I love wearing lace panties and bras."

Liz mocked a shudder. "Not me. My mother used to dress me in frilly underpants when I was little. She even used the threat of wetting the fancy panties for toilet training. I hated them. Ever since, I prefer plain, cotton undies."

Lucy could form an accurate mental image of Liz in a pretty dress and fancy panties because she had browsed Liz's photo albums during the lockdown. Baby Liz looked every bit as serious as the adult version, making Lucy wonder if she'd been an unhappy child. She looked so sad in some of the photos that Lucy wished she could reach back in time and give that little girl a hug.

"Don't get the wrong idea, Lucy. I love it when you wear fancy bras and panties." Liz smiled suggestively. "I like pretty women who enjoy being female."

"I was going to paint my fingernails today," Lucy said, extending her fingers. "I so seldom have a chance to do it. Somehow, I couldn't picture the skipper's mate wearing 'Bordeaux Lust.'"

"Oh, but I can."

"You and Erika and your nail polish fetish."

"Believe it or not, I once let Maggie give me a pedicure and put on polish. It was kind of sexy." Liz smiled when she spoke about Maggie, which was a good sign.

"You were going to tell me how it went today."

Liz shrugged. "Fine." Lucy recognized that tone—the vocal equivalent of a door being slammed shut in her face. It was so frustrating!

Lucy zipped up her parka and pulled up her hood. "You're cold, aren't you?" asked Liz. She took Lucy's hand and put it on the steering wheel. "Hold this while I crank up the heat. This vessel is built for winter fishing. The cabin should warm up quickly." Liz left her chair and turned on the two radiant heaters. The coils glowed orange, and soon the cabin began to warm.

"What made you think of taking the boat out this late in the year?"

"I've never done it before."

"A little danger to get your adrenaline pumping?"

"Exactly! Sometimes, I need to remind myself that there's still life in me. When I start becoming fearful and shying away from adventure, that's when I'll know I'm old."

"You're not old, Liz. You look fantastic." Lucy frowned. "You're not one who talks about getting old. What's going on?"

"I looked at Alina's kids today and saw how fast time is passing. Obviously, I'm closer to the end of my life than the beginning. When I look in the mirror, I can see how much I've aged. My hair is nearly white. The wrinkles are like chasms worn by a river. I'm not vain, so I don't really care about my looks, but I'm no longer the handsome, young butch who can turn heads."

"You turned mine," Lucy protested. "My heart skipped a few beats when I met you. I looked into those blue eyes and couldn't speak. Thank God, you opened your mouth, or we would still be standing in my church, staring at one another."

Liz patted Lucy's thigh. "I'm glad I haven't lost my touch, but today, when I was snipping the stitches to remove Maggie's drains, my hands felt clumsy. As my grandmother used to say when she was crocheting, and her hands were stiff from arthritis: '*Meine Finger sind dumm!*' Now that I've lost some manual dexterity, I understand. Watching Ellen operate made me wish I was back in the OR, but quitting surgery was the right thing to do."

Lucy thought for a moment before venturing a guess. "Is that why you haven't retired? To prove you're still able?"

"No. I haven't retired because there is a desperate shortage of doctors, and while I can still practice, I will. Part of me wishes I could skip the decline and work until I drop dead…like my brother. Heart disease runs in the family."

Lucy had been listening intently as she always did when people confessed their fears, but the memory of finding Erika lifeless in bed flashed into her mind. Liz apparently sensed the change. She slipped out of the skipper's chair and gave Lucy a little hug. "I'm scaring you. I'm sorry."

"I'm happy to listen."

"Who listens to you?" Liz asked.

"You do."

"Not enough, I think."

"Liz, you listen to people's problems all day. Why would you want to listen to mine?"

"Because I love you," said Liz, pulling her closer.

Lucy's eyes filled as the boat gently rocked them. There they were—two women, no longer young, clinging to one another in a small boat, floating on a vast ocean. Lucy forced herself to remember that they weren't insignificant. God saw them.

They managed to reach Portland by sundown. Liz put in to the marina. While they ate their tuna sandwiches, they watched the light fade. Lucy was grateful for the hot chowder left over from the church fair. The thermal containers steamed when they took off the lids.

"Will we have heat below deck tonight?" Lucy asked anxiously.

"Just our body heat."

"Seriously?"

Liz laughed. "No. Now that we're plugged into the dock, we have power. We'll have heat tonight."

After it got dark, Liz locked up the pilot house and they went below. At night, the reflection off the wood paneling made the cabin seem warm and inviting, but the waves lapping against the hull reminded Lucy that the cold ocean was just on the other side. "I'm not giving up my long johns," she declared. She unhooked her bra but wiggled back into the thermal shirt.

"I know how to find my way in, when I need to." Liz took off her jeans, giving Lucy a brief view of the white cotton briefs before they disappeared into thick, gray sweatpants.

"I'm a little anxious," Lucy admitted, getting into the snug bed under the prow. "This would have been the scene of the crime if I'd given in to your kiss."

"A missed opportunity, but it was a good thing you stopped me." Liz handed Lucy a glass of wine. "I don't know what I was thinking."

"Thinking didn't have much to do with it. I wasn't thinking either. I just wanted you to make love to me."

"You never told me that."

"I've only recently admitted it to myself."

Liz slouched in her seat, extending her long legs until they rested on the bench across from her. She crossed her arms, leaving one elevated to support her wine glass. "Maggie asked me to forgive her today."

*So, this is what Liz has been sitting on since she came back from Scarborough.* Lucy waited for her to say more, but of course, she didn't. "What did you say?"

"I said that I'd already forgiven her for coming on to me at Jenny's and for fucking Brad. And then, she admitted she had other flirtations besides her boy toy." Liz turned to Lucy. "Was that what you two talked about last night? Forgiveness?"

Lucy looked away to avoid confirming what Liz already knew. "Liz, you need to forgive her. All that anger is eating you up."

Liz inspected her fingernails with a closed fist like a man. "Talking to Tom has been helpful. I didn't realize that I never forgave Maggie for dating men in college. She wanted it both ways. She went out with the popular boys and left me back at the dorm, an embarrassment to be hidden. I was supposed to put up with that shit so she could feel normal. Then she just left me there. I was such a mess I almost didn't go to medical school. I even thought about killing myself. You didn't know that, did you?"

"No! Liz, I never realized it was that bad."

"Oh, it was bad. But I was on my own. In those days, if you had any history of mental illness, you couldn't get a license to practice medicine."

"Is that why you avoid therapy?"

"Among other reasons."

"I'm glad you're talking to Tom."

"Me too. I've found out that I'm still angry about something that happened almost fifty years ago. That's why I never felt guilty about our kiss. Part of me felt Maggie deserved it after all the pain she'd caused me."

"When you accused Maggie of being vindictive, was it projection?"

"No. She admitted she had an affair to punish her husband for cheating. That time, she chose a woman. She always designs her affairs to inflict the maximum damage."

"I have a hard time believing Maggie is so devious. My impression is she lashed out because she was angry and hurt."

"So was I, but we could have settled things years ago. After I got myself back together, I would have told her that I'd forgiven her for abandoning me, but she acted like I was a stalker and wouldn't answer my letters or take my calls. I just wanted her to acknowledge me. But she was still hiding me like a dirty secret, just like when we were in college. If she hadn't broken her fucking leg, she still wouldn't be talking to me. When she showed up in my office, I thought it was a sign that we belonged together. Now, I know I just wanted something I couldn't have. Then I found the cancer, and I couldn't escape."

Lucy didn't know what to say, so she remained silent, hoping the pity didn't show on her face. Liz drained her glass and got up to refill it. By that time, Lucy had found her voice. "How sad for both of you."

"Don't feel sorry for us. We had a good life together. It worked until it didn't."

"For your own sake, you should forgive her. Liz, I can't marry you with all that anger bottled up inside you." Once the words were out of Lucy's mouth, the air crackled like before a thunderstorm. "I didn't mean that," she added quickly.

Liz took a long swallow of wine. "Maybe you shouldn't marry me."

"Is that what you want?"

"No."

Lucy got up and tugged Liz's arm. "Come on. I'm sorry. Put away the wine and let me hold you."

Liz drained her glass and corked the bottle before disappearing into the tiny bathroom. Lucy waited in the cramped bed. The mattress was more comfortable than she'd expected, but she trembled under the comforter, cold and worried. She wondered if the heavy conversation spelled disaster for the trip.

The overhead light switched off, and Liz crawled on all fours into the bed. She let her body down with a thud and pulled her knees nearly up to her chin because it was such a tight squeeze.

"Come here," said Lucy, but Liz wouldn't budge. "Liz, I'm sorry I said I wouldn't marry you."

"You already apologized," Liz replied in an emotionless voice.

"Come on. Let me hold you." Finally, Liz rolled in her direction, and Lucy breathed a sigh of relief. She'd been prepared for rejection. When Liz was in one of these moods, she could be gruff and dismissive.

A warm hand snaked up Lucy's thermal shirt and cupped her breast. Her nipple instantly tightened to the light touch of Liz's fingers. Lucy felt slightly aroused, but she was worried that sex wouldn't be enough. She pressed Liz's hand closer to stop the motion. "Liz, you do know that I love you?"

"Yes," murmured Liz, but she didn't sound sure. She wiggled her hand free and took it back, which wasn't what Lucy had intended.

"Please believe me," Lucy whispered into the dark.

"I do." Again, the note of uncertainty. "Do you love me enough to marry me?"

Lucy swallowed a string of words that seemed too complicated to say. "Yes."

"Then let me make love to you."

Lucy could think of a multitude of reasons why they should keep talking instead, but sex seemed the simplest solution. Liz moved over her, covering her with her body, parting her legs with her knee. Her kisses were impatient. They became increasingly fierce, almost bitter. Her strong fingers moving inside her awakened unwelcome memories of the rape, but Lucy dismissed them. She opened wider to the insistent probing, willing herself to accept Liz's aggression as generously as she welcomed her tenderness. The climax came quickly and shook her entire body.

Afterward, Liz was still restless. She spooned Lucy for warmth, but she couldn't settle down. She adjusted her pillow twice. She swore when she threw Lucy's hair out of her face.

"I'm getting up. I'm just keeping you awake."

Lucy grabbed Liz's arm before she could get away. "No, you don't. If you leave me here without your body heat, I'll freeze to death."

"Then put these on." Liz picked up Lucy's thermal top and pants from the floor and tossed them in her direction. After she pulled on her own shirt and pants, she got back into bed.

Lucy rearranged herself in the tight space until they were eye to eye. "Do you want me to make you come again? That might relax you."

"I want you to go to sleep. You don't need to take care of me."

"Sure, I do. You're always taking care of other people. You deserve to be taken care of too. What will help you go back to sleep?" Lucy thought for a moment. "I could sing to you." She positioned herself higher on the pillow. "Come on. Scoot down, so I can cuddle you." After Liz made herself comfortable against her breast, Lucy began to sing Rachmaninoff's *Vocalise.* When she drew breath to begin the coda, she heard a faint, contented snore.

She drifted off to sleep, dreaming she saw a light flickering in the wind across the dark ocean. She identified it as Liz out on her boat, but she wondered how she could ever cross such a vast space to reach her.

# 15

Cherie studied her boss's face for signs that she had offended her. It was never easy to tell what was going on in Liz's head. Her silence was like a trap that lured you in and held you until you told her things she didn't need to know. Under the steady gaze of those blue eyes, Cherie couldn't keep herself from blurting out excuses. "We want to celebrate as a family. It's our first Thanksgiving with our babies. And if my aunt comes it will be so special!"

Liz finally blinked, breaking the tension. "Aren't you worried about a woman her age getting on a plane? The COVID numbers are rising again. People refuse to wear masks and act like assholes. They beat up flight attendants."

"Of course, I'm worried, but she's had all her shots. She'll wear a mask and be tested before she leaves, and she'll keep her distance until we're sure she wasn't infected on the plane. Oh, Liz, she really wants to come!" Cherie felt like she was pleading for permission, but she was really trying to persuade herself. "She might even stay if she likes it here. We have no family left in Louisiana. All my cousins moved away."

"That's hard on elderly people," Liz said. "How old is she?"

"Seventy-two. A very young seventy-two." Cherie wondered how it would feel for a woman that age to uproot herself from a warm, familiar place where she'd lived since birth and come to frigid Maine. Cherie still hadn't adjusted to its harsh winters. Once there was plowable snow, they wouldn't see the ground again until April. Cherie shivered just thinking about it. "Aunt Simone was an elementary school teacher all her life. She misses having kids in her life. She volunteered to watch mine when they come home from school."

"Not working out with Denise?" asked Liz, frowning.

"Oh, yes, it's great, but it's always good to have backup."

"Any word on the adoption?"

"Not yet. We're praying."

Liz raised a skeptical brow. Cherie wondered how Liz could marry the rector if she had that attitude about praying, but that was none of her business. She knew that Liz had a low opinion of psychotherapy too, but that didn't stop her from recommending patients. Most of Cherie's clients came through Liz.

"Well, Cherie," Liz said with a sigh. "We'll miss you and Brenda, but I understand. Know that you're always welcome. We still have all those pies in the freezer from the church fair."

"We only have a few left. Brenda loves pie." The words were out of her mouth before Cherie remembered the double meaning. The glint of mischief in Liz's eyes indicated she had too. "We've been pacing ourselves," Cherie continued, knowing she was digging herself in deeper. "I put Brenda on a diet. She's been developing a little pot belly, even with working out at the police gym."

"Marriage will do that to you. But don't worry. I won't mention the pie." This time Liz allowed herself a lewd grin.

Cherie laughed. "Since we're almost down to our last pie, maybe we could come for dessert."

"And you'd be welcome." Liz glanced at her watch. "Cherie, I'm keeping you. Don't you need to pick up the kids?"

"Yes, I've got to get out of here. Thanks for the invitation. I appreciate it."

"You're welcome. And now I need to see all those patients waiting for COVID shots."

"I feel guilty leaving you," said Cherie, getting up.

"Go. We'll manage."

Cherie hurried to get her coat and bag from the new locker room. It was unisex, but the only male member of the team was Liz's partner, Bill. He kept his stuff in his office closet.

"Off to your next job?" Ginny asked pleasantly as Cherie hurried to the front door.

"Yes, and I'm late again." Cherie looked out at the long line of parents waiting for vaccinations for their kids. "Liz is coming right down to see these patients."

"I hope so, it's getting cold out there."

Overhead, the sky threatened snow. Cherie wished there was a warmer place for people to wait, but with COVID, they didn't want people crowding the waiting room. The parents and grandparents waiting in line looked harried. Now that she had children, Cherie understood why. She resisted the urge to speed on her way to the elementary school. At least, she wouldn't have to wait while the buses pulled out into traffic. They'd be gone by now.

The crossing guard, one of Cherie's patients, was back at work. He waved as she passed. There were still parents picking up their kids from the front of the school, where Courtney waited with Keith and Megan.

"I'm so sorry to be late again," said Cherie, her breath emerging as vapor in the November cold.

"It's no problem. You're not really late, but I was just about to bring the kids inside."

"How's it going with you?"

Courtney shrugged. "The principal's out again with her mother. Fortunately, the cold weather has put a damper on the protests."

"Will the school board put in vaccine mandates?"

"I don't think so. The masks caused enough controversy."

Cherie looked through the glass doors into the enormous anteroom leading into the school. "Do you think we could get approval to run a vaccine clinic here?"

Courtney followed the direction of Cherie's gaze. "We can ask."

"I'll tell Liz. I don't know why we didn't think of it before. We ran one at the police station. It worked great."

"I'm sure if we hold it here, it will draw protests," said Courtney with a despairing sigh.

"I'm surprised they don't get bored with it."

"Some of them have nothing better to do. It's more than a cause. It's their only purpose in life—like the guys who drive around with flags flying from the back of their trucks."

Cherie didn't have time for a long political conversation. "Thanks for waiting, Courtney. I've got to get these two to choir practice."

On the way to the church, Keith talked about a fight on the playground. After listening for a while, Cherie asked, "What was this fight about?"

Keith's eyes engaged hers in the rearview mirror. "The kid's father died from the virus. Another kid said he really didn't die. He just left."

"That was mean. Why did he say that?"

Keith raised his shoulders.

"I hope you're nice to the kid whose father died. You know that's not an easy place to be."

Keith's lip began to tremble, and he glanced out the window. Cherie knew this subject needed deeper conversation, but not while they were racing to choir practice. She watched Keith in the rearview mirror, trying to decide whether having other kids in his class who'd lost parents made him feel less isolated or just brought up painful memories.

Fortunately, they would only be five minutes late. Since she'd become a foster mother, Cherie felt like she was late for everything. It bothered her because she prided herself on being punctual, but the kids moved to their own time, no matter how much she pushed and prodded them.

The other members of the children's choir were hard at work on a writing project. On the board were the musical symbols they were copying. "We're learning how to write music," Denise explained, handing the children pencils and sheets of blank score paper.

"That's ambitious," Cherie said, watching her kids find seats.

"Music is a language like any other. The earlier you start learning it, the better."

"My kids love coming here. They talk about it all the time. When they come home from choir practice, they have to sing what they learn for us." Cherie made a little face. "Not always well."

"Keith has a nice voice," said Denise. "Megan needs to learn to stay on key, but from what I've read, she's right at the developmental stage for her age."

Cherie realized that meant Denise had taken the time to research the subject. "You're really getting into this."

"I am."

Cherie lowered her voice. "I saw Lucy's door was dark when I passed. She's not here?"

"No, she rescheduled her afternoon appointments to meet with the bishop."

"Oh, is she in trouble?"

Denise laughed. "I don't think so. But you know Lucy. She can be unconventional."

"So's the bishop. He's gay too."

"I read that he made national news by calling the Holy Spirit 'She' at his consecration."

"I didn't hear that, but good for him." Cherie gave Denise's shoulder a pat. "I'll be back later. Hopefully, not late this time."

❋❋❋

The sleet pinged against the pavement as Lucy walked across the park. She didn't really care if she got wet, but she liked to look her best for the bishop. It was self-defense as well as respect. It was his job to care for his clergy, but since Olivia had shared her concerns, he'd been annoyingly attentive.

Lucy stepped carefully. High-heeled boots made her taller. At her height, any boost in stature was an advantage, although opera directors had appreciated that she didn't tower over the tenors like other sopranos. Today, the heels made walking on the icy sidewalk more treacherous. Lucy walked in the icy grass for better traction.

The admin's desk in the anteroom to the bishop's office was empty, and her computer screen was dark. For a moment, Lucy wondered if she'd arrived on the wrong day. She took out her phone to check her calendar.

The door to the bishop's office opened. "I thought I'd come out to see if you were here. Patsy's out for the day." He noted Lucy's instant concern. "Not to worry. It's not COVID. She had vacation time she wanted to use before the end of the year." He looked around. "Dr. Stolz didn't come with you?"

Lucy tensed. She'd been rehearsing her explanation on the way up and hoped it sounded convincing. At least, it was the truth. "She sends her apologies. They're vaccinating children at her office, and they're very busy."

The bishop had listened without reaction while she spoke, but she sensed his annoyance. "I'm trying to get in the pre-marital counseling around her schedule. Sounds like that's going to be harder than I thought." He guided Lucy by the shoulder into his office. "I hope, for both your sakes, that she's as serious about this marriage as you are." Despite the empty waiting room, he carefully closed the door behind them.

"Healthcare workers are under a lot of pressure right now," said Lucy. "I'm glad she's in counseling with Tom."

"That's good, and I want to hear all about it, but first, I'd like to discuss some business." He extended a hand toward a chair.

Lucy sat down, fiddling with her collar to make sure it was straight. When the bishop took off his mask, she took off hers.

He took a moment to look her over. Lucy guessed he was making a quick evaluation of her, much like how she assessed her counseling clients when they first came into her office. External appearance can reveal much about a person's mental state. He smiled warmly. "Lucy, you look much more rested than last time."

"Last time, I'd spent half the night with a dying woman. I'm surprised I could stay awake during the meeting."

He laughed. "But you did a great job of covering for yourself. Are you getting more rest?"

"I was able to get away on a little vacation. We took Liz's boat up to Casco Bay and cruised around for a few days."

"It's beautiful there."

"We slept on the boat one night, but it was so cold I thought I would never get warm again. We stayed on Peak's Island on the other nights."

"I hope you enjoyed it. I approve of you giving yourself time to re-charge your physical and spiritual batteries." He folded his hands on his desk. His smile was too perfect, almost as if he were posing for a portrait on the diocesan website. Lucy matched his smile, but she had an uneasy feeling. "Lucy, I have some big asks. I know that in our last visit, I was pushing you to take some things off your plate, but you seem to be managing well. You have that generous endowment from Olivia Enright, which was really smart of you."

"But I didn't…."

He raised his hand to stop her before she repeated herself. "I know you didn't solicit it, but she gave it because you ministered to her in exactly the way she needed. You have a gift for ministry. In fact, you have so many gifts that I hardly know how to deploy them all! We have a genuine opera star in our diocese, and yet we let her hide down there in Hobbs."

Lucy frowned, wondering where this was going. "I'm not hiding. I quit singing when I joined the church."

"You still sing.  You're singing a concert with Denise Chantal at the Webhanet Playhouse."

"It's a fundraiser. The Playhouse is barely scraping by after the pandemic closed them down for a season."

"This is fundraising, too, but think of it as a musical ministry. You could lift people up with your voice at a time when we all desperately need inspiration."

"What did you have in mind?" asked Lucy, using the shrewd tone she used to reserve for agents and opera house general managers.

"What do you think of joining our cathedral worship from time to time or perhaps a concert? We'd publicize it, of course."

"What does your director of music think about this?"

"It was his idea." He leaned forward. "Lucy, I always try to use the special talents of my clergy. Remember when Canon McMann, who's a physician, conveyed our messages about the pandemic? It was more effective because of her special expertise. Our music tradition attracts many people. You, yourself, said it was one of the reasons you became an Episcopalian."

Lucy tried to think of a way to politely deflect the request. "Jim, I have my hands full with St. Margaret's and the summer chapel. I also have a part-time counseling practice, which I haven't given up because there's so much need. My dissertation is written, but I still have to defend it. I can't possibly make a commitment until I finish school next year."

"Of course, and I know it's asking a lot of you. But I can offer some help. What do you think about taking a transitional deacon in your parish?"

"What?" asked Lucy, startled by the request. Taking on a transitional deacon sounded like help, but junior clergy needed close supervision. Lucy forced her brow to relax, so the bishop wouldn't see how much this idea distressed her.

"I mentioned it to Tom, and he seemed to like the idea. He even volunteered to mentor her." If Tom was already involved, this request would be difficult to refuse. Lucy scrambled to think of an appropriate response. The bishop jumped into the gap. "Tom assured me he could think of many ways the deacon could lighten your workload. She could help with the hospital and homebound visits. You could restart the morning prayer services the pandemic interrupted…I'm sure you'll find ways to put her to work. Won't you at least look at her resume?"

Lucy was happy to hear that the deacon was female, then scolded herself for being sexist. She gazed out the window to figure out what to say and noticed that the sleet had turned to snow. Meanwhile, the bishop was still waiting for an answer.

"Lucy, you can say no," he said. "I don't want to overburden you."

"After I finish school, I'll have more time. At least my book is with the publisher."

"And a fine book it is."

"You really think so?" asked Lucy, feeling suddenly insecure.

"Yes! It's brilliant, compassionate, and illuminating. I think it's going to be a big hit. You may find yourself more famous than when you were an opera singer. But be prepared. Some people won't like what you have to say. The old moralists will have their knives out for you. You saw how same-sex marriage nearly ripped apart the Anglican communion, and it's still not settled." A shadow of sadness passed over his handsome face. "Speaking of marriage, have you and Liz set a date for your wedding?"

Lucy shook her head. "Not yet, but it needs to be after school ends."

"You should come up with a date, so I can get it on my calendar." He opened his laptop. "Pentecost is on June fifth. How about the next Saturday? The eleventh?"

"Yes, let's try for that."

"At St. Margaret's?"

"No, the summer chapel, I think."

"St. Mary's by the Sea," he said aloud as he typed. "Do you want to consult Dr. Stolz first?"

Lucy shrugged. "Bride's prerogative."

"You're both brides," he reminded her with a smile.

In fact, Liz would probably snarl at being called a bride. "Let me text her to see if that date works for her," said Lucy, pulling out her phone. "You can probably pencil it in. It's so far out, I doubt she'll have a problem with it."

"Okay, and then I want to discuss why she didn't show up today."

Lucy flinched and sent her text before it was finished. She hurried to complete the message. Two seconds later her phone pinged with an answer. *Your call. Get your ass out of there. The weather sucks.*

"She says the date is fine," Lucy said, translating Liz's blue language into something more acceptable.

"Agreement is good," said the bishop, completing the entry in his laptop before closing it. He leaned back in his chair. "So, let's discuss why Dr. Stolz didn't come today. I understand that she's involved in the vaccination effort. Have you explained the importance of these meetings?"

"I have, but as you probably guessed from our last meeting, Liz is something of a rebel."

"Yes, and well-read, apparently. You said that she's has been talking to Tom. Tell me more, if you can."

"Liz is dealing with many issues—the pandemic, her many responsibilities to Hobbs, her mother's death last year, the end of her marriage."

"She's divorced?"

"Yes. I'm sorry, Jim. I thought I told you."

He frowned. "No, I don't think you did, but now I understand why you need to wait until spring. I'm assuming the date you set accounts for the waiting period after the divorce filing."

"Yes, it does." Lucy clasped one hand tightly in the other. *Why had she forgotten to mention Liz's divorce?*

"If I recall, your marriage to Erika Bultmann happened rather quickly."

"The church teaches that the only appropriate context for sex is marriage."

"Or, as you convincingly argue in your book, a loving, committed relationship. You shouldn't rush, Lucy. Until very few years ago, none of us could be married in the Church."

"It feels different to be married."

"It does, doesn't it?" said Bishop Green, looking reflective. "And yet so many people take it for granted." He focused on her face and looked intent. "Why did Dr. Stolz's marriage end? Do you know?"

"I'd rather let Liz tell you about it."

"Of course. So would I, but she's not here." He sounded irritated. By standing him up, Liz had apparently gotten under his skin.

"I can tell you this much," said Lucy. "Her wife had an affair with a man. Except for that, I think the marriage might have survived. Liz is still incredibly angry about it. Maggie, Liz's ex-wife, recently had a recurrence of cancer. Because Liz is a specialist in this type of cancer, Maggie asked for her support. Liz is finding it difficult for many reasons. I was tempted to intervene because I was Maggie's best friend, but I decided it was best not to involve myself."

"I note your use of the past tense."

Lucy took a deep breath. She was in this far. How could she get out of continuing? "Maggie blames me for breaking up the marriage."

He leaned forward expectantly. "Did you break up the marriage?"

"Not intentionally." Lucy couldn't imagine lying to the bishop. "There was one questionable incident. When Liz took her boat out fishing, I invited myself along. Without warning, she kissed me. Maggie found out about it somehow and was very upset."

"Understandably." The bishop's face maintained a neutral expression, but Lucy noticed a little pucker between his brows. "What did you do when Dr. Stolz initiated this kiss?"

Lucy felt her cheeks flame. She imagined the two bright red spots that showed like dabs of old-fashioned rouge whenever she blushed. She knew their appearance would confirm her guilt. "I ended it quickly."

"How quickly?"

"I responded at first, but I came to my senses and pushed her away."

"You knew she was married. You were also married."

"Yes," said Lucy in a small voice.

The pucker between the bishop's brows grew deeper. He leaned forward in his chair. "How long had this been going on?"

Lucy suddenly felt desperate. Wanting to flee, she glanced at the door trying to gauge its distance from her chair. When she looked back, she encountered the bishop's intense gaze. He was still waiting for an answer. "Probably since we met. Liz reached out to shake my hand when she introduced herself after my first carol service at St. Margaret's. They say when you're electrocuted you can't let go of the source of the current. It holds you in its grip until the power shuts off or you die. When our hands touched, neither of us wanted to let go."

"What you describe is a powerful attraction," said the bishop, his handsome face pale with concern.

"Powerful, yes, but not sexual. For years, I hadn't had so much as a twinge of interest in sex."

"Because of the rape you described in your book?"

"That and a relationship that ended in disappointment. I was nearly fifty when I was ordained, and I thought I would be content to live out the rest of my life as a celibate priest. That was the guidance at the time, and the ordination of gays and lesbians was still so controversial. I never expected to have an intimate relationship again."

"But that wasn't what God had planned for you."

"Apparently not. I met Erika at that carol service and Liz's wife. Maggie helped me get adjusted to life in Hobbs. She joined the choir and eventually became the music director at St. Margaret's. She and I shared so many interests—a life spent on the stage, dressing up, shopping, a love of musical theater. I wasn't as close to Liz at first."

"Why not?"

"She frightened me. She was scary smart and so intense. Erika came back that summer to finish writing her book on Habermas. They'd been friends for decades. I got to know Liz better because they spent so much time together. They would sit around, talking about things only they understood. Liz was with us so much that, when I married Erika, it was like getting a two-fer."

"Lucy, did you love your wife?"

"Oh, yes! Please don't misunderstand. Erika awakened a passion in me I thought had died forever. Despite her cool personality, she was a passionate woman. I truly loved her."

"And you were never intimate with Liz before her divorce or Erika's death?"

Lucy shook her head. "The closest we ever came was that steamy kiss on her boat."

"So, you were technically faithful." The bishop massaged his forehead as if he felt a headache forming. "Lucy, you have more formal training in psychotherapy than I do, and you wrote the best book on sex I've ever read. What would you say about this situation?"

"It's a mess."

He nodded enthusiastically, confirming her opinion. "Now, be honest. Are you responsible for the breakup of Liz's marriage? If you are, you are violating the guidance on remarriage after divorce." Lucy felt a flutter of panic, like a bird's wings beating inside her chest.

"I could have contributed to their breakup, but only peripherally. After Maggie forced me to tell her about the incident on the boat, she refused to let it go. She harped on it, alienating Liz. They seemed to reconcile for a while. Liz and I tried to stay away from one another, but we had to work together. And when Liz stayed away, Erika was hurt. I loved Erika. I loved Maggie too. She was my best friend."

"Lucy, I'm not judging you, but I don't need to tell you this is a serious problem. I'm not going to tell you what to do, but as a homework assignment, I want you to really look at this mess, analyze it until you see every aspect. Apply your expertise as a therapist. Pray for discernment. Then, if you still think marrying Liz Stolz is the right thing to do, you have my blessing. But while you're examining your conscience, please be kind to yourself. Remember that we're all sinners." He gazed out the window and instantly did a double take. "Good heavens! That snow is coming down hard. You should probably leave before the roads get bad."

Lucy couldn't get up at first, still stunned by the conversation. The bishop offered his hand, and Lucy finally got to her feet. "Call me if you need me. I'm happy to talk to you," he said. "God bless you, Lucy. I'm praying for you...and Dr. Stolz."

After she closed the office door, Lucy was grateful to be alone. She felt too wobbly to take the stairs and headed for the elevator. Suddenly feverish, she leaned her forehead against the stainless-steel wall to have its coolness. What had she done? She'd told the entire sordid story to her bishop, spilling all her anxiety and confusion in the process. *How stupid! And what a bad move for my career as a priest!*

She still felt shaky on her way to the parking garage. The sleet beneath the snow had left the pavement slick. She tried to plant each step firmly, but she was almost skating on the sidewalk. She headed toward the snow-covered grass for better footing. Just before she reached it, her leg suddenly skidded out from under her. Time passed in slow motion as the leaden sky overhead came into focus. When she landed, the impact was stunning. She saw a few valiant, red leaves still clinging to a maple before everything went black.

When she awoke, she was shivering from the cold. Her cheeks and her lips were numb. She blinked away the snowflakes that had settled on her eyelashes. A young female face with dark eyes and warm, brown skin hovered over hers. "Miss, miss, are you okay? Please be okay." The voice was anxious and emphatic.

"I fell," said Lucy, gingerly sitting up.

"I saw you go down," the woman bending over her replied. "You hit your head hard. We need to get you to a warm place. Can you stand?"

Lucy took an inventory of her body. She didn't think anything was broken, but it felt like someone had taken a hammer to the back of her head. She felt around tentatively and cringed as she brought her hand to her face, afraid to look. Fortunately, there was no blood. "Can you help me up?" Lucy asked.

The young woman reached into Lucy's armpit to give her a lift, and her black coat gaped open. Lucy's eyes fell on the collar. "You're ordained," she murmured, astonished.

"Just a deacon for now. I was heading to the bishop's office hoping to meet a rector who might have me, but she had to leave early because of the weather."

"That's me." Lucy zipped down her coat to show her collar. "Lucille Bartlett," she said, dusting off her backside.

"Bishop Greene said I might catch you if I hurried. Oh, Rev. Bartlett! I'm Reshma John. I'm so pleased to meet you!" Lucy blinked at the enthusiastic greeting. "I'm sorry," said the woman. "Let's save the introductions for later and get you to a warm place." She reached across the sidewalk for Lucy's purse. "Where were you going when you fell?"

"To the parking garage down the street."

"I'll help you."

"I can manage."

"Please, let me help you. As you know, it is a deacon's role to serve." The woman's dark eyes were kind, and her grip on Lucy's arm would allow no argument. Besides, Lucy's head ached, and she felt a little dizzy.

"Thank you. Please just help me to the parking garage."

"I've got you," said Deacon John, tightening her grip. Gingerly, Lucy took a few steps.

❋❋❋

Liz and Brenda drove around twice before they saw a young, black woman waving her arms furiously. She pointed to a parking space, and Liz recognized Lucy's car.

"Why didn't you just call 911?" Liz barked at the young woman as she hopped out of the police cruiser.

"She wouldn't allow it." The woman followed Liz back to Lucy's car. "She seemed okay to walk with my help."

"Who the hell are you?" asked Liz, eyeing the woman's collar.

"Reshma John. I'm the one who called you. I saw Mother Lucy fall."

Liz ripped open the passenger side door. Lucy looked at her mournfully. "Oh Lucy, what the hell did you do to yourself?" She reached over and turned off the engine, which they'd obviously been running for warmth. She shined a light into Lucy's eyes. To her relief, the pupils were the same size and responded to light. Lucy's eyes followed Liz's finger normally. "Did you black out?"

"Maybe," said Lucy. "I don't remember."

"She slipped on the ice," the stranger volunteered. "She hit the back of her head really hard."

"Thanks. I can take it from here," Liz said briskly. The woman in the collar didn't leave, so Liz ignored her. She eased Lucy forward, so she could examine the back of her head. There was no blood on the head rest, which was a good sign. Liz pulled out the black scrunchie holding Lucy's hair and examined the scalp. A purple bruise was blooming under the skin, but there were no open wounds. Liz's fingers lightly traced the vertebrae in her neck. "Any pain here?"

"No, but the back of my head really hurts."

"Is she okay?" Brenda called from the open window of the police car.

"She looks okay, but let's get her to an ED for x-rays. Do you have instant cold packs with you?"

Brenda got out and opened her trunk. She found a cold pack and handed it to Liz. "Do you need a back board?"

"They managed to walk here, so it's a little late for that." Liz gave the cold pack a sharp twist to mix the chemicals and positioned it behind Lucy's head. "Lean against it, but don't press hard. I didn't feel any fractures, but that doesn't mean you didn't crack your thick skull."

"Will she be all right?" the priest, or whatever she was, asked.

"She'll be fine," said Liz, standing up. "But next time, call 911."

"It's so cold. I couldn't leave her lying there on the ice," the young woman said in a voice more anxious than defensive. She opened her bag and took out a card. "Please call me and let me know how she is."

A quick glance at the card told Liz that Reshma John was an Episcopal deacon. "Thanks for helping her," Liz muttered, shoving the card into her pocket as she went around to the driver's side door. She started the engine and watched the woman in the black coat walk down the ramp to the exit.

"I'll give you an escort to the hospital," Brenda called. She pulled forward, so Liz could get out of the parking space. The police car shot off with Liz trying to follow. They were both going much too fast down the spiral ramp to the street.

"Liz, can you slow down a little? I feel dizzy."

"I'm sorry, honey. I'm trying to keep up with Brenda. We're almost out of here."

At the exit, Liz asked, "Where's your ticket?"

"I don't remember."

Rather than wait for Lucy to find it, Liz shoved her credit card into the machine, and the gate opened. Once outside the parking garage, Brenda turned on her flashers. In a matter of minutes, they were at the emergency entrance of Portland's biggest hospital. Brenda ran in and came out with two people pushing a gurney

"I can walk," Lucy protested.

"Why walk when you can ride?" said Brenda with a grin.

In the waiting room, they were separated from Lucy by someone who stopped them for a temperature check. Meanwhile, Lucy disappeared behind double doors.

"I'm a doctor," Liz protested, but that didn't seem to matter. "She's my fiancée," she added. "I'm her medical proxy."

"Sit down. We'll call you," said the attendant, unimpressed.

Brenda left, and Liz reluctantly took a seat. She loathed modern hospitals. Medicine had become unrecognizable. There were days when she wondered why she still practiced. Ten minutes passed before someone came by to ask for Lucy's information. The woman led Liz to a station with a plexiglass window. She impatiently watched the woman photocopy Lucy's insurance cards. Flipping through the sleeves to replace them, Liz found a picture of Erika. Across from it was a photo of herself. They did look like sisters, as Stefan had said. Liz gazed at Erika's photo. *I hope you're keeping an eye on her in there.*

*Oh, I am*, Erika replied in her mind. *Don't worry.*

Liz was sent back to the waiting room, where she texted a message to the rectory and called Amy to let them know they were at the hospital. Eventually, a woman in scrubs, who Liz guessed to be a nurse, called her name. "You can wait for her in the back. They've taken her in for a CAT scan to see if there's any fractures."

"Wouldn't a head x-ray be quicker?"

The woman shrugged. "It's what we do now. At her age, she could have broken a hip or fractured her spine."

Liz bristled. "She's only fifty-seven."

"Post-menopausal. It's standard procedure."

*And more revenue to the hospital*, Liz thought with contempt.

Clutching Lucy's purse to her chest like a proxy for its owner, Liz imagined Lucy in the CAT scan tube. Liz's only CAT scan was Jenny's doing, when an odd episode of bleeding a year after menopause made her worry about the possibility of uterine cancer. Since childhood, Liz had been claustrophobic and wanted to claw her way out of that cold, cramped space. Only heroic mind control had headed off a full-blown panic attack. After all that, the bleeding had turned out to be nothing.

The door opened. "She's fine. No fractures. No brain swelling."

"May I speak with her doctor?" Liz asked, getting up.

"She's fine," the nurse repeated firmly, indicating she had no intention of involving the doctor. "Your friend will be here in a few minutes. Don't rush, but we need the room. It's getting crowded out there." Liz hoped that didn't mean Lucy had been given cursory attention to move her along. She glanced at her watch. They'd already been there an hour.

An attendant wheeled Lucy through the door in a chair and placed some paperwork in a plastic bin by the door. "You're all set. Give this to the desk at the exit," he said, pointing to the right. "Remember to rest today, Lucy. Nice meeting you." He waved, and Lucy returned the wave.

Liz felt like a voyeur watching Lucy dress, so she busied herself with reading the paperwork the attendant had left. There was nothing medically useful, only instructions to rest for the remainder of the day and avoid drinking alcohol.

"Liz, can you help me with my boots? My head hurts when I bend over."

Liz pulled on and zipped her boots. "These aren't appropriate to wear in an ice storm," she scolded.

"It was clear when I left for Portland."

Liz wanted to ask why she hadn't read the weather report but decided against grinding in her point. "I'll wheel you to the entrance to wait while I get the car."

"I can walk," Lucy protested.

"Not a chance."

They were silent as Liz drove down the turnpike. The snow had stopped, but they passed cars in the ditch that ran along the highway. Liz swerved to avoid a car shimmying as they approached their exit. The car righted itself and headed on its way. "That was close," Liz muttered. "We've had enough accidents for one day."

"Thank you for coming to get me."

"Of course, I would come get you. I'm your friend, and we're almost married." Liz slowed down on the exit ramp and noticed Lucy staring at her. "What's the matter?"

"I'm not sure I can marry you."

"Wow. You really did get a bang on the head." The light turned red, forcing Liz to stop. She turned to look at Lucy's face. "Oh, my God. You're serious. Who put this idea in your head? That fucking bishop?"

Lucy sighed, obviously trying to be patient. "Please, Liz. He's not a fucking bishop."

"Lucy, we're not discussing this now. You're concussed and not thinking straight."

"All right. We'll talk about it when we get home."

"When we get home, you're going to rest. And I'm taking you to my house, so I can keep an eye on you." Liz glanced at Lucy, who clearly wanted to argue. Fortunately, she didn't.

When they passed the farm store on the way to Liz's house, Lucy asked, "Can we stop and get some cider donuts?"

"Now?"

"I'm hungry. I missed lunch."

"Bad girl," scolded Liz, but she pulled off the road into a parking lot and made a U-turn.

# 16

A faint sunbeam teased Lucy's eyes. She studied it through her eyelashes, which refracted the light into myriad tones of red and amber. Usually, Lucy would be awake by this hour. She would have sung her exercises and practiced a few pieces in her repertoire. If she were at home, and it wasn't too cold, she would have also gotten in a walk on the beach. But Liz had ordered her to rest today, and Lucy hadn't dared to argue.

It had taken most of the evening for Liz to calm down. After delivering a lecture about wearing shoes appropriate for the weather, she'd continued to hover. She'd parked Lucy on the living room sofa and wrapped her in one of her grandmother's colorful afghans. While she'd prepared dinner, she'd left Lucy with a pot of herbal tea. Alcohol was banned, along with studying. To make sure, Liz had hidden her tablet. Instead, they'd binge watched a PBS mystery series about an Anglican vicar.

Lucy didn't want to get out of bed. In addition to the unrelenting headache, her sleep had been interrupted by one of Liz's recurring stress dreams. They were always set in the hospital at Yale. In one version, Liz was leading young doctors and medical students on grand rounds, but her pager wouldn't stop beeping. It summoned her to the OR, where she had to watch her protégée remove Maggie's breasts again and again. In another variation of the Yale dream, Liz had brought her mother to work, but then couldn't find her. She asked the staff members if they'd seen the old woman, but no one had, leaving Liz to speculate that she'd wandered away.

The meaning of the dreams was as obvious to Liz as it was to Lucy. They both knew the nightmares were being dredged up by Liz's sessions with Tom. Lucy hoped that after helping Liz take herself apart, Tom was skillful enough to help her put herself back together.

Lucy finally opened her eyes and yawned. She stretched, feeling every part of her body. Her neck hurt more than yesterday, and the buttock on which she'd landed really ached. As every morning, she thanked God for the gift of awakening to a new day. She'd been especially diligent about this prayer since Erika's death.

Liz had gone to the office, so the house was silent. Lucy crept into the kitchen and found a note explaining where to find her tablet. The muffled sound of her phone ringing made her wonder if Liz had hidden that too. Then she remembered that she'd never taken it out of her bag. She fumbled trying to get it out before it stopped ringing. She cringed when the caller ID flashed the number of the diocesan office.

"Lucille Bartlett!" she answered smartly, hoping to sound more awake than she felt.

"Lucy, I was so worried after I heard what happened. How are you?" The hearty male voice belonged to Bishop Greene.

"Thank you, Jim. I'm feeling fine, but my doctor ordered me to take the day off."

The bishop laughed. "The hospital doctor or Dr. Stolz? If you listen to either one, I'm happy. You need to rest. Deacon John told me you really hit your head hard."

"They think I had a concussion, but according to the CAT scan, no real damage was done."

"We're all thankful that your injuries weren't more severe." She could hear exactly when the smile faded from his voice. "Lucy, I hope our conversation didn't upset you too much. The strict legalism of other denominations doesn't apply to us." Of course, he remembered that she'd been raised Roman Catholic. They'd spent many hours talking about the damage caused by guilt. "The guidance on marriage exists to help people make solid commitments, not to make them miserable. I'm only trying to help."

"I know, and our conversation has given me plenty to think about."

"Don't think too hard after that fall. There will be plenty of time to figure it out. That date on my calendar is many months away."

"Good thing, too, because I have some sad anniversaries before we get there."

He sighed. "Yes. Erika died around this time of year, didn't she?"

"The week before Christmas."

"Deaths at the holidays are so difficult." He paused, evidently to give his sympathetic message time to penetrate. "Lucy, I wonder if you could stand a visitor today. Reshma wants to stop by to make sure you're all right. She also wants to introduce herself under better circumstances…but only if you feel up to it."

"What time is she coming?" Lucy asked, panicking because she was still in her nightgown covered by Liz's enormous sweatshirt.

"At your convenience, of course. And only if you're feeling well enough."

"My doctor is allowing me to do only one thing today. My friend, Rabbi Morgenstern, is coming up from New York to head a congregation here. Her mother is having a brunch to welcome her to Maine."

"I'd forgotten that you know Rabbi Morgenstern. She mentioned it when she made the rounds of the Portland clergy. Sounds like we'll have lots of opportunities for interfaith services." A long pause ensued. "I'll tell Reshma to find a better day to visit."

"No, today's fine. I can meet her at the rectory after the brunch and show her around. I assume she'll be interested in living in one of the curate's studios."

"Yes, which is one reason I thought of St. Margaret's. Your parish is big enough to house junior clergy. But what about Dr. Stolz? Won't she be upset when she finds out you're working when you're not supposed to?"

"I won't tell, if you won't."

"Deal." That was one of Liz's favorite expressions, so it made Lucy smile. "I won't keep you, dear," said the bishop, winding down the call. "I'm so glad you're feeling better. Please give Rabbi Morgenstern my regards when you see her."

The screen went black, and Lucy noticed the time. Fortunately, years on the stage with its rapid costume changes had taught her to put herself together quickly. She debated on her way up the stairs whether to wear her collar. The affair was being catered by one of Hobbs' trendiest restaurants. Some of the town's most important people had been invited. A collar would probably be appropriate, except Lucy was at Liz's house, and there wasn't time to go home to get a fresh clerical blouse. In the side of the closet that Liz had allocated to her, Lucy found a cotton sweater that would fit nicely over the spare stock she left there for emergencies. Liz was right. Living in two houses was getting old.

Lucy showered quickly. She wasn't in the mood for bright red lipstick today, but she opened the tube and slicked some on because that's what people expected.

Yesterday's snow had already melted, leaving the roads merely wet. Freed of the need to concentrate on her driving, Lucy's mind wandered. While she appreciated the bishop's compassion, it would have been easier if he'd been more critical. He'd left flogging herself for her sins to her. Lucy wasn't looking forward to examining her conscience, never mind facing Liz, who would be furious if they couldn't marry. Lucy dreaded that conversation because it would only reinforce Liz's anger toward religion.

For all her rushing, Lucy ended up being early. Olivia was the only other guest in the enormous dining room. The sumptuous feast included an impressive array of smoked fish, baked goods of every description, casseroles in hot trays, a board of cold meats and cheeses, and sliced fruit arranged in a colorful design. A chef was standing by to make crepes to order. The night before, Liz had insisted on a light dinner because of the head bump. At the sight of all the gorgeous food, Lucy was suddenly ravenous. Yet no one seemed to be eating. To sustain her while she waited, Lucy surreptitiously snatched a small bunch of grapes.

"I caught you, and you look hungry," said Olivia, coming from behind. "You know, Lucy, this beautiful food isn't just for show. They do want us to eat it." She smiled and spoke directly into Lucy's ear. "I'm sure it cost a bundle."

"Everything looks delicious. But I can wait until more people get here. I don't want to ruin the effect."

"Let me get you a drink while you're waiting. There's champagne, mimosas, a breakfast punch that's quite potent, but the bloody marys are exceptional," said Olivia, raising a glass of red liquid.

"I don't think alcohol is a good idea. I fell on the ice yesterday and bumped my head."

Olivia's mouth gaped in alarm. "Oh, no, Lucy! Are you all right?"

"They did a CAT scan. No fractures. A concussion, Liz said."

"Poor Lucy," said Olivia, clucking solicitously. "You need to be more careful in bad weather. At our age, spills can be dangerous. We don't bounce like we used to." She cackled at her own joke. "Here. Try this." She offered the celery from her drink as a sample. Lucy found the taste pleasantly spicy, but now she was stuck with the leafy stalk.

More people had arrived, and the waiter passed out plates. At least, Lucy now had a place to park the celery.

"If you banged your head as hard as you say, I'm surprised Liz let you out today." Lucy gave Olivia a steely look, hoping to get her to back off. Olivia laughed, obviously pleased to get a reaction. "Oh, Lucy, don't look so annoyed. Everyone knows who runs things in that relationship. Clearly, you do."

"For your information, we both do. Someone doesn't always have to have the upper hand."

"There always needs to be a boss. Someone who has the last word and makes the decisions."

Lucy pressed her tongue against her teeth to prevent herself from saying, "And that worked so well for you with Sam." Instead, she sent darts of anger directly into Olivia's eyes, who evidently got the message. She glanced around the room, looking for a reason to escape.

"Excuse me, Lucy. I see Harriet Keene over there. Let me go over and say a quick hello." She gave Lucy's arm a pat and rushed off in Harriet's direction.

Lucy watched the Morgensterns greeting their guests. Rebecca was introducing her beautiful Israeli wife, Judith, and their teenaged twins to the manager of the senior center. Jack Dreyfus, one of Liz's friends and a former colleague, had his arm around Rebecca's mother. He beamed as if he were the patriarch of this beautiful family instead of a newcomer.

A waitress with tongs dangled a scone over Lucy's plate. Lucy nodded her permission to drop it. "Please start eating," the woman begged. "If someone starts, maybe the others will get the idea." Lucy recognized the waitress, who occasionally came to her church—one of those people, who showed up for Christmas and Easter and a few Sundays in between. She looked tired and harried. Lucy guessed the catering gig might be a second job for her.

"Does it help if people eat more food?" Lucy asked.

"If people look like they're enjoying themselves, the tips are usually better."

"In that case, I don't need any encouragement. I'm starving."

"The breakfast casserole with sausage is incredible," the woman confided near Lucy's ear.

"Sausage?"

"It's turkey sausage. Delicious and certified kosher. But you're Episcopalian, so why does it matter to you?"

"I'm engaged to someone who keeps an eye on my trans fats. What's your name?"

"Norma," said the woman, whose face lit up at being asked. Lucy always took the time to acknowledge service workers, knowing they were usually unnoticed and unappreciated.

"Thanks for the tip, Norma. I'm Lucy."

"I know who you are, Rev. Bartlett. Please eat!"

Lucy approached the food table. Finally, other people were heaping food on their plates. Lucy took a few spoonsful of the sausage casserole, and someone whispered behind her ear: "That's not enough to fill a cavity. Try the lox. We brought it up from Zabar's." Lucy turned around and looked into Rebecca Morgenstern's merry eyes. Lucy put down her plate to accept a hug but got more than a polite greeting. Rebecca enclosed her in a snug, full-body embrace. After Rebecca let go, she forked some lox onto Lucy's plate. She added a lump of cream cheese along with a bagel half. Then she helped herself to lox and the other half of the bagel. "Come with me," she said, taking Lucy's arm.

From the sunroom window, Lucy marveled at the unbroken view of the salt marsh. The tide was in, and the pools reflected the bright blue autumn sky like a mirror. Rebecca pulled out a chair for Lucy at the little breakfast table.

"You're the guest of honor. Won't you be missed?" asked Lucy, sitting down.

"I need to eat something before I faint," said Rebecca, taking the seat across from her. "And I'm so happy to see you! I've missed you." Her gaze was so full of affection that it brought tears to Lucy's eyes. "Most of these people are Mom's friends or the Hobbs bigwigs. You're the only person I know in this town."

"Is Judith okay out there by herself? She doesn't know anyone either."

Rebecca slathered cream cheese on her bagel. "Judith is a rabbi's wife. She can handle anything. And you laid-back Mainers are nothing compared to New Yorkers."

"This is a big move for you, Rebecca."

"Yes, no more care packages from Zabar's for Mom. I hear they make decent smoked salmon up here, but the bagels won't be the same. They say it's the city water that makes them crisp on the outside and chewy on the inside." She bit into her bagel with a satisfying crunch. "I thought I was moving up here to be closer to Mom, but now that Jack's in her life, it looks like she doesn't need me."

"You don't regret taking the congregation in Portland?"

Rebecca shook her head. "No, I was ready to move out of New York. Rents are ridiculous. The girls are in private school. The tuition is killing us. Change is good, right?"

"Sometimes," said Lucy, enjoying the salty taste of the tender fish against the cool tang of the cream cheese. "You're right. Our bagels are soft and mushy compared to these."

"Told you. It's the water," said Rebecca. "What's going on with you, Lucy? Melissa told me you're getting married again."

"That's the plan."

Rebecca looked up from her plate. "You don't sound too sure."

"I thought I was…until yesterday." Lucy gazed thoughtfully into the salt marsh. A blue heron alighted and approached on its stick legs toward a shallow pool.

"What happened yesterday?"

"I had a meeting with my bishop."

"Is he against the marriage?"

"Not exactly," said Lucy vaguely. "Rebecca, I know you just arrived, and you're really busy, but can you find some time to talk?"

"Sure," she said, her dark eyes full of concern. "For you, I always have time. When's good?"

"Saturday?"

Rebecca laughed. "Sorry, Lucy. Saturday's my busy day."

"Oh, my word! Of course, it is. What was I thinking?"

Rebecca followed the direction of Lucy's gaze and watched the heron. "I could do it on Sunday, but that's your busy day."

"Usually, I crash after services, but this Sunday is good. My fiancée is teaching an all-day handgun safety class."

"A gun class? One of those, huh?" She was trying to sound non-judgmental but didn't quite succeed.

Lucy didn't know how to explain, but she made an attempt. "Liz believes in strict gun control, but until we get it, she wants people to be as safe as they can."

Rebecca still looked doubtful. "Whatever you say. I hate guns."

"So do I."

Rebecca nodded. "Come up to Portland on Sunday. You can see the house we're renting. We're still moving in, but you don't mind boxes everywhere, do you?"

"No, I'd love to see your place."

"Good. I'm looking forward to it." Rebecca smiled warmly, then frowned. "Your problem can keep till then, can't it?"

Lucy wasn't sure it could, but she nodded.

✳✳✳

Leaning against the wall in the dining room, Melissa felt sidelined. She knew very few people in this group. Most of them were acquaintances from her mother's bridge club, town big shots, and neighbors she'd never met. She wished Courtney had been able to make it, but the principal was out again with her elderly mother. At least, if Courtney had come, Melissa would have someone her own age to talk to instead of standing there like a wall flower at the high school dance. She was familiar with that role. She'd been taller than almost all the boys, so she was hardly ever asked to dance.

She looked around for Lucy and was disappointed when she didn't see her. Lucy, with her natural warmth and chattiness, always made good company.

"Where did your sister go?" asked a familiar voice. Melissa looked down and saw Harriet Keene standing beside her.

"I have no idea," replied Melissa, "but when you're the queen, you can withdraw at will." After she said it, Melissa felt ridiculous sounding so bitter, like a caricature of the jealous, younger sibling.

Narrowing her blue eyes, Harriet studied Melissa's face. "Your sister obviously has a lot of personality. She's great with people, a good thing in her line of work."

"She's an extrovert. I'm not. That's why I chose trust practice. Most of the work is done in an office behind closed doors. I'm not really a people person."

"I don't know. You do fine when you need to," Harriet said in an encouraging voice that made Melissa remember why she liked this woman so much. Harriet had become a friend of the family during the Morgensterns' long fight to get a variance to build in the salt marsh. Although she really belonged to her mother's generation, Melissa considered her a friend too. She was always happy when Harriet called her to consult on local cases that involved trusts.

Melissa's phone vibrated in the pocket of her cardigan. The ID indicated the call was from the county court house. "Excuse me, Harriet. I've been expecting this call." Harriet politely stepped away to give Melissa privacy, while the family court clerk explained that the Benoit adoption had been approved. A hearing had been set to formalize the ruling on the Tuesday before Thanksgiving.

"From the look on your face, that was good news," Harriet said, returning to Melissa's side.

"That adoption case I was working on has been decided."

"The children whose parents died in the shooting? My God, I can't even imagine taking that on."

"Give me a minute to call the clients and let them know."

"Do you need privacy for your call?"

"No, stay. At least, it looks like I have a friend here."

Harriet smiled and patted her arm.

Brenda's voice sounded brisk when she answered the call, but when Melissa gave her the news, she yelped with joy. "We got them!" she shouted. "We got the kids!" In the background, Melissa could hear cheers and shouts of congratulations. She waited until things settled down on the other end before asking, "Will you call Cherie, or should I?"

"No, I'll call her right away. Thank you, Melissa. Oh, thank you so much!"

"See?" said Harriet after Melissa hung up the call. "Don't sell yourself short. You're very good with people."

"Oh, that was easy."

"No, it wasn't. You represented a lesbian couple in the adoption of kids who'd suffered profound trauma and you won. You may have a knack for family law."

"I did it pro bono."

"That doesn't mean you couldn't charge people with money. You could still do trusts. Maine is full of rich people who don't want the nursing home to clean them out when they land there. And there are hundreds of nonprofits who need help. Melissa, I'm seeing opportunities for you in the pine tree state."

"I don't know..." Melissa started to say.

"Your mother told me how hard you worked to make partner, but in a big firm, there's always pressure to make your quota. The financial rewards may be great, but so are your expenses. Look at all the money you put on your back to dress the part. Real estate is expensive in Boston. I bet you have a huge mortgage on your condo. Commuting costs big money. I'm no expert, Melissa, but I do know something about finance. You should ask Olivia to help you figure out if you'd be better off cutting your expenses and taking a lower salary. It might really pay."

Melissa frowned at the advice because it went against everything she'd been taught. In her world, success was measured by the prestige of the firm, the percentage of her draw, and her year-end bonus.

"I would be taking a big risk to leave my firm."

"Well, maybe you can have it both ways. Aren't they letting you work remotely?"

"Yes, but that won't last forever. They wanted us back in the office as soon as the COVID numbers went down."

"But now you're working at home again, and no one's squawking." Harriet folded her arms on her chest. "If you ask me, things will never be the same again. What we now call work will be changed forever." This wasn't the first time Melissa had heard someone express that idea. The business press was full of how people were quitting their jobs. "You could insist on a remote arrangement or threaten to take your clients with you."

"Except I'm not sure I'm well enough established to make good on that threat."

"Sure, you are. When I left my big firm, they gave me a hard time, but I came up to Maine and made a bundle on big-ticket real estate transactions. Now, it's my choice to take work that's less demanding."

"I didn't know that." To Melissa, Harriet had always seemed the epitome of a small-town lawyer.

Harriet elbowed her. "Check the real estate records if you don't believe me."

"No, I believe you."

"Look, Melissa. I have that empty office that's full of file boxes. We could clean it out and put the files in storage."

"Better yet, you could hire a high school kid to scan them."

"What a great idea! Let's put an ad online and see what we get." Melissa hadn't missed the fact that Harriet was already speaking collectively. "Listen to me, Melissa Morgenstern. Moving to Maine is the best thing I ever did. Why not give working out of my office a try? You don't have to cut the cord from your Boston firm right away. But sell that condo of yours. It's probably cheaper to stay in a hotel when you need to go into town."

"Hadn't thought of that."

"Sometimes, you need to look at things from another angle. We could share the cost of the secretary, now that I've finally hired one. I could throw you the legacy planning cases that are over my head anyway…"

"Yes, I can see it now." Melissa envisioned herself in the office next to Harriet's, sitting at the antique double desk rescued from the law office of another era.

"So?"

"So, I think you've got a deal," said Melissa reaching out her hand.

❄❄❄

Olivia was watching the door to see if Amy would show up. She knew the practice closed for an hour at lunchtime. Finally, a tall, gray-haired woman came into the room, accompanied by a younger Asian woman.

"Hey, Liv," said Liz, giving her a half hug. "Did you leave anything for us?"

Olivia gestured toward the table. Despite everyone feeding hungrily, the feast barely showed a dent. It had been ridiculously extravagant, but Olivia knew some people tried to advertise their wealth by serving guests excessive amounts of food. Olivia had diligently studied people with old money and knew that real wealth never bragged. It offered just enough.

"I'm ravenous," Liz declared. "Talk to you later." She headed straight to the food table and started filling a plate. That left Amy standing there, abandoned. Another person might feel awkward, but Amy had presence and poise, despite being in a place where she knew almost no one.

"I want to thank you again for dinner the other night," she said to Olivia. "Now that I have my kitchen set up and bought some new pots and pans, maybe I can return the favor."

"Oh, that would be lovely," Olivia said, meeting the woman's unnervingly calm gaze. The quiet intelligence in Amy's dark eyes fascinated her, and the fact that she chose her words with great precision. She never babbled like some people did to fill an uncomfortable silence. "Are you heading home for Thanksgiving, Dr. Hsu?"

"Please call me Amy." A sad look crossed Amy's face. "I was hoping to spend it with my parents, but they're flying to California to have Thanksgiving with my brother's family. I was surprised because my father has been so worried about the virus. There are rumors of a new variant."

"So, you'll be alone?"

"Liz invited me, but I've been thinking of spending a quiet holiday in my own place. It's been so busy since I landed in Hobbs, especially with Liz being away so much."

"She relies on you. Consider yourself privileged. It takes Liz time to trust people, but she's an excellent judge of character."

"Thank you, I guess." Amy narrowed her eyes slightly.

*And you are too,* Olivia thought. *You're not easily taken in by flattery.* Amy's stock went up a few points. Increasingly, she was looking like a good investment. An idea occurred to Olivia, but she took a moment to consider it, because she never liked to act on impulse. "There's an alternative, you know, to dining with your boss, which I imagine could be awkward."

"What's that?" Amy asked, looking curious.

"I'm considered a decent cook," said Olivia modestly. "I'm only entertaining my grandchildren for Thanksgiving. Perhaps you'd like to join us?"

The dark eyes blinked a few times in surprise.

"Don't worry. My granddaughters have been fully vaccinated, and Liz always makes sure we're all tested properly before and after they arrive."

"That sounds like Liz." Amy smiled. "Well," she said slowly. "Thanks for the invitation. I may just take you up on it, but there's something I have to tell you first—"

Liz barreled up with a plateful of food. "Have you seen a redhead about yay high?" She measured to her shoulder. "Probably wearing a collar, but maybe not. She's supposed to be off today. Forced sick leave."

Olivia pointed to the door where she had seen Lucy disappear with one of the Morgenstern daughters. "I think she went that way." Liz headed off, and Olivia returned her attention to Amy. She was dying to hear her big revelation. "You were saying?"

"I know that female relationships can be complicated. I've been burned in the past, so I always try to be transparent. Unfortunately, not everyone follows that policy."

The extended preamble was making Olivia impatient. She gave Amy the look she'd once used to encourage her staffers when they were choking on information they couldn't spit out.

"Before I accept your invitation," said Amy, "I want you to know that Sam McKinnon and I were seeing one another."

"You said 'were.' Does that mean you're no longer seeing her?"

"No, we decided we're better off as friends."

"I see," said Olivia with an unintentional sniff. She'd heard the rumors, but hearing them confirmed was difficult. "I'm sure you found Samantha as stubborn as I did."

That statement brought a look of surprise. "Actually, I found her fun and pleasant to be around." Amy scrutinized Olivia's face to see how this information had landed. "I'm only telling you because I understand you and Sam were together."

"We were, but she is just impossible."

Amy looked wary. "I'm sorry it didn't work out."

"It's irrelevant. Come for Thanksgiving, and we'll have a wonderful time."

"Are you sure?"

"Yes, and don't worry about the other thing. Thank you for telling me, but it doesn't really matter," said Olivia, trying to sound like it didn't.

# 17

Reshma's long legs made it hard to keep up with her as they walked across the quad. If not for her vocal training and walking every morning, Lucy would be breathless by now. When they reached the rectory, the young woman held the door open for her. "After you," she said with a flourish and a little bow. Her smile revealed perfectly even and brilliantly white teeth.

Lucy found herself thinking, *what a beautiful woman!* Aloud she said, "Thank you, and thank you for assisting at my Holy Communion this morning. I'm sorry I kept bumping into you."

"You were the celebrant," said Reshma. "It's my job to adjust to you."

"We'll find our rhythm. It took me a while when I was a deacon, but the dress rehearsal before becoming a priest was extremely helpful." She waited while Reshma made sure the door, which tended to stick, was tightly closed. She'd noted that Reshma observed small details, which would be of great help to her as she embarked on her ministry. "When will you be moving in the rest of your belongings?"

Reshma looked surprised. "Everything has arrived, Mother Lucy. I only need to unpack my bags and boxes."

"That's all you have? Nothing in storage somewhere? We probably have room in the basement."

"No, I find it's better to travel light." After hearing Reshma's story, Lucy understood why.

The new deacon was only ten when her mother, fleeing civil war and genocide in Sudan, brought her to Maine. Reshma's father was shot in front of his family and left to die while soldiers burned their village. Her little brother died of dysentery in the refugee camp. After Reshma and her mother arrived in Portland, they lived for months in a cramped hotel room while waiting for public housing. They had no clothing for the harsh Maine winter and had to depend on local charities.

An Episcopal Church in Maine chose two refugee girls to sponsor. Reshma was one of them. They arranged for a scholarship to an Episcopal boarding school in New Hampshire and paid her expenses. Reshma grew up among privileged white girls. She won a scholarship to Trinity College in Connecticut. She only returned to the refugee community when her mother was dying of cancer. Afterward, Reshma found solace in the Church that had nurtured her since childhood and decided to enter a seminary.

For all the misery she'd endured in her young life, she was always cheerful. Although Tom had volunteered to shoulder most of the burden of mentoring Reshma, Lucy made time for her because it lifted her mood, which had been dark since her conversation with the bishop.

"How are you getting along with your next-door neighbor?" Lucy asked.

"Oh, I love Denise. She invited me in for a glass of wine the first night, and it seems to have become a tradition. Sometimes, we cook together. Saves us both a lot of money." Lucy listened for criticism of the fact that the pay for deacons was skimpy, but she heard no complaint in Reshma's tone.

"I'm glad to hear Denise has reached out to you. Life can be lonely when you first come to a parish. I was lucky to make friends to introduce me to Hobbs." Lucy thought of Maggie Fitzgerald who had shown her around town and introduced her to people. Seeing her at the church fair had reminded Lucy how much she'd missed her.

"Denise is very gifted," Reshma said. "I've heard her practice in the church hall. Wow! I'd never heard a countertenor sing live before. What talent she has!"

"She told you about her background?" asked Lucy, a little surprised. The controversy about hiring a trans music director had mostly died down, but Denise had said she was keeping a low profile until people got to know her better.

"One of the first things she told me," Reshma said.

"I'm glad, it doesn't bother you."

Reshma raised her shoulders. "Should it?"

"No, of course not. But some people don't approve. She hasn't had an easy time here."

"The older generation finds it hard. So much has changed in such a short time." Lucy liked the note of compassion she heard in Reshma's voice.

"But you're comfortable here?"

"I love it!"

"Good," said Lucy, patting her arm. "That's what we like to hear. Tomorrow, I'll take you on my homebound visits."

"You will? Awesome!" Reshma replied with the enthusiasm of someone who'd just scored Super Bowl tickets. Watching a new deacon eager to begin her ministry was a vicarious pleasure. It reminded Lucy of a time when even the most mundane clerical tasks were new and exciting.

After Reshma had gone upstairs, Lucy locked up her work laptop in her office and headed out to her car. Any hope of decompressing on the drive up the turnpike fizzled when she found herself thinking of the previous night's tense conversation.

"That little sanctimonious prick! Fuck him!" Liz had spat when Lucy had finally told her about her discussion with the bishop. "We don't need him. We'll get married by a justice of the peace. Hell, I bet Olivia can marry us."

"You know why that won't work, and he didn't say that we can't marry, only that we needed to be really sure."

"I'm sure. What about you?"

When Lucy hadn't instantly answered in the affirmative, Liz had sulked on the porch with a bottle of Lagavulin. Watching her stare wordlessly into the flames of the propane stove, Lucy had considered going home to the beach house but realized that would be a mistake. By the time they went to bed, Liz had seemed calmer. Fortunately, she'd moderated her drinking because she had to teach a class today, but even after tentatively making love, she'd remained distant.

Lucy pulled over after the toll booth to turn on the GPS. The female voice, which Erika had set to British because it sounded more like her, crisply directed her to her destination. Rebecca's house was closer to the highway than Lucy had expected, probably why they were able to find this rental so quickly during a housing shortage. Rebecca and her family would hear the road noise when the windows were open during the summer. Of course, people accustomed to Manhattan's twenty-four-hour traffic, with its honking taxis and wailing sirens, probably wouldn't even notice.

Rebecca greeted Lucy with a warm embrace. "You can take off your mask, Lucy. We've had all our shots, and we were all tested yesterday before the Sabbath service."

The first thing Rebecca showed her was the partial view of the salt marsh from her bedroom window. "This is what sold us on this place. It reminds me of Mom's house in Hobbs," Rebecca explained, pulling up the duvet on the unmade bed. "I should have picked up, but I slept in this morning. With the twins, it's always busy around here."

"It doesn't matter to me. I'm not the neatest person myself."

"That's hard to believe, Lucy. You always look perfectly put together."

"It's part of my act," Lucy explained. "Where's Judith?"

"She took the girls to the school to sign up for basketball. They're tall like me, so they'll probably make the team, but I hope they have more athletic talent than I do, which is zilch."

Despite the unpacked boxes everywhere, she showed Lucy the rest of the house.

"Did you have lunch?" Rebecca asked as they descended the stairs.

"No, my service was over at eleven. I came straight here."

Rebecca smiled and yanked her arm. "Come with me, girlie. I have a pot of soup on the stove."

Lucy pushed aside a stack of mail to sit down at the kitchen table, while Rebecca spooned soup into two oversized mugs. She wasn't as tall as Melissa, but like her sister, her hair was a mass of unruly dark curls, and she had a perfect figure.

"There are many myths about chicken soup," said Rebecca, putting a steaming mug in front of Lucy. "I swear by it. It's an elixir that will heal whatever ails you."

Lucy inhaled the delicious fragrance. "It smells divine."

"Well, I am a rabbi, you know." Rebecca laughed heartily at her own joke. "Do you know the secret ingredient in every Jewish mother's soup?"

"Love?" Lucy guessed.

"Yes, love, of course, and chicken fat. If you skim off the fat, you lose all the goodness. Lucy looked down at the surface swimming with iridescent, golden bubbles and fresh parsley. "My grandmother would render chicken fat to spread on bread."

"Schmaltz," said Lucy. Rebecca looked curious, so Lucy explained, "When I lived in New York, I had lots of Jewish friends."

"Of course, you did. The arts are full of us." Rebecca sat down with her bowl of soup. "I always get kosher chickens. Otherwise, the fat isn't good for you. Those Talmud writers, who wrote our dietary laws, were on to something."

"Do you and Judith keep a kosher home?"

"Only for Passover. We're reform Jews. Besides, we like crustaceans too much. Now that we're in the land of 'lobstah,' I intend to eat lots of shellfish. I hear the peekytoe crabs aren't bad either. And I love butter," she said, spreading it generously on two slices of rye bread. She cut it into squares and put the plate between them on the table. "Go on, Lucy. Eat! You're too thin."

For several minutes, the only sound in the room was two women greedily slurping their soup. When Rebecca got close to the bottom of the mug, she drank the rest. "Ah!" she exclaimed, putting down the cup. She studied Lucy carefully. "I wish my soup could heal you, but that would be too easy. So tell me, what's going on with you? Is it your career, faith, pastoral work, love…?"

"Love," said Lucy, pouncing.

"But I thought you were engaged to that tall, good-looking doctor. I hardly know her, but Jack thinks the world of her. There's a problem with her?"

"Not with Liz. I love her with all my heart, and we're well matched in so many ways."

"She takes care of bodies. You take care of souls. I get it."

"I mean we're well-matched temperamentally. We both have strong personalities, but we know when to compromise...most of the time. She's reserved, and I'm...well, you know how I am. It's a good balance."

"Sounds like a good match," agreed Rebecca. "I can see her appeal for you. Jack says she's brilliant, and she's very sexy in a butchy kind of way. She has those intense blue eyes that look right into your soul."

"There's more to the story."

"There always is." Rebecca helped herself to a square of buttered rye bread.

"Gosh," said Lucy, staring at the ceiling. "This is hard. You should have seen me telling my bishop. I was shaking."

"Don't take this wrong, Lucy, but if you were in my congregation, I would have counseled you to wait before getting involved again. It's not even a year since Erika died."

"If I were in my congregation, I would have said the same thing."

"Then why are you in such a big hurry?"

"I'm not, but Liz seems to be."

"Don't tell me you're making her wait to have sex."

Lucy's cheeks started to warm. "No, but I did hold her off for months. Then my ex showed up, and Liz needed reassurance, and...."

"...one thing led to another." Rebecca gave Lucy a hard look. "Did you give in to Liz because of her needs or yours?"

"Both," Lucy admitted. "I couldn't wait any longer."

"Uh huh." Rebecca gave her a hard look. "Just keeping you honest, Lucy. So, it didn't work out on your timetable, but that's not the issue. What is?"

"Our church doesn't approve of remarriage when one partner caused the other partner's divorce."

Rebecca leaned on her hand. "Lucy, please tell me you weren't having an affair with Liz before her divorce."

Lucy blinked a few times, even though she'd rehearsed her answer to this question. "Not exactly. We had a silly flirtation going from the time we met. Everyone knew about it, including her wife. The closest we came to breaking our marriage vows was a passionate kiss, but I ended it before it could go anywhere."

"Had you been encouraging her?" asked Rebecca, giving Lucy the side eye.

"I don't think so. I played along because I thought it was harmless. She was married, happily it seemed, so I turned my attention to Erika, who was available and obviously interested in me. I never knew how deep Liz's feelings for me were until we were all living together during lockdown. She confessed that she loved me. We talked about it, and that seemed to be the end of it."

"But it wasn't. Okay, so spare me the suspense. What did break up the marriage?"

"Maggie had an affair with a man, a fellow actor. That was a red line for Liz."

"Is she with the man now?"

"No, I think it was just a fling. He was much younger. She's older than Liz, and I think she was feeling her age. Liz's interest in me, a woman who's a decade younger, must have been a real blow."

"So, Liz's ex committed adultery, and you didn't. That puts you in the clear, except there's a commandment against coveting your neighbor's wife. Infidelity doesn't need to be consummated to be real. You might be guilty of alienation of affection, which is still legal grounds for divorce in some states. Bear with me, Lucy, my father was a lawyer." Rebecca got up to get more soup. She pointed to Lucy's mug.

"Thanks. I still have some."

"You've got to eat, Lucy. You need fuel to do God's work. Take it from someone who knows." Rebecca sat down and looked thoughtful. "I can see why you might feel a tiny bit guilty about the kiss. But it was just a kiss, right? One time?"

Lucy nodded emphatically.

"Obviously, you shouldn't have allowed another woman's spouse to kiss you. The flirting and teasing may have been bad judgment, but it sounds harmless. All the parties knew it was going on and it was out in the open."

"But I should have stopped it."

Rebecca shrugged. "Once that kind of behavior is accepted, it becomes part of the culture, and it's hard to stop. Lucy, you do know that you are drop-dead gorgeous, and you sing like an angel, but if Liz's relationship had been satisfying, she never would have looked at you. Were you aware of problems in the marriage?"

Lucy thought back. "I heard them argue, like all couples. As close as Maggie and I were, she never mentioned any problems."

"Maybe you weren't as close as you thought."

"Maybe not," Lucy agreed with regret. "Maggie was Liz's first sexual experience, which can have a powerful hold on people. They were just beginning to explore their second chance, when Liz discovered a lump in Maggie's breast."

"Don't tell me it was cancer." Rebecca's face softened with sympathy. "How horrible!"

"After that, Liz felt she couldn't leave. She proposed to assure Maggie that she would stand by her. Liz has an overdeveloped sense of responsibility."

"That guilt thing. Jewish girls are experts, but you and your friends are giving me stiff competition." Despite the quip, Rebecca's face remained serious. "It sounds like the marriage was on shaky ground from the beginning."

"I wasn't there. I can't say. For obvious reasons, I'm sympathetic to Liz's side of the story."

"But you were all friends, living your happily ever after, and then there was a tipping point. What happened after Liz told you she loved you?"

"I explained that I would never break my marriage vows. Liz and I had this knight and lady game we were playing. Liz liked me to sing Elsa's dream from *Lohengrin*. She once asked me to sing "*Liebestod*" on her boat in the middle of the harbor."

"Sounds like you two were sublimating all over the place, but I bet that only made it worse."

Lucy nodded sadly, remembering Liz weeping after she sang on the boat.

"No wonder Maggie picked up on what was going on. You two were probably transmitting your attraction like a cell tower. Lucy, this is the stuff they write operas about."

"Don't I know it," said Lucy with a sigh.

Rebecca took a sip of soup. "How else could you have handled it?"

"I don't know. Liz and I worked together. Liz and Erika were friends. It's a small town… I will say that Liz really tried to save the marriage. She stayed away from me, but Erika missed her so much. I felt bad about that too, separating two people who'd been friends for decades. Erika was going through a transition. She was finally going to retire. She could have used Liz's advice, but she wasn't there for her because of me."

"If Erika had wanted to see Liz, she could have reached out to her. She was an adult. Everyone in this story is an adult. Not only an adult, but old enough to be a grandmother!"

That made Lucy smile. "You'd think we're old enough to know better."

Rebecca shrugged. "Age has nothing to do with it. Look at my mother making a fool of herself over Jack. Love. It's a terrible thing."

"No, it's not!"

Rebecca laughed. "Just yanking your chain." Rebecca's face became serious again. "Lucy, the only thing you did wrong was fall in love with someone else's spouse. Attraction doesn't always play by the rules. It was Liz's job to defend her marriage. You should probably thank Maggie for ending it, because if it was up to you and Liz, you'd still be singing Wagner on her boat." Rebecca's dark eyes studied Lucy. She let out a long sigh. "Oh, Lucy. That's the best I can offer. You're the expert on sexual ethics. When your book is published, people will be lining up to ask for your advice."

"Which only proves how flawed so-called experts can be, and how desperate we are to believe them."

"Give yourself credit, Lucy. Your book is wonderful, and its message of compassion will help many people. Try giving some to yourself. You can continue to beat yourself up over your mistakes, or you can accept the gift of love that God has given you. It's pretty simple."

There was the sound of people talking in the entry foyer. Judith and the girls had returned.

"I should let you get back to your family," Lucy said, getting up. "Thank you so much for your time, Rebecca."

"Why do I feel I haven't helped you?"

"Oh, you have. I needed to talk to someone who has no stake in this. Someone willing to ask the hard questions."

"Except I don't have any answers." Rebecca opened her arms. "Come here. Give me a hug."

"Pray for me," Lucy whispered into her ear.

"I'll pray that you forgive yourself. Remember. None of us is perfect. We are all still learning."

Lucy tried to leave, but Judith wanted to chat, so she stayed for a few minutes longer. Rebecca followed her to the door.

"If you need me, just call. And now you know where to go for chicken soup."

Feeling lighter, Lucy smiled on her way to her car. The conversation hadn't solved her dilemma, but it had changed her relationship with Rebecca. Once they had been two faith leaders united for a common cause. Now, they were really friends. Lucy saw it as a reminder that a problem can often be a blessing in disguise.

As she turned onto Route 1, Lucy saw the sign for Scarborough and remembered that Maggie lived nearby. She pulled off the road and entered the address into the GPS, trusting its directive British voice to get her to the right place.

When she arrived at the house, there were no cars in the driveway. Lucy scrutinized the raised ranch for signs of activity but saw none. She was about to leave when a figure appeared at the picture window. A moment later, the front door opened.

"I thought it was you," Maggie's dark-haired daughter called to her as she approached. "I recognized your car."

"Is your mother home?"

Alina waved her closer before saying more. "She's not here. She's been down at Sam McKinnon's for almost a week. I think she needed a break from the kids. They won't leave her alone." Alina opened the door wider. "Want to come in?"

"Thanks, but not today. I just wanted to say hello to your mother and see how she's doing."

"From what I hear, Sam's taking good care of her. You could stop by on your way home."

"Good idea. I might do that."

"Sure, you don't want to come in?" Alina looked like she could use some company, but Lucy was determined to see Maggie.

"Another time, but thank you. Next time, you're down in Hobbs, give me a call. We'll get together for coffee."

Alina seemed to like that idea. She stood on the front porch while Lucy got back into her car. Hugging herself against the cold, the tiny woman looked like a lost girl. Lucy felt remiss for not spending more time with her, but she felt stripped bare after talking to Rebecca, and her emotional reserves were low.

As she drove back to Hobbs, she wondered whether it was wise to visit Maggie while she felt so fragile, but maybe it was an ideal time. Maggie was in a weakened state too. Their shared vulnerability might help them remember they had once been friends. Lucy rehearsed a little speech to explain the unplanned visit but then decided it was better to arrive with no preparation. "Let the chips fall as they may," her father used to say. Lucy heard his voice in her head as if he were sitting beside her. "I love you, Daddy," she whispered aloud.

Driving down the driveway, she saw Sam's truck parked in front of the barn. The plow had been mounted, which reminded Lucy that more snow was predicted. As she got out of the car, she gazed at the leaden sky and realized that it might arrive soon.

There was no doorbell, only a replica of a ship's bell hanging on a chain from the porch ceiling. After Lucy rang it, she had to wait a long time before Sam came to the door. "Lucy!" she said with an enormous grin. "How nice to see you." Sam pulled her into a fierce hug, and Lucy felt the strength of the hard muscles in her arms.

"Sam, I'm sorry to bother you, but Alina said Maggie is here."

"No bother. And yes, Maggie's here. Come on in."

Lucy entered the warm house. It smelled of spice and savory meat. "What are you cooking that smells so good?"

"Maggie is teaching me to make a Tagine. I'm cooking and she's giving orders. It does smell good, doesn't it?"

"I miss Maggie's cooking," said Lucy wistfully.

"Maggie's in the living room. I'm sure she'll be glad to see you." Lucy was less sure, but she took a deep breath and followed Sam. "Hey, Mags. Look who showed up on our doorstep." Lucy noted the nickname and the collective possessive. Obviously, things had progressed while Maggie was recuperating at Sam's.

Maggie winced trying to raise herself from the sofa. "You don't need to get up," Lucy said, touching her cheek to Maggie's. "I would have come to you."

"You have come to me," Maggie said with a mysterious little smile.

"Can I get you something to drink, Lucy?" Sam asked, playing the attentive hostess. "We're trying this new chardonnay." Sam held up the bottle, as if Lucy could read the label from that distance. "Would you like a glass?"

Lucy glanced at the standing clock against the wall. It was almost three, a little early to start drinking, but maybe some alcohol would help her relax. "Sure, Sam. Thank you."

Maggie patted a seat beside her on the couch. "Sit next to me, Lucy."

"How are you feeling?" Lucy asked, sitting down beside her.

"Every day a little better. I'm glad Sam rescued me. It was hard to recuperate and still be the full-time grandma the girls expected. I love them to pieces, but..."

"…you need to take care of yourself. And that's what you're doing, Maggie. I'm proud of you."

Maggie smiled warmly at the compliment. She raised her arm to put it around Lucy but let out a sharp whimper. "I wanted to give you a hug, but I can't do that right now."

"Here, let me." Lucy put her arm around Maggie's shoulders and hugged her gently.

"I think I should go in and check on dinner," Sam said, getting up.

"Don't open the pot!" Maggie ordered. "It needs to cook undisturbed."

"Maggie, I was only going to prep the squash." Sam made a deep theatrical bow. "With your permission, Madam."

"Yes, that's fine," said Maggie, waving her off.

When Sam left the room, Lucy had no doubt her hasty departure was intended to give them privacy. Lucy's smile was meant to encourage conversation, but there was an extended silence before Maggie spoke. "It's so nice to see you, Lucy. How did you know I was here?"

"I was up in South Portland visiting Rebecca Morgenstern. I remembered your house was nearby, so I stopped in. Alina told me you were here."

"How are they doing up there? I think Alina's angry I ran out on her."

"She seems to be doing all right."

Maggie glanced at her furtively. "And how's Liz?"

"She's okay. Very involved in the effort to vaccinate the younger children. Busy as always."

"I like that new doctor she hired. Does that mean she'll finally retire?"

"I don't know," Lucy said honestly.

"So, she doesn't talk to you either. Don't let her get away with that, Lucy. She'll bring out her bottle of scotch and brood before she'll tell you what's going on. Sometimes, you have to dig it out of her with a shovel." Lucy nodded, remembering last night's episode. What she didn't understand was why Maggie was offering her advice. "Maybe you'll have better luck communicating with Liz," Maggie continued. "At least, she respects you."

"You thought she didn't respect you?" Lucy felt herself frowning and willed her brow to relax.

"She had me on a pedestal for a long time. It's not the same. She listens to you, really listens. With me, she only paid attention to be polite, but I don't think she heard half of what I said."

If what Maggie said was true, her relationship with Liz must have been lonely. "I'm sorry, Maggie," Lucy said, taking her hand.

"I know, Lucy, and I don't blame you." Maggie took in a deep breath. "Liz has been good to me. She treats my grandkids like they're her own. When I got sick again, she could have told me to go to hell, but she didn't."

"No, she didn't. Liz makes mistakes, like all of us, but at heart, she's a good person."

"You are too." Maggie's eyes searched her face. "Lucy, while I'm down here staying with Sam, would it be too awkward if I came to St. Margaret's?"

"Not at all. I'd love you to meet our new deacon and Denise. What an amazing voice she has. We're planning the carol service, and we could really use your advice."

"You could?" asked Maggie in a small, hopeful voice.

"Yes!"

❋❋❋

*Where the hell is Lucy?* Liz wondered as she rummaged in the refrigerator for something to eat. She was ravenous after her gun safety class despite the sandwich she'd wolfed down at lunchtime. She hardly remembered eating it because she was trying to moderate a debate about what constituted self-defense. The news was crowded with coverage of a high-profile court case of a boy who'd brought an assault rifle to a BLM protest. He was too young to own a gun in his home state, and he'd crossed state lines, supposedly to help police defend property. The liberal view was he had gone to the demonstration looking for trouble. The second amendment people saw him as a patriotic citizen.

Liz usually avoided politics in her gun classes, but she'd allowed this conversation to continue because it pertained to the students' responsibilities as gun owners. She'd been surprised to discover most of the students in this class were liberal women. Some said they wanted to protect themselves against domestic violence. Others were afraid of other gun owners and fearful of political chaos.

"The way I see it," said a well-dressed woman who owned a high-end Kimber, "there are a lot of guns in this country, and it's an arms race. We can't let all the crazies have the guns. We need them too."

Although she completely agreed, Liz didn't dare even nod in response. Instead, she shifted the conversation to why it was important to use hollow points for self-defense instead of target ammunition.

Liz's search of the refrigerator turned up the plate of pork chops from last night's dinner. She unwrapped it and stood at the island, eating a cold chop. She flipped open a beer and drank it out of the bottle, taking pleasure in the fact that there were no witnesses to her uncivilized behavior.

The sound of the door from the garage closing told her that Lucy had arrived. "I'm home!" she called through the house. "I'm so sorry," she said. "I thought I'd be home hours ago."

Liz wiped her mouth with the back of her hand before she allowed Lucy to kiss her.

"So what was this important mission? Feeding the hungry? Sheltering the homeless? Burying the dead?"

"Don't be a smart ass. I went up to see Rebecca and then stopped at Sam's to see Maggie."

"Comforting the sick," said Liz with a nod and took another swig of beer. "You know, you were supposed to make dinner tonight."

"Oh, no! I forgot. I'm sorry, Liz. I'll go back to town to get takeout."

"Don't be silly," said Liz, grabbing her arm. "You're home now. There might be something in the freezer. I'll go down and look."

"Are you sure?" Lucy gave her a hard look. Liz guessed she was trying to evaluate where things stood after last night's difficult conversation.

"Positive."

Lucy reached up and put her arms around Liz's neck. "How about a kiss before I go up to change. Then, I'll help you get dinner ready." Liz lost herself in Lucy's sweet mouth, but when the kiss ended, Lucy made a face. "You taste like beer."

"Yes, and it's a great IPA. Want another taste?"

"No, thank you," said Lucy, "but you can pour me a glass of wine. I'll be right down."

Liz finished her beer and turned on the oven to high before heading downstairs to see what she could find in the freezer. She pulled out a frosty aluminum tray from the bottom of a pile. She always tried to use the oldest food first. She scraped the frost off the label with her fingernails and saw the date and identity of the contents. The careful round-lettered handwriting confirmed that the eggplant rollatini dated from before the pandemic. Maggie had made it.

Liz's fingers stuck to the icy tray, so she put it down quickly. She stared at the label and recalled that summer before her marriage ended. It had been a good year for gardening. Before the first frost, she and Maggie had processed the abundance of tomatoes, peppers, and eggplant as they did every year. Side-by-side, they'd made stacks of dinners to use on busy nights when one of them had a meeting or a rehearsal. Liz even remembered the conversation while they were making the rollatini. Maggie had talked about going back to work part time as a drama coach at the high school.

Liz had thought all of that year's food had been used. Somehow, she had missed this tray. She knew it was edible, despite its age. The professional freezer in the basement was set to the coldest temperature and could keep food nearly indefinitely.

"Liz, did you find something?" Lucy called down the basement stairs.

"I did. I'll be right up." Liz hurried because the frozen aluminum was stinging her fingers. She dropped it on the counter and massaged her hands to get the circulation going again. She pulled back the foil to remove the plastic wrap beneath it.

"What's for dinner?" Lucy asked, looking curious.

"Eggplant rollatini. Maggie made it." Liz shoved the tray into the oven. The preheat gauge pinged the moment she closed the door. She turned around and saw Lucy scrutinizing her face. "Don't worry, Lucy. It's still good to eat."

"I'm not worried about the food. I'm worried about you. You look like you're ready to cry."

Liz's nose began to run, so she sniffled. Then her eyes filled. She wiped them with the cuff of her sweatshirt.

"Come here," said Lucy, reaching up.

Liz buried her face in the soft skin of Lucy's neck and began to sob.

# 18

Brenda was busy mixing the batter for pumpkin bread, but she could feel Cherie's aunt watching her. When the scrutiny became unnerving, Brenda finally asked, "Simone, am I doing something wrong?"

"No, in fact, you're doing everything right. I couldn't do it better myself. The loaves in the oven smell delicious! I love pumpkin pie spices." Cherie's Aunt spoke with a distinctive, educated tone because she'd been a schoolteacher, but you could still hear the warmth of the South in her voice. Although she was a shade darker than Cherie, like her niece, Simone could pass for white. She was in her early seventies but looked younger. Her noble face was finely featured, and she had clear, hazel eyes. Brenda didn't have to look hard to see Cherie in this still beautiful woman.

"This bread makes a good breakfast on Thanksgiving morning when everyone's working in the kitchen," said Brenda.

"Very practical," agreed Simone. "Now, I'm glad I didn't make pumpkin pies. It would have been too much."

"Pecan pie is my favorite. Cherie doesn't make it often enough."

"Brenda, you need to watch yourself. Cherie shows love through her cooking, just like her mama, and if you're not careful, all that goodness will settle right in your middle."

"Oh, I'm afraid it's too late for that," said Brenda, patting where the department cook-off apron covered her little belly. She picked up the bowl and distributed the batter into the waiting pans.

Simone sat down and resumed the task of peeling yams, which she'd adamantly pointed out were NOT sweet potatoes, despite what the sign in the store said.

"Brenda, you're not at all what I expected," said Simone in a casual tone.

Brenda looked up, waiting for clues to where this comment was leading. When none were forthcoming, she decided to probe. "I hope I'm not a disappointment."

"No, girl, not a bit, but you're not what I pictured either."

"How so?"

"You're much better than I had hoped. It did not make a good impression on us when Cherie told me you were from New York. Even worse, when she told us you were the chief of police." Simone pronounced the word with a hard accent on the first syllable, proof she came from Louisiana, despite her refined elocution. "I expected a hard woman. Tough and masculine, but you're a right pretty thing, despite being so tall." Simone measured Brenda's height with her eyes.

"Well, thank you." Brenda felt her cheeks warm at the compliment.

"I'm surprised you got Cherie to even talk to you. After that trooper shot her sister, we were all angry, but not like Cherie. Her sister was shot right in front of her. It must have been terrifying. The bullet went right through Sisi and hit Cherie. I bet she still has that scar."

Brenda visualized the hard, bright circle in the soft flesh of Cherie's thigh. "Yes, she does."

"Her sister, Sisi, was named after me. She was my godchild as well as my niece. We all miss her, but especially Cherie. After the shooting, Cherie hated the police. How did you ever get her to marry you?"

"I persisted until she saw me, Brenda, and that I wasn't anything like that trooper who killed her sister. It hasn't been easy. Every time a cop shoots someone, I have to hear about it."

"The horror she experienced is something you never forget. None of us will." Simone nodded knowingly. "But it's obvious that you adore her, and my Cherie adores you. She's so happy, which would have been enough, but then you brought home those beautiful babies for her to love. When that judge said they were hers, her eyes lit up like fireworks on the fourth of July. You know what she needs to be happy. That's what matters."

"I try," said Brenda. She opened the oven door and tested the baked loaves with a toothpick. They were done, so she set them on a wire rack to cool. She slid the unbaked loaves into the oven. "I think that's enough. What do you think, Simone?"

Simone glanced at the half dozen loaves sitting on the racks. "I think so too. They smell good. Brenda, I never expected you to be so handy in the kitchen."

"Why not?" Brenda turned off the water in the sink, where she was washing the mixing bowl, so she could hear better.

"Isn't it usual that one does the cooking and housework and the other the outside work?"

Brenda reminded herself that this woman was from another generation. "We share the chores. Cherie's such a good cook it's hard to compete, but we alternate making dinner. I cook on the nights she has therapy appointments. I mow the lawn and prune the trees, but she loves flowers, so she does most of the gardening. We don't have assigned roles like some straight couples. We just do what each of us likes to do and does best."

"Doing what you like best. Hmm. Makes sense." Simone picked up another sweet potato and inspected it for insect holes. She found one and gouged it out aggressively with the tip of her paring knife. "Honey, I hope you don't mind my asking so many questions."

"It's fine," Brenda assured her. "Asking questions is how people learn."

"I admit I'm still getting used to this gay marriage thing." Simone shook her head. "No one would ever have imagined such a thing when I was young."

"Me neither," said Brenda.

"When that judge said yesterday that you were both new mothers, it took some rearranging in my mind, but I'm getting there. What I couldn't mistake is how happy you both were, and those kids too. You were just beaming with joy and pride. Those babies are going to have a hard time growing up after what they've been through, but I have every confidence in you and Cherie."

Brenda smiled. "That means a lot, coming from you, Simone. Thank you."

"You're welcome. Just do a good job."

"How are you girls doing?" Cherie walked in, carrying a small stock pot. "Mmm. Smells real good in here." She bent to sniff the cooling loaves. "Can't wait to taste those. Did you put raisins and walnuts in?"

"I sure did."

Cherie set the pot on the stove. "Liz sent over some soup. She made it from one of those enormous Blue Hubbards, the kind you have to open with an axe. She said it made enough soup to feed an army, and since we won't be there to help eat it, she insisted on giving us some."

"I don't mind," said Brenda, looking in the pot. "We can have some for dinner tonight."

"Good idea to eat light on the day before Thanksgiving," said Simone, glancing at Brenda's little tummy. "Save some room for tomorrow."

Cherie looked around the kitchen. "Everything under control here?"

"We're doing just fine," Simone assured her.

"Good," said Cherie. "That's what I like to hear. Where are the kids?"

"Watching *The Lion King* for the fiftieth time. Good thing we kept all those old Disney DVDs from when my nieces and nephews were young."

"I'll just peek in before I go up to change, and then we'll get started prepping the turkey. Sound good?"

They nodded. Cherie gave them each a curious look before leaving. Once she was gone, Brenda turned to Simone with a conspiratorial grin.

✳✳✳

Liz almost collided with Lucy on her way back from the porch. "I was looking for you," Lucy said. "What were you doing out there?"

"I'm brining the turkey. It's way too big to fit in the fridge, but it's cold enough to keep on the porch."

"Won't it freeze out there?"

"It will barely get down to freezing tonight. Besides, it's in a salt brine, which won't freeze unless it's really cold. I added some cider too. My secret ingredient." Liz looked at her watch. "So, they finally let you out for good behavior?"

"I had some phone calls to make. They took longer than I expected." Lucy reached up. "I need hugs. Lots of hugs." Liz's strong embrace lifted her off the floor a little. "Pray we have a peaceful Thanksgiving. At least two of my parishioners are in hospice. One's not doing too well."

"Here's hoping they both make it through Thanksgiving." Liz raised her crossed fingers.

"It's so hard on families when people die during the holidays. The memory always makes them sad. Remember when you went on that house call on Easter and thought you came back with COVID?"

"I sure do," said Liz, although the first Easter of the pandemic now felt like ancient history. So much had happened since. Liz was dreading the Christmas season, which would also bring the anniversary of Erika's death.

Lucy looked sad. Obviously, she was thinking about that too. "Let me change. Then I'll help you however I can." She pulled out her tab collar and stuck it in her pocket.

"No, you don't," ordered Liz. "Put that where Ellie can find it."

Lucy stared over her shoulder. "Bossy tonight, aren't you?"

"I have a lot to do, and I'm not used to doing it all by myself." Realizing what she'd said, Liz rubbed her forehead with the heel of her hand. "I'm sorry, Lucy. I didn't mean that the way it came out."

Lucy looked at her thoughtfully. "I know you miss Maggie's help, and I understand. I'm not the cook she is, but I'll do what I can. After I change, you take a break. We'll have a glass of wine. I want to talk to you about something."

"But—"

"But nothing. I'll help you. It will all get done. I promise."

Liz grumbled, shredding red cabbage for slaw while she waited for Lucy to return.

"Stop that!" Lucy ordered, coming into the kitchen. Liz defiantly finished cutting up the little heel of cabbage and covered the bowl with plastic wrap. Her fingers were purple from the cabbage, so she scrubbed them in the kitchen sink with a surgical brush.

Lucy put a glass of wine at her elbow. "I opened another bottle," said Liz, nodding to where the wine stood on the counter.

"We'll get to that. I'm sure we'll need it after we talk."

Liz looked up from drying her hands. "That doesn't sound good."

"It's all good. Come out and sit down and you'll find out what I mean," Lucy said, picking up the glasses. She cocked her hip before she headed down the hall to the living room. After that, Liz had no choice but to follow her. "Nice fire," said Lucy, patting a space next to her. "Sit down, Liz. This is important."

Liz eyed her cautiously before sitting down beside her. "Lucy, what's going on?"

"I was talking to the bishop before I came home. That's why I'm late."

"Oh, really? And what did that little prick want?"

"Liz! He may be little compared to you, but he's not a prick. He's a very kind, decent man, and I called him. Now, stop that." Liz growled. Lucy waited until she wiped the belligerent look off her face before continuing. "I asked him to confirm the date for our wedding."

"So, we are getting married."

"Yes, of course we are. We need to wait until it's a year since your divorce because those are the rules. I'll be finished with school, and the weather will be better in the spring. Maybe we could have the reception outside. I was hoping for a small wedding, but we could have a big crowd."

"Don't we have anything to say about it?"

"Liz, you're a prominent citizen of Hobbs. So am I. Fame and glory come with a price." Liz made a sour face. "Now, that's enough. This is good news. I told the bishop I had worked through my concerns with the help of a friend, which he was glad to hear. But he said you need to show up for our next meeting. No excuses."

"Oh, fuck."

Lucy stared at her. "You want to marry a member of the clergy? This is part of the deal. And stop making faces. It's what you signed up for."

"Did Erika have to go through all this?"

"Yes, but she wasn't as stubborn as you are. I thought you'd be happy."

"I am happy."

"Good. Because I have more news. I've decided where we're going to live after we get married."

"*You've* decided?" said Liz, crossing her arms. "I thought this was supposed to be a joint decision."

"You've already made your wishes known. You'd rather live here, and so we will. But I'm not selling the beach house. I'm going to rent it. Melissa and Courtney have been looking for a place to live. It's big enough for two women and a child. I think they'll be comfortable there. The garage isn't included in the rental. When I was at Sam's, I talked to her about turning it into a cottage for us. That way we'll have a place on the beach in the summer. Otherwise, we can rent it."

"You've thought of everything. I'm impressed." Liz raised her glass.

"There has to be some benefit to those logic lessons you've been giving me."

"Judging from your sermons, I wasn't sure."

Lucy gave her a little jab with her elbow. "After dinner, I'd like to invite Melissa and Courtney over for a drink. We can tell them about the beach house. Is that all right with you?"

"But Lucy, I have so much work to do!"

"Liz, you need to chill. We're having a small group tomorrow. It's only family."

"And Denise and that new deacon of yours. And Stefan..."

"Stefan is family. It's only six, Liz, a small group. And I'll help you. I may not be a gourmet cook like Maggie, but I can peel and cut up vegetables and do other useful things. Just be patient with me. It might take longer, but I'll get it done. I promise." Lucy reached out and took Liz's hand. "Okay?"

Liz put her wine glass on the table. She took Lucy's glass and put it down too. "I love you, Lucy, and I'll even go to see your fucking bishop."

"You'd better, if you want him to marry us." Lucy pulled Liz's face closer.

"You still want to marry me, don't you?" she asked and teased Liz's lips with the tip of her tongue.

"Oh, yes," said Liz fervently and kissed her.

***

"But I'm so tired," protested Courtney. "The kids are always crazy before a holiday. The teachers are distracted and exhausted. Do we really have to go?"

Melissa's height always made her look formidable, but she emphasized her determination by putting her hands on her hips. "Yes, we do. They have been nothing but kind to us. It's just a little holiday drink. I think we owe them that much. We don't have to stay long."

"But I really don't want to," Courtney whined. After being an adult all day, pretending to be a child sometimes felt so good.

Melissa sat down beside her. "Please, Court. They have some news for us."

Courtney frowned. "This had better be good if I'm going to drag myself over there after such an awful day."

"I know what it is, but I didn't want to spoil the surprise." It was obvious that Melissa wanted to tell her. She only needed a little encouragement.

"If you want me to go, you'd better tell me."

"Okay, I'll tell you, but you'd better act surprised. Promise?"

"I promise."

"Lucy called this afternoon while you were at school. Remember that place she thought might come available? Well, it did."

"Took long enough. When can we move in?"

"Might be a while. It's Lucy's beach house."

"Really!" shrieked Courtney. "A house on the beach? That's fantastic!" Courtney started doing a happy dance. Then she froze. "But won't it cost too much?"

Melissa shrugged. "You made the deal when you told her how much rent you can afford."

"But that's not fair to Lucy. That place is worth so much more."

"Well, we can pay more. Yesterday, I had an offer on my condo in Boston. One that I can accept. That's the other big news."

Courtney gripped her arms. "Oh, Melissa, are you sure you want to sell the place? You might need to move back to Boston for your job."

Melissa slowly shook her head. "I gave them an ultimatum. I won't go back to the office full time. What could they say? They don't want to lose my clients or the revenue I bring in. It was Harriet who explained that I hold all the cards. I decided to play them. And if I don't like the game they want to play, I'll leave," said Melissa, looking resolute. "I'm tired of the commute and all the demands from the senior partners. Do you know how many people are quitting their jobs in this country? People are fed up."

"I wish I could quit mine." Courtney sank down on the sofa and put her face in her hands.

"I know, baby," said Melissa, rubbing her back. "You're new at this, and you've had a trial by fire because of the pandemic. It wasn't fair, but everyone is under so much stress."

"Fortunately, the principal will be coming back for another term. Barbara found homecare for her mother. I'd really like to be principal someday, but not next year."

"Once you have more experience, you'll make a great principal. Hopefully by then this insane pandemic will be behind us."

Courtney patted Melissa's thigh. "Let me ask Kaylee to do the dishes, so we can get going." She got up, but Melissa pulled her back.

"Before we go, we should talk. Do we want to offer Lucy more rent?"

"I think we should," Courtney said. "She's so kind, and she means well, but I don't want to take advantage of her."

"I wonder if she has any idea what she could get for that house. I asked Harriet. She quoted a figure neither of us could afford alone. If we pay the rent the place is worth, it means we're in it together. Are you ready for that?"

Courtney searched Melissa's eyes. "Are you?"

"I don't know. My track record with women isn't great."

"Neither is mine. You're my first female lover in years," said Courtney. "And you're still worried I might change my mind and go back to men."

"No, I'm not," Melissa protested. "I know you're not looking for anyone else. You're with me now."

"Oh, thank God. You finally get it! What happened?"

"I realized I don't have to understand why you're attracted to both men and women. You love me now, and that's enough."

"How did you figure this out?"

"I had a glass of wine with Lucy the other night…when you were at school for the big meeting about the vaccinations. We were talking about trans sexuality. She told me she doesn't understand it, but she doesn't need to. She just has to love everyone the way they are. Then it clicked. It's the same way with bi people. I don't have to understand."

"Are you sure, Melissa? This really bothered you."

"It bothers me more that you won't acknowledge me in public, but I understand why. I won't pressure you about it anymore. Maybe someday, you'll feel more comfortable, but I'm not counting on it."

"Wow! It's like Christmas."

Melissa laughed "We'll get there soon enough. It's only Thanksgiving. So, are we agreed? We'll pay Lucy a fair rent. She'll push us to pay less because she agreed to the lower rent, so we have to present a united front."

"Melissa, I can't afford it on my own. Living together and splitting the expenses is a big commitment. Are you sure you're ready?"

"Not completely, but I love you, so I'm going to try." Melissa frowned and looked thoughtful. "No, I'm going to do more than try. We're going to do this, aren't we?" Melissa's eyes were bright with enthusiasm.

"Yes, we are," said Courtney, caught up in Melissa's excitement. "Let's go tell Lucy we accept. Oh, I can't believe this! We're going to live on the beach!"

"The dishes," Melissa reminded her. "You wanted to ask Kaylee to do them."

"Right!" said Courtney, jumping up from her seat.

# 19

"Make sure to get some poultry seasoning inside the cavity," said Maggie. "I mean way up inside, Sam. Get your fingers in there."

Alina snickered softly. Her face was hidden behind her dark hair, but Sam could guess what she was thinking. If her mother weren't present, she probably would have laughed out loud.

"Now rub the olive oil on the skin," Maggie said. "Rub it like you mean it!" Sam grinned. She was glad Alina had left the room, or she would have burst out laughing. "The salt and pepper come next, then sprinkle on the poultry seasoning. Rub it in good." Maggie got up to inspect. While waiting for her to decide if the bird was seasoned to her satisfaction, Sam stood with her oily hands raised like a surgeon waiting to go into the OR.

"Good job," Maggie finally pronounced.

"What's next?" asked Sam.

"Use the wide, heavy-duty aluminum foil to make a tent for the breast."

"It does have a fine breast!" Sam declared, then glanced at Maggie to make sure the innuendo hadn't offended her, but she appeared to have missed this double meaning like all the others.

"I feel so helpless not being able to lift anything," said Maggie in frustration. "I always made the Thanksgiving turkey."

"That's why I volunteered to be your arms." Sam struck a bodybuilder post.

"And strong arms they are," said Maggie in a tone of admiration. "But wash your hands before you handle the aluminum foil."

Sam made a face because it was so obvious, but she opened the kitchen tap with her elbow and scrubbed her hands in scalding water. "I thought Liz always brined the turkey."

"She did, but you can't make good gravy from a brined turkey. I'm using my mom's recipe. I like it better."

Sam didn't argue. Where the kitchen was concerned, Maggie was the boss. Sam was barely the sous chef today. She wiped her hands on her jeans, measured the aluminum foil by eye, and constructed a neat tent. "What's next?"

"Slide the bird into the oven." Maggie glanced at the clock. "Three and a half hours should do it."

"Mom, are you and Sam okay by yourselves? I forgot to get some whipping cream for my pie. I'm going to run out quick and pick it up," said Alina, snatching her car keys from the counter.

"Good luck finding a store open today," said Sam. "All the supermarkets had signs saying they were closed on Thanksgiving."

"I think the convenience store at the gas station might be open. I'll take the kids to give you a break. Be right back."

Sam began to wipe up the countertop where she'd been working, spraying white vinegar straight from the bottle.

"I hope she finds an open store," Maggie said. "She put a lot of work into that pumpkin pie."

"I'm sure she'll be fine," said Sam. She bent to give Maggie a kiss. "Thanks for being patient with me. I've never made a turkey before. I always went home or to a friend's house for Thanksgiving dinner."

"Well, now you know how." Maggie reached out for Sam's hand. "Thanks for all your help. You're so sweet. How did Olivia let you get away?"

"She tried too hard to keep me."

"I'll remember that." Maggie reached up and grazed Sam's cheek with her fingertips. "You've been taking such good care of me. When I'm able, I promise to pay you back." She winked and smiled seductively.

The doorbell rang. "I'll get it," Sam said, running down the stairs. She looked out the side window and saw a familiar figure breathing vapor from standing in the cold. "It's Liz! Should we let her in?"

"Of course, we should let her in."

Sam opened the door, and Liz reached out a small stock pot. "Squash soup. I made a vat of it. The Hubbard was huge this year. Twenty-six pounds!"

"Impressive."

Sam turned and saw Maggie standing at the top of the stairs, smiling warmly. "Invite her for a cup of hot cider, Sam. She came all this way to bring us soup. It's the least we can do."

"Hi, Maggie," said Liz, showing her discomfort by shifting from one foot to the other. "Happy Thanksgiving."

"Happy Thanksgiving. Who's cooking dinner?"

"I am, but it's a big turkey, and it's got hours to go. I figured I could sneak out to make a delivery."

"How did you fit that big squash in the oven?" Maggie asked. "Did you break it up with your axe as usual?"

"I sure did."

"Why don't you come in?" said Maggie, gesturing toward the kitchen. "We've got a crock pot full of hot cider."

"I can spike it for you," offered Sam with a grin.

"I would love some, but I left Lucy and Emily in charge, which is always dangerous. Maggie, if it works for you, I'll come up next week to make sure everything's healing okay."

"Thanks, Liz. I appreciate it."

"And thanks for the soup," Sam called after Liz as she headed down the front walk. Liz waved over her shoulder, and Sam closed the door. "Now, what was that about? Why would she drive all the way up here to bring us soup?"

"Well, Sam. I'm sure you know the answer to that." Maggie winced as she tried to cross her arms. Since she'd been feeling better, she kept forgetting things she wasn't allowed to do.

As Sam climbed the stairs with the pot of soup, she tried to figure out what Maggie meant. "I think I get it now. She still cares about us. She wants us to know that some things may have changed, but others haven't."

Maggie nodded. "Your turkey is beginning to smell good."

❋❋❋

"Mom, is it all right with you if I stay at our house tonight?"

Lucy looked up from her laptop. She was trying to get some work done on her final term paper while the turkey was cooking. It took effort to bring herself down from the heady world of hermeneutics to focus on Emily's question.

"Aren't you comfortable here, sweetheart? I thought you liked the seashore room." The ocean-facing bedroom had the best view from the second floor. The decorations—a comforter with starfish and shells and lamp bases fashioned like glass fishing buoys—bordered on kitsch, but it was a beautiful and airy place. In the morning, the sunrise over the ocean flooded the room with golden light. When Lucy couldn't go to the beach for a walk, she often went there to pray.

Emily refused to give her mother eye contact, which meant she was stressed and retreating into old behavior. "Mom, I love it here, and I really like being with you and Aunt Liz, but can't you understand? I need *privacy*."

Lucy did want to understand but she did. "Sweetie, sit down and let's talk."

"Mom, we don't have to have the sex talk. We already did that."

"I know, but let's talk anyway." Lucy pointed to a chair. "Sit down."

Slouching, Emily headed toward the table and pulled out the chair. She stared forward, focusing on the tabletop. Up till now, Lucy had noticed a significant improvement in her social skills. Although Emily might not always feel the emotions, she could reproduce them accurately. Lucy reached out to touch her, but she flinched away. "I'm sorry, baby. I won't touch you if you don't want me to."

"If I have sex, I have to touch. It's good to practice." Emily tentatively held out her hand. She closed her eyes and looked pained as Lucy took it.

"Emily, you know you can talk to me about anything. Anything at all," Lucy said, enclosing her daughter's warm hand in hers. "Please talk to me." She sounded desperate, because she was, but she needed to dial back the emotion because it would only frighten Emily away.

"I know you're an expert on sex, Mom, but I don't think you can help me with this."

"Denise isn't pushing you, is she?" asked Lucy, leaning down so she could see Emily's eyes.

"No. I'm pushing her. I want to know how it feels."

Lucy nodded, understanding that Emily really wanted to do this experiment, but she was afraid. "Do you like Denise, Emily?"

"I like her very much. More than anyone I've met so far."

"Is she good to you?"

"Yes."

"Do you care for each other?"

"I don't know what that means, but I think so. I like to be with her. We talk about music. When I can't sleep, I call her on the phone, and she sings to me." Lucy thought of the nights when she sang Liz to sleep.

"Music is a special language," Lucy said. "It helps us communicate thoughts and feelings we can't express any other way."

"Yes!" This time, Emily wasn't mimicking pleasure. Her smile was genuine. "That's how Denise and I talk. We speak music!"

Lucy looked into Emily's blue eyes. Redheads with blue eyes were so rare, and so was Emily. She was a gifted musician and a brilliant mathematician, but it was Emily's determination to grow as a human being that impressed Lucy most of all.

"Sweetie, if you give Denise your body, you'll be using a different language, the language of touch. It can give you great pleasure, but it's at its most beautiful when you really love someone. Do you understand?" Emily nodded. "Yes, you can stay at our house tonight, but promise me one thing. You won't do anything that doesn't feel right for you. Give yourself a chance to find your way. And if you have any questions, please ask me." Lucy emphasized the invitation by squeezing her daughter's hand.

"Don't tell Denise I said anything to you."

"Of course not." Lucy got up and kissed her forehead. "I love you."

"I promised Denise I would take a walk with her on the beach. What time is dinner?"

"Liz said the turkey will be ready at five o'clock, but we invited the new deacon to come around four. Can you be back before then? Maybe you can pick up Stefan at the senior residence."

"I can do that." Emily got up and hugged Lucy from behind. "Thanks, Mom."

Lucy listened to Emily's rapid footsteps on the stairs. She could tell she was happy.

When the front door closed, Lucy began to cry. She'd barely had a chance to get to know the child she'd given away so many years ago. She hoped Emily was making good choices, but making mistakes was part of growing up. Lucy couldn't stop her beautiful daughter from becoming a woman.

Wiping away her tears, Lucy opened her laptop and reread what she had written before Emily had interrupted. The words now seemed so far removed from what she'd just experienced, and she struggled to make sense of them. Without love, all the theological exegesis in the world was meaningless.

The door from the garage opened. "How's my turkey doing?" asked Liz, striding into the kitchen. "Smells good." She opened the door of the oven to look. When she stood up, she noticed the tears on Lucy's face. "Hey, baby," she said softly, kneeling beside her. "What's the matter?"

"Emily just left."

"Did you have a fight?"

"No. We talked. She asked to stay at the beach house."

"Are we making her uncomfortable?"

"It has nothing to do with us. She wants to be with Denise tonight."

"Oh," said Liz, understanding. She got to her feet, massaging her knees as she stood. "Your baby's going to lose her virginity tonight. Are you upset?"

"No, I knew it would happen eventually, but it will be so much harder for her."

"Change is hard for everyone," said Liz and kissed the top of her head.

***

"Negative," Amy pronounced, reading the rapid test strip.

"You cannot imagine how grateful I am that you came to test my girls," said Olivia.

"You invited me for dinner. It's the least I can do." Amy gave her hostess a hard look. "You do realize you could have gotten the kits in the pharmacy and done it yourself?"

"Yes, but you're a doctor and can make sure it's done right."

"Are we finished now, Grandma?" asked Olivia's older granddaughter impatiently. She was in the full bloom of adolescence, her cheeks still showing a little baby fat, but her hair was dark and sleek. You could almost smell the pheromones emanating from her moist skin.

"Yes," said Olivia. "Sharon, don't forget to thank Dr. Hsu."

"Thank you, Dr. Hsu," said the girl in a mocking, sing-song voice before leaving the room.

"Kids," complained Olivia, shaking her head. "But I'm glad they're here. I missed them when I was at odds with their mother. It's taken years to get to this point. We're not exactly best friends, but at least, we're talking." Amy tried to look attentive, but she had no idea what Olivia was talking about. "You don't know the story, do you? Can there really be a single person alive who hasn't heard it?"

"I'm sorry, Olivia. You need to fill me in."

"Maybe it's arrogant of me to think everyone knows about it. You know that I founded the Enright Fund?"

"Yes, and you were forced to sell it. Insider trading like Martha Stewart."

"Oh, Martha. She got such a raw deal. A man would have gotten away with it, but they had to make an example of her. Poor woman. I've known her since she was on the Street. Savvy investor, but few people remember her for her financial acumen. They only think of her media empire and her cooking show. By the way, I'm making her stuffing today. Simple but delicious."

Amy tried to make sense of the bits and pieces Olivia was throwing at her. She had never seen Olivia so scattered. She wondered if it was the children's presence or hers.

"You're looking at me like I'm a criminal," Olivia said, which confused Amy because she was wearing her usual expression, which was completely neutral. "I did nothing illegal, nothing at all," Olivia continued breathlessly. "Whatever you read about me in the papers isn't true. Well, some of it is. It was my son, the girls' father, who was charged with insider trading. Since it was my company, and he worked for me, I had to divest myself of my controlling interest, but I'm innocent of any wrongdoing."

Amy patted Olivia's arm, "It's okay. I believe you."

"You're new here and don't know the real story. I don't want those women to poison you with their nasty opinions. I'm not as bad as everyone says."

"Olivia, take it easy. No one is talking about you."

"They're not?"

"No."

Olivia looked disappointed. "Then I hope you'll reserve judgment and get to know me for who I am, which is not what you think."

"Olivia, you don't have to tell me this today. It's Thanksgiving. I'm glad to be here, and share Thanksgiving with your family."

Olivia's face suddenly twisted in pain. "My family. There's a part of my family I haven't seen in years. I heard this morning that my last sister died. It was COVID. She wasn't vaccinated. She had other problems—drugs, obesity. All my siblings ended up with diabetes, alcoholism, drug addiction. I haven't talked to any of them in decades."

"I'm sorry," said Amy, putting her hand on Olivia's shoulder. "We can't choose our families. Sometimes, they have problems, and we need to walk away."

"I walked away because they're white trash and never tried to better themselves. I wanted to make something of my life, so I left. Now, they're all gone, except some nieces and nephews who don't even know me." Olivia compressed her lips and looked away, obviously holding back tears.

"Why are you cooking this big Thanksgiving dinner after getting such bad news? Why didn't you cancel? I would have understood."

"I've got to pull myself together. It's Thanksgiving. I invited you, and you expect a good meal. The girls expect it. They've been through so much already. Did you know my son killed himself?" Olivia suddenly asked, looking distracted.

"Because he was caught on insider trading?"

"No, because he was accused of abusing his daughters."

Amy opened her mouth, but no words came out. She didn't know what to say, although she was sure her face expressed her horror.

"I probably disgust you now," said Olivia, reading her expression. "Yes, I raised a monster. You haven't heard any of this from the others?" she asked suspiciously.

"No, not a word." Olivia looked flushed, then pale. She was shaking. Amy reached out. "You don't look well. You should sit down."

"I'm all right," Olivia insisted, waving her off. "I need to get the turkey in the oven."

"I'll help you," said Amy. "I might not be a gourmet chef like you, but I can cook a meal."

Olivia nodded and turned to head toward the kitchen. She took a few steps and staggered. "I feel dizzy," she said, reaching out for the wall. Amy grabbed her by the arm before she fell. Olivia leaned heavily against her as Amy helped her to a nearby chair. She reached for Olivia's wrist to take her pulse and found it erratic.

"Do you have pain in your chest? How about your arm or your jaw?"

"It feels like someone is pressing against my chest with a fist," said Olivia, trying to catch her breath.

"Do you have aspirin in the house?"

"In my bathroom. In the medicine cabinet."

"Sharon!" Amy called. "Sharon!" The girl came into the room. "Go upstairs to your grandmother's bathroom and find some aspirin. Read the labels and don't bring anything but aspirin. Go!"

Sharon's eyes grew wide. "Is Grandma all right?"

"Get the aspirin. Now!" ordered Amy, taking out her phone to call 911.

By the time Amy had finished answering the dispatcher's questions, Sharon had returned with the aspirin. Amy cursed the child-protection cap but finally managed to open the bottle. She handed a tablet to Olivia. "Chew this slowly." Olivia put it into her mouth. She made a face as she began to chew. "Yes, I know it doesn't taste good, but it can help prevent damage to your heart."

"Grandma's having a heart attack?" Sharon asked shrilly.

"I don't know yet," Amy answered. She wished she had her stethoscope, but it was back in the office. "Sit back, Olivia. I want to listen to your heart." Amy leaned her ear on Olivia's chest. Her heart rhythm was odd, but she couldn't hear well though Olivia's sweater.

Amy pulled out her phone to see how much time had elapsed since she'd called 911. Less than three minutes had passed. She felt so helpless without equipment and drugs. She dialed Liz's number.

"Amy! Happy Thanksgiving," Liz announced cheerfully. Amy could hear laughter in the background.

"Liz, Olivia Enright is having a cardiac event. Which hospital should I send her to?"

"Olivia? Oh, shit. Have them take her to Southern Med. Is she conscious?"

"Yes, I have her chewing aspirin. Oh, I wish I had a stethoscope."

"That's why I still carry a bag. Old-fashioned, but in an emergency, you never know what you might need." Amy heard the mild criticism in Liz's voice, but it was gentle, merely a strong suggestion. "Can she speak?" Liz asked.

"Yes, she's lucid, and her color is better. Does she have a heart condition?"

"Not that I know of. I have her on Losartan for hypertension."

Amy heard the wail of a siren. "The ambulance is here. I have to go."

"Call me when they're gone. Tell Olivia that Lucy is praying for her."

Two young men and a woman dragged enormous black bags of equipment into the house. When Amy saw the array of drugs and instruments they contained, she finally breathed a sigh of relief. One of the paramedics unlocked a plastic case and removed a portable ultrasound. Olivia was suddenly modest, so he had to unbutton her blouse. His dark brows furrowed slightly as he moved the probe over her chest.

"May I see? I'm a doctor," said Amy. He held up the screen for her to see. Amy recognized the erratic pattern of cardiac distress.

"Bring in the stretcher," the head paramedic ordered the others. "We're going for a ride to…" He looked up at Amy expectantly.

"Southern Medical Center," she said, glad to have a ready answer.

"You heard the doc." Despite the urgency of his message, the paramedic's voice was low and calm. He arranged the leads for a heart monitor while the other members of the crew brought in the stretcher. Minutes later, Olivia was strapped in, and the paramedics were carrying her out the door.

Amy finally noticed the girls standing in the doorway of the living room. "Is Grandma going to be all right?" asked the older one in a shaky voice.

"Yes, I think so," said Amy approaching. "The paramedics will take good care of her." Amy sounded calm, but as she assessed the situation, she realized she was alone in the house of someone who was practically a stranger, with two children whom she barely knew.

"What about Thanksgiving?" asked the younger girl. "Grandma was going to cook the turkey."

"Don't worry," said Amy. "We'll still have Thanksgiving." She said it with great confidence, but Olivia hadn't even begun cooking the meal. And if Olivia was admitted to the hospital, which was likely, she had left behind two minors too young to be left unattended. Amy had felt completely in control handling Olivia's medical situation. That's what she'd been trained to do, but she had no idea what to do with two young children.

Her phone vibrated in her pocket. Amy took it out and saw it was Liz calling. "Are they gone?"

"Yes, they were amazing, and so well-equipped."

"We have a great emergency service in Hobbs. Did they take her to Southern Med?"

"Yes. Her granddaughters are here with me." She looked at their pale, anxious faces and fought down a feeling of panic. "Do you have any suggestions?"

"Sure. Bring them over here. Hold on. I'm sorry, but I'm in the middle of cooking. I'll put Lucy on."

Amy heard a loud thump—the phone being put down on a hard surface. Then a higher pitched, pleasant voice came on the line. "Hello, Amy. I'm sorry you had to go through this today," said Lucy. "I had the number of the girls' mother because they were in counseling with me. I explained what had happened and promised her that I would look after them until she can get here. She's in Florida with her parents, so she probably won't arrive until tomorrow. We'll keep them with us tonight." Listening to Lucy's level-headed plan, Amy felt her anxiety level plummet.

"Thank you, Lucy. I can't even tell you how relieved I am."

"Just tell Sharon and Jessica that you're coming to Mother Lucy's house for Thanksgiving. Hopefully, that makes them feel better. Now, tell Liz what you know about Olivia's condition, so I can pass on the information to the girls' mother. Hold on. Liz is putting in her earpods, so she can talk to you while she cooks. It's kind of busy here."

***

The level of noise at Liz's house reminded Cherie of childhood Thanksgivings. She brought an apple pie into the kitchen and found Lucy and Rhesma wrapping up the leftovers.

"Where's Liz?" asked Cherie.

"In her office. She's on the phone with Southern Med. Amy's with her."

"Amy?" Cherie put down the pie. Brenda came in with a pecan pie and set it beside the others.

"I just heard from the dispatcher that Olivia was taken to Southern Med," Brenda said. "What's going on?"

"Sounds like Olivia had a heart attack. Amy was there. She can tell you more," said Lucy, carefully arranging the covered plates in the refrigerator.

Liz came into the kitchen, followed by Amy. "They've already restored a normal rhythm," said Liz. "Sounds like a CAS."

"Coronary artery spasm," said Cherie, translating for Brenda.

"Even though they're almost full because of COVID, they're going to keep her for the night," Liz explained. "Tomorrow morning, I'll head down to see how she's doing. If they're ready to release her, I'll bring her home. They're hurting for beds, so I'm sure they'll be glad to get rid of her."

"I'll go with you," Amy volunteered. "If you can pick me up at Olivia's house, I'll leave my car there. When she comes home, I can help her get settled."

Liz gave Amy a curious look. "That's taking house calls to a whole new level, but it's kind of you, Amy. I'll pick you up at ten after I make breakfast for this gang." Liz looked around the kitchen. "Wow, Lucy, you got everything put away. I'm impressed." She opened the door of the refrigerator and looked in.

"We wrapped up the turkey well and put it on the porch. Reshma carried it out. Emily and Denise set the table for dessert. We've been busy while you two have been playing doctor." Lucy gave Liz a warm smile that took the edge off the little dig.

Liz gave Brenda a pat on the shoulder. She bent to hug Cherie. "Happy Thanksgiving. Thanks for the pies. Let me round up the rest of the troops and we can have dessert."

Once the pies were devoured, everyone moved to the living room to enjoy their food comas. Liz lured the children into the media room with the promise of a Disney movie. The Enright girls had monopolized Lucy's attention, but she gently urged them to join the other children in the media room.

Once Lucy was free, her daughter approached and whispered something in her mother's ear. Lucy tried for a happy face, but her attempt at a smile couldn't completely mask the frown. Lucy held Emily's hand for a moment, then took Denise's. Cherie couldn't hear what Lucy was saying, but her intense look indicated she was trying to impress something important on them.

"Happy Thanksgiving, everyone," the tall redhead announced. "Denise and I have to go." Emily kissed her mother and Stefan. When the young people walked away, they were holding hands. Cherie realized with surprise that they were a couple. They looked so sweet together, tenderly gazing into one another's eyes. Lucy's eyes followed them. Her bittersweet smile lasted only a moment before she turned to Aunt Simone and resumed their conversation.

The noise and activity in Liz's house seemed to make Megan insecure. She'd refused to go with the other children. Her bony backside poked into the soft flesh of Cherie's thigh, and she squirmed, making it worse. Cherie held her daughter closer, which seemed to calm her. She noticed that Megan was staring at something across the room and followed the direction of her gaze. Megan's eyes were focused on the new deacon, who, sensing she was being watched, got up and sat beside Cherie.

"I'm sorry my daughter is staring at you," Cherie apologized. "Before my aunt came to visit, my kids had never seen a real black person. People say I don't count because I'm so fair."

Reshma studied Cherie's face and looked at her hands. "I would never have guessed. There are so few people of color in Maine."

"It must be hard for you. Why do you stay?"

"Because my mother brought me here. She used to repeat that old saying: 'You've got to grow where you're planted.'"

Megan finally squirmed her way out of Cherie's arms, so she let her down. She headed directly to Brenda, who let her climb into her lap. Her face registered pain as Megan settled her bony rear.

"How do you find our parish?" Cherie asked Reshma.

"I love it here, and now that I've met you, I know I'm not the only one. That's a great comfort to me."

"I think my aunt is staying here. She's waiting to see how the winters are before making a final decision."

"Ah, she's in for a treat, isn't she?" said Reshma with a grin.

Cherie chuckled conspiratorially. "She has no idea, but she's about to find out."

Across the room, Cherie heard Stefan's mellow baritone. "Come on, Elizabeth. Take me home. I want to see what the mummies are doing. Maybe some of them are still awake."

Lucy turned to her father-in-law with fake disapproval. "Papi, is that any way to talk about your neighbors?"

"Ah, some of them are so old they should be embalmed."

Liz got up and helped the old man to his feet. "Don't be such a grump, Stefan. That's my job."

"You have no reason to be grumpy. You have Lovely Lucy, and she loves you." He blew a kiss to Lucy. "Come on, Elizabeth. Take me home, so you can get back to your company."

"Please excuse me. Don't any of you go anywhere." Liz pointed around the room to each person in turn. "I'll be right back."

"As if we could move after all that pie," groaned Brenda.

Reshma turned to Cherie. "Will you be at the Open Kitchen to give out food tomorrow?"

"I'm hoping to come if I can find a sitter."

"Bring the children. The older ones can look after them in the nursery, and we can take turns looking in on them."

"In the morning, Brenda is going to Olivia's to get the turkey that never made it to the oven. We'll add it to the others we're cooking."

"The homeless will be happy to have a good meal, wherever it comes from. Gratitude often brings unexpected abundance. And we have so much to be thankful for."

Cherie gazed around Liz's cozy living room, warmed by the blazing fire. Brenda, with Megan on her lap, sat between Lucy and Aunt Simone. She turned and smiled before blowing Cherie a kiss.

"Yes, we do," Cherie agreed, patting Reshma's arm. "Yes, we do."

# Also by Elena Graf

## THE HOBBS SERIES

### HIGH OCTOBER

Liz Stolz and Maggie Fitzgerald were college roommates until Maggie confessed to her parents that she'd fallen in love with a woman. Maggie gave up her dream of becoming an actress and married her high school boyfriend. Liz became a famous breast surgeon. Maggie is performing in a summer stock production near the Maine town where Liz is now a general practitioner. When Maggie breaks her leg in a stage accident, she lands in Dr. Stolz's office. Is forty years too long to wait for the one you love?

### THE MORE THE MERRIER

#### A HOBBS CHRISTMAS STORY

Maggie and Liz have been dreaming of a quiet Christmas since they got back together after being separated for forty years. This year they are determined to celebrate a romantic holiday alone. Their plans of sitting by the fire, drinking mulled wine and watching old Christmas movies get scuttled by surprise visits from friends and family. The Christmas chaos provides some holiday cheer and a touching lesson in the real meaning of Christmas.

### THIS IS MY BODY

The new rector of St. Margaret's by the Sea Episcopal Church has a secret. Lucille Bartlett was a rising star at the Metropolitan Opera, but she disappeared from the stage, and no one knows why. Philosophy Professor Erika Bultmann is a confirmed agnostic, who doesn't have much use for religion, but she is fascinated by Mother Lucy. When Erika returns to her summer cottage in Hobbs to finish her last book before she retires, Lucy is drawn to the enigmatic professor, but she wants much more than a casual affair. When Lucy's secret is revealed, she needs Erika's support more than ever.

### LOVE IN THE TIME OF CORONA

It's midwinter in Maine, and the biggest problem is a snowstorm. Only Liz Stolz, the senior doctor of Hobbs Family Practice, is paying attention to the strange virus in China that's roiling the financial markets. She tries to alert the town leaders to the potential danger, but police chief, Brenda

Harrison, is distracted by Liz's new physician's assistant, Cherie Bois. The friends are pushed together during the lockdown, straining friendships and relationships.

## THIRSTY THURSDAYS

Hobbs, Maine, is gradually reopening after the lockdown. Liz has begun a new tradition—Thirsty Thursdays, a weekly cocktail party on her deck, designed for her friends to socialize safely. An impulsive kiss shakes up friendships and relationships. Pretentious, overbearing Olivia is pursuing Sam and trying to find her way into the tight-knit group. Will the down-to-earth, independent women of Hobbs accept an outsider who's so different?

## THE DARK WINTER

The residents of Hobbs are relieved to have gotten through the summer relatively unscathed. Liz agrees to help architect Sam McKinnon build a soundproof practice room for Erika Bultmann's wife, former opera singer Rev. Lucy Bartlett. Fortunately, the early Christmas gift is ready before tragedy strikes. In the process of keeping a promise to a friend, Liz causes stress in her marriage, which has been rocky since an impulsive kiss. As the women of Hobbs pull together to help a beloved friend deal with her loss, the dark winter brings tension and realignment in their small community.

## SUMMER PEOPLE

After a dark winter of loss and isolation, the summer people are returning to Hobbs, including forty-something Melissa Morgenstern, a trust lawyer from Boston. Liz introduces her to the new assistant principal of the elementary school, Courtney Barnes. Courtney has a daughter and considers herself bisexual, which raises red flags for Melissa. Liz and Rev. Lucy Bartlett seem headed for a relationship when their courtship is interrupted by the arrival of Lucy's ex, the woman who inspired her to become a priest. Susan secretly wants to rekindle the relationship, but that's not the only secret she's keeping.

# THE PASSING RITES SERIES

## THE IMPERATIVE OF DESIRE

A coming-of-age story that takes a young woman from La Belle Époque, through a world war, a revolution that outlawed the German nobility, the roaring twenties, to the decadent demimonde of Weimar Berlin. A quirk of inheritance law allows Margarethe von Stahle to inherit her family's titles. Margarethe reluctantly marries, but that doesn't prevent her from finding solace in the arms of women. She trains under the best surgeons and rises to prominence as London's infamous "Lady Doctor." Finally, duty requires her to return to her homeland and take the reins of the family fortunes.

## OCCASIONS OF SIN

For seven centuries, the German convent of Obberoth has been hiding the nuns' secrets—forbidden passions, scandalous manuscripts locked away, a ruined medical career, perhaps even a murder. In 1931, aristocratic physician, Margarethe von Stahle, is determined to lift the veil of secrecy surrounding her head nurse, Sister Augustine, only to find herself embroiled in multiple conflicts that threaten to unravel her orderly life.

## LIES OF OMISSION

In 1938, the Nazis are imposing their doctrine of "racial hygiene" on hospitals and universities, forcing professors to teach false science and doctors to collaborate in a program to eliminate the mentally ill and handicapped. Margarethe von Stahle is desperately trying to find a way to practice ethical medicine. She has always avoided politics, but now she must decide whether to remain on the sidelines or act on her convictions.

## ACTS OF CONTRITION

World War II has finally come to an end and Berlin has fallen. Nearly everything Margarethe von Stahle has sworn to protect has been lost. After being brutally abused by occupying Russian soldiers, Margarethe must rely on the kindness of her friends to survive. Fortunately, the American Army has brought her former protégée, Sarah Weber, back to Berlin. As Margarethe confronts painful events that occurred during the war, she must learn both to forgive and be forgiven.

# About the Author

In addition to the books in the Hobbs series, Elena Graf has published four historical novels set in Europe in the early 20th century. Lies of Omission, the third volume in the Passing Rites Series, won a Golden Crown Literary Society award for best historical fiction and a Rainbow Award. The fourth volume, Acts of Contrition also won a Goldie and a Rainbow Award.

The author pursued a Ph.D. in philosophy but ended up in the "accidental profession" of publishing, where she worked for almost four decades. She lives with her wife in coastal Maine.

If you liked this book and would like more stories about the people of Hobbs, Maine, write to Elena at elena.m.graf@gmail.com.

Elena Graf is a member of iReadIndies, a collective of self-published independent authors of Sapphic literature. Please visit our website at iReadIndies.com for more information and to find links to the books published by our authors.